Praise for Elizabeth Bear's
Hammered

"*Hammered* is a very exciting, very polished, very impressive debut novel." —Mike Resnick

"Gritty, insightful, and daring—Elizabeth Bear is a talent to watch." —David Brin, author of the Uplift novels and *Kiln People*

"A gritty and painstakingly well-informed peek inside a future we'd all better hope we don't get, liberally seasoned with VR delights and enigmatically weird alien artifacts. Genevieve Casey is a pleasingly original female lead, fully equipped with the emotional life so often lacking in military SF yet tough and full of noir attitude; old enough by a couple of decades to know better but conflicted enough to engage with the sleazy dynamics of her situation regardless. Out of this basic contrast, Elizabeth Bear builds her future nightmare tale with style and conviction and a constant return to the twists of the human heart." —Richard Morgan, author of *Altered Carbon*

"*Hammered* has it all. Drug wars, hired guns, corporate skullduggery, and bleeding-edge AI, all rolled into one of the best first novels I've seen in I don't know how long. This is the real dope!" —Chris Moriarty, author of *Spin State*

"A violent, compulsive read...[Bear is] a welcome addition—not only to 'noir sci-fi' but to sensational fiction in general....Compulsively readable...Bear's greatest talent in *Hammered* is writing about violence in a way that George Pelecanos, Robert Crais and [the aforementioned] Parker would envy....Bear isn't just a writer to watch, she's a writer to applaud." —*Huntsville Times*

"Bear's twenty-first century has some intriguing features drawn from ongoing events...desperate and violent urban centers, artificial intelligences emerging in the net, virtual reconstructions of famous personalities, neural augmentation, nanotech surgical bots. Bear devotes admirable attention to the physical and mental challenges that radical augmentation would likely entail, and *Hammered* certainly establishes Bear as a writer with intriguing potential." —*Fantasy & Science Fiction*

"With Jenny Casey, author Elizabeth Bear delivers a kick-butt fighter who could easily hold her own against Kristine Smith's Jani Killian or Elizabeth Moon's Heris Serrano. Jenny is deadly but likable, someone readers can both relate to and root for. As she and her appealing cast of sidekicks skate close to the edge of disaster, the suspense of *Hammered* rises.... What Bear has done in *Hammered* is create a world that is all too plausible, one wracked by environmental devastation and political chaos. Through Jenny Casey's eyes, she conducts a tour of this society's darker corners, offering an unnerving peek into a future humankind would be wise to avoid." —SciFi.com

"*Hammered* is a tough, gritty novel sure to appeal to fans of Elizabeth Moon and David Weber....In Jenny Casey, Bear has created an admirably Chandler-esque character, street-smart and battle-scarred, tough talking and quick on the trigger.... Bear shuttles effortlessly back and forth across time to weave her disparate cast of characters together in a tightly plotted page-turner. The noir universe she creates is as hard-edged as the people who inhabit it. The dialogue and descriptions are suitably spartan, but every one of her characters has their own recognizable voice. It takes no effort at all to imagine *Hammered* on the big screen." —sfrevu.com

"A sobering projection of unchecked current social, political and environmental trends... Although a careless reader might be lulled by the presence of drugs, the hard-edged narration, and the run-down setting of the opening scene into thinking this novel is dystopian or even cyberpunk in nature, such expectations are quickly undercut by Bear.... Without giving too much away, it can be said that the underlying theme of Bear's novel is *salvage,* in all its senses.... Indeed, every character in *Hammered,* even the villainous, has their own powerful motives for their actions; and conversely, the hands of the 'good' characters are never entirely clean, and they make fearful moral bargains and compromises simply because they can't see any better way to do what they must. They all try to salvage what they can... [which] embodies the novel's central theme of how what we would choose to preserve and what we wish to discard are sometimes inextricable." —*Green Man Review*

"[An] enjoyable dystopian thriller... The nicest thing about this novel is the rich characters... every character is identifiable and unique. It's rare to find a book with so many characters you genuinely care about. It's a roller coaster of a good thriller, too. There's plenty of intrigue and a few climactic gun fights and an intriguing love triangle involving Jenny and an old friend. Everyone involved seems to have genuine motives for all the things they do and aren't just pawns in the author's game. Jenny Casey is an excellent protagonist, reaching fifty, tired and crippled and liking it that way, unwilling to admit that she needs people. Elizabeth Bear manages to create an anti-heroine you still care about, despite her reluctance to take part in events. Plus she has an intriguing history that is occasionally delved into, along with that of the planet, that always leaves you wanting that little bit more....I, for one, will be looking forward to that next book. Elizabeth Bear has carved herself out a fantastic little world with this first novel. Long may it continue." —SFcrowsnest.com

"*Hammered* is a well-written debut, and Bear's deft treatment of the characters and their relationships pushed the book up to keeper level....I would gladly hand it over to anyone who would appreciate a broader spectrum of strong female characters to choose from, particularly in the realm of speculative fiction." —broaduniverse.org

"An enthralling roller-coaster ride through a dark and possible near future." —*Starlog*

"Bear has done a bang-up job re-arranging a few squares of the here-and-now into a future that's guaranteed to raise the blood pressure of readers in the present. Sure, we all want heart-pounding suspense, and Bear offers that in spades. But she also provides the kind of pressurizing prescience that doesn't exactly see the future so much as it re-paints the most unpleasant parts of the present into a portrait of a world that knows and loathes itself all too well....Bear is apparently so familiar with darkness that she can elucidate many shades of black, and peel them away in such a manner as to keep the reader intrigued but still in the dark. And though the novel stays firmly in rooms without proper lighting, the plot and the science fiction eventually come out into the open.... She manages to include a number of hoary ideas from the treasure troves of past science fiction writers, but unpacks them in such a way that they seem once again fresh and exciting. Having set the readers' expectations on earthly matters such as bad drugs and run-down prostheses, she shows no hesitation to go a good deal beyond them. And the gritty underpinnings she establishes make her flights of fancy all the more believable." —*Agony Column*

"[Bear] does it like a juggler who is also a magician."
—Matthew Cheney, *Mumpsimus*

"Packed with a colorful panoply of characters, a memorable and likable anti-heroine, and plenty of action and intrigue, *Hammered* is a superbly written novel that combines high tech, military industrial politics, and complex morality. There is much to look forward to in new writer Elizabeth Bear." —Karin Lowachee, Campbell Award–nominated author of *Warchild*

"Even in scenes where there is no violent action, or even much physical action at all, the thoughts and emotions of Ms. Bear's characters, as well as the dynamic tensions of their relationships, create an impression of feverish activity going on below the surface and liable to erupt into plain view at any moment.... The language is terse and vivid, punctuated by ironic asides whose casual brutality—sometimes amusing, sometimes shocking—speaks volumes about these people and their world.... This is a superior piece of work by a writer of enviable talents. I look forward to reading more!" —Paul Witcover, author of *Waking Beauty*

"*Hammered* is one helluva good novel! Elizabeth Bear writes tight and tough and tender about grittily real people caught up in a highly inventive story of a wild and wooly tomorrow that grabs the reader from the get-go and will not let go. Excitement, intrigue, intelligence—and a sense of wonder, too! Who could ask for anything more?" —James Stevens-Arce, author of *Soulsaver*, Best First Novel 2000 (*Rocky Mountain News*)

"In this promising debut novel, Elizabeth Bear deftly weaves thought-provoking ideas into an entertaining and tight narrative." —Dena Landon, author of *Shapeshifter's Quest*

Praise for
Scardown

"Bear deftly creates believable characters who walk into your heart and mind easily.... [Her] prose is easy on the mind's ears, her dialogue generally crisp and lifelike." —Scifi.com

"*Scardown* is a wonderfully written book, and should be a prerequisite for anyone who wants to write intrigue. Although it doesn't reinvent the cyberpunk genre with radically new science or philosophy, it uses the established conventions to tell a thoroughly engaging story, and tell it with a high degree of skill. It's engaging brain candy with surprising emotional insights—and some cool gun fights—and you won't be able to put it down." —*Reflection's Edge*

"For all the wide-screen fireworks and exotic tech, it is also a tale in which friendships and familial relationships drive as much of the action as enmity, paranoia and Machiavellian scheming.... Here there be nifty Ideas about natural and artificial intelligences; satisfyingly convoluted conspiracies; interestingly loose-limbed and unconventional interpersonal relationships; and some pretty good jokes.... I will simply warn the tenderhearted that Bad Things great and small will indeed be allowed to happen, but that those who come through the other side will have exhibited that combination of toughness and humanity that makes Bear one of the most welcome writers to come over the horizon lately." —*Locus*

Praise for
Worldwired

"Elizabeth Bear... has forged a peculiar and powerful path with her tripartite novel. By sheer force of will and great writing, Bear has pulled off a rather remarkable feat without drawing attention to that feat. That is, beyond the attention you get when you nab a John W. Campbell Award... What we didn't expect was that she'd manage to sort of re-invent the novel and re-invigorate the science fiction series... [a] rip-roaring tale of detection, adventure, aliens, conspiracy and much more told in carefully-turned prose with well-developed characters." —*Agony Column*

"Elizabeth Bear is simply magisterial. She asserts firm control of her characters, her setting, and her research (for the novels). She creates flourishes of style and excitement; not one time does this novel bore its characters or readers.... It really is a fine thing to see a writer mature as well and as successfully as Elizabeth has—

and in only her third published book. I can pay her the ultimate compliment a reader can make a writer: I will purchase and read each of her books. Yes, I trust her insights and talent that much.... Run, do not walk, to your nearest bookseller, buy this book, and then sit back and enjoy." —Las Vegas SF Society

"Most of *Worldwired* is about attempts to find common ground—whether within a broken family, between countries on the brink of war, or with aliens so truly alien that humans may not be able to communicate. Bear excels at breaking world-altering political acts and military coups into personal ambitions, compromises, and politicians who are neither gods nor monsters.... *Worldwired* is a thinking person's book, almost more like a chess match than a traditional narrative.... Hard-core science fiction fans—especially those who read David Brin and Larry Niven—won't want to miss it." —*Reflection's Edge*

"The language is taut, the characters deep and the scenes positively crackle with energy. Not to mention that this is real science fiction, with rescues from crippled starships and exploration of mysterious alien artifacts and international diplomatic brinksmanship between spacefaring powers China and Canada. Yes, Canada!" —James Patrick Kelly, author of *Strange but Not a Stranger* and *Think Like a Dinosaur*

CARNIVAL

Elizabeth Bear

BANTAM BOOKS

CARNIVAL
A Bantam Spectra Book / December 2006

Published by Bantam Dell
A Division of Random House, Inc.
New York, New York

This is a work of fiction. Names, characters, places, and incidents
either are the product of the author's imagination or are used fictitiously.
Any resemblance to actual persons, living or dead, events, or locales
is entirely coincidental.

All rights reserved
Copyright © 2006 by Elizabeth Bear
Cover art by Steve Stone / Bernstein & Andriulli, Inc.
Cover design by Jamie S. Warren Youll

Bantam Books, the rooster colophon, Spectra, and the portrayal of a
boxed "s" are trademarks of Random House, Inc.

ISBN-13: 978-0-553-58904-7
ISBN-10: 0-553-58904-0

Printed in the United States of America
Published simultaneously in Canada

www.bantamdell.com

OPM 10 9 8 7 6 5 4 3 2 1

For Stephen and Asha

car•ni•val (kär'nə-vəl) n.

[Italian carnevale, from Old Italian carnelevare:
carne, meat (from Latin caro, carn-)
+ levare, to remove (from Latin levare, to raise) .]

lit. "farewell to the flesh"

Contents

CONTENTS

Acknowledgments

The author would like to thank, in no particular order, Kenneth D. Woods (for the conversation that started this whole idea), Sarah Monette, Ursula Whitcher, Michael Evans, Dr. Stella Evans, Kathryn Allen, Dr. Ian Tregillis, Chelsea Polk, Amanda Downum, Leah Bobet, Dr. Avi Ornstein, Dr. Peter Watts, Dr. Jacqueline A. Hope, Larry Klein, Greg Wilson, Terry Karney, S. K. S. Perry, the Online Writing Workshops' "Zoo," Faren Bachelis, Anne Lesley Groell, Kit Kindred, Jennifer Jackson, and others too numerous to name.

BOOK ONE

The Festival of Meat

1

MICHELANGELO OSIRIS LEARY KUSANAGI-JONES HAD BEEN
drinking since fourteen hundred. He didn't plan on
stopping soon.

He occupied a bubbleport on the current observation
deck of *Kaiwo Maru*, where he had been since he
started drinking, watching a yellow main-sequence star
grow. The sun had the look of a dancer swirling in veils,
a Van Gogh starscape. Eons before, it had blundered
into a cloud of interstellar gas and was still devouring
the remains. Persistent tatters glowed orange and blue
against a backdrop of stars, a vast, doomed display of
color and light. Kusanagi-Jones could glimpse part of
the clean-swept elliptical path that marked the orbit
of New Amazonia: a darker streak like a worm tunnel
in a leaf.

Breathtaking. Ridiculously named. And his destination. Or rather, *their* destination. Which was why he
was drinking, and why he didn't intend to stop.

As if the destination—and the mission—weren't bad enough, there was the little issue of Vincent to contend with. Vincent Katherinessen, the Old Earth Colonial Coalition Cabinet's velvet-gloved iron hand, far too field-effective to be categorized as a mere diplomatic envoy no matter how his passport was coded. Vincent, whom Kusanagi-Jones had managed to avoid for the duration of the voyage by first taking to cryo—damn the nightmares—and then restricting himself to the cramped comforts of his quarters...and whom he could avoid no longer.

Vincent was brilliant, unconventional, almost protean in his thinking. Unless something remarkable had changed, he wore spiky, kinky, sandy-auburn braids a shade darker than his freckled skin and a shade paler than his light-catching eyes. He was tall, sarcastic, slender, bird-handed, generous with smiles as breathtaking as the nebula outside the bubbleport.

And he was the man Michelangelo Kusanagi-Jones had loved for forty years, although he had not seen him in seventeen—since the *last* time he had betrayed him.

Not that anybody was counting.

Kusanagi-Jones had anticipated their date by hours, until the gray and white lounge with its gray and white furniture retreated from his awareness like a painted backdrop. If Kusanagi-Jones captained a starship, he'd license it in reds and golds, vivid prints, anything to combat the black boredom of space.

Another man might have snorted and shaken his head, but Kusanagi-Jones didn't quite permit himself a smile of self-knowledge. He was trying to distract himself, because the liquor wasn't helping anymore. And in addition to his other qualities, Vincent was also almost pathologically punctual. He should be along any tick—and, in fact, a shadow now moved across

Kusanagi-Jones's fish-eye sensor, accompanied by the rasp of shoes on carpet. "Michelangelo."

Kusanagi-Jones finished his drink, set the glass in the dispensall, and turned. No, Vincent hadn't changed. Slightly softer, belly and chin not as tight as in their youth, gray dulling hair he was too proud to have melanized. But in the vigorous middle age of his sixties, Vincent was still—

"Mr. Katherinessen." Kusanagi-Jones made his decision and extended his hand, ignoring Vincent's considering frown. Not a gesture one made to a business associate.

Through the resistance of their wardrobes, fingers brushed. Hands clasped. Vincent hadn't changed his program either.

They could still touch.

Kusanagi-Jones had thought he was ready. But if he hadn't known, he would have thought he'd been jabbed, nano-infected. He'd have snatched his hand back and checked his readout, hoping his docs could improvise a counteragent.

But it was just chemistry. The reason they'd been separated. The reason they were here, together again, on a starship making port in orbit around a renegade world. *Old times,* Kusanagi-Jones thought.

Vincent arched an eyebrow in silent agreement, as if they'd never parted.

"Kill or be killed," Vincent said, next best thing to a mantra. Kusanagi-Jones squeezed his fingers and let their hands fall apart, but it didn't sever the connection. It was too practiced, too reflexive. Vincent's gift, the empathy, the *sympathy* that turned them from men into a team. Vincent's particular gift, complement of Kusanagi-Jones's.

Vincent stared at him, tawny eyes bright. Kusanagi-

Jones shrugged and turned his back, running his fingers across the rainbow lights of his subdermal watch to order another martini, codes flickering across neuromorphed retinas. He stared out the bubble again, waiting while the drink was mixed, and retrieved it from the dispensall less than a meter away.

"Oh, good." Vincent's Earth patois—his com-pat— was accentless. "Nothing makes a first impression like turning up shitfaced."

"They think we're animals anyway." Kusanagi-Jones gestured to a crescent world resolving as *Kaiwo Maru* entered the plane of the ecliptic and began changing to give her passengers the best view. "Not like we had a chance to make them like us. Look, crew's modulating the ship."

"Seen one reconfig, seen them all." Nevertheless, Vincent came up to him and they waited, silent, while *Kaiwo Maru* reworked from a compact shape optimized for travel to something spidery and elegant, designed to dock with the station and transfer cargo— alive and material—as efficiently as possible.

"Behold," Vincent teased. "New Amazonia."

Kusanagi-Jones took a sip of his martini, rolling the welcome rawness over his tongue. "Stupid name for a planet." He didn't mind when Vincent didn't answer.

Bravado aside, Michelangelo did stop drinking with the one in his hand, and Vincent pretended not to notice that he checked his watch and adjusted his blood chemistry. Meanwhile, *Kaiwo Maru* docked without a shiver. Vincent didn't even have to put his hand out to steady himself. He pretended, also, that he was looking at the towering curve of the station beyond the bubble, but really, he was watching Michelangelo's reflection.

There had been times in the last decade and a half when Vincent had been convinced he'd never exactly remember that face. And there had been times when he'd been just as convinced he'd never get it out of his head. That he could feel Michelangelo standing beside him, glowering as he was glowering now.

One wouldn't discern it casually; Angelo wouldn't permit that much emotion revealed. His features were broad and solemn, his eyes stern except when bright. He seemed stolid, wary, unassuming—a blocky muscular man whose coloring facilitated his tendency to fade into the shadows. But Vincent *felt* him glowering, his displeasure like the weight of an angry hand.

Michelangelo glanced at his watch as if contemplating the colored lights. Vincent knew Michelangelo had a heads-up; he wasn't checking the time. He was fidgeting.

Fidgeting was new.

"I don't love you anymore." Michelangelo pressed his hand to the bubble and then raised it to his mouth.

"I know. I *can* still read your mind."

Michelangelo snorted against the back of his fingers. "I'm a Liar, Vincent. You'll believe what I want you to believe."

"How generous."

"Just true." Then the irony of his own statement seemed to strike him. He dropped his head and stared at the tips of his shoes as if hypnotized by the rainbows reflected across them. When he glanced back up, Vincent could read laughter in the way the crinkles at the corners of his eyes had deepened.

Vincent chuckled. He touched his watch, keying his wardrobe to something more formal, and stilled momentarily while the program spread and the wardrobe rearranged itself. "Do you *want* me, at least? That would make things easier."

Michelangelo shrugged, impassive. Vincent turned, now watching him frankly, and wondered how much of the attraction was—had always been—that Michelangelo was one of the few people he'd met that he *couldn't* read like a fiche.

"They offered me a choice. Therapy or forced retirement."

Michelangelo's coloring was too dark for his face to pale, but the blood draining made him ashen. "You took therapy."

Vincent stifled a vindictive impulse. "I took retirement. I don't consider my sexuality something that needs to be *fixed*."

"Sign of persistent pathology," Michelangelo said lightly, but his hands trembled.

"So I've been told. The funny thing is, they couldn't make it stick. I didn't even make it home before I was recalled. Apparently I'm indispensable."

Michelangelo's thumb moved across his inner wrist, giving Vincent a sympathetic shiver at the imagined texture of the skin. Another glass appeared in the dispensall, but from the smell, this one was fruit juice.

He sipped the juice and made a face. "I heard."

Vincent wondered if the license was off. "And you?"

"Not as indispensable as Vincent Katherinessen." He put the glass back and watched as it recycled: the drink vaporizing, the glass fogging. A waste of energy; Vincent controlled the urge to lecture. If they got what they needed on New Amazonia, it wouldn't be an issue—and anyway, they were on a starship, the one place in the entire OECC where conserving energy wasn't a civic duty as mandated as community service. "I took the therapy."

Vincent swallowed, wishing he could taste something other than the tang of atomizing juice. He picked a nonexistent bit of lint off his sleeve. "Oh."

Michelangelo lifted his chin, turned, and gave Vincent a smile warm enough to melt his implants. He glanced over his shoulder, as if ascertaining the lounge was empty, then leaned forward, slid both hands up Vincent's neck, and pulled Vincent's head down to plant a wet, tender kiss on his lips.

It's a lie, Vincent told himself, as his breath shortened and his body responded. Michelangelo was substantial, all muscle under the draped knits his wardrobe counterfeited. They both knew he controlled Vincent the instant Vincent let him close.

Just as Vincent knew Michelangelo's apparent abandonment to the kiss was probably as counterfeit as his "hand-knitted" sweater. *It's a lie. He took the therapy.* It didn't help. His body believed; his intuition trusted; the partnership breathed into the kiss and breathed out again. Sparkles of sensation followed Michelangelo's hands as they cupped Vincent's skull and stroked his nape. He *knew* Michelangelo wanted him, as he had always known. As Michelangelo had always *permitted* him to know.

He wondered what the ship's Governors made of the kiss, whether they had been instructed to turn a blind eye on whatever illegalities proceeded between the diplomat and his attaché. Or if their interaction had been logged and would be reported to the appropriate agencies within the Colonial Coalition when *Kaiwo Maru* dispatched a packet bot.

The relationship between the Cabinet and the Governors was complex; the Cabinet did not carry out death sentences, and the Governors did not answer to the Cabinet. But after the Great Cull, they had begun performing some of their Assessments in accordance with planetary laws. There was détente; an alliance, of sorts, by which the Cabinet maintained control and the Governors, with their own inhuman logic and society, supported an administration that maintained ecological balance.

Once, there had been many governments on Old Earth. Industrialized nation-states and alliances had used more than their share of resources and produced more than their share of waste. But Assessment had ended that, along with human life in the Northern Hemisphere. In the wake of an apocalypse, people often become reactionary, and the survivors of Assessment were disproportionately Muslim and Catholic. And in a society where being granted permission to reproduce was idealized—even fetishized—where every survivor meant that someone else had *not* lived...those who were different were not welcome.

Over a period of decades, in the face of necessity, resistance to the widespread use of reproductive technology and genetic surgery waned. The Governors did not care about the morality of the human-made laws they enforced. Or their irony either.

So, throughout Coalition space, that kiss was the overture to a capital case. But just this once, its illegality didn't matter. That particular illegality was why they were here.

Michelangelo leaned back, but his breath stayed warm on Vincent's cheek, and Vincent didn't pull away. "They'll just separate us again when this is over."

"Maybe. Maybe not. We were useful to them once."

"Politics were different then."

"The politics are different now, too."

Michelangelo disengaged, stepped back, and turned away. "Can't honestly think we will be allowed within three systems of each other. After New Earth"—Michelangelo's weight shifted, a guilty tell Vincent could have wasted half a day on if he'd been in the mood to try to figure out how much of what Michelangelo gave him was real—"we're lucky the Cabinet thought us useful enough to keep alive."

By Michelangelo's standards, it was a speech. Vincent stood blinking for a moment, wondering what else had changed. And then he thought about therapy, and the chip concealed in—but isolated from—his wardrobe. *Don't love you anymore.*

That would make things easier, wouldn't it?

"If we pull this off"—Vincent folded his hands behind his head—"The Cabinet won't deny us much. We could retire on it. I could finally introduce you to my mother."

A snort, but Michelangelo turned and leaned against the bubble, folding his arms. "If we don't wind up Assessed."

Vincent grinned, and Michelangelo grinned back reluctantly. The sour, sharp note in Michelangelo's voice was a homecoming. "If we bring home *just* the technology we're to negotiate for—"

"Assuming it is either portable or reproducible?"

"—we're unlikely to find ourselves surplused. I know what a cheap, clean energy source will mean to the Captaincy on Ur. And to appeasing the Governors. What will it mean on Old Earth?"

Michelangelo had that expression, the knitted brow and set muscle in his jaw that meant he agreed with Vincent and wasn't happy about it. He had to be thinking about Old Earth's tightly managed population of fifty million, about biodiversity and environmental load and Assessment. *Culling.*

"On Earth?" Michelangelo would never call it *Old Earth,* unless speaking to someone who wouldn't know what he meant otherwise. "Might mean no culls for fifty, a hundred years."

"That would pay for a lot." Michelangelo could do the math. Nonpolluting power meant that a larger population could be supported before triggering the Governors' inexorable logic.

The Governors did not argue. They simply followed the programs of the radical environmentalists who had unleashed them, and reduced the load.

Assessments were typically small now. Nothing like the near-extermination of the years surrounding Diaspora, because Old Earth's population had remained relatively stable since nine and a half billion citizens had been re-duced to organic compounds, their remains used to re-claim exhausted farmland, reinvigorate desertified grassland, enrich soil laid over the hulks of emptied cities—or simply sealed up in long-abandoned coal mines and oil wells.

Michelangelo's nod was curt, and slow in coming. Vincent wondered if he'd been mistaken in pushing for it, but then Michelangelo made him a little present of the smile they both knew tangled Vincent's breath around his heart. "And if we manage to overthrow their government, steal or destroy their tech, and get a picture of their prime minister in bed with a sheep in bondage gear?"

A heartbeat, but Vincent didn't even try to keep the relief off his face. "They'll probably give you another medal you're not allowed to take home."

Michelangelo's laugh might have been mistaken for choking. He shook his head when he stopped, and

waved a hand out the bubble at the light over the dock-
ing bay, on Boadicca Station's side. "Light's green.
Let's catch our bus."

Pretoria household's residence was already bannered
and flowered and gilded to excess when Lesa arrived
home, but that wasn't limiting the ongoing application
of gaud. The street-level entrance opened onto a wide
veranda, and one of Pretoria household's foremothers
had wheedled House into growing a long, filigreed lattice from floor to roof around it. It was a pleasant, airy
screen that normally created a sense of privacy without disrupting sight lines, but currently it was bur-
dened with enough garland to drift scent for blocks,
without considering the sticks of incense thrust in
among the flowers. Those would be lit two evenings
hence. In the meantime, misted water would keep the
blooms fresh.

Lesa climbed the steps along with the household
male who'd accompanied her on her errand. Xavier
carried a dozen bottles of wine in a divided wicker
holder slung over his shoulder. He was a steady, careful
sort; they didn't clink.

Lesa herself had two bags—the pick of fresh fruit
and vegetables from the morning's markets—and two
live chickens in a flat-bottomed sack, slumbering
through their last hours in artificial darkness. It paid to
get there early, especially near Carnival, and Elena
wouldn't trust the males or the servants with anything
as important as buying for a holiday meal.

Besides, they were all busy decorating.

Katya, Lesa's surviving daughter, supervised the activity on the veranda, her glossy black hair braided off

her neck, unhatted in the sun. "Melanoma," Lesa said, kissing her on the back of the head as she went by.

Katya was fifteen Amazonian years—twenty-odd, in standard conversion—and impatient with anything that smacked of responsible adulthood. And she wouldn't wear her honor around the house; her hip was naked even of a holster. Of course, Lesa—both hands full of groceries, unable to reach her honor without dropping chickens or fruit—wasn't much of an example, whatever her renown as a duelist twenty years and three children ago.

Katya blew her fringe out of her eyes. "Sunblock." She rubbed Lesa's cheek with a greasy finger. "Hats are too hot."

"On the contrary," Lesa said. "Hats are supposed to keep you cool." But it was like arguing with a fexa; the girl just gave her an inscrutable look and went back to braiding a gardeneid garland, the sweet juice from the crushed stems slicking her fingers. "Want help?"

"Love it," Katya said, "but Claude's in there. The Coalition ship made orbit overnight. You're on."

"They got here for Carnival? Typical male timing." Lesa stretched under her load.

"See you at dinner." Katya ducked from under her lapful of flowers and turned so she could lean forward mockingly to kiss the ring her mother wore on the hand that was currently occupied by the sack of chickens.

Inside the door, Lesa passed the groceries to one of the household staff and sent her off with Xavier once he'd kicked his sandals at the catchall. Lesa balanced on each foot in turn and unzipped her boots before hanging them on the caddy. In Penthesilea's equatorial heat, all sorts of unpleasant things grew in unaired shoes.

She dug her toes into the cool carpetplant with a

sigh of relief and hung up her hat, grateful to House for taking the edge off the sun. Claude and Elena would be in the morning room at breakfast, which was still being served. Lesa's stomach rumbled at the smell as she walked through seashell rooms and down an arched corridor, enjoying the aviform song House brought in from the jungle along with filtered light.

Elena Pretoria was exactly where Lesa had imagined her, on the back veranda with her long hands spread on the arms of a rattan chair— real furniture, not provided by House—her silver-streaked hair stripped into a tail and her skin glowing dark gold against white lounging clothes. For all the air of comfort and grace she projected, however, Lesa noticed the white leather of her holster slung on her waist and buckled down to her thigh. Elena had a past as a duelist, too, and as a politician. And she wasn't about to let Claude Singapore forget it, even if Claude's position as prime minister was enough rank to let her enter another woman's household without surrendering her honor.

Claude was tall and bony, a beautiful woman with blunt-cut hair that had been white as feathers since she was in her twenties, and some of the lightest eyes Lesa had ever seen—which perhaps explained the depth of the crow's-feet decorating her face. They couldn't all be from smiling, though Lesa wasn't sure she'd ever seen Claude *not* smiling. She had an arsenal of smiles, including a melancholy one for funerals.

"Lesa," Claude said, as Lesa greeted her mother with a little bow. "I'm here—"

"I heard. The grapevine's a light-minute ahead."

Claude stood up anyway, extending her hand. Lesa took it. Claude had a politician's handshake, firm but gentle. "I don't know why we even have media on this planet."

"It gives us someone to blame for scandals," Lesa answered, and Claude laughed even though it hadn't been funny. "I'm ready. When will they make landfall?"

"Tomorrow. We're shuttling them down. You'll come by this evening for a briefing?"

"Of course," Lesa said. "Dinnertime?"

"Good for me."

Claude stepped away from her chair, and Elena took it as a cue to stand. "Leaving us already?"

"The Republic never sleeps. And I can hear Lesa's stomach rumbling from here. I imagine she'd enjoy a quiet breakfast with her family before the madness begins."

"Claude, I don't mean to chase you out of your chair," Lesa said, but Claude was turning to shake Elena's hand.

"Nonsense." Claude stepped back, and adjusted her holster. It was a Y-style, and they had a tendency to pinch when one stood. "I'll see you tonight. I can show myself out—"

"Good-bye." Lesa did walk a few steps toward the door with the guest, so as not to give offense. When Claude was safely gone, she tilted her head at Elena. "Why did she come herself?"

"Probably a subtle message not to try anything tricky. She hasn't forgiven me for getting her wife ousted from the Export Board, and she still thinks the Coalition can be appeased." The twist of her mouth revealed what she thought of that idea. It made Lesa restrain a smile: it was also Katya's moue, and Lesa's son Julian made the same face when he was concentrating.

Lesa used that image of Julian to keep her voice under control. "As soon as they have what they want, the

Coalition will scorch us off the surface. They're distracting us while they set up the kill."

"They'd have to justify the ecological damage from an orbital attack to the Governors, and that would be...hard to get approval for, I imagine. They might convince the Governors that we need to be Assessed, however, and brought under control. We'd fight."

Lesa caught the glint of Elena's smile. "You heard from Katherine Lexasdaughter."

"Coded. A packet concealed in the *Kaiwo Maru*'s logburst as she made orbit."

Lesa could imagine the resources required to arrange for treason and insurrection to be transmitted in a ship's identification codes on a governed channel. Katherine was head of the Captain's Council on Ur, and held a chair in the Colonial Cabinet on the strength of it.

"He's coming." Lesa's chest lightened and tightened both at once. Elena might think she was the saltspider at the center of the web, but Lesa couldn't allow her to recognize all the layers of machinations here. Elena was not going to be happy with Lesa when things shook out.

Elena's smile was tight with guarded triumph. "I hate hanging our hopes on a man, even if he is both gentle *and* his mother's son. But he came."

2

BOADICCA WASN'T THE LEAST CIVILIZED STATION
Kusanagi-Jones had seen, but its status as a cargo transfer point rather than a passenger terminal was evident.
New Amazonia's trade was with other Diaspora worlds,
a ragtag disorganization of colonies beyond the reach of
Coalition growth—for now, anyway. (Kusanagi-Jones
occasionally wondered if the Governors' long-dead pro-
genitors had understood that in their creation, they had
delivered unto Earth's survivors a powerful impetus to
expansion.)

Boadicca reflected that isolation. The curved pas-
sageways were devoid of decoration, creature comforts,
carpeting, kiosks, and shops. The only color was vivid
stripes of contack, which scanned the watches of
nearby pedestrians to provide helpful arrows and
schematics. Kusanagi-Jones paused to study the patterns, and frowned. "Security risk," he said, when
Vincent looked a question. "Too easy for a third party

to match up destination with traveler. Must be short on saboteurs and terrorists here."

Vincent smiled, and Kusanagi-Jones read the comment in the air between them. *Not anymore.*

"Good old Earth," Kusanagi-Jones agreed, lapsing out of common-pat and into a language that wasn't taught in any school. "If you can't bring it home, blow it up."

Secrets within secrets, the way the game was always played. If they couldn't find a way to bring New Amazonia under OECC hegemony with at least the pretense of consent—the way Vincent's homeworld Ur had fallen—they would weaken the local government through any means necessary, until the colonials came crawling to Earth for help.

Colonies were fragile, short on population and resources. On Ur, for example, there had been the issue of sustainable agriculture, of a limited gene pool further damaged by the exigencies of long-distance space travel, of the need for trade and communication with other worlds. Where Ur maintained a pretense of sovereignty and had significant representation on the OECC's Cabinet, successful sabotage leading to a failure of strength would result in a worse outcome for New Amazonia in the long run. And if Vincent and Kusanagi-Jones did their jobs as ordered, that was the plan, just as it had been on New Earth.

And just as on New Earth, Kusanagi-Jones didn't intend to allow the plan to come to fruition. He also wasn't foolish enough to think that a second act of self-sabotage would evade his superiors' notice.

Vincent defocused as he checked his watch. "I'd kill for a coffee. But our luggage is on the lighter."

"I hope it was well packed." *Luggage* was an inadequate term; the cargo pod that Vincent had shepherded

all the way from Earth under diplomatic seal carried
what their documents euphemistically identified as
samples. Those samples included, among other objects,
Fionha Dubhai's holographic sculpture *Ice Age* and an
original pastel by the Impressionist Berthe Morisot.
Irreplaceable didn't even begin to cover it. And *bargaining chip* was only the beginning of the story.
There was more back on Earth; this shipment was only
to prove goodwill—to show willing, as Vincent would
say. Whatever their history, the OECC wasn't stinting
on the tools to do its job, either by bargaining or by
blowing things up.

Vincent put a hand on Kusanagi-Jones's elbow as
they drew up before a loading bay, one identical
among many. Two green lights blinking beside the
archway indicated their destination. "This is the end
of the line."

"You said it." They walked forward, side by side, to
link their documents into the lighter's system so the
pilot could tell them where to go.

The long New Amazonian day was inconvenient for
creatures whose biorhythms were geared toward a
twenty-four-hour cycle. Lag became a problem in
more temperate climes, but Penthesilea was fortunate
in that high heat provided a supremely adequate excuse for a midafternoon siesta. During more than two-
thirds of the year, it was followed by the afternoon
rains, which signaled the city's reawakening for the
evening round of business.

Lesa cheated and let Julian stay with her while she
napped. Walter, the big khir that usually slept in her
rooms, was nowhere in evidence—probably off with
Katya—and Julian at six and a half local years was of

the age when naps were an abomination before the god of men. He sat up at Lesa's terminal while she flopped across the bed and closed her eyes. She'd seen the problem he was working. He said it was a minor modification of House's program, though Lesa didn't have the skills to even read it, let alone solve it, but Julian was so thoroughly engaged that she let him keep tapping away as she dozed, lulled by the ticking of the interface.

That sound blended into the patter of the rain on her balcony so that she didn't rouse until House pinged her. She opened her eyes on yellow walls shifting with violent sunlight—entirely unlike the gray skies outside—and winced. "House, dial it down, please."

The light dimmed, the walls and ceiling filling with the images of wind-rustled leaves and vines. She stretched and rubbed her eyes. "Hello, Mom," Julian said without looking up from the monitors. "Did you sleep well?"

She rubbed at her eyes and padded across the carpetplant to the wardrobe. "Too well," she said. "I'm late. Save your work, Julian, and go eat."

"Mom—"

She paused, a fistful of patterned sylk drawn out into the light, and turned to stare at the back of his head. "You know you can't stay down here while I'm gone."

His shoulders drooped, but his hand passed quickly over the save light, and he powered the terminal down before sliding, monkeylike, out of the chair. It was a little too tall for him, so he had hooked his toes over a brace while he worked, and the disentangling turned him into a study in conflicted angles. "All right," he said, and came to hug her before vanishing through the door, gone before it had entirely irised open.

Lesa dressed for business in the warmth of the evening; the rain would be over before she left. She chose a tailored wrap skirt and the sylk blouse, and belted her honor over the skirt. Claude could take offense at anything, even if Lesa were of a mind to show up anywhere public unarmed. And the skirt would be cool enough; she couldn't face trousers after the rain, with the hottest part of the year beginning.

Downstairs, she passed Xavier in the foyer, coming in from the decorating. Lesa had taken her own turn earlier in the day. At least it was better than pulling the flowers down, which was the part she truly hated.

She told House she was leaving, and asked it to summon a car. The vehicle was waiting by the time she reached the end of the alley that fronted Pretoria house; a diplomatic groundcar with a male driver, his street license prominently displayed on his shoulder— marking a gentle male, rather than a stud like Xavier. He smiled as she slid in. "Government center?"

"Singapore house," she said. "I have a dinner invitation."

He drove carefully, politely, through the rain-flooded streets. Water peeled away under the groundcar's tires on long plumes, but the only people outside during cloudover were one or two employed stud males with street licenses hurrying back to their households or dormitories for dinner, and the householders on their porches under umbrella-covered tables, sipping drinks and enjoying the brief cooling.

The household Claude Singapore shared with her wife, Maiju Montevideo, was on the seaward side of the city, overlooking the broad, smooth bay. By the time Lesa arrived, the clouds had peeled back from the tops of Penthesilea's storied towers. The rays of the westering sun penetrated, sparking color off the ocean, brightening it from gray to the usual ideal blue.

Lesa Pretoria was not Claude Singapore, and her own rank as a deputy chief of Security Directorate did not entitle her to carry her honor inside another woman's house. She paused at the top of the steps to Singapore house's door and surrendered it to the woman who waited there, along with her boots. Both were hung neatly on a rack, and Lesa smiled a thanks. There was a male servant present, too, but he could not touch firearms.

She must come armed, to show her willingness to use her strength in defense of Pretoria household's alliance with Singapore, and she must be willing to lay that strength aside to meet with Claude. There were forms, and to ignore them was to give offense.

Lesa wasn't particularly concerned about offending, however prickly Claude might be. Lesa could outduel her. But it was also polite. She gave the male servant her overcoat and followed the woman inside.

Although the rains were barely breaking, Lesa was the last to arrive. Claude and Maiju and the other guests were gathered around a table under a pavilion in the courtyard, sitting on low carpet-covered stools to keep the dampness off their clothes.

In addition to the prime minister, there was Miss Ouagadougou, the art expert who would be working directly with the Coalition diplomat. She was joined by her male confidential secretary, Stefan—a striking near-blond, almost unscarred, though Lesa knew he'd had a reputation during his time in the Trials. Beside them sat Lesa's superior, Elder Kyoto, the head of Security Directorate.

Claude stood as Lesa emerged from the passageway, disentangling her long legs from the bench, and

ushered Lesa to a seat—one strategically between
Maiju and Stefan, Lesa noticed with a grin. Maiju was
separatist; she'd as soon see all the males—stud *and*
gentle—on New Amazonia culled down to the bare
minimum and confined to a gulag. Or better yet, the
widespread acceptance of reproductive gene splicing.

It would take a revolution to make that happen. Lesa
wasn't the only Penthesilean woman who honestly enjoyed the company—and the physical affection—of
males. And artificial insemination and genetic tamper-
ing were banned under the New Amazonian constitu-
tion. On Old Earth, before the Diaspora, there had been
extensive genetic research, and it had led to the birth
of people who would be considered abominations in
Lesa's culture. Human clones, genetically manipulated
people—their descendents might still be alive on Old
Earth today.

One of the representatives the Coalition Cabinet
was sending was an Old Earth native. Lesa tried not to
think too much about that, about what could be lurk-
ing in his ancestry.

Maiju was a radical. But her wife was prime minister, and so she kept her opinions to herself.

"Good evening, Elder Montevideo, Elder Kyoto,
Stefan," Lesa said, as she helped herself to a glossleaf
to use as a plate. The dining was informal, and Stefan
served her without being asked, graciously playing
host.

The dark green leaf curled up at the edges, a convenient lip to pinch her food against. She was hungrier
than she had realized, and once Claude resumed her
place and began eating, Lesa joined in, rinsing her fingers in the bowl of water by her place to keep them
from growing sticky with the sauce. The wine was

served in short-stemmed cups, and she kept her left hand dry for drinking with.

At a more formal meal there would have been utensils, but this was family style, intended to inform those assembled that they might speak freely and conduct business with candor. Nevertheless, Lesa waited until Claude pushed her glossleaf away before she spoke. "Tell me about the delegates," she said.

"You know the senior diplomat is Vincent Katherinessen, the son of the Captain of Ur."

"Reclaimed peacefully by the Old Earth Colonial Coalition some fifty-seven standard years ago," Lesa said, "and, though there are Governors on-planet, generally granted unprecedented freedoms by the Cabinet because they keep their own population down, accept Old Earth immigrants, and practice a religion that encourages ecological responsibility. Katherinessen is a superperceiver, which is why he'll be my especial problem."

"Yes," Claude said. "We requested him. He's the only admitted gentle male in the Coalition's diplomatic service. There was a scandal——"

"Something on New Earth, wasn't it?"

Stefan stood as the women talked and began whisking used glossleafs off the table, piling them to one side for the convenience of the service staff. Meanwhile, Maiju did them all the honor of serving the sweet, an herb-flavored ice presented in capacious bowls, with fluted spoons, and accompanied by real shade-grown Old Earth coffee—a shrub that flourished in the New Amazonian climate.

"A Coalition warship, the *Skidbladnir*, was destroyed by sabotage during a diplomatic mission headed by Katherinessen. The lack of military assets allowed New Earth to walk away with its sovereignty intact.

Another mission was sent, but by the time it arrived, New Earth had managed to scramble enough of a military operation to make the cost of retaking the world excessive, and the Governors would not permit a full-scale use of force because of the ecological impact. New Earth is marginally habitable at best—it's cold and has a low oxygen rating and not a lot of water, which made it a poor investment from the Governors' point of view, as they will not permit Terraforming. During the investigation it came out that Katherinessen had what they would call an improper relationship with his attaché." Claude's habitual smile drifted wider as her left hand crept out to take Maiju's possessively. "I don't know why they weren't culled for the...'crime.'"

"And here he is," Lesa said, and then slipped her spoon into her mouth and let the ice melt over her tongue, spreading flavors that shimmered and changed as it warmed.

"Guess who they sent along with him?"

Lesa's spoon clicked on the bowl. "The attaché?"

"Amusing, isn't it?" Claude steepled her fingers behind her untouched dessert. "They seem to have taken us at our word when we said we would only accept women, or gentle males."

Lesa shook her head, and drank two swallows of scalding coffee too rapidly, to clear her palate before she spoke. "It's got to be a trick."

"Of course it is," Claude said. "No smart woman would expect the Coalition to deal in goodwill."

"We're not either," Miss Ouagadougou said, who had been so quiet. "We can't give them what they're trading for. It's unexportable."

"Don't worry," Claude said. "We have that covered.

We're not going to give them anything at all. Anything they want, in any case."

The meeting continued long past midnight. Afterward, Lesa returned home, changed clothes, and rode the lift almost to the top of the towering spire of Pretoria house. She slipped past Agnes and into the Blue Rooms, saying she was going to check on Julian. She stopped, though, and crossed to the outside wall, where she climbed into an archway and watched the snarled sky turn toward sunrise. Lesa's hair was tangled, leached to streaked black and gray in the nebula-light. The Gorgon stretched overhead, a frail twist of color like watered silk, far too permeable a barrier to hold anything at bay for long. Pinprick glows slid against it, red and green, and she wondered if the cargo lighter descending across the dying nebula carried the Colonial diplomats.

Lesa hugged herself despite her nightshirt sticking to her skin, despite the jungle beyond the city walls still steaming from afternoon rains. It wasn't safe to stand here half clothed, her honor left with Agnes outside and nothing between her and a messy death except her reflexes and a half-kilometer of space.

But she needed the air, and she needed the warmth. And she could hear the stud males sleeping, their snores and soft breath soothing enough that she almost thought about lying down to sleep beside them. Her mother would have her hide for a holster in the morning, of course, but it might be worth it. Elena Pretoria was almost sixty; she was still sharp and stubborn and undeniably in charge, but Lesa was more than capable of giving her a challenge, and they both knew it.

And the men knew which member of the household

looked out for them, and they knew there were gentles
and armed women beyond the door. Some women
were frightened of men—hopelessly old-fashioned, in
Lesa's estimation. Stud males might be emotional, tem-
peramental, and developmentally stunted, at the mercy
of their androgens, but that didn't make them incapable of generosity, friendship, cleverness, or creativity.

It wasn't their fault that they weren't women. And
Lesa knew better than to provoke them, anyway. Like
any animal—like the house khir that had been Lesa's
responsibility before Katya took over—they could be
managed. Even befriended. They simply demanded
caution and respect.

Which was something many women were not willing to offer to stud males, or even gentle ones, but Lesa
found she preferred their honesty to the politics of
women. An eccentricity—but that eccentricity was one
reason why she would be the one to meet the Colonials
when they came.

The reason besides Katherinessen. She was looking
forward to that. She stroked the archway and felt
House shiver its pleasure at the touch.

Some people couldn't sense the city's awareness of
their presence and its affection. Lesa found it comforting. Especially as she considered the thorniness of the
problem she faced.

Her mother believed in the process. No matter what,
no matter how much wrangling went on between
Elena and Claude, Elena believed in the process. In the
New Amazonian philosophy.

And Lesa no longer did.

She stepped back. The wall stayed open and a warm
breeze chased her, bringing jungle scents and the calls
of a night-flyer. She'd worry about the Colonials tomorrow. Tonight, she picked her way past the sleeping

men, brushing a finger across her lips when her fa-
vorite, Robert, lifted his head from his arm and
watched her go by. He winked; she smiled.

The boys' quarters were at the back of the Blue
Rooms. She pushed past the curtain and held her palm
to the sensor so House could recognize her and let her
pass. The boys slept even more soundly than the men.

None of them woke. Not even Julian, when she
climbed over him and the yearling khir curled against
his chest, slid between his body and the wall, and
pushed her face into his hair as if she could breathe his
rag-doll relaxation into her bones.

*Timeslip. Cold currents on unreal skin. The flesh-
adapted brain interprets this as air on scales, air tickling
feathers.*

*Kii had wings once. Eyes, fingers, tongue. No more.
Now, Kii watches the aliens through ghost-eyes, tastes
their heat and scents and sounds through ghost-organs.
No skin-brush, tongue-flicker, swing of muzzle to inhale
warmth through labial pits.*

*The aliens are that. Alien. Unscaled, unfeathered.
Tool users with their soft polydactyl hands. They totter
on legs, bipedal, hair patchy as if with parasites. But after Kii has seen a few, Kii understands they are supposed
to look that way.*

*Sudden creatures, and so strange, with their hierar-
chies and their false Consent that leaves them unhappy,
untribed.*

*But they know combat for honor, and the care of
young, and they keep the khir. And they know art for its
own sake.*

They are esthelich, *cognizant of order. And that is new.
The ghost-others think Kii's fascination strange. But*

*Kii is explorer-caste, a few still remaining—still needed
even among the ghosts—and Kii is not content with experiment, manipulation, analysis. The others may engage with cosmoclines, programming, reordering the
infrastructure of their vast and artificial universe. They
may manipulate wormholes, link branes, enhance control. They have mistressed power enough to manufacture
entire branes—objects similar to a naturally occurring
four-dimensional universe—and learned finesse enough
to program them. They have aspired to leave their shells
and embrace immortality.*

*Nothing they are or desire cannot be made or remade
on a whim. They are beyond challenge. They no longer
evolve.*

*And yet Kii watches the alien curl around its cub as
the cub curls around the khir, and Kii sees something
new. Perhaps Kii is in need of a programming adjust-
ment, but it is not violating Consent to wonder.*

And things that are new are things that Kii's caste is for.

On fourteen worlds, Vincent Katherinessen had never
seen a city like Penthesilea.

The limousine they'd transferred into after the
lighter's splashdown came in low, skimming over the
wind-ruffled bay and the densely verdant forests that
grew against the seashell walls of the ancient, alien
city. The pilot was giving the emissaries the view; she
brought the craft up on an arcing spiral that showed
off three sides of the skyline.

Vincent leaned against the window shamelessly and
stared. The structures—if they *were* individual structures, given how they flowed and merged together,
like tall colonies of some sea animal with calcified ex-
oskeletons—were earth-shades and jewel-shades, re-

flecting a dark oily iridescence like black opal or treated titanium. Vincent wondered if they were solar. The colors were suggestive, but could be decorative—though he couldn't think of a human culture that would choose that color scheme or the chaotic, almost fractal architecture that put him in mind of something arranged by colony insects, Ur-hornets or Old Earth termites.

No one really knew. As the OECC had reconstructed from its incomplete access to New Amazonian records, Penthesilea looked more or less as it had when the New Amazonians arrived—the only evidence of nonhuman intelligence that had been found on any explored world. There were four other cities, each miraculously undamaged and thrumming after centuries of abandonment, each apparently designed by an intelligence with little physical resemblance to humans. And each cheerfully polymorphous and ready to adapt to the needs of new occupants who, in the hard, early days of the colony, had determined convenient shelter to be the better part of caution, and who had not been proven wrong in the decades since. Arguments about their nature and design possessed the OECC scientific community and proved largely masturbatory. New Amazonia wasn't about to allow a team in to research their construction, their design, their archaeology, or—most interesting of all to the OECC—their apparently clean and limitless power source.

So Vincent and Michelangelo were here to steal it. And if they couldn't steal it—

There were always fallback options.

Vincent glanced at his partner. Michelangelo sat passive, inward-turned, as if he were reading something on his heads-up. He wasn't; he was aware, observing, thinking, albeit in that state where he seemed to have become just another fixture. Vincent nudged him—not physically, exactly, more a pressure of his attention—and Michelangelo turned and cleared his throat.

Vincent gestured to the window. "Change your clothes. It's time to go to work."

Michelangelo ran fingers across his watch without looking, and stilled for a moment as the foglets in his wardrobe arranged themselves into a mandarin-collared suit of more conservative cut than Vincent's, ivory and ghost-silver, a staid complement to Vincent's eye-catching colors. "Kill or be killed," he murmured, his mouth barely shaping the words so neither the pilot nor the limousine would hear them.

Vincent smiled. *That's what I'm afraid of.*

Michelangelo nodded, curtly, as though he had spoken.

The first thing Kusanagi-Jones noticed as he stepped down from the limousine was that the pavement wasn't exactly pavement. The second thing was that there were no plants, no flowers except the freshly dead garlands twined with ribbon or contack that hung from every facade. No landscaping, no songbirds—or the New Amazonian equivalent—just the seemingly wind-sculpted architecture, buildings like pueblos and weathered sandstone spires and wind-pocked cliff faces. He stood, tropical humidity prickling sweat across his brow, and arched his neck back to look up at the legendary Haunted City of New Amazonia.

He didn't see any ghosts.

He'd done his threat assessment before the door of the limousine ever glided open, and he reconsidered it now, as his wardrobe wicked sweat off his skin so quickly he barely felt damp and his toiletries combated the frizz springing up in his hair. He blocked the door of the limousine, covering Vincent with his body, and turned like a shadow across a sundial to scan roofs and the assembled women with his naked eyes and an assortment of augments.

The Penthesilean security forces stood about where he would have stationed them, and that was good. It was good also that the women in the greeting party stayed back and let him make sure of the surroundings rather than rushing in. He hated crowds.

Especially when he was with Vincent.

He moved away, and a moment later Vincent stood beside him. Kusanagi-Jones's skin prickled, but there was nothing but the dark opalescent *something* under his feet, the punishing equatorial sun, and the three women who detached themselves from the dignitaries and started forward. The one in the middle was the important one; older, with what Kusanagi-Jones identified——with a bit of wonder——as sun-creases decorating the edges of long black eyes distinguished by epicanthic folds. Her hair was straight and shoulder length, undercut, the top layer dyed in stained-glass colors, shifting to reveal glossy black. She wore dark vibrant red, what Kusanagi-Jones thought was a real cloth suit——a blatant display of consumption.

The two behind her were security, he thought; broadshouldered young women in dark plain wardrobes or clothing, with the glow of animal health and stern expressions calculated to give nothing away. All three of them were openly armed.

Kusanagi-Jones knew how to use a sidearm. He'd received training in *all* the illegal arts, although he'd never been a soldier. And he'd been on planets raw enough that citizens were still issued permits for long weapons. But he'd never been in the presence of people—especially women—who wore their warcraft on their sleeves.

He wondered if they could shoot.

It made him unhappy, but he stepped to one side and allowed Vincent to take point. The older woman stepped forward, too. "I'm Lesa Pretoria," she said in accented com-pat, tendering a hand.

Vincent reached to take it as if touching strangers were something he did every day. He shook it while Kusanagi-Jones hurried to adjust his filters so he could follow suit. "Vincent Katherinessen."

"That's not a Coalition name," Miss Pretoria said.

"I was born on Ur, a repatriated world. This is my partner, Michelangelo Osiris Leary Kusanagi-Jones. He *is* from Old Earth."

"Ah." A world of complexity in that syllable. Vincent had answered in nearly flawless New Amazonian argot, which owed less to Spanish and Arabic and more to Afrikaans than com-pat did. She extended her hand to Kusanagi-Jones. "I'll be your guide and inter-preter."

Warden, Kusanagi-Jones translated, taking her hand and bowing over it, painfully aware of her considera-tion as his wardrobe considered her and let them touch. "The fox."

She blinked at him, reclaiming her appendage. "Beg pardon?"

"Lesa," he said. "Means *the fox*."

Her lips quirked. "What's a fox, Miss Kusanagi-Jones?"

The Amazonian patois had no honorific for unmar-ried men, and his status here was at least diplomatically speaking better than that of a *Mister*. So being called *Miss* relaxed him, although he caught Vincent's sharp amusement, an undertone flavored with mockery.

Just another mission, just another foreign land. Just another alien culture to be navigated with tact. He smiled at Vincent past Miss Pretoria's shoulder and bowed deeper before he straightened. "An Old Earth animal. Beautiful. Very clever."

"Like what we call a *fexa*, then? A hunting omnivore?" she continued as he nodded. "All gone now, I suppose?"

"Not at all. Seven hundred and fourteen genotypes preserved, of four species or subspecies. Breeding nicely on reintroduction." He gave her a substandard copy of Vincent's smile number seven, charming but not sexually threatening. "Featured in legends of Asia, Europe, and North America."

"Fascinating," she said, but she obviously had absolutely no idea where those places were, and less interest in their history. "Those are nations?"

"Continents," he said, and left it at that, before Vincent's mirth could bubble the hide off his bones like lye. He stepped back, and Miss Pretoria moved to fill the space as smoothly as if he'd gestured her into it—no hesitation, no double-checking. They fell into step, Vincent flanking Pretoria and himself flanking Vincent, her security detail a weighty absence on either side: alert, dangerous, and imperturbable. Pretoria ignored them like her breath.

Kusanagi-Jones caught Vincent's eye as they headed for the reception line. *Your reputation precedes you, Vincent. She's like you.* Neither an empath nor a telepath; nothing so esoteric. Just somebody born with a greater than usual gift for interpreting body language, spotting a lie, a misdirection, an unexpected truth.

A superperceiver: that was the technical term used in the programs they'd been selected for as students, where Michelangelo was classified as *controlled kines-thetic,* but the few with the clearance to know his gift called him a *Liar.*

He almost heard Vincent sigh in answer. Irritation: *do something, Angelo.* Not words, of course—just knowing what Vincent *would* have said.

Kusanagi-Jones took his cue as they entered the receiving line and tried for a conversation with Miss Pretoria between the archaic handshakes and watch-assisted memorization of each name and rank. He knew as soon as he thought it that he shouldn't say it, but it was his job to be the brash one, Vincent's to play the diplomat.

He leaned over and murmured in Miss Pretoria's ear, "How does a planet come to be called New Amazonia?"

Her lip curled off a smile more wolf than fox. "Miss Kusanagi-Jones," she said, the dryness informing her voice the first evidence of personality she'd shown, "surely you don't think we're *entirely* without a sense of humor."

He shook another stranger's hand over murmured pleasantries. There was a rhythm to it, and it wasn't unpleasant, once you got the hang of it. The New Amazonians had firm grips, sweaty with the scorching heat. He wished he'd worn a hat, as most of the women had.

He decided to risk it. "I admit to having worried—"

She didn't laugh, but her lip flickered up at the corner, as if she *almost* thought it was funny. "You'll be pleasantly surprised, I think. You're just in time for Carnival."

3

THEY HAD NOT BEEN LIED TO. THE MEN WERE GENTLE; when one leaned, moved, spoke, the other one mirrored. She sensed it in the energy between them, their calm failure to react on any visceral level to her smile, the swell of her breasts, the curve of her hips—or to the more youthful charms of her security detail. She knew it as surely as she would have known fear or hunger. Not only were they gentle, they were *together*.

She'd been afraid the Coalition would try to send stud males, to pass them off—even to replace Katherinessen with an impostor. These weren't quite like the gentle males of her acquaintance, though. They were wary, feral, watching the rooflines, eyes flickering to her honor and to the weapons of the other women. She shouldn't have been surprised. Without women in a position to protect them, gentle males would find rough going in a society dominated by stud males and hormonally driven aggression. She liked the

way they backed each other, the dark one and the
tawny one, shoulder to shoulder like sister khir against
a stranger pack. She wondered how old they were,
with their strange smooth faces and silken skin, and
the muscled hands that didn't match their educated
voices.

They survived the receiving line without a diplomatic incident, but both men seemed relieved when she
ushered them inside. Even filtered by the nebula—invisible in daytime—the sun was intense at the equator,
and they weren't accustomed to it. She'd read that on
Old Earth the cities were small, widely spaced, and
densely packed, the population strictly limited—
through culling and fetal murder, when necessary—
and the regenerated ecosystems were strictly off-limits
without travel permits.

She shuddered, thinking of that circumscribed existence, locked away from the jungle for her own protection and the world's—unable to pick up a long arm,
sling it over her back with a daypack and a satphone,
and vanish into the bush for a day or a week, free to
range as far as her daring would support. She could
have been like these men, she realized: coddled, blinking in the bright sunlight—or worse, because a woman
wouldn't rise to their position in the OECC. They'd
probably never been outside a filter field in their lives.

Good. That was an advantage. One she'd need, given
what Claude had told her about Katherinessen. The
legendary Vincent Katherinessen, and his legendary
ability to know what one thought before one knew it
oneself.

She collected herself and focused on the deal at
hand—which was, after all, a deal like any deal.
Something to be negotiated from the position of
strength that she was fortunate to have inherited.

"We've arranged a reception before we sit down to dinner. And some entertainment first. If you're not too tired from traveling."

Katherinessen's gaze flicked to his partner; Kusanagi-Jones tipped his head in something that wasn't quite a nod. The communication between them was interesting, almost transparent. Most people wouldn't have even seen it; *she* couldn't quite read it, but she thought she might learn. In the meantime, it was good to know that it was going on, that the dynamic between the two men was not quite the leader-and-subordinate hierarchy they projected. Something else developed for navigating a male-dominated space, no doubt.

"I think we're acceptably fresh," Katherinessen said, "as long as our licenses hold out. We both got a lot of sleep on the ship. But it would be nice to have a few moments to relax."

Lesa wanted to ask if he meant cryo, but wasn't sure if it would be in poor taste, so she nodded. "Come with me. The prime minister is eager to greet you, but she can wait half a tick."

"She thought it best not to overdignify our arrival with her presence?" Katherinessen asked. A sharp, forward question; Lesa glanced at him twice, but his face stayed bland.

"I've negotiating authority, Miss Katherinessen. Parliament, of course, will have to ratify whatever we agree."

"On our end, too. I'm assured it's a formality." His shrug continued, *but so are we always assured, are we not?* The raised eyebrow was a nice touch, including her in the conspiracy of those who labor at the unreasoning whim of the state. "Am I supposed to inquire as to the nature of the entertainment?"

She smiled back, playing the game. "It's the day

before Carnival. We thought you might like a real
frontier experience, and the Trials began at first light
today. If that meets with your approval."

His smile broadened cautiously. He was really a
striking man, with his freckles and his auburn hair.
Pity he's gentle, she thought, and then mocked herself
for thinking it. If he wasn't, after all, he wouldn't be
here. And she shouldn't be anywhere near him, honor
on her hip and security detail or not.

"We are at your disposal, Miss Pretoria," he said,
and gestured her graciously ahead. The security detail
followed.

One reason Kusanagi-Jones trained as rigorously as he
did was because it speeded adaptation. He could have
taken augmentation to increase or maintain his strength,
but doing the work himself gave additional benefits in
confidence, balance, and reflex integration. His brain
knew what his body was capable of, and that could be the
edge that kept him, or Vincent, alive.

That never changed the fact that for the first day or
two in a changed environment, he struggled as if finding his sea legs. But as far as he was concerned, the less
time spent tripping over invisible, immaterial objects,
the better.

So it was a mixed blessing to discover that wherever
Miss Pretoria was taking them, they were walking. It
would help with acclimation, but it also left Vincent
exposed. Kusanagi-Jones clung to his side, only half an
ear on the conversation, and kept an eye on the windows and the rooftops. To say that he didn't trust the
Penthesilean security was an understatement.

"Tell me about these Trials," Vincent was saying.
"And about Carnival."

Lesa gave Vincent an arch look—over Kusanagi-Jones's shoulder—but he pretended oblivion. "Your briefings didn't cover that?"

"You are mysterious," Vincent answered diplomatically. "Intentionally so, I might add. Are they a sporting event?"

"A competition," Lesa answered. "You'll see. We're in time for a few rounds before high heat."

Around them, the atmosphere had textures with which Kusanagi-Jones was unfamiliar. The heat was no worse than Cairo, but the air felt dense and wet, even filtered by his wardrobe, and it carried a charge. *Expectant.*

"It gets hotter than this?" Vincent asked.

Lesa flipped her hair behind her ear. "This is just morning. Early afternoon is the worst."

They crossed another broad square that would have had Kusanagi-Jones breaking out in a cold sweat if the heat wasn't already stressing his wardrobe. Here, there were onlookers—mostly armed women, some of them going about their business and some not even pretending to, but all obviously interested in the delegates from Earth. Kusanagi-Jones was grateful that Vincent knew how the game was played and stuck close to him, using his body as protection.

Smooth as if they had never been apart.

Miss Pretoria led them under cover at last, into the shade of an archway broad enough for two ground-cars abreast. The path they followed descended, and women in small, chatting groups emerged from below—settling hats and draping scarves against the climbing sun—or fell in behind, following them down.

This place was cooler, and the air now carried not just electric expectation, but the scent of an arena. Chalk dust, sweat, and cooking oil tickled Kusanagi-

Jones's sinuses. He sneezed, and Miss Pretoria smiled at him. He spared her a frown; she looked away quickly.

"Down this way," she instructed, stepping out of the flow of traffic and gesturing them through a door that irised open when she passed her hand across it. Kusanagi-Jones stepped through second, because the taller of the two security agents beat him to first place.

This was a smaller passageway, well lit without being uncomfortably bright. With a sigh, he let his wardrobe drop its inadequate compensations for the equatorial sun.

"Private passage," Miss Pretoria said. "Would you rather sit in my household's box, or the one reserved by Parliament for dignitaries?"

Vincent hesitated, searching her face for a cue. "Is yours nicer?" he asked.

Her mouth thinned. "It is," she said. "And closer to the action."

Kusanagi-Jones caught the shift in Vincent's weight, the sideways glance, as he was meant to. Miss Pretoria didn't approve of them, or perhaps she didn't approve of the "action."

Kusanagi-Jones stepped aside to let her take the lead again. It wasn't far: a few dozen yards and they could hear cheering, jeering, the almost inorganic noise of a crowd.

There must have been other concealed side passages, because this one led them directly to the Pretoria house box. They emerged through another irising door and among comfortable seats halfway up the wall of an oblong arena. The galleries were severely raked, vertiginous, and one of the security agents reached out as if to steady him when he marched up to the edge. He stepped away from her hand, and she let it fall.

When he leaned out, he looked down on the heads of the group seated immediately below. And Vincent was just as unprotected from anybody watching from the next tier above.

While the immediate security concerns distracted Kusanagi-Jones, Vincent touched his elbow. He didn't need to be told to follow Vincent's line of sight; he did it automatically, his alerted interest becoming a startle and a reflexive step closer as another cheer went up.

The floor of the arena was divided into long ovals, each one bounded by white walls that were thick, but not higher than a man's waist. And in each of the pits were men.

Young men, judging from the distance, paired off and engaged in contests of martial arts, each pair attended by an older man and a woman—referees or adjutants. Kusanagi-Jones, his hands tightening on the railing, had the expertise to know what he was seeing. These were men trained in a sort of barbaric amalgam of styles, and they were not fighting for points. He saw blood on the white walls, saw at least one individual fall and try to rise while his opponent continued kicking him, saw another absorb a punishing roundhouse and go down like a dropped handkerchief.

Beside him, Miss Pretoria cleared her throat. "There are screens," she said, and touched the wall he leaned against. "Please sit."

Vincent did, back to the wall, and Kusanagi-Jones was comforted when he saw Vincent surreptitiously dial his wardrobe higher. Kusanagi-Jones wasn't the only one feeling exposed.

Miss Pretoria continued fussing with the wall, and images blossomed under her hands. These were the same combats being carried out below, close-up, in real time. Nothing here was faked, or even as ritualized as the pre-Diaspora bloodsports that had masqueraded as contests of athletic prowess.

It was a public display of barbarism that Kusanagi-Jones should have found shocking if he were at all well socialized.

Vincent shifted slightly, leaning back in his chair, but Kusanagi-Jones wouldn't allow himself to give away so much. Instead, he placed himself in the seat before Vincent, beside Miss Pretoria, and leaned forward to speak into her ear as another roar went up from the galleries and—on the sand, on the monitors—another man fell. Medics came to him, capable women checking his airway and securing him to a back board, and the view on the monitor shifted to the weary champion feted by the referees. Around them, Kusanagi-Jones saw women consulting datacarts and bending in close conversation.

"What's the prize?"

Miss Pretoria considered him for a moment. "Status. To the victors go a choice of contracts; households with more status will bid for preferred males. Which benefits both them, and their mothers and sisters—"

Kusanagi-Jones didn't need to turn to see Vincent's expression. He hadn't let his fisheye drop since they set foot planetside.

Vincent reached past him, leaning forward, and indicated the monitor. "You're selecting *for* aggressive men?"

Miss Pretoria showed her teeth. "We're not docile, Miss Katherinessen. And we're not interested in forcing males to conform to standards that ignore what nature intended for them."

She said it easily, without apparent irony. But the look Vincent shot the back of Kusanagi-Jones's head had enough of that for all three of them and the self-effacing security agents, too.

They lingered at the arena for an hour or so longer than Vincent really wanted to be there, although he supposed it was beneficial in terms of information gathered—both regarding the society they found themselves contending with, and what Miss Pretoria chose to show them about it. Angelo, of course, watched the bloodsport with as much appearance of interest as he might have mustered for a particularly tiresome political speech. Even Vincent wasn't certain if he was analyzing the technique of the duelists and finding it wanting, musing on the ironies of this open display of arts that on Old Earth would be considered illegal, or sleeping with his eyes open.

Vincent, by contrast, let himself wince whenever he felt like it. Which was fairly frequently. Eventually, Miss Pretoria chose to take note of her guest's discomfort, and suggested she show them their quarters so that they could take advantage of siesta to get ready for the reception and dinner.

The walk back was quiet and uneventful, though the still-increasing heat left Vincent feeling unwell enough that he was grateful it wasn't long. He recognized the courtyard where they'd first emerged from the limousine by its colors and layout. The particular building they approached—if any given portion of the city could be called a separate building—had a long sensual single-story arch rising into a slender tower with a dimpled curve like that of a hip into a high-kicked leg. The tower was even shaped like a human leg—a strong, shapely one, with a pointed toe and a smooth swell of calf near the peak. An oval window or door opened into that small valley; Vincent would have liked to see a garden there, pots and orchids, maybe. On Ur, on Old Earth, there would have been flowers, great waterfalls of them growing up the wall. The swags and garlands of dead, cut flowers were another alien grace note, a funereal touch. They even smelled dead, sweet rot, although if you ignored the fact that they were corpses they were pretty.

Miss Pretoria smiled a quiet professional smile. "We think the Dragons were fliers. That's one of the reasons we call them Dragons; half the access points to the dwellings are above ground level, some of them at the tips of spires. It used to be more like four-fifths of them, but now that people have been living here for a hundred years, things have changed."

A hundred New Amazonian years; 150, give or take, of Earth's. "I was noticing the lack of plants."

"Oh," she said. "We don't really—well, I'll show you." She gestured them inside, through a curtain of cool air that ruffled the fine hairs on Vincent's neck. The doorway was simply open to the outside, air exchange permitted as if it cost nothing in resources to heat or cool. He bit his lip—and then lost his suppressed comment totally as they walked through the dim entryway and he got his first glimpse of the interior.

For a moment, he forgot he was inside a building at all. The walls seemed to vanish; he had the eerie sensation of standing in the center of a broad, gently rolling meadow bordered on three sides by jungle and on the fourth by the sunlit curve of the bay. A dark blue sky overhead poured sunlight, but less brilliantly. Vincent's headache eased as his squint relaxed. He no longer had to fight the urge to shade his eyes with his hand; this was like the sunlight he was accustomed to, the tame sunlight of Ur or Old Earth.

"Better?" Pretoria asked, pulling off her shoe.

"Very much so." He glanced around, aware of Michelangelo's solid presence on his left side, and pressed his foot into the flooring. It was soft, living. Not grass, of course, or the tough broad-turf of home, but a carpet of multiple-leaved, short-stemmed plants sprinkled with bluish-gray trefoils. He gestured at the ceiling and walls. "This is...awesome."

He adjusted his wardrobe so he, too, was barefoot. Michelangelo did the same, without seeming to have noticed anyone else's actions.

Miss Pretoria placed her shoes on a rack by the door, and Vincent stole a look at them. He couldn't identify the material. The security detail kept their boots, custom bowing to practicality.

"This is the guests' quarters of government center. The lobby is yours to make use of as you please. For your safety, we ask that you do not venture out unescorted."

"Is Penthesilea so dangerous for tourists?" Vincent asked. It had seemed tame enough on their two brief jaunts, and he was interested by how casually the local dignitaries ventured out in public. The culture, in that way, reminded him of pre-Repatriation Ur, a small town society in which everybody knew everybody else. He craned his neck, looking through the almost-invisible ceiling, and watched some small winged animal dart overhead.

"Dangerous enough," Miss Pretoria said, with a smile that might almost have been flirting, before she beckoned them on.

Somewhere between shaking Miss Pretoria's hand and being shown to their quarters so they could get ready for dinner, Vincent started to wonder if he was ever going to hit his stride. Normally, he would have felt it happen, felt it fall into place with an almost audible click. Still, he had some advantages. Pretoria didn't know how to respond to his relentless good humor. He didn't rise to her provocation, and it set her back on her heels. Which was all to the good, because he needed her off-balance and questioning her assumptions. If nothing else, it would make it easier to keep up appearances for Michelangelo, who needed to see Vincent doing what they had come here to do: *the* job. The damned job, so important it took a definite article.

Angelo was restless again, fidgeting as he pretended to examine documents in the hours they were given to themselves. Vincent pretended to nap, his eyes closed, and listened first to the silence of heavy heat and then to the patter of rain on the sill of the windowless frame that looked out over Penthesilea.

For a moment, Vincent felt a pang at the necessity of that deceit. And then he remembered the *Kaiwo Maru*, the transparency of Michelangelo's desire to bloody him. *I took the therapy.*

It explained, at least, why Michelangelo had never tried to contact him, even through their private channels. They were spies, for the Christ's sake. They'd kept their affair secret for thirty years; Michelangelo could have passed a note without getting caught. If he'd wanted to. If the job and the goddamned Coalition hadn't been more important than Vincent. Probably the job, frankly. Michelangelo had never cared for politics, for all he'd been willing to sacrifice just about anything to them.

That was fine. There were things that were more important to Vincent than the Coalition, too.

Such as bringing it down.

He sat up, rolled off the bed, and—without looking at Angelo—began to putter around their quarters. The suite was halfway up one of the asymmetrical towers. A single bedroom, with a bed big enough for four; a recreation area; and a fresher so primitive it used running water. Vincent had never actually *seen* one, apart from in antique records. The walls had the same simulated transparency as the "lobby" of the building, although now they showed the dark jungle and the phosphorescent sea. Overhead, blurred stars glowing through the dying nebula. Vincent paused for a moment to wonder at that—how the city itself vanished, except the bit he could see through the open window frame, and was replaced by the sensation of being alone in a reaching space.

The New Amazonians must have adapted, but he found it disconcerting. It wasn't something a human architect would design for a living space. There was no coziness here, no safety of walls and den. This was a lair for a beast with wings, whose domain and comfort were the open sky.

Vincent grinned at Michelangelo, and nodded to the bed. "Do you want a nap before dinner?"

Michelangelo tapped his watch. "I'm on chemistry. And three months of cryo. I'll be fine." As if cryo were rest.

"Do you suppose the mattress squeaks?"

"We'll find out, won't we?" The smoke in Angelo's voice was enough to curl Vincent's toes. *All lies.* "Besides, I need to do my forms. Do you want first turn in the fresher?"

Vincent knew when he was beaten. He shrugged and switched his wardrobe off, pretending he didn't notice Michelangelo's lingering, to-all-appearances-appreciative glance as the foglets swarmed into atmospheric suspension, misty streaks across his body before they left him naked. "If I can figure out how to work it," he said, and walked through the arch into the antechamber, Michelangelo's eyes on every step.

The fresher was primitive but the controls were obvious, the combined bath and shower a deep tub with dials on the wall, handles marked blue and red, a nozzle overhead. A washbasin and a commode completed the accommodations, and Vincent had the technology worked out in three ticks.

He stepped down into the tub—there were stairs, very convenient—and set the dial for hot.

Lesa didn't have time to go home and change before dinner. Fortunately, the government center was all smart suites, and she'd had the foresight to stash a change of clothes in her office. She wouldn't even have to commandeer one of the rooms for visiting dignitaries.

She ordered the door locked and stripped out of her suit, leaving it tossed across the back of her chair. She placed her honor on the edge of the desk, avoiding the blotter so she wouldn't trigger her system, and turned to face the wall. "House, I need a shower, please."

There had been no trace of a doorway in the transparent wall before her, but an aperture appeared as she spoke and irised wide. She passed through it, petting the city's soap-textured wall as she went by. It shivered acknowledgment and she smiled. Lights brightened as she entered, soothing shades of blue and white, and one wall smoothed to a mirror gloss.

House was still constructing the shower. She inspected her hair for split ends and her nose for blackheads as she waited, but it didn't take long. The floor underfoot roughened. The archway closed behind her and warm rain coursed from overhead. Lesa sighed and closed her eyes, turning her face into the spray. Her shoulders and back ached; she arched, spread her arms, lifted them overhead and stretched into a bow, then bent double and let her arms hang, pressing her face against her knees, waiting for the discomfort to ease.

The water smelled of seaweed and sweet flowers; it lathered when she rubbed her hands against her skin. She could have stayed in there all night, but she had things to do. "Conditioner and rinse, please," she said, and House poured first oily and then clean hot water on her, leaving behind only a faint, lingering scent as it drained into the floor.

Her comb and toiletries were in her desk. She dried herself on a fluffy towel—which House provided in a cubbyhole, and which she gave back when she was done—and sat naked at her desk, wrinkling the dirty suit on her chair, to comb through her tangles and spy on her guests while she planned her attack.

"Show me the Colonial diplomats." There was always a twinge of guilt involved in this, but it *was* her job, and she was good at it. Her blotter cleared, revealing the guest suite.

Miss Kusanagi-Jones stood in the center of the floor, balanced and grounded on resilient carpetplant, his feet widely spaced in some martial-arts stance. Eyes closed, his hands and feet moved in time with his breath as he slid sideways and Lesa leaned forward, fascinated. She'd suspected he was a fighter. He held himself right, collected, confident, but without the swaggering she was used to seeing on successful males.

As if he didn't feel the need to constantly claim his space and assert his presence.

She wondered if this was what combat training looked like on a gentle male, one whose strength wasn't bent on reproduction and dominance. It suited him, she thought, watching his stocky, barrel-chested body glide from form to form without rising or falling from a level line. He finished as she watched, then paused, a sheen of sweat making his dark skin seem to glow in comparison with his loose white trousers. Then he bowed formally and dropped into slow-motion push-ups, alternating arms.

Male arm strength. Which made it no less impressive.

Katherinessen came from the shower a moment later, naked and dripping slightly. Wisps of mist hung around him, and green, gold, and blue lights glowed through the tawny skin in the hollow of his left wrist. He touched them; the mist drifted in spirals about his body, and his hair and skin were dry. Even the water droplets on the leaves of the carpetplant ended abruptly, five steps from the shower door.

He was older than she'd thought, Lesa realized. He was a ropy man, long and lean, the fibers of his muscles clearly visible under the skin, but that skin had a soft, lived-in look. He moved in his body unselfconsciously. She thought he might be showing himself off to his lover a little, which made her smile.

He could be anywhere from thirty-five New Amazonian years to fifty; if he were a native she would have guessed thirty from the sparse gray in his hair and his relatively unlined face, but the Colonials stayed out of the sun; he might be much older.

And that was without accounting for the OECC's medical technology. She'd heard they could live into their second century in vigorous health. It worried her;

these men were the equivalents of Elders, if men had Elders, and if the Colonial Coalition had any sense at all, they would be as wily and problematic as anyone in the New Amazonian Parliament.

And they were *men*. Men with education and resources and the power of a multiworld organization behind them. But *men*, half crazy with evolutionary pressures half the time. The OECC couldn't *conquer* New Amazonia; they'd proven *that* to everyone's satisfaction. But if it ever decided that what New Amazonia had to offer wasn't worth the trouble and loss of face its existence created—and if they could find enough reasons to justify their actions to the Governors—they could destroy it.

Bang. As easily as Lesa could lay down her comb, open the closet door with a word to House, and pull out her formal dress.

Lesa didn't believe her mother's confident prediction that the Governors would protect them. For one thing, as long as they remained an ungoverned world, they weren't under the OECC's ecological hegemony. The Governors might easily decide it was better to shoot first and reconstruct later, and they might be willing to destroy the Dragons' legacy to do it.

She dressed and found her evening holster on the hanger. It was supple red leather, detailed in gold, and it stood out against the sea-snake sequins of her flowing trousers.

Kusanagi-Jones was finishing his push-ups when she turned back to the image in her blotter. He came up on his knees and rose with casual power, standing in time to hook Katherinessen around the waist as Katherinessen went by, and pulled him close.

Lesa flicked the desk off and reached for her honor

in the same gesture. Bonding the pistol into her holster, she frowned.

All right, they were cute. But she couldn't afford to start thinking of them as human.

Angelo's body was warm and firm through his gi. His hair tickled Vincent's cheek and the crook of his neck smelled of clean sweat, quickly fading into the same toiletry licenses he'd been using for the last thirty years. Vincent wondered what he'd do if they ever took that particular cedar note off the market. It was a *known* smell, viscerally, and Vincent's body responded. "Go get clean. It's pleasant. Decadent. You'll like it."

Michelangelo stepped back, his gi vanishing into curls of foglets. His body was still hard under it, blocky, the pattern of moles and tight-spiraled curls on his chest at once familiar and alien, like coming home to a place where you used to live.

"Figures. We have to come to the last outposts of civilization for our decadence." Tendons flexed as he glanced at his watch. "Be out in a few ticks. I've given you access to my licenses. Figure out what I should wear, won't you?"

Vincent smiled to hide the twisting sensation. Dressing Angelo had always been Vincent's job. Left to his own devices, Michelangelo would probably walk around naked most of the time. Not that most people would object—

Mind on your job, Vincent reprimanded himself, and set about trying to figure out what the New Amazonians would consider "formal."

Uncertain what cultural conditions would apply, their offices had issued each of them a full suite of licenses, which, of course, did not include any hats.

Formal fashions on Old Earth tended to be more elaborate than those on colonial planets, which cleared about half the database, but Michelangelo had the advantage of his complexion and looked wonderful in colors that Vincent couldn't remotely carry off.

Vincent chose a wrap jacket and trousers in rusty oranges and reds, simple lines to offset the pattern, the shoulders flashing with antique-looking mirrors and bouillon embroidery. That should dazzle a few eyes—and hearts, if Vincent was reading Miss Pretoria's admiring glances accurately. He had absolutely no objections to using his partner's brooding charisma as a weapon.

For himself, he chose a winter-white dinner jacket and trousers instead of tights, because he didn't want to risk slippery feet if they were expected to go barefoot again. The jacket was plain, almost severe, with understated shaded green patterning on the lapels.

He'd wear a shirt and cravat to dress it up. Let them stare at Michelangelo's chest; it was prettier than Vincent's, anyway.

He was already dressed, toiletries arranging his hair and moisturizing his face, when Michelangelo emerged from the fresher. He flicked his watch, sending Michelangelo the appropriate license key. Michelangelo's wardrobe assembled the suit in moments; he glanced at himself in the mirrored wall and nodded slightly, as if forced, unwilling to admit that Vincent had made him handsome. "I look like a Hindu bride," he said, fiddling with his cuffs.

"I don't think we have a license for bangles," Vincent answered. "If we'd known how conspicuously the New Amazonians consume, I would have requisitioned some."

Michelangelo's disapproval creased the corners of his eyes. When he spoke, it was in their own private code, the half-intelligible pidgin of one of Ur's most backwater dialects and a random smattering of other languages that they'd developed in training and elaborated in years since. It had started as a joke, Vincent teaching Michelangelo to speak one of his languages, and Michelangelo elaborating with ridiculous constructions in Greek, Swahili, Hindi, and fifteen others. It was half-verbal and half-carrier, tightbeamed between their watches—practiced until, half the time, all they had needed was a glance and a hand gesture and a fragment of a sentence.

It had saved their lives more than once.

"A planet like this," Michelangelo said, "and they're wearing nonrenewables and doing who-knows-what to the ecosystem. Haven't seen forests like that—"

—outside of old 2-D movies and documentaries about pre-Change, pre-Diaspora Old Earth. Vincent knew, and sympathized. The frustration in Michelangelo's voice couldn't quite cover the awe. Ur didn't have forests like that, and neither did Le Pré, Arcadia, or Cristalia. Never mind New Earth, which was about as dissimilar to Old Earth as it could be, without being a gas giant.

"See the logging scars when we came in?" Michelangelo continued. "Bet you balcony passes to the Sydney Bolshoi that those outgoing lighters are exporting *wood*."

"Not to Old Earth. Not legally."

They'd dealt with their fair share of environmental criminals in the past, though. And it wasn't even necessarily illegal trade; there were other colonies, not under OECC oversight—and there are idiots on every planet who considered possession more important than morality.

Michelangelo knew it, too, and knew his denial was reflexive. "So smuggling happens. More to the point, what do you expect from a bunch of women? Short-term thinking; profit now, deal with the consequences later."

Vincent shrugged. "They can be educated. Assisted."

"Perhaps. You saw her shoes, right?"

Vincent nodded. "Pretoria's? I didn't recognize the fiber. What about them?"

"*Leather*, Vincent." Michelangelo's stagy shudder ran a scintilla of light across the mirrors on the yoke of his jacket. "I'm trying very hard not to think about dinner."

4

FOR THE THIRTIETH TIME, KUSANAGI-JONES WISHED THEIR downloads on New Amazonian customs had been more in depth. Although, given this was the first *physical* contact between the New Amazonians and a Coalition representative since the Six-Weeks-War almost twenty years ago, he was lucky to get anything.

He'd guessed right about the food, and he hadn't even had to wait until dinner to prove it. There were crudités—familiar vegetables in unusual cultivars, and some unfamiliar ones that must be local produce amenable to human biochemistry. But he didn't trust anything else, even if he'd been rude enough to wardrobe up an instrument and stick it in a sample.

Usually mission nerves killed his appetite and he struggled with the diplomatic requirements of eating what was set before him. As the gods of Civil Service would have it, though, when the options included things he was unwilling to consume even in the name of détente, he was practically dizzy with hunger.

And the wine the New Amazonians served at the reception was potent. So he crunched finger-length slices of some sweet root or stem that reminded him of burgundy-colored jicama and stuck at Vincent's elbow like a trophy wife, keeping a weather eye on the crowd.

Penthesilea was the planetary capital, and there were dignitaries from Medea, Aminatu, Hippolyta, and Lakshmi Bai in attendance, in addition to the entire New Amazonian Parliament, the prime minister, and the person whom Kusanagi-Jones understood to be her wife. There was also a security presence, though he was not entirely certain of its utility in the company of so many armed and obviously capable women.

Even that assembly—at least three hundred individuals, perhaps 95 percent female—didn't suffice to make the ballroom seem crowded. They moved barefoot over the cool living carpets, dancing and laughing and conversing in whispers, with ducked heads, while the musicians sawed gamely away on a raised and recessed stage, and handsome men in sharp white coats bore trays laden with what Kusanagi-Jones could only assume were delicacies to the guests. It could have been an embassy party on any of a dozen planets, if he crossed his eyes.

But that wasn't what provoked Kusanagi-Jones's awe. What kept distracting him every time he lifted his eyes from his plate, or the conversation taking place between Vincent and Prime Minister Claude Singapore—while Singapore's wife and Miss Pretoria hovered like attendant crows—was the way the walls faded from warm browns and golds through tortoise-shell translucence before vanishing overhead to reveal a crescent moon and the bannered light of the nebula

called the Gorgon. The nebula rotated slowly enough
that the motion was unnerving, but not precisely apparent.

When the silver-haired prime minister was distracted by a murmured comment or question from an
aide, Kusanagi-Jones tapped Vincent on the arm, offered him the plate, and—when Vincent ducked to examine what was on offer—whispered in his partner's
ear, "Suppose they often feel like specimens on a slide?"

"I suppose you adapt," Vincent answered. He selected a curved flake of something greenish and crispy,
and held it up to inspect it. Light radiated from the
walls—a flattering, ambient glow that did not distract
from the view overhead.

"Are you admiring our starscape, Miss Kusanagi-
Jones?"

He glanced at the prime minister, hiding his blink
of guilt, but it wasn't Singapore who had spoken.
Rather, her wife, Maiju Montevideo.

"Spectacular. Do I understand correctly that
Penthesilea is entirely remnant architecture?"

Montevideo was a Rubenesque woman of medium
stature. Regardless of his earlier comment regarding
Hindu brides, Kusanagi-Jones was minded to compare
her to the goddess Shakti grown grandmotherly. Her
eyes narrowed with her smile as she gestured to the
domed, three-lobed chamber. "All this," she said. She
led with her wrist; Kusanagi-Jones wondered if New
Amazonia had the sort of expensive girls' schools
where they trained apparently helpless young women
to draw blood with their deportment. These women
would probably consider that beneath them, but they
certainly had mastered the skills.

Her eyes widened; he tried to decide if it was calculated or not. From the shift of Vincent's weight, he

thought so. "Miss Pretoria hasn't taken you to see the frieze yet?"

"There hasn't been time." Miss Pretoria slid between them, a warning in the furrow between her eyes. *Interesting*.

"No," Vincent said. Vincent didn't look up, apparently distracted by the vegetables, but he wouldn't have missed anything Kusanagi-Jones caught. His nimble fingers turned and discarded one or two more slices before he abandoned the plate untasted on a side table.

Elder Montevideo showed her teeth. Kusanagi-Jones couldn't fault New Amazonian dentistry. Or perhaps it was the apparent lack of sweets in the local diet.

"After dinner?" she asked, a little too gently.

Kusanagi-Jones could still feel it happen. Vincent's chin came up and his spine elongated. It wasn't enough motion to have served as a tell to a poker player, but Kusanagi-Jones noticed. His own tension eased.

Vincent had just *clicked*. He was on the job and he'd found his angle. Everything was going to be just fine.

Vincent tasted his lips. "Perhaps *instead of* dinner?" he said lightly, a quip, beautiful hands balled in his pockets.

"The food isn't to your liking, Miss Katherinessen?"

Vincent's shrug answered her, and also fielded Kusanagi-Jones's sideways glance without ever breaking contact with Singapore. "We don't eat animals," he said negligently. "We consider murder barbaric, whether it's for food or not."

Perfect. Calm, disgusted, a little bored. A teacher's disapproval, as if what he said should be evident to a backward child. He might as well have said, *We don't play in shit.*

Michelangelo's chest was so tight he thought his control might crack and leave him gasping for breath.

"Strange," Montevideo said. The prime minister—Singapore—towered over her, but Elder Montevideo dominated their corner. "I hear some on Coalition worlds will pay handsomely for meat."

"Are you suggesting you support illegal trade with Coalition worlds?" Vincent's smile was a thing of legend. Hackles up, Montevideo took a half-step forward, and he was only using a quarter of his usual wattage. "There's a child sex trade, too. I don't suppose you condone that."

Montevideo's mouth was half open to answer before she realized she'd been slapped. "That's the opinion of somebody whose government encourages fetal murder and contract slavery?"

"It is," Vincent said. He pulled his hand from his pocket and studied the nails. Montevideo didn't drop her gaze.

Kusanagi-Jones steadied his own breathing and stretched each sense. Every half-alert ear in the room was pricked, every courtier, lobbyist, and spy breath-held. Elder Montevideo's hand was not the only one resting on a weapon, but it was hers that Kusanagi-Jones assessed. Eleven-millimeter caseless, he thought, with a long barrel for accuracy. Better to take Vincent down, if it came to it, risk the bullet on his own wardrobe and trust that the worried, level look Miss Pretoria was giving him meant she'd back his play if the guns came out.

He wondered about the New Amazonian rules of honor and if it mattered that Vincent was male and that he didn't *seem* armed.

And then Vincent looked up, as if his distraction had been a casual thing, and gave her a few more watts. He murmured, almost wistfully, "Now that we've established that we think each other monsters, do you suppose we can get back to business?"

She blinked first, but Kusanagi-Jones didn't let himself stop counting breaths until Claude Singapore nudged her, and started to laugh. "He almost got you," Singapore said, and Montevideo tipped her head, acknowledging the touch.

Just a couple of fairies. He gritted his teeth into an answering smile. Apparently, it would have been thought a victory for Vincent if he provoked the woman enough to make her draw. A Pyrrhic victory, for most men in their shoes—

Singapore glanced at her watch—an old-fashioned wristwatch with a band, external—and then laced her right hand through Montevideo's arm. "We'll be wanted upstairs."

Vincent fell in beside her and Kusanagi-Jones assumed his habitual place. He didn't think Singapore was used to looking up to anybody, and she had to, to Vincent. "What I'd like to do instead of dinner is get a look at your power plant."

"Unfortunately," Singapore said, "we can't arrange that."

"Official secrets?" Vincent asked, not *too* archly. "We'll have to talk about it eventually, if we're going to work out an equitable trade arrangement."

Kusanagi-Jones could have cut himself on Singapore's smile. "Are you suggesting that the Cabinet will resort to extortion, Miss Katherinessen? Because I assure you, the restoration of our appropriated cultural treasures is a condition of negotiation, not a bargaining chip."

She ushered them through the door. A half-dozen people around the room disengaged themselves from their conversations and followed them into the hall.

"It would make a nice gesture of goodwill," said Vincent.

And Elder Singapore smiled. "It might. But you can't get there from here."

The route to the dining room wound up a flight of stairs and across an open footbridge, almost a catwalk. Kusanagi-Jones breathed shallowly; his chemistry was mostly coping with the alien pollen, but he didn't want to tax it. He leaned on Vincent's arm lightly as Vincent fell back beside him. "Why are we antagonizing the people in charge?"

"Did you see Montevideo glance at her wife?"

Kusanagi-Jones didn't bother to hide his shrug.

"They're not the ones in charge. Maybe a little fire will draw the real negotiators out." Vincent paused and smiled tightly. "Also, aren't you curious why they wanted us to see these friezes and Miss Pretoria was all a-prickle about it? Because I know I am."

Kusanagi-Jones's hands wanted to shake, but he wouldn't let them. They entered a banquet room, and he saw Vincent seated on the prime minister's left and took his own seat next to Miss Pretoria, touching the glossy wood of the chairs and table as if he were used to handling such things. He sat, and discussed his dietary needs with Pretoria, then allowed her to serve him—which she did adroitly. The food was presented family style, rather than on elaborately arranged and garnished plates, whisked from some mysterious otherworld to grace the incredible solid wooden table.

There *were* vegetarian options, although most of them seemed to contain some sort of animal by-products. But the scent of charred flesh made eating anything—even the salad and the bread with oil and vinegar that Miss Pretoria assured him was safe—an exercise in diplomatic self-discipline. It smelled like a combat zone; all that was missing was the reek of scorched hair and the ozone tang of burned-out utility fogs.

The cheese and butter and sour cream were set on the table between plates laden with slices of roasted animal flesh, like some scene out of atavistic history—the sort of thing you expected to find in galleries next to paintings of beheading and boiling in oil and other barbaric commonplaces. Michelangelo brushed his sleeve up and touched his watch again, adjusting his blood chemistry to compensate for creeping nausea, and kept his eyes on his own plate until he finished eating.

He shouldn't be huddled in his shell. He should be talking with Miss Pretoria and the assembled dignitaries, walking the thin line between interest and flirting. He should be watching the women—especially Elena Pretoria, a grande dame if he'd ever met one, and most likely Lesa Pretoria's mother—and the two reserved, quiet men at the table, picking out what he could about the social order, trying to understand the alliances and enmities so he could exploit them later.

The women seemed interested in Vincent and himself—by which he meant, attracted to—and a glance at Vincent confirmed he thought so, too. Elders Singapore and Montevideo were the obvious exceptions to the rule. They had eyes only for each other, and Kusanagi-Jones might have found it sweet if he hadn't suspected they'd cheerfully have him shot the instant he wasn't conforming to their agenda.

The more he watched Montevideo, the more he thought—despite her apparent spunk—that she was like politicians' wives everywhere: intelligent, intent, and ready to defer—at least publicly—to her mate's judgment. Vincent was right; she looked at Singapore every time she said something.

Kusanagi-Jones bit his lip on a pained laugh; he recognized no little bit of himself in her behavior.

It didn't hurt that Vincent was now paying an

outrageous and obviously insincere court to the prime
minister that still seemed to entertain her enormously.
She had switched to treating them like indulged children; Kusanagi-Jones found it distasteful, but Vincent
seemed willing to play the fool. The women were asking
interested questions about the Colonial Coalition, seeming shocked by things in absolute disproportion to their
importance.

Montevideo was particularly fascinated by eugenics
and population-control legislation, and kept asking
pointed questions, which Vincent answered mildly.
Kusanagi-Jones pushed his plate away, unable to face another mouthful of red-leaf lettuce and crispy native fruit
mixed with imported walnuts. It wasn't so bad when he
wasn't trying to eat, and it was amusing to eavesdrop as
Montevideo tried to get a rise out of Vincent.

"Well, of course the Cabinet tries to limit abortions,"
Vincent was saying. "Ideally, you control population
through more proactive means—" He shrugged, and
speared a piece of some juicy vegetable that Kusanagi-
Jones couldn't identify with a perfectly normal Earth-
standard fork—except Kusanagi-Jones would bet the
forks were actual metal, mined and refined, and not fogs.
"But even medical bots fail, or can be made to fail.
Biology's a powerful force; people have a reproductive
drive."

"You don't think . . . *people* can be trusted to make their
own decisions, Miss Katherinessen?" Arch, still sharp.

Kusanagi-Jones didn't need to look at Vincent to
know he would be smiling that wry, gentle smile. He
looked anyway, and didn't regret it, although Vincent's
expression made it hard to breathe. Again. Dammit.

He could not afford to care, to trust Vincent. He was
here to destroy him. New Earth, all over again. Only
worse this time.

"No," Vincent said, as Kusanagi-Jones picked the remainder of his bread apart. "We evolved for much more dangerous times, and memory is short. Just because Old Earth survived pandemics and famines and Assessments during the Diaspora to achieve a few modern ideas about stewardship doesn't mean that enlightenment trickles down to everybody. And it's very hard for most people to postpone an immediate want for a payoff they won't see, and neither will their grandchildren."

"Thus the Governors," Elder Montevideo said, folding plump, delicate hands. The prime minister watched, silently, and so did Elder Pretoria, who was seated at the far end of the table.

"The Coalition," Kusanagi-Jones said, to demonstrate solidarity. He would *not* show pain. "So the Governors don't intervene again on a large scale. They *are* still watching."

He knew better than to attempt Vincent's trick of speaking as if to an idiot child, but it was tempting.

"The Coalition isn't allied with the Governors, then?" asked one of the other women at the table, an olive-skinned matron with cool hazel eyes who never stopped smiling. Elder Kyoto, if Kusanagi-Jones had the name right. He'd logged it; he could check his watch if needed.

"The Coalition is interested in...minimizing the impact the Governors have on human life. And the Governors permit the Coalition Cabinet that latitude."

"And the Governors must be prevented from intervening?"

"If you know your history." Vincent smiled right back. "It keeps us on our toes."

Elder Singapore covered her partner's hand with her own. "If it wasn't for Diaspora, New Amazonia wouldn't be here. And we would be robbed of the pleasure of each other's company. Which would be a great pity indeed."

Vincent asked, "Was yours one of the private ships?"

"The Colony craft? Yes. Ur was also, wasn't it?"

He turned his fork over as if fascinated by the gleams of light on the tines. "My great-grandmother was disgustingly rich. It was an experimental society, too. The colonists were all pregnant women. No men. And there was a religious element."

Elder Montevideo leaned forward, although she wasn't quite overcome enough to rest her elbows on the table. "What was the purpose of the experiment?"

"To prove a point of philosophy. To establish an egalitarian matriarchy based on Gnostic Christian principles." He glanced up, twinkling. "My mother is the only woman on the Colonial Coalition Cabinet. We're not so different."

She sat back, picked up her silver knife, and gave minute attention to buttering a roll. "Our founding mothers believed that it was possible to live in balance with nature," she said. "And by balance, they did not mean stasis. They meant an evolving dynamic whereby both the planet's Gaian principle and her population would benefit. Not exploitation, as it was practiced on Old Earth: women do not *exploit*. We take care when we practice forestry, for example, to leave renewal niches, and we practice sustainable agriculture and humane animal husbandry." The knife went down with a *clink*. "Of course, the impact of our activities is attenuated because we didn't need to bootstrap through a fossil-fuel economy. We've been fortunate."

At least they know it, Kusanagi-Jones thought. He sipped his wine and watched her eat.

"I'm curious," Vincent said. "Something you said

earlier hinted to me that you find eugenics distasteful."

Miss Pretoria laughed out loud and glanced at the prime minister for permission to continue. Kusanagi-Jones saw the elder Pretoria lean forward, but she still held her tongue. *A watcher.* Dangerous, if the mind was as sharp as the eyes. "If Old Earth gave women reproductive autonomy, I don't believe you'd have a population problem. *We* don't—"

"*You* have an undamaged ecosystem," Kusanagi-Jones said. Vincent might have been the one to guess that a bold-faced refusal to temporize was one way to carn their respect, but Kusanagi-Jones wasn't too shy to capitalize on it. Vincent didn't quite smile, but the approval was there between them, warm and alive. "For now, at least, until you overrun it."

Kusanagi-Jones, who had been about to continue, closed his mouth tightly as Elder Montevideo spoke. "One of the reasons our foremothers chose to emigrate was because of Earth's eugenics practices. They did not feel that a child's genetic health or sexual orientation determined its value. Do *you*, Miss Kusanagi-Jones? Miss Katherinessen? Because I assure you, the mothers at this table would disagree."

Vincent's eyes were on Montevideo, but Kusanagi-Jones could tell that his attention was focused on Miss Pretoria. And even Kusanagi-Jones could feel her discomfort; she was *buzzing* with it. "I think," Vincent said, carefully, "the health of a system outweighs the needs of a component. I think prioritizing resources is more important than individual well-being."

"Even your own?" Miss Pretoria asked, laying down her fork.

Vincent glanced at her, but Kusanagi-Jones answered.

"Oh, yes," he said, directing a smile at his partner.

He was a Liar; neither his voice nor his expression betrayed the venom he'd have liked to inject into them. He projected pride, praise, admiration. It didn't matter. Vincent would know the truth. It might even sting. "Especially his own."

Lesa shouldn't have been taking so much pleasure in watching Katherinessen bait Maiju and Claude, but her self-control was weak. *And a small gloat never hurt anyone,* she thought. Besides, even if the enemy of Lesa's enemy wasn't necessarily Lesa's ally, the prime minister richly deserved to be provoked—and in front of Elena. Lesa saw what Katherinessen was playing at. He lured them to underestimate and patronize, while picking out tidbits of personal and cultural information, assembling a pattern he could read as well as Lesa could have.

He was also staking out space, while getting them to treat him like a headstrong male. Clever, though confrontational. Lesa often used the same tactic to manipulate people into self-incrimination.

Just when she thought she had their system plotted, though, Kusanagi-Jones turned and sank his teeth into Katherinessen, hard. And Lesa blinked, reassessing. A quick glance around the table confirmed that only she had caught the subtext. And that was even more interesting—a hint of tension, a chink in their unity. The kind of place where you could get a lever in, and pry.

She wondered if Kusanagi-Jones was aware of Katherinessen's duplicity, and if he was, if Katherinessen *knew* he was aware, or if there was a different stress on the relationship. They'd been apart for a long time, hadn't they? Since New Earth. Things changed in seventeen years.

Then as fast as it had been revealed the flash of anger was gone, and Lesa was left wondering again. Because it was possible she'd been intended to see it, that it was more misdirection. They were good enough to keep her guessing, especially when Katherinessen smiled fondly across the table at Kusanagi-Jones, not at all like a man acknowledging a hit.

Lesa was aware of the other dynamics playing out around the table. They were transparent to her, the background of motivations and relationships that she read and manipulated as part of her work, every day. But none of them were as interesting as Katherinessen and Kusanagi-Jones. Their opacities, their complexities. She could make a study just of the two of them.

And something still kept picking at the edge of her consciousness, like Katherinessen picking at Maiju, like a bird picking for a grub, though she didn't quite know what to call it. She wondered if they could have fooled her, if perhaps they weren't gentle after all. The idea gave her a cold moment, as much for fear of her own capabilities eroding as for the idea of a couple of stud males running around loose.

Even the best of them—even Robert, whom she loved—were predators. Biologically programmed, as a reproductive strategy. Uncounted years of human history were the proof. In previous societies—in *all* recorded societies, other than the New Amazonian— when a woman died by violence, the perpetrator was almost always male. And almost always a member of the woman's immediate family, often with the complicity of society. The Coalition was a typical example of what men did to women when given half an excuse: petty restrictions, self-congratulatory patronization, and a slew of justifications that amounted to men asserting their property rights.

Two stud males—if they *were,* and she honestly didn't think so—on the loose and unlicensed in Penthesilea were unlikely to bring down society. But by the same token, Lesa wouldn't let a tame fexa run loose in the city. There was always the chance somebody would get bitten.

The irony of that concern, compared to the gender treason she was plotting, made her smile bitterly.

"Miss Pretoria," Katherinessen said, as the waiter removed his plate, "you're staring at me." He hadn't looked up.

"Are there circumstances under which the well-being of a minority *does* matter? Circumstances of gross injustice?"

"Oppression? Such as the status of men on New Amazonia?"

Elder Kyoto, the minister of security, waved her fork. "There are sound behavioral——"

"Just so," Claude said. The other guests went quiet. "Or what the Coalition would like to do to New Amazonia, to bring it under hegemony. Setting all that aside for the moment—as civilized people should be able to do"—and it seemed to Lesa that Claude reserved a particularly bland smile for Kusanagi-Jones—"is it still an interesting question on its own merits?"

Katherinessen steepled long fingers. Dessert was being served. He declined a pastry just as Lesa warned them that there was most likely butter in the crust, but both males accepted coffee without cream.

Katherinessen tasted the coffee as soon as it was set before him, buying a few more moments to consider his answer and unconcerned with his transparency. "Whichever group is in ascension at a given moment is, historically speaking, both unlikely to acknowledge even the *existence* of abuses or bias, and also to justify the bias on any grounds they can—social, biological, what have you. May we agree on that?"

Claude's smile slid from bland toward predatory. "Mostly."

"Then let me raise a counterquestion. Do you believe an egalitarian society is possible?"

"Define *egalitarian*."

"Advancement based solely on merit." Katherinessen smiled at his partner, who was stolidly stirring his coffee over and over again. "As Angelo is fond of pointing out to me, I have certain advantages of birth. My family is well regarded in society on Ur. By comparison, on Old Earth before Assessment, any of us would have been disadvantaged due to our skin tone—if we lived in the industrialized world."

"Protected by it, later," Kusanagi-Jones said under his breath. He was leaning on the arm of his chair, toward Lesa; she thought she was the only one who heard it.

Claude didn't answer immediately. She nodded around the excuse of a bite of pastry, forked up in haste, as if inspecting Katherinessen's words for the trap. "So even Assessment wasn't an equalizer. Not a fresh start."

"It was the opposite of an equalizer." Katherinessen shrugged. "Each round of Assessed were chosen on the grounds of arbitrary standards programmed into the Governors before they were released. It was the epitome of unnatural selection, for an elite. Agriculturists, scientists, engineers, programmers, diplomats, artisans, and none of them Caucasian—what more arbitrary set of criteria could you imagine for survival?"

Lesa laid her fork down. "I don't believe equality exists."

Elder Kyoto glanced around. "Why not?"

"Because Miss Katherinessen is right, but doesn't take it far enough. Not only will whoever's on top fight to stay there, but if you reset everyone to equality, whoever wins the scramble for power will design the rules to stay there."

Katherinessen nodded. "So what do you think *is* possible?"

"If I were the oppressed?"

A short pause, with eyebrow. "Sure."

Lesa wondered if she could startle him. The Colonials *did* think everybody on New Amazonia was an idiot, or at least naive. That much was plain. "Conquest. Revolution. Dynamic change would ensure that nobody ever wound up holding too much power. Fortunately for me, as a member of the ruling class, people tend to prefer the status quo to unrest unless they're very unhappy. Which is why the Coalition isn't entirely welcome here."

She picked her fork up again and began flaking apart the buttery layers of pastry, not so much eating as pushing them around on the plate to cover the gilding. Katherinessen sighed. She thought it was satisfaction. She didn't want to feel the answering glow in herself, as if she'd just done well on a test.

"You are so very right." Katherinessen glanced at Kusanagi-Jones, who had stopped stirring his coffee, but wasn't drinking.

"You know what they say," Kusanagi-Jones quipped. "Détente is achieved when everybody's unhappy."

The bipeds communicate. There are the new ones, the males in their dual-gender system. Kii supposes one biologically convenient system for randomizing genetic material is as good as another, but the bipeds also use

*theirs as a basis for an arcane system of taboos and re-
strictions. At first Kii thinks this is adaptively obligated,
that the child-bearing sex was responsible for the protection of the offspring, and the society was structured
around that need. There are local animals with similar
adaptations—unlike the Consent, unlike the khir—
where the greatest danger to cubs is posed by unrelated
males, which prey on the offspring of other males.*

*Kii is startled to find an intelligent species retaining
such atavistic tendencies. But then, Kii is also startled to
find an intelligent species evolve without also evolving
the Consent, or something like it. And since the territorial dispute, Kii is forced to acknowledge that no matter
how developed their technology and aesthetics, the
bipeds have no Consent.*

*Kii wonders if the other population of bipeds, en-
croaching again on the ones Kii thinks of as Kii's bipeds,
intend another territorial dispute. The timeslip is
threads that converge and threads that part; patterns of
interference. It is a wave that has not collapsed. The nonlocal population may transgress, driven, Kii thinks, by
outstripping its habitat. There may be another dispute.
The probability is not insignificant that the local population of aliens will be overrun. Kii is possessive of the
aliens, and Kii's possessiveness informs the Consent.*

*If the other population encroaches, Kii wishes to in-
tervene again, more strongly than before. The Consent is
not so sanguine.*

Yet.

5

EVEN VINCENT WAS RELIEVED WHEN DINNER ENDED, though it segued without hesitation into another endless reception. This one at least had more the air of a party, and finally there were a number of other men present.

As soon as they left the table, the elder Pretoria cut Michelangelo off Vincent's arm as neatly as impoverished nobility absconding with an heiress at a debutante's ball. Despite Michelangelo's long-suffering eyeroll, he went, flirting gamely.

Vincent took this as a sign that the business portion of the evening had ended, and availed himself of the bar. He wasn't going to get drunk—his watch would see to that—but he would examine the options. It would give him something to do with his hands while considering the evening's haul.

He accepted the drink he'd pointed to in a moment of bravado—something greenish-gold and slightly cloudy, a spirit infused with alien herbs, if his nose didn't mislead him—and leaned into a quiet corner, for the moment observed by no one except the security detail, who appeared to be making sure he didn't wander off.

It was a reversal of his and Michelangelo's usual roles, but not an unpracticed one. Michelangelo could pretend to charisma as effectively as anything else, and dominate a room with ease. And the dynamics of an assembly such as this could be revealing. It was like watching a dance that was also combat and a game of chess.

Miss Pretoria, for example, was leaving a conversational cluster that included the person Vincent had tentatively identified as the minister of the militia—of Security, he corrected himself, which was a significant choice of title on its own—and crossing to the group that encompassed Michelangelo and Elena Pretoria, and a tall, beautifully dressed, dark-skinned man with a shaved-slick scalp. With whom, Vincent noticed, Michelangelo was now flirting. Vincent's fingers curled on his glass, and he pressed his shoulders against the warm, slightly vibrating wall of the building, feeling it conform to his body.

The prime minister and her entourage occupied a space that was more or less on the left center of the ballroom, and somehow managed to give the impression of being off in a corner—and one diametrically opposed to the Pretoria household at that. And there was something else interesting: as Lesa crossed the room, nobody wanted to catch her eye, despite her occasional nods and words she shared with those she passed. Unobtrusively, a path opened before her, but it wasn't the standing aside of respect. It was a withdrawal. *I wonder what she is when she's not a tour guide and turnkey.*

He dug his toes into the groundcover and watched. People could give themselves away in the oddest manners. Even simply by the ways in which they made sure of their guard. For example, the faint discomfort with which Lesa responded to a broad-shouldered, bronzed man who entrapped her a few steps from the relative haven of her mother's enclave. He had long hair cut blunt at his shoulders, the fair, blondish-brown color and coarse wavy texture even more unusual than Vincent's auburn, and his hands were knotted whitely with old scars. He spoke softly, eyes averted, and Lesa reached out and tucked a strand of that wonderful hair behind his ear in a good counterfeit of flirtation before excusing herself to join her family.

Vincent was just finally getting around to paying some attention to his drink when the minister of Security—the one who had been about to bring biology into the dinner argument until Singapore shut her down—appeared at his elbow. "Miss Katherinessen," she said, mispronouncing his name *kath-er-in-ES-sen,* "I'm sorry to see you've been abandoned."

She held out her hand and he took it gingerly. The wine on her breath bridged the distance between them easily. The New Amazonian disregard for personal space, but also something more.

He would have stepped back, but he was already against the wall. "I'm self-amusing," he said, and met her gaze directly, the way Penthesilean men did not.

She edged closer, oozing confidence. She expected him to be intimidated and perhaps flattered as she laid her hand on his arm. He'd seen the expression on her face on enough old warhorses cornering sweet young things at embassy parties: a predator gloating over trapped prey.

He was supposed to blush and look down, and maybe sidle away. Instead, he pictured Michelangelo standing where he was standing now, and burst out laughing.

She stepped back, abruptly, covering her discomfiture with a scowl. "I wasn't aware I was so amusing."

"Actually," Vincent said, stepping around her now that he'd bought himself room, "I find the corner by the door's the best place to be. Are you attending the ceremony tomorrow, Elder?"

He turned to face her, which put his own back to the room—but that wasn't too unsettling when Michelangelo had it covered. And now she was the one trapped against the wall, which was a tactical gain.

"I wouldn't miss it," she said. "We've arranged a meeting with some technical specialists afterward, who can explain what we're prepared to offer for our part of the deal. I'm sure Lesa's made sure you have a copy of the schedule."

"She functions as a secretary, too?" Vincent asked with a thickly insincere smile. He stepped back as Kyoto stepped forward. Miss Pretoria was coming up behind him, and he sidestepped, as if accidentally, opening the tête-à-tête. *One, two, three, four*— "A multitalented individual."

"Why, thank you, Miss Katherinessen," Pretoria said, and then let her eyes rest on the minister of Security. "Oh, Elder. I didn't see you back there, behind this great wall of a man. I'm sorry to interrupt, but his partner asked me to fetch him—"

She smiled, and Vincent wondered if the venom was as apparent to Kyoto as to him. Perhaps not, because Kyoto excused herself and brushed past them with every indication of calm.

Vincent tilted the glass against his mouth, inhaling redolence that stung his eyes, and smiled at the warden as he licked a droplet off the cleft of his lips. The liquor, now that he finally tasted it, was good, warm on the tongue. And if he wasn't mistaken, it had enough kick to shift a moon in orbit.

He shifted the glass to his left hand to extend the right. He was adapting to *that* local quirk, at least. Her clasp was still warm and firm. "I am indebted beyond words."

"She's good at her job," Pretoria said.

"Did Angelo really send you to the rescue?" Vincent would have expected Michelangelo to take a special kind of lingering pleasure in watching him twist, actually, but he would take pity if it was on offer.

"I suggested to him that he—and you—might want to sneak downstairs and indulge in a little tourism... I mean, inspect the gallery space. What do you say?"

Vincent finished his drink. So Pretoria was avoiding the fair-haired man, and Vincent's own presumed desire to avoid Elder Kyoto was a convenient excuse. "Grab your security and let's go."

Kusanagi-Jones glanced up as Vincent laid a gentle hand on his arm and insinuated himself into the conversational circle. "We're escaping," Vincent murmured against his ear, and Kusanagi-Jones nodded while Miss Pretoria made excuses to her mother involving long trips and early rising.

"Whatever the warden wants," Kusanagi-Jones replied, using Vincent's body to cover the shape of the words. Vincent steered him out of the group as he made his farewells. There was a scent of liquor and herbs on Vincent's breath, and Kusanagi-Jones sighed wistfully. "Don't suppose you saved me any of that."

"Sorry. We'll get room service later."

"They overcharge for the licenses in hotels."

Vincent laughed under his breath and gave Kusanagi-Jones's arm a squeeze. "Miss Pretoria wants to show us the gallery."

"That's *the warden* to you," she said, falling into step. She met Kusanagi-Jones's guilty look with a toss of her rainbow hair, but she grinned. "Oh, yes, I heard that."

"Just as well," Vincent said, releasing Kusanagi-Jones's arm after one more caress. "What do you do when you're not shepherding visiting dignitaries, Warden?"

She shrugged. "You just met my boss. I'm security directorate. I review licensing for gentle males and others."

"Political officer," Vincent said. She wasn't tall, but she moved with direction and strength. If she had been wearing boots, they would have been thumping on the groundcover. Even the security detail was hustling to keep up.

She flipped her hair behind her ear again. It kept escaping in ways a grooming license would not permit. "You could say that."

The curved corridor opened into a bell-shaped chamber. She selected a side corridor. Kusanagi-Jones noticed she was running the tips of her fingers down the left-hand wall. "Just here—"

Another room, this one long and narrow like a gallery. The walls were the faux-transparent type, the ceiling view of a perfect, cloudless night sky.

"This is the museum?" Kusanagi-Jones asked. "Where's the art? Doesn't the sunlight damage it?"

Miss Pretoria smiled, seeming pleased that he'd broken his silence, but she addressed them both as she waved them forward. "It's downstairs," she said. "Underground. Come along."

Penthesilea looked small on the surface, but Kusanagi-Jones had gained a hard-won appreciation for how rarely appearances matched actuality. After the arena, he wasn't surprised by the scale of the underground city.

They stepped from a lift into a cavernous space. The air here was cool, the illumination indirect, bright but soothing, with long splashes of light reflecting from scrollworked eggshell-white walls. Vincent cleared his throat. After glancing at Miss Pretoria for permission, Vincent reached out and softly ran his hand over the decorations, if that was what they were. Kusanagi-Jones resisted the urge, despite the tactile charm.

Vincent said, "If the original inhabitants—"

"The Dragons."

"The Dragons. If they could fly, why the lift?"

"It's new."

"Do you understand the technology that well?" And Vincent made it sound casual, startled. Natural. Kusanagi-Jones wondered if Pretoria was fooled.

Truthfully, though, he listened with only half an ear to the conversation. His attention was on the security detail, the multidimensional echoes caused by the cavern's organic shapes, the possibility of an attack. He was surprised by how freely they were permitted to move; on Earth, there would have been an entourage, press, a gaggle of functionaries. Here, there was just the three of them, and the guards.

Convenient. *And* indicative of even more societal

differences that would be positively treacherous to navigate. As if the openly armed women hadn't been enough of a hint.

"...this seems like a very fine facility," Vincent said. He moved casually, his hands in his pockets as he leaned down to Miss Pretoria, diminishing her disadvantage in height. "Controlled humidity and temperature, of course."

"Yes. These are the galleries that were emptied by the OECC robbers in the Six-Weeks-War," she said. Her body language gave no hint that she considered any potential to offend in her phrasing. It was matter-of-fact, impersonal.

And this is a diplomat, Kusanagi-Jones thought. He trailed one hand along the wall; the texture was soapy, almost soft. He imagined a faint vibration again, as before, but when he tuned to it, he thought it might just be the wind swaying the fluted towers so far overhead. *They've been alone out here a very long time. Long enough that awareness of ethnocentrism is a historical curiosity.*

He stroked the wall again, trying to identify the material. It didn't come off on his fingers, but it felt like it *should.* Like graphite or soapstone—slick without actually being greasy. There was a geologist's term, but he couldn't remember it.

"These galleries?" Vincent said. "This is where the Coalition troops..."

"Were killed, yes." *This* subject, Miss Pretoria seemed to understand might be touchy. "The ones who came to repatriate the art. And New Amazonia. Seven hundred. Give or take."

"A ship's complement of marines."

"We warned them to withdraw. They attempted to disarm us."

Kusanagi-Jones glanced over in time to catch that predatory flash of her teeth once more. Vincent was watching her, his hands still in his pockets, his face calm.

"There's been a lot of practical experiment on what happens after the occupiers disarm the locals. Just because we've disavowed Old Earth history doesn't mean we fail to study it. You can file that one with *sense of humor*, if you like."

Kusanagi-Jones felt the thrum between them, Vincent and Pretoria. Her chin was up, defiant. Vincent stood there, breathing, smiling, for her to bash herself against. For a moment, Kusanagi-Jones pitied her; she didn't stand a chance. Vincent's silences were even more devastating than his sarcasm.

He ended this one with a soft, beckoning gesture, something that invited Miss Pretoria into the circle of his confidences. "I don't suppose you'd consent to tell me how you managed to herd or lure an entire ship's complement into these chambers, Miss Pretoria? Just as a goodwill gesture, something to get negotiations off on a congenial foot?"

She tilted her head. "You never know when we might need it again. And speaking of goodwill gestures, do you have a list of the art treasures you're returning?"

"One wasn't sent ahead?"

"One was," she answered. She started walking again. Vincent accompanied her and Kusanagi-Jones fell in closer to the security detail. "But since we've planned that repatriation ceremony for tomorrow, it doesn't hurt to make sure we're all working from the same assumptions."

Her tone made it plain she knew they weren't, but was willing to play the game. Kusanagi-Jones found himself admiring her a little. More than a little; she had sangfroid, an old-fashioned haggler's nerve. Maybe she'd known exactly what she was doing with that too-sharp word *robbers*.

Her next comment clinched it. "If you'll follow me," she said, "I'll show you some things that *weren't* stolen."

Vincent, surprising everyone except Kusanagi-Jones, laughed like it was the funniest thing he'd heard in a week. Kusanagi-Jones laughed, too. But he was laughing at the startled expression on Pretoria's face. "About that sense of humor—"

She grinned, and he remembered the sharpness with which she'd returned the volley after overhearing the unflattering nickname. "You're not going to tell me men have one, too?"

Vincent shot him a look; Kusanagi-Jones answered with a shrug. They passed through three chambers, each one with soft full-spectrum light and stairs ascending to a gallery, each with white walls bare and smooth as the walls of a chalk cave.

"How much did they take?" Vincent asked. Even hushed, his voice echoed into many-layered resonance. "All this?"

"You don't know?"

"I know what we brought. The lists I transferred."

She smiled. "That's maybe a twentieth of it—"

"The *Christ*."

"Mmm. These vaults were on the surface then, public galleries. A museum. We brought what we could from Old Earth—"

"Women's art," Kusanagi-Jones said, but he was thinking *On the surface? All this?*

She stopped and turned, her shoulders square and

her chin lifted. She folded her hands behind her back. "Do you have a problem with that?"

"I wondered why your ancestors limited the collection."

She gave him that smile again, the toothy one. "Somebody else was taking care of the rest."

"You're content with the bias?"

She turned and kept walking. Another half of one of the big rooms in silence, until she paused beside a wall like any other. She lifted her hand and pressed the palm against the surface. "Are you content with yours?"

Before he could answer, the wall scrolled open and a door created itself where there hadn't been a door a moment before. She stepped through before the edges had finished collapsing seamlessly into themselves, and Kusanagi-Jones had an awful moment of clarity. It came to him, lead-crystal sharp, that he needed to be thinking of this city not as static structures, but as the biggest damned fog this side of a starship. But Vincent didn't look worried, so Kusanagi-Jones made sure he didn't look worried either and followed Pretoria through the gap. He stopped so fast that Vincent ran into him.

The contents of this room were intact. It was a hundred meters long, with three galleried levels of well-hung walls, plinths and stands scattered about the floor. He had taken three steps forward, sliding out from under Vincent's steadying hand on his shoulder, before he even thought to turn and ask their warden for permission. Still smiling, she waved him forward. Vincent dogged him, and he couldn't even be bothered to be offended when Pretoria called after him, "Don't touch!" although he did growl something about being housebroken, under his breath.

He folded his hands ostentatiously in the small of his back, and tried to remember not to hold his breath. There were pieces here Michelangelo couldn't even name, although he had—many years since—taken a class in the treasures that had been lost during Diaspora, and he'd chipped all the relevant records before he left Earth.

Vincent leaned over his shoulder, breath warm on his ear, resting a hand on his shoulder where the skin of his fingers could brush Michelangelo's neck. It was scarcely a distraction. He paused in front of a case with a long, chain-linked silver necklace, as much sculpture as it was jewelry, hung on a display rack like a barren branch. His chip told him the name.

"Matthesen," he said, pointing with his chin so as not to give Pretoria an excuse to shoot him. "*Fear Death by Water*. Supposed to be lost." He knew the white marble miniature of a nude and pensive woman beside it without help. "Vinnie Ream Hoxie's *The Spirit of the Carnival*. These must all be North American. That's Jana Sterbak's *The Dress*—"

Vincent didn't even comment on the power required to keep the lights that shimmered words in archaic English burning across the wirework form. "That's art?"

"Heathen," Michelangelo said, more fondly than he intended. "Yes, it's art. And oh..."

It caught his eye from across the room, a swirl of colors that seemed at first an amorphous form on a starry field, a nebula in dank earthen green and mahogany. A heavy tentacled brown arm reached from the upper left-hand corner of the canvas, shoving at the sky like an oppressive hand. Michelangelo gasped with the power of it, the vault, the weight, the *mass*.

Just paint on canvas, and after he practically ran across the room to it, it shoved him back a step.

Vincent, who had followed him, swallowed but didn't speak.

"*The Lawrence Tree,*" Michelangelo said. He didn't need to look at the plaque. "Georgia O'Keeffe."

"I've heard of her," Vincent said. He almost sounded surprised. "What's this one?"

Michelangelo didn't know. He waved a question at Pretoria.

The warden came to them, as if reluctant to shout now that they were thick in the spell of the gallery. "Saide Austin is the artist," she said, and Michelangelo took a moment to appreciate the irony of a woman named after a city named after a man. "It's called *Jinga Mbande.*"

It was wood, Michelangelo thought, darkly polished, the image of a well-armed woman with upthrust breasts pointed like weapons, the strong curve of her belly hinting at fecundity. She held a primitive firearm in one hand, a spear in the other, and had the sort of classically African features that were rarely even seen on Earth anymore. "An Amazon heroine?"

"A freedom fighter," Pretoria said. She stood silent on his left hand as Vincent waited on his right, and they all breathed in the silence of the rich gleam of light on polished wood. The air was cool and smelled faintly of lemon oil.

"Old Earth history," she said then, and stepped away as if she needed to cut the camaraderie that had almost grown between them. "Follow me, and I'll show you the friezes."

They went. Up a spiral stair—*neck-breaking-type,* Vincent mouthed at him as they climbed—to the third and final gallery. As they reached the landing, Miss

Pretoria about a dozen steps ahead of them, Kusanagi-Jones leaned forward and whispered in Vincent's ear, "If this is where the marines were killed, was Montevideo's comment a veiled threat?"

Vincent coughed. "Pretty well-cursed veiled." And then he looked up and fell silent.

Kusanagi-Jones hadn't been prepared to be struck dumb again. *You'd think you'd run out of awe eventually.* And perhaps one would. But not right away.

The friezes, as Montevideo had so blithely called them, were a single long strip about three meters tall that ran the entire perimeter of the room. They had subtle detail and deep refractive color that washed to white when you weren't looking at them directly, so they faded out as one glanced along their length, ghosts emerging and vanishing. At first he wasn't sure if the images actually moved, but he occasionally stopped and stared at one detail or another, and became aware that the scene shifted, playing itself out in slow animation.

And he understood why the New Amazonians called the long-lost native aliens *Dragons.*

The pictured creatures were feathered almost-serpents, four-limbed counting the wings and the legs that helped anchor the flight membranes. The wings were bony and double-jointed, shaped for walking on and manipulating things as well as flight. The vane was stretched skin over an elongated pinkie finger that formed the longest part of the leading edge of the wing, five more fingers making a grasping appendage at the front of the joint. They were neither bat-wings nor bird-wings, despite the hairy feathers—or feathery fur—that covered the creatures' backs and napes and heads.

The Dragons flocked through the spires of what

must be one of the other cities of New Amazonia, because it was far taller and more towered than
Penthesilea, and they raced clouds in jewel-bright colors. The ones in the foreground were as detailed as
Audubon paintings. The ones in the background were
movement itself. In among them were wingless animals, four legged, like lean reptilian jackals. They reminded Michelangelo of some kind of feathered
dinosaur, what a theropod would look like if it ran on
all fours.

A scientist—an anthropologist or biologist—might
have cautioned him against jumping to conclusions.
But to Michelangelo, it was breathtakingly obvious
that the winged animals were the city builders, the native inhabitants. Even if several of them did not hold
objects in their hands that he tentatively identified as a
light-pen, a paintbrush, a chisel, the eyes would have
given them away. They were all iris, shot through with
threads of gold or green—but even in the thing the
New Amazonians inadequately called a *frieze*, they
were aware.

The Dragons towered three or four feet taller than
he, even with their long necks ducked to fit into the
frieze. They moved in the animation, the three humans
the focus of their predatory attention. Michelangelo
felt them watching, and it took the gallery railing
across his lower back to make him realize that he had
backed the entire width of the catwalk away.

6

AFTER THEY RETURNED TO THEIR ROOMS, MICHELANGELO took his time finishing his report to *Kaiwo Maru* and getting ready for bed. Vincent waited until he ordered the lights off and slid in beside him. He turned under the covers, cloth brushing his skin, and pressed himself against his partner's back, draping an arm around Angelo's waist. Michelangelo stiffened in the darkness.

"This is twice now," Vincent said. "Are you going to tell me why you're angry?" Again in their own private language, needlessly complicated, half implied and half tight-beamed, the parts of speech haphazardly switched and vocabulary and syntax swiped from every language either one of them had encountered.

For a moment, he thought Michelangelo wouldn't answer. But his hand covered Vincent's, and he said, "Twice?"

"On *Kaiwo Maru* and at dinner. I can't think what I

said to anger you, but it must be something." He kissed Angelo's neck.

Michelangelo didn't respond. Not even a shiver, and this time he let the silence drag. Vincent was just about to retreat to his own side of the bed when Michelangelo stretched, turning so their eyes could meet, the transmitted light of the nebula revealing his expression. Which, as usual, admitted nothing.

"If we're going to work together—" —*you have to talk to me.* It was more than talking, though. He wanted what they had once had, the trust and the knowledge that Michelangelo would be where he was needed. And it was unfair to ask.

Vincent was the one keeping secrets that could get them both killed. The betrayal had already happened, and Angelo inevitably was going to find out about it and have to live with the consequences. *How many times are you going to make his choices for him?*

Whatever lies Michelangelo was implying, they were for the job; he had made that plain on *Kaiwo Maru.* The smallest dignity Vincent could do in return was not to lie to Michelangelo about Vincent's honorable intentions.

So Vincent leaned forward, instead, and kissed his partner. There was a moment of resistance as their wardrobes analyzed the situation, but as he'd suspected after *Kaiwo Maru,* they were still keyed to each other. Vincent had never changed his program, and apparently Michelangelo hadn't either. The resistance faded, and Angelo took Vincent into his arms.

Sounds drifted into the room from outside, attenuated by height. Music, laughter. A woman singing, the nauseating reek of scorched flesh from some restaurant, people getting the jump on Carnival. The colored sky shone through the false skylights, filling the room with a faint glow. Michelangelo's mouth opened. He kissed hard, well, fluently, his hands soft and warm on Vincent's back. And Vincent . . . wished he believed.

Lesa undressed herself and hung her clothes up to air without bothering House to raise the lights. The night was cloudless and there was enough illumination through the ceiling that she had no problem maneuvering in her own bedroom. But it was dark enough that she was surprised to find the bed already occupied when she tugged the covers back.

Surprised, but not terribly so. "Hello, Robert."

He was awake. He propped himself on his elbows, the sheets gliding down his chest, revealing curly hair. Glossy scars contrasted with the oiled smoothness of his scalp. His teeth flashed in the darkness. "I thought you'd be longer."

She shrugged, and slid into bed beside him, rolling onto her stomach, voice muffled in the pillow. "Let me guess. I forgot to tell Agnes that I wanted you tonight?"

"She said to check in with her in the morning, because she thought you'd be late, too, and didn't feel like waiting up. Arms down by your sides, please?"

His hands were strong; he slicked them down with the oil from the bedstand while she shrugged her nightshirt off, and started work on her shoulders first. Maybe not safe to give him so much autonomy, so much freedom. Maybe not wise to be as permissive with him as she was. But this was Robert, after all, and he was as much hers as he could be without a transfer and a marriage, and she trusted him more than any woman she knew.

She didn't doubt his temper, or his capacity for violence. They were marked on his body, and his status as males figured such things was significant. But he'd never directed either of those things at her, or any woman.

Not gentle, no. But *smart*.

"Thank you," he said.

Her spine cracked under his weight. "Mmph." It might have stood a better chance of being a word if she hadn't had a mouthful of pillow. Robert pulled the cushion out of the way, straightening her neck, and ran his thumbs down her spine, triggering a dizzying release of endorphins. "You heard something? Or is this a social call?"

"Would that it were, my lady."

She laughed at his pretend formality. "It can be a social call, too."

"Business first." But the kiss he planted between her shoulder blades promised pleasant business, at least. He stayed bent down, nuzzling through her hair to brush his lips across her ear. "Did you meet the Colonials?"

"Yes. And yes, it's them. Well, I'm as sure as I can be."

"And what do you think? Can we trust Katherinessen?"

His hands forestalled her shrug. Flinty, dangerous hands, the gnarled scar across the palm of the left one rough when it caught on her skin. "Do we have another choice? I can't tell, Robert. I don't know. Claude won't risk it. There's no guarantee about Katherinessen. Kusanagi-Jones is hard-line Old Earth, though I don't understand it and it makes me sick to think about, and Claude's bound to think placating the Coalition is safer than open opposition, especially if it means allying ourselves with Coalition worlds in open revolt."

"Appeasement has such a glorious history."

"This isn't about glory. And it worked for Ur. Sort of."

"Which is why they're so eager to be rid of the Governors now?"

His tone was arch and dry. She matched it. "Keep it in your pants, Robert."

"I'm not wearing any pants," he said reasonably.

Somewhere, she found the energy to snort. "Anyway, if Mother finds out I've been letting you read history, she'll—"

"Have your hide for a holster. I know." His caresses became more personal and she rolled over, looking up through the dark. He touched the tip of her nose. "What are you going to do?"

She shrugged, and sighed. "I'll know tomorrow. If we miss the meeting, it's not like we'll get another chance—"

"No." He kissed her. "Not in time for Julian, anyway."

Kusanagi-Jones was long past feeling guilt about *lying*. Conscience was one of the first things to go. If he'd ever had much of one to begin with, the job had burned it out. So it was with a certain amount of amusement that he identified the emotion he was feeling over telling the truth—as guilt. Well, a limited sort of truth, with the limitations carefully obscured, but still. Unmistakably the truth.

The fact that he was doing it selfishly didn't enter into it, he told himself. The fact that Vincent was right, and what he really wanted was to punish—

Of course, Vincent only knew that because Kusanagi-Jones wasn't bothering to hide it. Pretoria had probably picked up on it, too, but with luck she'd think it was jealousy, male games.

Oh, hell.

An omission was as good as a lie, and he had told
Vincent he'd chosen the therapy. He was justifying.
Justifying, because if Vincent didn't think Kusanagi-
Jones cared for him anymore, that was one less way
Vincent could hurt him. Justifying, because if he
hadn't cared, if he was doing his job, then he was a
much better actor than this. Justifying because he,
Kusanagi-Jones, deserved Vincent's loathing and anger
for other reasons entirely—reasons Kusanagi-Jones
was too good a Liar for Vincent to suspect, even years
later.

Justifying, and it was the sort of thing, the sort of
self-delusion, that got you killed. He knew it.

And so did Vincent, apparently, because Vincent
pushed against his hand and looked up, leaving an
arc of moisture cooling on Kusanagi-Jones's skin.
"Something's wrong," he said. "Or else I'm more out
of practice than I thought."

The dry tone, brittle enough to break an edge and
cut yourself on. It still worked, too; Kusanagi-Jones
laughed, an honest laugh. Startled into it, though
nothing Vincent said was surprising. It was just very
Vincent, and Kusanagi-Jones had been so deep in his
own bout of self-pity that he'd forgotten.

"Tired," he said, not bothering to hide the fact that
it was a lie.

Warm hands stroked his thighs. "Mmm. You were
the one who said you didn't need rest; you had chemistry."

"Rub it in." It could only be fraught if he let it.
He was a professional. And *Earth* needed what they
had come for. The Coalition needed it; the Governors
were ruthless in balancing population and consumption against their programmed limits. Even wind
farms and geothermal caused impact. Action, reaction,

as incontrovertible as thermodynamics. And—seemingly abrogating those laws—clean, limitless New Amazonian energy could change the fate of two dozen worlds.

And Kusanagi-Jones needed their mission to fail. Or more precisely, *he* needed a win—because he *wasn't* Vincent Katherinessen, and he wasn't getting any younger, and accepting therapy had kept him his job, but it hadn't done enough to lift the cloud after their last awful failure, the mess on New Earth. Kusanagi-Jones needed a win.

And meanwhile, ethics and—sod it, *humanity*—demanded he take a fall. Just like New Earth. But a win here was the only way he could count on staying alive. The only way he might be allowed to stay with Vincent. It left him cold from throat to groin to think of losing that again.

Vincent had always been worth paying attention to in bed. And Vincent had noticed that he still wasn't doing so. "Angelo," he complained, "you're *thinking*."

"And that's supposed to be your job?" Not quite Vincent's dry snap, but enough. "Really want to know?"

Vincent nodded, his depilated cheek smooth on Kusanagi-Jones's skin. "I've no right to ask."

Somehow, in their own private language, it was possible to talk. "You never came," Kusanagi-Jones said, as if his betrayal hadn't happened. And as far as Vincent knew, it hadn't. "I know. Unrealistic expectations. You couldn't have come. Couldn't have found me, and there was nowhere to run. Doesn't help."

Kusanagi-Jones felt Vincent flinch. "I failed you."

"Didn't—"

"I did," he said, as if he needed to. "But you took the therapy."

"I did," he said. Six months of biochemical and

psychological treatments. Kusanagi-Jones wouldn't call it torture; they'd both experienced torture. Profoundly unpleasant. That was all. And he wouldn't let his hands shake talking about it now. "They said I was a model patient. Very willing."

Vincent tensed, shoulder against his thigh, the long muscles of his body tightening. "If this is—"

"Vincent," he said, "I don't want to lie to you."

That shudder might have been relief, or pain. Or the flinch of a guilty conscience. But Vincent nodded and shifted his weight, moving back, pulling his warmth away. Kusanagi-Jones stopped him, tightening his fingers on Vincent's head.

"I can counterfeit anything," he said, and waited for the realization to settle in. He knew it would, although it took longer than he expected. But he felt it take hold, felt Vincent understand what he meant, felt his grief turn to disbelief.

"You're amazing," Vincent said, quiet voice vibrating with excitement, suppressed laughter, his breath both warming and cooling Michelangelo's skin. "A therapy team. A cursed therapy team. You beat *reeducation*. You son of a bitch."

"S'what I do. Not just you who's good at his job."

Vincent shook his head. "I see why you would be mad at me."

"It's done." And it was. Gone and past mending, but maybe leaving room. If Michelangelo decided Vincent was worth more than his ethics.

Michelangelo drew one knee up and pressed his palm into the coarse, rich nap of Vincent's braids, urging silently. And Vincent, after a thoughtful pause, acquiesced.

Later, he slid over Michelangelo, lithe body warm as he straddled his hips, fumbling their bodies into connection before pinning Michelangelo's hands to the bed. Fingers flexed through fingers and the sheets bunched in strangely *material* ways as Vincent exerted the strength that had always excited them both, and Michelangelo pushed back, spreading his arms to draw Vincent's mouth down on his own. Vincent groaned, breath rasping, and Michelangelo slurped sweat off his neck—quickly, before his wardrobe could wick it away—and left banners of suck-marks purpling on Vincent's golden-brown chest. The Gorgon's radiance, bright as moonlight, cast diffuse shadows rather than razored ones, colors layered on Vincent's skin like a Secunda sunset, and Vincent's meticulous nails gouged crescents on the backs of Michelangelo's hands.

It was good.

But it wasn't what it had been. It couldn't be; there was too much moving under the surface now, and Kusanagi-Jones couldn't set it aside. Vincent was a professional, but he wasn't a Liar, and he was keeping back something. Once, Kusanagi-Jones wouldn't have minded. Once he would have known it was orders, and Vincent would tell him when he should.

But that had been before Kusanagi-Jones learned just how badly he'd screw Vincent over, when it came down to orders. And not even official orders.

No. Orders on behalf of Free Earth, in opposition to the Cabinet.

Angel walks beside giants. The nearest is warm and smells sour, sweat and fear, but under the scent is the warmth and the familiar spices of home. Mama holds his hand to keep him close, but it isn't needed; you couldn't pry him from her side.

Her palm is cold and wet, and her hand is shaking. She

calls him *On-hel,* like she did, a pretty nickname. She
shushes him. They come into a bright room and she picks
him up, swings him off his feet and holds him close. Not
balanced on her hip, but pressed to her chest, as if she can
hide him in the folds of her wardrobe.

Someone says big words, words he doesn't understand. They boom, amplified. They hurt his ears, and
he hides his head in Mama's breast. She cups a big
palm against the back of his head, covering his ears,
making the hurt go away. He knows not to cry out loud.
He curls up tight.

Mama argues. Her arm around him is tight. But
then someone else speaks. He says *they won't take the
boy,* and Mama staggers, as if someone has struck her a
blow, and when he looks up she's swaying with her
eyes closed. "The boy is not to blame," the man says,
the man Angel's never seen before. "The Governors
say, let the punishment fit the crime."

Then someone pulls Angel away from her, and she
lets him go as if her arm has numbed. She turns away,
her round brown face contracted. She seems caught
midflinch.

He cries her name and reaches for her, but somebody has him, big arms and a confused moment of
struggling against strength. He kicks. He'd bite, but
whoever has him is wise to that trick. He's held tight.

"Close your eyes, Angel," Mama says, but he doesn't
listen. She's not looking at him. He dreams his name
the way she said it again, the fond short form nobody
else has ever called him.

Whoever's holding him says something, some
words, but he's screaming too loud to hear them, and
then Mama takes a deep breath and nods, and there's a
pause, long enough that she opens her eyes and turns

as if to see why what she was anticipating has not come
to pass—

—and she falls apart.

She makes no sound. She doesn't show pain or even
squeak; the Governors are programmed to be humane.
But one moment she is whole and alive and letting out
a held breath and taking in another one to speak to
him, and the next she pitches forward, boneless, her
central nervous system disassembled. Within moments, the thing that was Angel's Mama is a crumbling dune in the middle of a broad white empty floor,
and the man who is holding him, too late, thinks to
step back and turn Angel's face away.

He already knows not to cry out loud. He couldn't,
anyway, because his breath won't move.

The adult holding him soothes him, strokes him,
but hesitates when he seems to feel no emotion.

He wasn't too worried, the adult Kusanagi-Jones understands. The boy was too young to understand what
he'd seen, most likely. And everywhere, there are families that want children and are not permitted to have
them.

Someone will take him in.

Angelo's breathing awoke Vincent in the darkness. It
was not slow and deep, but a staccato rhythm that
Vincent had almost forgotten in the intervening years,
and now remembered as if it were merely hours since
the last time he lay down beside Michelangelo.

Angelo was a lucid dreamer. He had learned the
trick in self-defense, with Vincent's assistance, decades
before. Angelo could control his dreams as easily as he
controlled his emotions. Just more irony that it turned
out not to help the problem.

Because it didn't stop the nightmares.

Vincent had hoped, half-consciously, they might have eased over the passing years. But judging from Angelo's rigid form in the bed, his fists clenched against his chest, his frozen silhouette and panting as if he bit back panicked sobs—

—they were worse.

"Angelo," he said, and felt the bed rock as Angelo shuddered, caught halfway between REM atonia—the inhibition of movement caused by the shutdown of monoamines in the brain—and waking. *"Angelo,"* Vincent snapped, bouncing the bed in preference to the dangerous activity of shaking his partner.

Angelo's eyelids popped open, dark irises gleaming with reflected colors. He gasped and pushed his head back against the pillow, sucking air as if he'd been dreaming of being strangled.

He might have been. All Vincent knew about the nightmares was that they were of things that had happened, or might have happened, and between them they had enough unpleasant memories for a year's worth of bad dreams.

Vincent put his hand on Angelo's shoulder; when he breathed out again he seemed calm. "Thank you," he said. He closed his eyes and swallowed.

"Think nothing of it," Vincent answered, and put his head down on the pillow again.

Lesa sat cross-legged on the bed, a cup of tea steaming in her hands, her breakfast untouched on the tray beside her, and watched the Coalition diplomats disentangle themselves from the sheets. She had a parser-translator running on their coded conversation of the night before, but it hadn't been able to identify the language. It *had* tossed out some possibles, based on cognates, but its inability to provide a complete translation was frustrating. It could put together a word here, a word there—Katherinessen, laughing, calling Kusanagi-Jones a *son-of-a-bitch* in plain Ozglish, not even com-pat—and she got a sense that they were talking about personal history, some old hurt or illness that was tied to the hesitations in their sex.

Just the sort of thing you'd expect recently reunited long-term lovers to discuss when they were safe under the covers, warm in each other's arms. But something tugged her attention, something she couldn't quite call an irregularity, but an...eccentricity. They were together, but strained—by history, she thought, secrets, and maybe the mission itself.

She smiled, watching Katherinessen unwind himself from the bed and pad across the carpetplant to the window, where some delicate tool rested in the sun, dripping tiny solar panels like the black leaves of an unlikely orchid.

Secrets. Of course, Katherinessen *was* keeping secrets.

He rested his arm on the window ledge, squinting in the sunlight, and began to fuss with the interface on his implant. Recharging its battery, she realized, after a moment. Clever—and she thought it might have a system to capture the kinetic energy of his body when he moved. Meanwhile Kusanagi-Jones checked something on his own implant, then stood and glided toward the bathroom. She shook herself free of her urge to watch him go about his morning routine; he wasn't as pretty as Katherinessen, but he moved like a khir, all coiled muscle and liquid strength. Instead she stood, drank off her tea—kept hot by the mug—and clicked her fingers for Walter. The khir poked its head

from the basket beside the door and stretched regally,
long scale-dappled legs flexing nonretractable claws
among the carpetplant. Its earfeathers flickered forward and up, trembling like the fronds of a fern, and
when it shook itself, dust motes and shreds of fluff
scattered into the sunlight like glitter.

Lesa snapped her fingers again and crouched, holding out a piece of her scone. Walter trotted to her,
dancing in pleasure at being offered a share of breakfast. It inspected the scone with nostrils and labial pits,
then took it daintily between hooked teeth as long as
Lesa's final finger-joint. She dusted the crumbs off the
khir's facial feathers, and it chirped, dropping more
bits on the carpetplant. Standing, its nose was level
with hers when she crouched.

She bumped its forehead with her hand, petting
for a moment as it leaned into her touch, then stood
and walked toward the fresher. The door irised into
existence; the shower created itself around her. She
hurried. She had things to accomplish before the repatriation, and it *was* the first of Carnival.

Vincent sat on the window ledge, wearing the simplest
loose trousers and shirt he had licensed. He sweated
under them, the rising sun warming the moist air on
his back. His face and chest were cool; his body was
breaking the air curtain, but it didn't seem to disrupt
the climate control.

"Angelo," he called, loud enough to be heard over
running water, "do you get the feeling we're being
watched?"

Michelangelo's voice drifted over splashing. "Expect
we wouldn't be?"

Silly question, sarcastic answer, of course. But there

was something picking at the edge of his senses. Something more than the knowledge that there were video and audio motes turned on them every moment. More unsettling than the knowledge that somewhere, a technician was dissecting last night's lovemaking via infrared and voice-stress.

Vincent frowned, imagining too vividly the expression on some cold-handed woman's face as she analyzed the catch in Michelangelo's breath when he'd finally consented to thrust up into Vincent with that particular savagery. It was rare that Angelo allowed glimpses of the man under his armor. And Vincent worked for them, he did. He always had.

"Such a gentleman," he called back as the water cut off, filing the shiver at the nape of his neck under *deal with it later*. The Penthesileans said their city was haunted, and Vincent did not wonder why. It wasn't just the wind or the trembling in the walls when you brushed them with your hand.

Sound carried in these arched, airy chambers. Vincent's first reaction was that they would be prohibitive to heat. Of course, that didn't mean much at the equator, and they *would* catch a breeze—but these were people so energy-rich they let the tropical sunshine splash on their streets and skins unfiltered by solar arrays, like letting gold run molten down the gutters, uncollected.

He thought of Old Earth, her Governors and her painstakingly, ruthlessly balanced ecology, and sighed. If generating power were removed from the equation, that would leave agriculture and resources as the biggest impactors, and a utility fog was a very efficient use of material. One object, transfinite functions.

Michelangelo stepped out of the shower, making it Vincent's turn. Their wardrobes could handle sweat and body odor, but bacterial growth and skin oil were beyond them. Besides, Vincent had an uneasy suspicion he was getting hooked on warm water flooding over his body. It was a remarkable sensation.

He kissed Michelangelo in passing, and keyed his wardrobe off before he stepped under the shower. Michelangelo would start complaining about the clothes Vincent had chosen for him soon enough, and then, if they hurried, they could make it to the docks and check out the cargo before their command appearance at breakfast and the repatriation ceremony.

"Angelo——" Hot water sluiced across Vincent's neck, easing discomfort he hadn't noticed. He checked his chemistry. He could afford an analgesic. And a mild stimulant. Something to tide him over until breakfast, where he hoped there would be coffee.

"Here." He was in the fresher, his voice pitched soft and echoing slightly off the mirror as if he were leaned in close.

"I need an Advocate."

Michelangelo's silence was indulgence.

Vincent listened to the water fall for thirty seconds, and then said, "Kyoto. She never got to say her piece at dinner."

"The terrifying old battleaxe? What topic?"

"Biological determinism. Can you do it?"

"Right." Michelangelo cleared his throat. "The only significant natural predator that human women have is heterosexual men. The Amazonian social structure, with its strictures on male activity, has nothing to do with masculine intelligence or capability."

"Good." Vincent started to key a toiletry license, and saw a bar of soap resting in a niche in the wall. "Do you suppose this soap is animal fat?"

"Probably," Michelangelo said, dropping his cheerfully didactic voice of Advocacy. "How's it smell?"

"Nice." But Vincent, having sniffed, put it down again and ran his hand under the water until his skin tingled. "So if it's not that men suffer under reduced capacity, what's it about?"

"Biology. Self-defense. Reasonable precautions."

"Keep going."

"Traditionally, the responsibility for safety falls on the victim. Women are expected to defend themselves from predators. To act like responsible prey. Limit risks, not take chances. Not to go out alone at night. Not talk to strange men. Rely on their own, presumably domesticated men for protection from other feral men—in exchange for granting them property rights over the women in question." He laughed. "How's that?"

"And the New Amazonian system is superior in what way?"

"Punishes the potential predator and arms the potential victim. If men cannot control themselves, control will be instituted. Potential predators are caged, regulated."

"But?"

Michelangelo fell silent again. Vincent heard the splash of water, the rustle of the towels. "What do I think, or what would Elder Kyoto say?"

"Kyoto."

"It could have happened centuries ago, but women were soft," Michelangelo said. "Too soft for revolution. Too willing to believe the best of men. Unwilling to punish all for the sins of many, so they took that onus on themselves, and endured the risks. And a certain percentage of human males acted the way some males of most species will act: infanticide, rape, kidnapping, and the general treatment of females as chattel."

"And what do *you* think?"

More quiet. The water cut off.

Vincent ducked his head out of the shower without rinsing the soap from his hair. "Angelo?"

Michelangelo was leaned against the wall, palms on either side of the mirror, inspecting the whites of his eyes. He turned around and set his backside on the basin between pale-knuckled hands. "Think we're all prey. And all predators, given half a chance. What about you?"

After a certain amount of trouble, Kii accesses the space-ship. Timeslip reveals emergent properties; the ship is named Kaiwo Maru, *and* Kaiwo Maru *will have been important to the resolution, eventually. The threads lead through her, swirl around her. They are altered when they cross her path, and tumble away in alien directions.*

They are altered since the moment she arrived, and Kii understands the implications. This is a cusp. There are others such, that are collapsed. There will have been others again.

The Consent is that Kii examine Kaiwo Maru. *She uses a simple quantum computing engine, Bose-Einstein condensates similar to the ones implanted in the en-croaching bipeds. She is constructed of modular units, foglets, and is transfinitely adaptable.*

And she is aware.

Kii is at first excited to find that she hosts conscious-ness. There's more here than Kii has understood; the bipeds are more advanced than Kii could have realized.

But Kii comes to understand that the consciousnesses she hosts are problematic. They are intelligent, focused, with a developed and balanced value system. They are disinterested.

They have only goals and directives, and while they wait for the opportunity to carry out those directives and continue to achieve those goals, they play endless, complicated games.

They find Kii unremarkable. They are incurious.

They are intelligent, Kii decides, not esthelich. *They have no art. Which perhaps means the bipeds are not* esthelich *either, if they are associated with these consciousnesses, which they call the Governors.*

If they are not esthelich, *not people...*

That would simplify things.

7

THE DOCKS WERE TARRED WOOD, AN ARCHAIC EXTRAVA-
gance. Vincent kept wanting to crouch and run his fingers across the surface to verify the size of the logs.
They were laid side by side, countertapered, each one
meters in diameter at the base. The whole thing shivered faintly when the sea foamed around the pilings.
The cargo pod—detached from the lighter, now—
bobbed at the end of the pier, squeaking against the
bumpers. Vincent was grateful for the hats that Miss
Pretoria had had in her hand when she arrived that
morning. If he'd been planning on going back to the
OECC, he'd have made a note to get them to design licenses for headgear for future diplomats.

Michelangelo stood impassive on his left hand, two
steps away and half a step behind. Miss Pretoria was
on his right side, her security detail flanking the three
of them. They'd taken a surface car here from the government center, a fuel-cell vehicle. They must use the

native power to compress hydrogen for charging it, instead of the processes that had led to such vehicles being banned on Old Earth. There was no tang of combustion products anywhere near the city, and his wardrobe reported clean air. Particulates were limited to dust and organics—skin flakes, pollen, microscopic organisms, the inevitable detritus of man and nature.

Vincent leaned closer to Miss Pretoria and asked, "What will you do when your population increases beyond the capacity of the remnant cities?"

"We haven't even identified their limits yet. Our problem has been keeping our population on an upcurve."

"And yet, no eugenics laws."

"Women who work historically have fewer children than those who don't," she said. "And we work *very* hard. Many women get their Obligation out of the way as early as is legal, or don't even bother with it if they don't *want* to head a household. Three babies isn't a big investment for a man, but—biologically speaking—it's an enormous one for a woman. At least until the children are crèched. Also, there's the Trials. Only our best males breed, and they're in demand."

"Stud males," Vincent said quietly.

Michelangelo glanced at him, and then at Miss Pretoria. " 'Gentle' males don't reproduce?"

"There are women who make arrangements. But we won't stoop to intervention to conceive. And you won't find a market for implants like yours here." Her shrug bordered on a shudder.

"Moral objections to implanted tech?"

"After the first Assessment? I don't know how you can walk around in a utility fog that could start disassembling your body anytime your Governors decide they're done with you."

Vincent raised an eyebrow. Michelangelo opened his mouth and shut it again. They walked quietly, the sea breeze ruffling the fine hairs on Vincent's skin, the pier echoing with the cries of some white-winged flying animal. Parallel evolution; it looked enough like an Old Earth tern that Michelangelo did a double-take over the first one, but the rear limbs were feathered as well, and seemed to act as auxiliary wings. Vincent pointedly continued to say nothing when he saw them scavenging among buckets of offal lined up stinking at the quayside.

The reek was astounding. Vincent breathed through his mouth until they were out where the breeze off the bay blew away the worst, and Michelangelo gritted his teeth, swallowed hard, and touched his watch to adjust his blood chemistry. *He's doing that too much.* But this wasn't the time to say it.

The murmur of conversation swelled and dropped as they passed each cluster of bystanders—men and women, finally, although far more of the latter. Vincent stole sideways glances right back. *These* men were tough looking, muscular, most of them strikingly scarred. They were dressed distinctively, trousers and vests, each of them wearing a leather bracelet on his left wrist with a brightly colored badge. "Household allegiance?" Vincent asked, nodding to the badges.

"License," Miss Pretoria said.

Vincent bridled at the faint disapproval in her voice. *So she doesn't think they should be out on their own even with a tag in their ears?* "For work, or transit?"

"Yes," she said, eyes forward. "My own—that is to say, the male I plan to take with me when I found my household, when I can buy his contract from my mother—he's street-licensed, but doesn't work. We don't need the income." She said it with a certain amount of pride, and Vincent thought of Old Earth men he'd heard say: *but my wife doesn't work, of course.*

He shook his head. "These are laborers?"

She nodded as they passed a light security cordon and drew up before the cargo pod. "Usually, they're of the household that operates the fishing boat."

The pod had a massive hatchway for unloading, and a tight-squeeze access port. Both were sealed. A woman standing by in a severe beige suit extended her hand. Vincent surreptitiously keyed his wardrobe to allow contact and met her handshake.

"Miss Ouagadougou," Pretoria said. "Miss Katherinessen, Miss Kusanagi-Jones."

"A pleasure," Miss Ouagadougou said, winning Vincent's affection by entirely failing to notice that she was shaking hands with a man.

"Charmed," Michelangelo said, sounding as if he meant it, and also shook her hand. She was slight and brown-skinned, with a bit of desk-job pudge, her gray-streaked hair twisted into a straggling knot at the nape of her neck. She wore a weapon, just like every woman in Penthesilea, but the leather on the safety strap was cracked as if she didn't oil or use it often.

"Miss Ouagadougou is one of our leading art historians," Miss Pretoria said, standing aside. She gestured Vincent toward the sealed hatch on the pod.

He deferred, glancing at Michelangelo. "Angelo's the expert on the team. I've got a layman's knowledge, but he has a degree in art history from the University of Cairo, on Old Earth."

Michelangelo's slight smile reflected amusement as Miss Pretoria blinked at them, obviously conducting an abrupt field rearrangement of her assumptions. "I beg your pardon," she said. "There's room for all of us in the capsule."

"That's all right. I'll stay outside." Vincent folded his arms and pointed with his chin across the water, its serene blue surface transparent enough that he could see rippled golden sand underneath. Penthesilea sprawled and spiked behind him, embraced by the green crescent arms of the bay. In the shadow of his hat, the sun wasn't even so bad. "It's a beautiful day."

Miss Pretoria stared at him for a moment, then nodded. "Don't wander far. I'd hate to see you kidnapped by pirates. They have an eye for a pretty man."

"Pirates?" Of course, where there was shipping, there was piracy, but...

"Even New Amazonia has terrorists and renegades," she said. "By the way, should you have the opportunity to be kidnapped by radicals, you'd rather fall in with the Right Hand Path than with Maenads, if you get the choice."

Vincent laughed. "I won't pass the security cordon." Miss Ouagadougou's eyes flicked sideways, her lips tightening as if she was about to say something, and Vincent wondered exactly what it might be. Regarding the Right Hand Path, by the timing of her gesture. Michelangelo also shot him a look, and Vincent returned it. *Of course I have an ulterior motive. Run with it.*

Michelangelo nodded, took the handoff, and turned away, ducking to murmur in the historian's ear before he produced the key for the cargo pod's seal. She laughed, bubbling excitement and enthusiasm, almost vibrating with her eagerness to run her gaze over the treasures.

They filed inside, leaving the door open, and Vincent sighed in an unanticipated intensity of relief. *Alone at last*, he thought, self-mocking, and leaned against a piling, tilting his hat forward to produce a little more shade. To anyone observing, he might have seemed to be drowsing in the sun, halfheartedly watching the bustle the length of the pier.

He wasn't surprised to see a man he recognized from the reception round the pilings at the land end of the pier and walk up the path between bustling fisherwomen, obviously intent on the cargo pod. The man was dressed like the laborers, although his trousers and vest were of better quality, embroidered, and the badge on his left wrist looked more elaborately decorated. His shaven head gleamed black as basalt under the heat of the sun, and he was big and fit, but none of that was unusual. Neither the scars pale against his complexion nor the swagger in his stride set him apart among Penthesilean men.

What startled Vincent was the man's companion; a leggy teal-green-and-gold-dappled animal, maybe sixty kilos, all long bones and prancing angles under the windblown fuzziness of what was either a pelt or hairlike feathers. One of the raptor-creatures from the Dragon's frieze, it looked more predatory in the flesh. Two large front-facing eyes would provide binocular hunter's vision, sheltered under fluffy projecting eyebrows. Something like a moth's fronded antennae protruded from the top of its long head, and its limbs, muzzle, and belly were scaled, a sleek contrast to the warm-looking fluff on its back.

"Pets," Vincent said, under his breath, watching the way the beast leaned its shoulder on the man's thigh as they moved down the pier. "They have *pets*."

Well, of course. They ate animal flesh, and while some of it must be harvested from the wild—witness the bustle and the stench of death on this pier—they also must have domestic animals. And it was a short step from one perversion to another, from enslaving animals for their meat to enslaving them as toys.

Vincent kept his face carefully calm in the dappled shade of his hat, and swallowed to fight the taste of bile.

And this is better than the Governors? The beast nosed the man's hand as they paused by the security cordon and the man rewarded it with a quick ruffle of its feathers. It was like watching a grown man in diapers; the process of infantilization was complete. There was no way an animal so crippled could have a life outside of human control.

This is what we are when we're left to our own devices—savage, selfish, short-sighted. Vincent squared his shoulders, thought of Michelangelo, and frowned. *But free. Any government founded on a political or religious agenda more elaborate than "protect the weak, temper the strong" is doomed to tyranny,* he quoted silently, and made himself look away from the tame animal. He slipped an etched-carbon data chip no larger than his thumbnail out of his pocket and concealed it in his lightly sweating palm. It was steady-state material, not a fog, and fiendishly expensive, but there were too many security risks entailed in using his watch to transport data as sensitive as this. And he could afford it with his mother footing the bill.

They'd have to make the trade quickly, invisibly, without detection by the security agents, Michelangelo, or Miss Pretoria. The New Amazonian habit of indiscriminate handshaking proved itself useful for once.

Vincent checked his watch as the black-skinned stranger showed the security guards his license, displayed a data pad of archaic design, and was waved through. No doubt, he was ferrying a message for Miss Pretoria or Miss Ouagadougou.

Eight hundred hours, as arranged.
Right on time.

Lesa hung back by the hatch, inside the cool darkness of the shuttle, and watched Nkechi Ouagadougou and Michelangelo Kusanagi-Jones code-key open cargo lockers with the sort of reverence she associated with wrapping a funeral shroud. Lesa herself wasn't an artist or a scientist. Her aesthetic sense was limited. If it weren't for her empathic gift, if her foremothers hadn't had the resources for Diaspora and she'd been born on Earth, she'd have been Assessed.

But as Ouagadougou and Kusanagi-Jones paused before each freshly opened chamber and waited for the utility fog that served as packing material to fade to transparency, she could feel their awe. It rolled off them in bittersweet cataracts, Kusanagi-Jones's flavored with a faint reluctance and Ouagadougou's dripping eagerness. It was a held-breath sort of moment for both of them, and Lesa didn't want to intervene.

Besides, enjoyable as the overflow of their quiet glee was, she was only pretending to watch them. Practically speaking, she was watching Katherinessen. And Robert, who paused beside the step up to the door to introduce himself. They shook hands—Lesa's smile never showed—and Katherinessen's hand slipped back into his pocket. "They're inside," he said. Quietly, but his voice was crisp enough to carry.

Robert bowed, his manners impeccable, and glanced at the hatch. Lesa knew she was invisible in the darkness within. She stepped forward so the light would catch on her cheekbones and held out her hand. "Hello, dear."

He didn't step inside the pod, just held out a

datacart and bowed as she accepted it. Something else fell into her palm—a chip, which had been pinned between his thumb and the cart. She flipped her hand over, opening the cart. "Anything important?"

He looked demure, or a convincing approximation. "Elder Elena Pretoria sends her regards," he said, folding his hands behind his back. "And requests her daughter inquire as to whether the emissaries would consent to join the household for supper and Carnival tonight in the absence of other plans."

Lesa thumbed the cart and slipped the chip into her pocket casually with the opposite hand. "All I can do is ask."

Michelangelo swung down from the pod in a state of elation, feeling light and taut enough that he actually checked his chemistry to make sure it wasn't a malfunction. The twin expressions of concern that Vincent and Miss Pretoria wore stopped him short before he was firmly grounded. His foot skipped on the wood underfoot, and he reached up and tilted his borrowed hat to cut the glare.

"Problem." His eyes were on Vincent, but it was Miss Pretoria who answered.

"A small one," she confirmed, and moved forward with one hand upraised to stop Miss Ouagadougou from running into Kusanagi-Jones's back. Which was fortunate. Kusanagi-Jones was not looking forward to apologizing to the first unwary New Amazonian who bounced off his wardrobe or was shocked by it . . . but he also wasn't about to dial the safety features down unless he was actively engaged in shaking someone's hand.

"Nkechi," Miss Pretoria said, "I've been asked to hurry Miss Katherinessen and Miss Kusanagi-Jones back to the government center. Can you see to the relocation of the cargo?"

Kusanagi-Jones stepped aside and turned in time to see her nod and vanish back inside. He crossed the slight distance between the landing and his partner and took up station at Vincent's side. His shadow still stretched long on the dock beside him, but the sun was climbing enough to sting where it snuck around the shade of his hat. "Is everything in order?"

"Perfectly," Michelangelo answered.

Miss Pretoria turned back to them and held up a datacart. She ducked her head, speaking under the shadow of her hat. "A message from my mother, in her role as opposition leader. Countersigned by Antonia. Elder Kyoto, I mean."

Their habitual security detail flanked them, just far enough away not to overhear if they kept their voices down. Two more women in plain black uniforms remained by the lighter.

"I'm not sure we ever heard her Christian name." Despite his height, Vincent's heels rang on the docks with the effort of keeping up with Pretoria; the warden could move when she had to.

She frowned. "That's an odd term for it."

Kusanagi-Jones didn't have to look at Vincent to know he'd led her into that particular trap on purpose, although his purpose was mysterious. "The first emigrants to Ur were religious refugees," he said. "It's just a turn of phrase."

"Pregnant religious refugees? Miss Katherinessen—"

"Vincent."

"—I suspect you're pulling my leg."

"Some of them were political refugees—"

"Some of *us* are still waiting to hear about the crisis," Kusanagi-Jones said irritably. It wasn't Miss

Pretoria's leg Vincent was yanking. It was Kusanagi-Jones's chain.

"Sorry," Vincent lied, biting back a widening of his smile.

I never should have fucked him. But he had, whatever advantage it gave Vincent. And he'd do it again.

At least the crisis couldn't actually be a crisis. Vincent wouldn't be playing cat-and-mouse games with him if it were.

It was a measure of his own stress and his reactions to the New Amazonian culture that his brain spent a full half-second pinwheeling on the atavistic roots of the phrase *cat-and-mouse,* as archaic to Earth's governed culture as saying *hoist on his own petard.* The New Amazonians probably had cats, or the native equivalent. And they probably set them on local herbivores for entertainment, too. When they weren't enjoying a good duel or a round of cockfighting.

Savages.

Anyway, Vincent was enjoying toying with him far too much for the crisis to be anything overwhelming. In fact, confounding Pretoria's careful observation of them into that slightly furrowed brow could be Vincent's entire objective. In which case, Kusanagi-Jones was content to play the game. He cleared his throat, deciding the silence had gone on long enough.

"In the car," Pretoria said.

It waited where they had left it, a low-slung honey-brown groundcar complete with a wet bar and seats more comfortable than most armchairs. The doors hissed shut after they entered—a perfect seal—and Kusanagi-Jones used every iota of his craft to appear as if he relaxed against the upholstery, while trying not to picture the animal it must have come from. Cool air shocked the sweat on his neck.

The car rolled forward like a serpent sliding over grass.

"The repatriation ceremony has been postponed," Miss Pretoria said, and leaned forward in her chair to pull glasses and a decanter of cloudy gray-green fluid out of the refrigerator. One at a time, she poured three glasses and handed the first two to Vincent and Kusanagi-Jones. "Any allergies?"

If there were, the nanodocs should handle it. He shook his head and sipped; it looked like swamp water, but tasted tart, with complex overtones. "The reason for the postponement?"

Vincent said, "Officially, a delay in negotiations."

The artifacts in the cargo pod, *officially*, were an expression of goodwill—not termed a gift because they already belonged to the New Amazonian people. Negotiations had nothing to do with it. "Unofficially?"

"A threat against the prime minister's life," Miss Pretoria said, after a glance at Vincent to see if he was going to speak. "And Miss... and Vincent's."

That moment of communication unsettled Kusanagi-Jones. There was something behind it, and he thought if he had Vincent's gifts he would know what it was. But Vincent's hazel eyes were undilated and he met Kusanagi-Jones's gaze easily. "Do we know the source of the threat?"

"We suspect the Left Hand. A radical free-male group. Although it could as easily have been one of the Separatist movements; they put Claude in power, and they can't be pleased that she's negotiating with..." Lesa shrugged apologetically.

"Men," Vincent finished. "These Maenads you mentioned. Is that such a group?"

"The most radical of them. Claude doesn't actually believe there's much of a threat, you understand. If enough people wanted to get rid of her badly enough to risk their lives to do it, you'd hear no end to the challenges." Lesa didn't quite smile. "We've never had an assassination on New Amazonia, though two prime ministers have been shot down in the street when they weren't fast enough on the draw. So no, we're cautious, but not too worried."

"Then why the rush?"

"The ceremony is delayed, but we're still expected for breakfast. And we might as well see the art installed in the gallery, since we have the time after all."

"And in the evening?" Kusanagi-Jones asked, folding his hands around the moist, cold glass. Vincent might not be worried, but when it came to his own personal safety, Vincent was sometimes an idiot. And additionally, Kusanagi-Jones suspected that Vincent wouldn't show concern in front of the New Amazonian women.

She smiled. "My mother has invited you to dinner and sightseeing tonight. And of course, there's Carnival."

They attended the state breakfast, which thankfully involved less probing-out of territorial limits and more honest gestures toward détente, and a generous quantity of sliced fruit and plain porridge, which Vincent was assured had been prepared without any animal products. He even got Michelangelo to eat, and drink half a pot of tea laced heavily with sugar, and *almost* managed it without pausing to wonder how his partner had survived seventeen years without him.

They'd returned to the gallery by the time Miss Ouagadougou arrived with three lorry-loads of repatriated art. It came under heavy guard by New Amazonian standards: six armed women and the driver. Vincent couldn't help comparing the way politicians and dignitaries walked everywhere, attended only by one or two personal retainers, and wondered how the death threat would affect that. On Old Earth, there would be a renewed frenzy of security preparations. Here, with the New Amazonians' culture of macha, they might just flaunt themselves more. Bravado seemed to be the most likely response.

Michelangelo was going to have a few stern words to say about that, Vincent imagined.

An armed population might cut down on personal crime—although he wasn't willing to gamble on it unless he had the analyzed statistics graphed on his watch—but apparently property crime was still a problem.

Strike two for Utopia. *The problem with the damned things always comes when you try to introduce actual people into your philosophical constructs.*

At the gallery, Vincent attempted to assist with the unloading and the decisions on what would be displayed and where, but there were burly men with laborer's licenses and handcarts and floatcarts for the former, and Michelangelo and Miss Ouagadougou for the latter. And Miss Ouagadougou finally clucked at Vincent and told him that he might as well go for a walk, because he was more in the way than she wanted.

He'd thought he might find a quiet corner and go over his notes from the last day, and attempt to present the appearance of a serious diplomat, but half an hour's restless flipping through the information on his watch and trying not to distract Michelangelo left him pacing irritably in the anteroom. His focus was compromised. It wasn't just the variations in gravity, daylight, and atmospheric balance, or the unfamiliar food—in fact, New Amazonia's oxygen-rich air was a vast improvement over New Earth's, to choose a world not particularly at random. He was as accustomed to those things as he was to the slightly folksy Colonial Christian persona he'd been using on Lesa all morning. Adaptation was his stock in trade.

No, he had mission jitters like a first-timer, aftermath of what he'd just set in motion, and the fact that it was now out of his control. With luck, Robert would see the message in the chip into the right hands, the ones who could *decode* it. With luck, they would get a message back to him, and the alliance he'd come to broker—the one in contravention of his supposed OECC loyalties, the one that could allow Ur, New Amazonia, and several other outlying colonies to resist repatriation and governance—could become reality. He might even learn who Katherine Lexasdaughter's opposite numbers were, if they trusted him enough to arrange a face-to-face introduction.

Which they had to if this was going to work. Because the assurances and promises he carried weren't recorded anywhere except in his head, and he wouldn't commit them to anyone else.

It was out of his hands, in other words. And there was little Vincent cared for less than trusting to luck.

And the jitters were compounded by standing here, looking at Michelangelo bent in close, professional conversation with Miss Ouagadougou, remembering the smoothness of his skin, the tingle of their wardrobes meshing—

Stop it. He turned away and padded through the other, still-empty chambers of the museum. One of the security detail detached herself and followed at a respectful distance. Vincent checked his stride to allow her to catch up, folded his hands behind his back, and turned. The chalky surface of the floor felt soft and slick under the balls of his feet. He wondered if the

Amazonians ever used carpets or mats, or only bare floors and ubiquitous carpetplant.

The agent was another tall woman, broad-shouldered and muscular, with a beaked nose, arched eyebrows over dark eyes, and coarse-grained skin. "I'm sorry, Miss——"

"Delhi." She didn't quite smile, but she was thinking about it. "Shafaqat Delhi, Miss Katherinessen."

"Vincent," he said. "If I may call you...Shafaqat?"

And there went the smile. She had broad lips, small teeth, very white. A radiant smile. "What's your pleasure, Vincent?"

No stumble. Much more comfortable with him than Miss Pretoria was. But then, also not personally responsible for the success of negotiations. Vincent had no illusions who would be the sacrifice if the whole careful structure of half-truths and unmade promises came down on the New Amazonian's ears.

She still might benefit from revolution. Vincent wanted to see the remnant technology remain in *human* control, not that of the Governors. At least the Governors' directive of ecological balance kept their powers in check. But he could envision a Coalition in which those limits did not apply. One in which further growth of the species was allowed, within limits, but every human was fitted not just with a watch, but with an entire series of governor-controlled utility fogs. It wasn't the most reassuring concept of the future he'd ever entertained.

And the human government, the Colonial Cabinet, was worse. The Governors were unconcerned with one's *mores*, as long as one didn't reproduce illegally or steal energy, though they'd enforce Coalition laws. *God granted Adam and Eve free will and the first damned thing they did with it was find the nearest snake and hand it back.*

The agent looked vaguely concerned. "Vincent?"

"I beg your pardon," he said. "You asked my pleasure."

"Within my professional capacity, of course." There was definitely a flirtatious edge on that smile. He might have lost his mind but at least he hadn't lost his charm.

"Miss Ouagadougou suggested that it might be all right for us to do a little exploring, as long as it wasn't unaccompanied." He waved backhanded the way they'd come. Miss Ouagadougou's laugh followed Michelangelo's reassuring rumble, their voices echoing from high arched spaces so reverberation obscured the words. "Would you do me the honor of escort?"

She laughed, and he thought he saw respect shade her expression at his willingness to venture out in spite of the threat. And that was important, too; he was sure now that he needed to show himself fearless if he wanted to be in a position to bring these women into an alliance with Ur.

Shafaqat said, "What a delightful invitation. Although I am detailed to protect you. You could have just told me where you wanted to go. It's Carnival. You should get to play a little."

"But that isn't as much fun."

"I'll let them know we're going," Shafaqat said. "And find out what time your partner wants you home."

8

WHEN SHE DISCOVERED THAT SHAFAQAT AND MISS
Katherinessen were going for a walk, Lesa opted to
join them. They left Miss Ouagadougou so enamored
of her task that the abandonment barely drew a grunt.
Miss Kusanagi-Jones was less sanguine about the unescorted trip, arguing with Katherinessen in low tones.
His unease didn't seem assuaged by Lesa's comment
that she was capable of squiring Vincent undamaged
through the streets, even on the first of Carnival.

As they returned through the galleries, Lesa noticed
that Katherinessen was stealing surreptitious sideways
glances, and she got the impression that he was looking for some evidence of the fate of the Colonial
marines who had died here.

There wasn't any. House wouldn't permit lingering
damage—and whatever damage there had been, had
been from the marines' weapons. The ghosts didn't
leave scorched or melted walls.

They paused on the carpetplant in the antechamber so that Lesa could slip into her boots, Katherinessen could adjust his wardrobe, and they could both retrieve their hats. The Coalition diplomats seemed to have adapted to the need to keep the sun off their heads. Which was more than she could say for Robert. Lesa could no more keep a hat on him than on their daughter.

Shafaqat seemed relieved to be part of the expedition, although Lesa was aware that the agent bore a certain healthy respect for herself. And that as they stepped outside, she was hovering protectively close to Katherinessen and not to Lesa.

At least, nothing in her manner suggested that she anticipated trouble. Lesa glanced over her own shoulder, made sure of the street, and led them along a latticed walkway that swung thick with garlands, threads of smoke from the incense swaying in the sultry air. "Is there anything in particular you'd like to see?"

"Carnival." He ticked his fingernails along the lattice. "I'm familiar with a Christian holiday of the same name—"

"We celebrate it in honor of the Gaian Principle," Lesa said. "Ten days of party before the summer fast of Contemplation. Not a complete fast," she hastened to add, as Katherinessen turned to her, lips parting. "But we make a point of a bit of spiritual cleansing and contemplation."

"But it's not a religious holiday?"

"It's a *spiritual* observance," she said. "Some follow it more than others. Simple food, no alcohol, meditation, and a focus on community service and charitable giving. A time of renewal, when the jungle dries in the heat before the rains."

"Contemplation," he said, shaping it with his lips as if tasting it. "How long is that?"

"Fifty days," she said.

She saw him running conversions in his head—day length, and year length. "That's a long time."

"It's a pretty good party," she answered, and met his wrinkled nose with a grin. "It takes awhile to recover."

She took him on a tour of the administrative center first, Shafaqat trailing them attentively. Seeing her own city through new eyes was an interesting process. He asked questions she'd never considered at any depth, although she was sure there were scientific teams at work on every one of them, and she knew some of the common speculations about this and that and whatever the Dragons might have intended: *What are the colors for? Do you have any idea what the shapes of the buildings represent?*

It was her city, after all. She'd been born here, and what seemed to Katherinessen alien and fabulous was to Lesa no more than the streets she'd grown up on, the buildings in whose shadows she had played.

"Why do the walls hum?" he asked eventually, when she'd been forced to shake her head and demur more times than she liked to admit.

"The ghosts," she said, pleased to finally have an answer.

He laughed, as she'd intended, and lifted his fingers to his face to sniff whatever trace of the blossoms lingered there. "You'd expect them to smell sweet," he said, gesturing to a heavy, wax-white bloom. "Ghosts?"

Lesa knew what he meant. The New Amazonian pseudo-orchid had a citruslike scent, not floral at all. "The haunted city, after all," she said. "The walls hum. Sometimes you see shadows moving from the corners of your eye. Sometimes House takes it upon itself to make arrangements you didn't anticipate. We still don't know everything Penthesilea is capable of."

"But you live here?"

"In a hundred years, it's never acted in any way contrary to our interests. When the foremothers arrived, there was nobody here but the khir. It took care of them, too."

"The pets."

"Domesticated by the Dragons. We think. Symbiotes or pets."

"And left behind when the Dragons—"

"Went wherever they went. Yes."

"Reading the subtext of your remarks, the city *adapts*?"

"House. We call it House. And yes. It understands simple requests, makes whatever we need that's not too complicated—appliances or electronics or fluffy towels—and cleans up. Most people don't notice the hum. You must have sensitive hands."

"The hum is its power source?"

"Or maybe its heartbeat. If it's alive. But it's probably just a vast, abandoned fog, still cleaning up after the family dog millennia later."

Katherinessen didn't answer for a minute. They were leaving the government center and the streets were starting to fill up. Not just the pedestrian galleries, but the roadways themselves were full of women and men, heads crowned with garlands and necks hung with beads, swathed in gaudy, rustling paper costumery that Katherinessen seemed to be making an effort neither to reach out for nor flinch away from.

"That's sad," he said. "When you think about it. You don't know what happened to the Dragons?"

"We don't," she said, both alert to his prying for information and fighting the urge to trust him. Everything she could read on him said he was honest—

as honest as a double agent could be—and the chip's information confirmed everything she thought she knew. She had to raise her voice to carry over the street noise, the melodious thunder of a steel drum. "But I believe they died. Somehow."

His eyes were shadowed under the hat when he turned them on her, but they still caught fragments of light and glowed like sunlit honey. "You have a reason to think so?"

"Miss Katherinessen," she said, leading him around the crowd gathered about the musicians, out of the shade gallery and into the hotter, less-crowded street, while Shafaqat followed five steps behind. "I guess you've never had a pet?"

It could have been a facetious question, but he saw by her eyes that she was serious. "No," he said. "Tamed animals aren't permitted in the Coalition. It's unnatural."

"A lot of animals have symbiotes," she said, threading through the pressing crowd.

Michelangelo would have a fit. All these people, and not just close enough to touch, but packed together so that one could not avoid touching. The streets were a *blur* of people, brightly clothed, drenched in scent or sweat or both, hatted and parasoled against the consuming light. The clamor of music was everywhere, instruments he recognized from historical fiche and instruments he didn't recognize at all, and ancient standbys like saxophone, trombone, and keyboard synthesizer, as if the entire city had spontaneously transformed into something that was half marching band and half orchestra.

Pedestrians threw money to some musicians. Others had no cup out, and accepted beads or garlands of flowers or offerings of food. He couldn't follow one song for more than a bar or two—they laddered up each other and interwove, clashing. The sheer press of people was as dizzying as the heat.

Vincent surreptitiously dialed his wardrobe down and hurried to keep up with the warden. "You don't think it's immoral to enslave animals?"

"I don't think it's slavery." She paused by what he would have called a square, a pedestrian plaza, except it was anything but square. Or geometrically regular, for that matter.

He should have known better than to continue the same old argument, but if he could resist an opening, he wouldn't have the job he did. "And what about treating your husband as chattel? Is that not slavery?"

"I'm not married," she snapped, and then flushed and looked down. Shafaqat coughed into her hand.

Vincent concealed his smile, and filed that one under *touchy subjects*. "And?"

"No," Pretoria said. "It's not slavery either. You hungry?"

She looked him straight in the eye when she changed the subject, which was how Vincent knew she was lying. And her smile when he rocked back said she saw him noticing. *That would be entirely too convenient.*

"I could eat," he said, though the bustling mall reeked of acid sweetness and perfumes and scorched flesh.

"This is the place to get lunch. I think we can find you something that was never self-aware, although you may be forced to eat it seasoned with a flying insect or two." She extended her arm, which he took.

"I can live with the death of a few bugs on my conscience."

"Hypocrite," she said. But she laughed. "Doesn't it get tiring being so damned morally superior all the time?"

Kusanagi-Jones managed to forget Vincent's absence quickly. Miss Ouagadougou was pleasant, efficient, and capable, and there was a lot of work to accomplish. The three largest pieces would form the backbone and focal point of the display. Two of the three were twentieth-century North American—one just a fragment, and both remnants of a much larger public artwork.

Kusanagi-Jones didn't think those anything special. Perhaps they'd be more meaningful in context, but it seemed to him that their status as cultural treasures was based on their provenance rather than on their art. They were historical works by women; it might be enough for the New Amazonians, but Kusanagi-Jones hoped his own aesthetic standards were somewhat higher.

The third piece, though, he couldn't denigrate. Its return was a major sacrifice, big enough to make him uneasy. The level of commitment betrayed by the Cabinet permitting such a treasure to slip beyond its grasp indicated desperation. Desperation, or no actual intent to let the sculpture go for long.

Officially, Catharine Kimberly was considered a minor artist, but Kusanagi-Jones had seen some of her other work, and he didn't think *Phoenix Abased* was the aberration that most scholars maintained. It was a marble sculpture—real marble, quarried stone, one of the last. Larger than life-size, it depicted a nude woman overcome with grief, her hips twisted by a drawn-up knee, her upper body thrown forward as if she had been knocked down or she was prostrating herself, sprawled into the abject line of her extended

arms, which she seemed—by the sprung muscles of
her neck, buttocks, and torso—to be fighting the mir-
ing stone.

They weren't precisely arms, though. Where reaching fingers should have splayed, consuming stone gave
the suggestion of wings. Broken feathers scattered the
base of the sculpture, tumbled down her shoulders,
tangled in the mossy snarl of hair framing her pain-
saturated face. Her head was turned, straining upward,
her mouth open in a hurtful *O* and her eyes—roughly
suggested, thumbprint shadows—tight shut. As if her
wings were failing her, crumbling, shed, leaving her
mired in unhewn stone.

And now that her wrappings were off, and he stood
before her in person, he could see what the fiche
couldn't show. She did not merely grovel, but struggled, dragging against the inexorable stone and wailing aloud as it consumed her.

Her body was fragile, bony, imperfect. She was too
frail to save herself. She was devoured.

Perhaps the artist was only a woman. Perhaps she'd
never created another work to compare to this raw
black-and-ocher-streaked masterpiece. But then, she
might have, might she not? If she had lived.

And this was enough. It had *impact*, a massive
weight of reality that pressed his chest like a stone. His
eyes stung and he shivered.

Whatever the evidence of her name—and Kusanagi-
Jones would be the first to admit that pre-Diaspora naming conventions were a nightmare from which he was
still trying to awaken—Catharine Kimberly had been a
dark-skinned South African woman who lived at the
time of first Assessment and the rise of the Governors.

Operating under their own ruthless program, the
Governors had first subverted the primitive utility

fogs and modulars of their era, turning industrial and agricultural machines to the purpose of genocide. Domestic animals and plants had been the first victims, destroyed as the most efficient solution to a hopeless complex of ethical failings. Better to die than reproduce as chattel.

Then the Northerners had been Assessed, for their lifestyle and history of colonial exploitation. Following that, persons of European and Chinese descent, regardless of talent or gender.

Billions of corpses produced an ecological dilemma resolved through the banking and controlled release of organic compounds. Salvage teams were allowed to enter North American, Asian, and European cities, removing anything of cultural value that they could carry away, and then the cities were Terraformed under layers of soil produced by the breakdown of human and agricultural detritus.

After that, the tricky work began.

During the Vigil—the seven-year gap between first Assessment and the final extensive round—those survivors who could find a way were permitted to take flight. At the end of the Vigil, those remaining on Earth had been culled, using parameters set by the radicals who had created the Governors and died to teach them to kill.

The exempt were an eclectic group. Among them were poets, sculptors, diplomats, laborers, plumbers, scientists, engineers, surgeons. Those who created with their minds or with their hands. A chosen population of under fifty million. Less than one in two hundred left alive.

Catharine Kimberly had been spared that first Assessment. And so she had completed *Phoenix Abased*. And then she had taken her own life.

Which was a sort of art in itself.

Kusanagi-Jones reached out, left-handed, and ran his fingers down the cool, mutilated stone. It was smooth, flinty to the touch. He could pretend that he felt some energy in it, a kind of strength. Mysticism and superstition, of course, but Kimberly's grief gilded the surface of her swan song like a current tickling his fingertips. He sniffed and stepped back, driving his nails into his palm. And looked up to find Miss Ouagadougou smiling at him.

"It's a powerful piece," she said, kindly patronizing. Just an emotional male, after all.

He smiled, and played to it. "Never actually seen it before. It's revered—"

"But not displayed?"

"Not in Cairo," he said. "We don't travel to other cities much. Wasteful. It's different to touch something." He shrugged. "Not that I would rub my hands over it normally, but—"

"Curator's privilege," she said. She bent from the waist, her hands on her knees, and stared into the wailing woman's empty eyes. "Tell me about your name."

"My name?"

She turned, caught him with a smile. Like all the New Amazonians, she seemed old for her age, but also fit, and his threat-ready eye told him that she was stronger than she looked. "Michelangelo Osiris Leary Kusanagi-Jones. Quite the mouthful. Are those lineage names?"

"Michelangelo—"

"For the artist, of course. Michelangelo di Lodovico Buonarroti Simoni."

"Show-off," he said, and her smile became a grin. She straightened up, hands on her hips, and rolled her shoulders back. Volatile male, he thought, and Lied to her a little. It wasn't hard. If he didn't think about it, if he wasn't consciously manipulating someone, it happened automatically. He wasn't sure he'd know an honest reaction if he had one. And if Miss Ouagadougou wanted to flirt, he could flirt with the best.

Second-best. There was always Vincent.

"Yes," he said. "For the artist."

"And Miss Katherinessen is named for Vincent van Gogh?"

He backed away from *Phoenix Abased* and framed it with his hands. "Named for the twentieth-century poet. Edna St. Vincent Millay. Ur has its own conventions. And his mother is a fan."

"And what about the rest of it?"

"Katherinessen?"

"No, I understand a matronymic. Osiris."

"Egyptian god of the dead. After the Vigil and the second Assessment, most of the survivors...you understand that it was rare for more than one member of a family to survive."

"I understand," she said. "I think the Glenna Goodacre piece should be in the middle. The Maya Lin fragment to block sight lines as one enters"—it was an enormous mirror-bright rectangle of black granite, etched with a list of men's names—"and then as you come around, Goodacre and Kimberly beyond."

"Saving the best for last."

She paced him as he continued to back away, trying the lay of the hall from various perspectives. "Precisely. So your ancestors...constructed new families? Renamed themselves?"

"After heroes and gods and historical figures."

"And artists."

"Sympathetic magic," Michelangelo said. "Art was survival."

"For us it was history." Miss Ouagadougou slid her fingers at full extension down glossy black granite. "Proof, I guess—"

"Of what came before."

"Yes." The tendons along the side of her neck flexed as she turned to stare at him. "Do you wonder what it was like?"

"Before the Governors? Sometimes."

"It must be better now," she said. "From what I've read. But still, the price."

"Too much." *Michelangelo Osiris Leary Kusanagi-Jones.* The futility of his own name stunned him. Five meaningless words. Five cultures, five entire *races* of people. And all that was left of them, the living re-memberer of all those millions of dead, was the sylla-bles of a Liar's name.

He swallowed. It hurt.

Her fingers brushed the wall again and fell away from the black granite. "It's lunchtime," she said. "I understand you have some dietary restrictions to consider. Shall we see what we can find to eat while the staff re-arranges the display? We'll come back to it after."

"I'd like that." He looked away from the wall, which was a mistake, because it put him face to face with Kimberly's murdered angel. "I'd like that very much."

9

VINCENT'S WARDROBE COULDN'T KEEP UP WITH THE
sweat. It slicked his neck, rolled in beads down his face,
and soaked the underside of his hair and a band where
the borrowed hat rested on his head. His hands
were still greasy from a lunch of some fried starchy
fruit and tubers, served in a paper wrapper, and his
wardrobe was too overwrought to deal with it.

He mopped his face on his sleeve, further stressing
foglets already strained by the jostling crowd and the
press of his escort on either side, and tried to regulate
his breathing. The nausea was due to the heat, he
thought, and not the food; his watch didn't report any
problems beyond mild dehydration and a slightly elevated body temperature, which he was keeping an eye
on. It wasn't dangerous yet, just uncomfortable, but
Miss Pretoria was tireless. She tugged Vincent's sleeve
to direct his attention to a Dragon costume operated by
two men, the one managing the front limbs walking

on stilts and operating paired extensions from his wrists that simulated the beast's enormous wings. "How could something that big fly?" he asked, checking his step to let the puppet shamble past.

"They must have been somewhat insubstantial for their size," Miss Pretoria said. "The khir, which are the Dragons' closest living relatives, have a honeycombed endoskeleton that leaves them much lighter than an equivalent terrestrial mammal. So the Dragons would have been about the same weight and wingspan as the largest pterosaurs. And we think they soared more than flew, and may have been highly adapted climbers." She turned to watch the puppet proceed down the street, bowing and dancing, bells shimmering along the span of the wings.

Her eyes widened as she turned to him. "Miss Katherinessen, you should have said something."

"I'm sorry?"

"I think we'd better get you out of the heat." She turned to Shafaqat, gesturing her forward. "Would you call for a car, Miss Delhi? And get Miss Katherinessen something to drink? We're going to find some shade."

"I'm fine," Vincent said, as Pretoria latched onto his wrist and tugged him toward a side street where the buildings would block most of the glaring light. "Nothing a cold shower and a glass of ice water wouldn't cure."

Pretoria clucked her tongue and bulldozed over him. "You're not adapted to this climate, and I'm *not* explaining to my mother why it is that a Coalition diplomat suffered heat exhaustion under my care, no matter how manly you need to prove you are."

He checked over his shoulder. Shafaqat moved through the press of bodies efficiently, her height, bearing, and uniform gaining a certain deference even from costumed, staggering merrymakers. Vincent had never seen a crowd like this on a Coalition planet: jostling, singing, shouting, raucously shoulder to shoulder and yet decorously polite. He wondered if it was a side effect of living packed into their alien cities, encircled by the waiting jungle, or of their rigid social strictures and their armed obeisance to the *code duello*.

Pretoria's hand cooled his skin as she pulled him into the shady side street, which wasn't any less crowded than the square. She pulled his wrist out and up as he made the choice to let her touch him without resistance. It was foreign, invasive. His skin crawled and stung when she pulled back, steadying his hand with her other one, and bent over it.

"You're burned," she said. "Not too badly, I think, but it's going to hurt by tonight."

"That's impossible. My wardrobe should filter UV—"

But his wardrobe was overstressed, and of course he'd had to dial it down to keep it from zapping pedestrians—or Miss Pretoria, with her frontier touchiness. She squeezed his wrist, and the cool pressure of her palm turned to shocking heat. He yelped and yanked his hand away.

"Sunburn," she said. "Good thing you wore long sleeves." And then she reached out and caught his shoulders, pushing him against the wall, and he would have shrugged her away but the blood roared in his ears and the orange status lights flickered in his watch. The street swam around him, aswarm with people who might have been staring at him curiously if he could have focused on their faces. "You know," he said, uncertainly, "I don't feel too well at all."

Her hand closed on his wrist again, searing, as she tugged him into motion. Shafaqat reappeared on his other side. "Miss Pretoria?" Something icy and dripping touched his hand.

"Drink that, Vincent. Miss Delhi, did you call the car?"

"I'm *fine*," Vincent insisted, even though he couldn't quite lift his feet. He broke Pretoria's grip, more roughly than he had intended, and ducked his head, blinking, as he tried to get a good look at the display on his watch. Nausea made him gulp. "I don't think I should drink anything."

They ignored him. "It's on the way," Shafaqat said. "Where are we going?"

"Redirect it to Pretoria house. We can get him there and into a cold shower by the time it could reach us and find a place to land in this crowd, and it'll be a huge flap if we have to send him to the clinic." Miss Pretoria cursed. "I'm an idiot. I thought he would tell me if it got to be too much."

"Men," Shafaqat said. Vincent could picture the twist of her mouth from her tone.

"Angelo would tell you it's Vincent in particular, not men in general," Vincent said.

"Vincent, can you walk a little way?" Pretoria said, concerned, carefully pronouncing his given name.

"I can walk." He wove slightly, but steadied. "How far?"

Shafaqat answered, pressing the cold, sweating thing into his hand again. He closed fingers that didn't want to tighten around the coolness of the globe. "Less than a kilometer. And you have to drink this."

"I feel sick."

"You feel sick because you're dehydrated. You need fluids. If you can't keep it down you'll need an IV. Slowly, just a sip at a time. But *drink*."

Her tone reminded him of Angelo's. Not exactly

hectoring, but assured. Somebody steadied his hand as he raised the globe to his mouth, found the straw, and sipped.

Once the fluid—something tart, with bubbles—flooded his mouth, it was an act of will not to gulp it all. Temperature shock chilled his teeth in the bone, replacing the dizzy headache with a stabbing one. He found his footing. "Better."

Now that he'd become aware, the prickle of warmth across his shoulders and back and thighs took on new significance. He'd worn long sleeves, but if his wardrobe's UV blocking had failed, those sleeves wouldn't have protected him.

He was going to have one hell of a radiation burn.

"Drink more," Pretoria reminded, keeping him on the shady side of the street. He obeyed, the sugary fluid a relief. He finished the globe quickly despite his attempts to regulate his intake. They'd stopped walking, pausing in a much smaller side street—more of a service access route, too narrow for a hovercar and tight even for ground transport—without the press of foot traffic. As Shafaqat pressed another globe into his hands—this one a little warmer, but also dripping condensation—Miss Pretoria turned aside and placed one hand on the wall of a nearby structure.

"House," she said, "I need cold water, please, in a basin."

He still felt unwell—disconnected—but it was his body, now, and not his mind. He sipped the second beverage, and asked, "Is this Pretoria house?"

"It's the back wall of a marketplace," Miss Pretoria said, and a cubbyhole appeared about a meter up the violet-gray wall.

Shafaqat urged Vincent toward it. He went, finishing the second drink before relinquishing the spent globe into the security agent's hands. She crushed it and made it vanish.

"Roll up your sleeves," Miss Pretoria said. He didn't bother; his wardrobe didn't mind wet. He plunged arms webbed with distended veins in water as frigid as if it flowed from a cave. The cold first saturated his arms and ached in the depths of the bones, and then the slug of chilled blood struck his heart and spilled up his throat. He gasped and remembered to knock his hat off before sticking his face into the water.

When he straightened, water dripping down his forehead and under the collar of his shirt, he was suddenly clearheaded. He turned and slumped against the wall, tilting his head back to encourage the water to run from his braids down his neck and not into his eyes. He coughed water, blew it from his nostrils, and panted until the last of the dizziness faded. His wardrobe, out of the sun now and given half a chance to work, cooled him efficiently, evaporating sweat and water from his skin, drawing off excess heat.

"Thank you," he said, when he dared open his eyes and try to focus. It worked surprisingly well. First he saw Shafaqat, and then, over her shoulder, he saw something less encouraging. Five women, sidearms drawn, faces covered by Carnival masks.

"Miss Pretoria?" He surreptitiously dialed his wardrobe up.

She turned, following his gaze, and stiffened with her hand hovering above her weapon.

"There's only five of them," Shafaqat said.

"Good odds," Pretoria said. She sounded as if she meant it. Vincent pushed away from the wall and stepped up to cover her flank. If it were *his* target, he'd have another team covering the side street. "Three more."

"Thank you." Pretoria's right hand arched over her weapon, a gunslinger pose, fingers working. She'd unfastened the snap; Vincent hadn't seen her do it.

Pretoria and Shafaqat shared a glance. Shafaqat nodded. "Run," Pretoria said. Flat command, assumed obedience.

"I don't know where I'm running to."

"Pretoria household." Miss Pretoria stepped diagonally, crowding him back.

"Lesa, there's *eight*—"

Her grin over her shoulder was no more than a quick flash, but it silenced him. He looked again, saw the way the masked women paused to assess every shift of balance—Pretoria's even more so than Shafaqat's.

He recognized that fearful respect. Lesa Pretoria had a *reputation*. And for whatever reason, they didn't want to kill her. He acquiesced, though she probably couldn't see him nod. "How do I get there?"

"Follow the ghosts," Pretoria snapped, as the first group of adversaries picked closer, fanning out. If Vincent were in Pretoria's shoes, he'd wait until they were close enough to get in each other's way. If he were gambling that they didn't want to kill him.

"Ask House," Shafaqat clarified. Slightly more useful. She stood with one shoulder to the street, narrowing her profile, her hand also hovering over her holster. "We'll delay them. Go left"—through the line of three, rather than the line of five—"Go on. *Go*."

Vincent went.

Angelo might *look* like the dangerous one, but that didn't mean that Vincent had no idea how to take care of himself in a fight. He charged, zigzagging, and trusted his wardrobe to soak up any fire he didn't dodge.

When the fire came, it wasn't bullets. A tangler hissed at his head, but his timing was good, and his wardrobe caught it at the right angle and shunted it aside. Gelatinous tendrils curled toward him, and sparks scattered where they encountered the wardrobe and were shocked off. Two of the masked women grabbed for him as he sidestepped the tangler, and his wardrobe zapped their hands. He shoved past them as shot from a chemical weapon pattered behind him, spreading the sharp reek of gunpowder, while he twisted against grabbing hands.

Firearms echoed again, and one of the women who was clinging to his arm despite the wardrobe's defenses jerked and fell away. Vincent shouldered the other one aside and ran.

Leaving a couple of women to do his fighting for him. But they were security, and they had ordered him to clear the area.

If it had been Michelangelo, he would have done the same.

Once he reached the crowded street, he could no longer hear the footsteps behind him. He wove between clusters of merrymakers, half expecting some good Samaritan to trip him as a purse-snatcher or runaway, but it was Carnival, and other than a few turned heads, bright laughter, and a startled exclamation—no one paid him heed.

He couldn't run for long. His head started spinning again, and he'd left his hat lying in the damp dust. He let himself drop into a jog, then a walk, sidestepping drunks and Dragon dancers and wandering musicians. The toe of his shoe dragged on the pavement and he stumbled, his wet hair steaming. But Miss Pretoria had also told him that her household was close, and Shafaqat had told him how to get there.

He ducked down a side street strung with more cut flowers, past three men and five women carrying shopping bags, and stepped into the shade. "House," he said, feeling ridiculous, although he'd waited until there was a gap in the flow of people, "show me how to get to Pretoria household."

At first there was no reaction. But then a shimmer formed along the wall, neither an arrow nor a trace, but something like a ripple on water. It was a pale sheen of blue luminescence, dim in shadow and brighter in sunlight, and it led him further along the street he had ducked down.

It didn't take him long to realize that he wasn't being led by the most direct route. Instead, House brought him down side streets, less populated ways, and through shadowing courtyards. It concerned him, but he didn't know which other way to go, and so he followed. The shimmer ran along walls, or sometimes immediately underfoot, always a half-step ahead until it brought him back into sunlight on a quiet byway with only a little pedestrian traffic, not broad enough for a car. There, at the bottom of a set of broad shallow steps leading to a screened veranda, it abandoned him, vanishing into the pavement like oil dispersing on water.

He looked up the steps at the front door, which glided open. Behind it stood a young woman with Lesa's broad cheeks but a darker complexion and curlier hair. "House said to expect you," she said. "I'm Katya Pretoria. Come in off the street."

That's a bit more than a goddamned giant utility fog, Vincent thought, but he didn't hesitate to climb the steps.

"Your mother might need help," he said, pausing to glance over his shoulder, back in the direction from which he'd come.

"Household security's on the way."

10

"MISS KUSANAGI-JONES," MISS OUAGADOUGOU SAID AFTER he had entirely managed to lose track of the time after, "do you need to check in with your ship?"

He glanced up from sketching schematics on his watch, refocusing on Miss Ouagadougou through shimmering green lines that overlaid the physical gallery. His watch identified her as an individual rather than a part of the landscape, and backgrounded the display plan behind her. It looked odd, sandwiched between her and a Gerónima Cruz Montoya casein-on-paper painting. "Sorry?"

"It's past teatime. And the station should be overhead in a few ticks. We'll eat upstairs, and I thought you might—"

"Very kind," Kusanagi-Jones said, recollecting himself. "Does this suit?"

"The schematics?" Her hair bobbed on the nape of her neck. "If you finalize them, I'll upload them to the ministry net, and they'll keep a crew in tonight to finish the setup. It actually works out better this way."

"It?" He was already sealing the plans, satisfied with the exhibit. Miss Ouagadougou had a good eye. "Lead on," he said, before she finished fussing with her headset.

They ascended the lift in companionable silence, Miss Ouagadougou still fiddling and Kusanagi-Jones pulling up a sat-phone license on his wardrobe menu. He'd need a relay station; his watch couldn't power orbital communication.

If he was lucky, his communication would reach *Kaiwo Maru* before she dispatched a packet-bot back to Earth to swap mail. It would still take six months to send a message and get an answer, assuming *The Pride of Ithaca* or one of the other inbound ships was close enough to relay the bot's signal. But at least this way the message would be in the queue.

If anything happened.

He coded two reports. The first used a standard diplomatic cipher, and detailed a strictly factual, strictly accurate report of his and Vincent's doings since landfall. The second, concealed in the first and still largely innocuous to Coalition eyes, concerned itself with a perceived obstructionist element in New Amazonian government.

There was a third message, contained not in a discrete data stream, but in the interplay of the others. In the cracks between. Kusanagi-Jones concealed an ironic smile.

This one, of necessity brief, must be sent when Vincent wasn't present to record it. It was sealed eyes-only, quantum coded. When Kusanagi-Jones broke the seal on his own end of the code, a quantum entanglement triggered a wave-state collapse on the other end

of the system, alerting his principal that a message was
en route. The only man in the universe who could read
the message was the one who held the other half of
the key.

That man was Siddhartha Deucalion Hunyadi
Lawson-Hrothgar. He was a senior member of the Earth
Coalition Cabinet. And its contents, if they *could* have
fallen into the wrong hands, would have meant surplus-
ing and execution not only for Kusanagi-Jones, but for
Lawson-Hrothgar as well.

Kusanagi-Jones understood Vincent's position. The
great-grandson of a Colonial Founder, the son of
Captain Lexasdaughter—the most powerful head of
state remaining under Coalition control—Vincent
would work *within* the system, attempt to ease the
Coalition's stranglehold through diplomatic means.

Kusanagi-Jones, with the assistance of a revolutionary patron, had chosen another path.

Which was the thing Vincent could never be permitted to learn about New Earth, and the destruction
of the starship named *Skidbladnir*, and why they had
been separated: that it had happened so because
Michelangelo had planned it that way.

"When you report," Miss Ouagadougou said, as they
stepped out into brilliant sunlight, "I'll have something to add."

Kusanagi-Jones wouldn't show startlement. Instead,
he stepped aside to give her a line of travel and fell into
step behind. "Something about the plan I'd like to discuss. May I uplink the new version to your datacart?"

"Of course." She pulled it out of her hip pack and
flipped up the cover. "Password?"

He gave her one, and established a single-photon
connection. The security detail hung back, just out of
earshot if they spoke in level tones. New Amazonian

courtesy. But there were some things you didn't say out loud.

Green letters flashed across his vision and vanished. *The director of security is a radical*, Miss Ouagadougou said. *Get her to enlist.*

Kyoto? he asked. *That old dragon?*

She's inclined pro-Coalition. A free-maler. Claude's a loss. Saide Austin holds her purse strings, and Saide Austin... He glanced at her as the text scroll hesitated. She shrugged, a slow rise of her shoulders, a quick tilt of her head. He recognized the name from the gallery. Saide Austin.

More than an artist, apparently. *You're a Coalition agent.*

Since before the war.

He wondered what they'd given her to buy her loyalty—money, access to Coalition art treasures—or if hers was an ideological treachery.

She put her hand on his arm. *I've imbedded an information packet in your copy of the plan.* She transmitted a code key, which he saved. "I'm starving," she said. "It's been hours since lunch."

"Miss Ouagadougou?"

Kusanagi-Jones looked up. One of the agents had stepped forward. He might as well have been a shadow on the wall.

"Cathay." Miss Ouagadougou smiled. "Problem?"

"Miss Pretoria requests you and Miss Kusanagi-Jones join her at Pretoria house." Cathay—Kusanagi-Jones was uncertain if it was her first name or last—smiled. "A car is waiting."

Miss Ouagadougou wet her lips, and Kusanagi-Jones's pulse accelerated. Problem.

"My uplink," he said. He'd been hoping, frankly, to get another look around the galleries and see if he could find whatever passed for a power conduit. Wherever they had the power plant hidden, there had to be *wiring*. Electricity didn't transmit itself, and he'd seen no signs of microwave receivers. Room temperature superconductors, he'd guess.

"Do it in the car," she said, fingers closing on his wrist.

Problem. Yes, indeed.

Kii touches the cold illation machines that populate Kaiwo Maru's core. They are intelligent, in their own way, but Kii is not of interest to them. They process Kii, and ignore.

Kii contemplates, and the Consent observes. There is no determination yet, as Kii analyzes the Governors' decision trees. The Governors are aware. They are adaptive. They are goal driven, and they are improvisational.

But their entire purpose, Kii soon understands, is the maintenance of the encroaching bipeds. They are a predator. A constructed predator, a coolly designed one. They exist to assure the bipeds do not overburden their habitat. They are ruthless and implacable, and their disregard for Kii is not founded on a lack of intelligence or awareness. Rather, Kii is external to their parameters. Their only interest is the bipeds. They are created creatures, as Kii is a created creature, a program contained in a virtual shell. But unlike Kii, they are not alive.

They are not esthelich. *They are not alive. In this fragment, Consent is reached with ease.*

Vincent shouldn't have been so relieved that it was Robert who took charge of him once they were inside. It was unprofessional. But for all his size, scars, and shaven head, the big man was a calming presence, revealing no threat-registers. It was the easy kind of personality that deservedly confident, competent, unthreatened people projected, and Vincent really was not feeling well at all. He let Robert bring him into the cool depths of the house, under more of those swags of dead flowers, and show him into the fresher. Or... make one for him. Now that he was watching for it, he could see how it worked, the way the building anticipated and fulfilled requests. A limited teachable AI, at least, if not sentient.

The city was not so much haunted as programmed.

"Take off your shirt," Robert said as the door irised shut behind them. He reached to grab cloth, and Vincent, who hadn't dialed his wardrobe down, stepped back fast and tilted his chin up to look Robert in the eye. White teeth shone in contrast to Robert's plum-colored lips, and Vincent sighed.

"No," Robert said. "That's not a proposition."

Vincent knew. There was no erotic interest at all, either predatory or friendly. "It doesn't work like that."

Robert backed off, and Vincent touched his wrist and made his wardrobe vanish, dialing down the protection, too. He turned, showing Robert his back, and bit his lip not to shiver away when Robert reached out, slowly, making sure Vincent could see him in the mirror as he paused his hand a centimeter from Vincent's shoulder blade. The heat of his palm made Vincent flinch; when Robert drew his hand back, he scrubbed it against his vest as if to rub the radiant warmth away. "That's going to blister. Have you ever had a sunburn?"

"No," Vincent said.

"You'll feel nauseated, achy, tired. You'll experience chills. House, some burn cream, please? Miss

Katherinessen, into the shower. Cold water will help. Essentially, you're experiencing a mild radiation burn."

"I've had those," Vincent said. His watch would handle the worst of it: he could manage his chemistry to alleviate the flulike symptoms, and his licenses included both powerful painkillers and topical analgesics.

Another aperture expanded before him, leading him into a smaller chamber. He ducked through, stepping over the ridge while it was still opening, and sniffed hard. The pull of raw skin across his back and thighs was an unsubtle reminder toward caution. He paused a moment, giving his wardrobe enough time to collect its foglets so they wouldn't wash away. There were no controls in the stall and no obvious showerhead.

"House," he said, experimentally, as the aperture closed between him and Robert. "Cool water, please."

It pattered on his head like rain.

Once Miss Ouagadougou had ascertained that Vincent was well, Kusanagi-Jones breathed a sigh of relief and set about working out how to adapt his watch to the car's hub. He'd have to piggyback on its signal, which meant all the more opportunities for the transmission to be intercepted, but it wasn't as if there were a secure channel on the entire damned planet. You closed your eyes and put your trust in cryptography.

He sent the message with Miss Ouagadougou's addendum, unlinked, and sat back against the upholstery. Cloth rather than leather. He permitted himself to sag into it. "What happened?"

In spare details, Cathay told him. "Miss Pretoria?" he interrupted, when she paused to draw a breath.

"Fine," she said. "Uninjured. She has arranged to meet us at Pretoria house. You and Miss Katherinessen are asked to limit your movements until we sort out which faction is responsible for the kidnapping attempt."

"Of course." And of course, the attempt itself could be nothing more than a smokescreen to justify tightening the leash. But that was Vincent's department, not his.

He was still going to shave thin strips off Vincent.

The car ride was brief. It still amused Kusanagi-Jones that the automobile had to be *put* somewhere when they arrived rather than vanishing in a blur of fogs. It was, in point of fact, too large to fit down the narrow alley that led to Pretoria house, and he and Miss Ouagadougou and Cathay disembarked at the bottom of the street so the driver could take it away. Cathay, he noticed, stuck as close to his side as he would have stuck to Vincent's, shielding him with her body.

He'd expected Lesa Pretoria. The young woman who waited at the top of the stairs looked tolerably like her, but younger and softer around the eyes. "Katya Pretoria," she said, beckoning. She didn't step out into the sun, and Kusanagi-Jones didn't blame her. The brief walk from car to porch was enough to make his skin sting. "It's a pleasure to meet you, Miss Kusanagi-Jones. Your partner's being seen to——"

"Vincent wasn't injured?"

"He just got a little too much sun," she assured, extending her hand. Kusanagi-Jones brushed his wrist to dial his wardrobe down and accepted the handshake as he crested the stairs. She pulled him up the last step easily. He wasn't tall, but he weighed more than he seemed to and probably had twenty kilograms on her.

She braced to take the weight, but didn't grunt. "You can speak with him as soon as he's out of the shower."

"Sorry to be so early to dinner."

Her smile broadened, unmistakably flirtatious. Miss Ouagadougou cleared her throat from the bottom of the steps, but Katya ignored it. "It's good to have fluid plans, don't you think? Miss Ouagadougou, thank you for a safe delivery. We'll have him home in time for the ceremony tomorrow, I promise."

And before the historian could quite answer, Katya took Kusanagi-Jones's wrist and drew him into the house, security following. As soon as they were inside, though, Kusanagi-Jones stepped away from her to get a sense of the space. The house was cool inside, shadowed by the broad verandas and rich with breezes. "How much seeing to did Vincent require?"

"Miss Katherinessen has made himself quite at home," she said, and the grin turned into a wink. "One of the senior males is seeing to him. He's in good hands."

Kusanagi-Jones snorted. He let a little jealousy show. It couldn't hurt, and it was easy enough to feel jealous of Vincent. He had a way of getting what he wanted, after all. "The question is, is your male safe at Vincent's hands?"

"Robert's my sire," she said. "He's safe most places. He's a three-time Trial champion, all city, and before he retired he was third overall."

A gleam of pride reflected through her voice. He wasn't likely to forget the Trials quickly. And he remembered Robert from the docks, and Robert had had scars. And had been beautiful and dark.

Just to Vincent's taste.

But interesting, that pride. *My sire.* A young woman proud of her father, even here. He supposed just because you kept someone as chattel, it didn't mean you didn't care for him. Especially if you thought it was for his own good. "Well, I hope he's not driven to defend his honor at Vincent's expense," he joked, waiting for her response.

Which was a chuckle. "Don't you envy him that? That sense of . . . entitlement?"

She'd picked that up on a moment's acquaintance, had she? Kusanagi-Jones snorted hard enough that it stung. "Envy Vincent? Not the entitlement. Sometimes maybe the privilege that produced it. Trying to drive a wedge between us, Miss Pretoria?"

"Of course not," she said, maintaining a perfect deadpan. "That's what they hired my mother for."

11

AFTER THE SHOWER, VINCENT LET ROBERT SMEAR HIS BACK
with a gelatinous yellow substance that stung and
soothed, and smelled of cucumbers and mint. He could
have pulled up a license, but there was no reason to give
away more of the capabilities of his wardrobe than he
needed to. Robert worked steadily and quickly, and when
he was done and Vincent summoned a new outfit from
his wardrobe, he made sure he programmed it not to absorb the gel. It slid and stuck, but it did help. He turned
back and offered his hand to Robert for yet another of
the endless New Amazonian handshakes. "Thank you."

"You're welcome," Robert answered. His clasp was
firm.

Vincent was unsurprised to feel the edged corners of
a chip pressed into his palm as he dropped his hand,
and he cupped his fingers slightly to hold it. The outfit
he'd chosen had pockets suitable for the nonchalant
shoving of hands, so he did.

"Your partner's arrived," Robert said. "Shall we meet him?"

Vincent's wardrobe dried the water from his braids and tidied his hair. He took a breath and drew himself up, the carpetplant cool under the soles of his feet.

He'd erred, and taken chances. And he didn't have anything to show for it, in terms of his public mission or either of his private ones. Angelo was going to kill him. Slowly. Probably by ripping strips off his slow-roasted back.

He might as well get it over with. "Ready as I'll ever be. Have you heard from Miss Pretoria and Miss Delhi?"

Robert nodded. Vincent had known the answer before he asked. While he was in the shower, Robert's affect had changed, from controlled concern to concealed relief. There was something else under it, though— a sidelong glance, an even breath. Vincent honestly couldn't say *how* he knew—it was a complex of cues too subtle to verbalize—but there it was. Robert was withholding information.

And he was concerned for Vincent, too. Not in quite the same way as he was concerned for Miss Pretoria. Of course, he wouldn't be, if Vincent understood the relationship. This would be the man Lesa intended to marry, when she established her own household and become an Elder in her own right. He had special status in Pretoria house, the way, historically, a . . . a house dog would have had more status than a hunting dog.

He wasn't livestock. He was a pet.

And he was also the one passing Vincent data chips. Which meant that he could either be operating as an agent on behalf of someone in the household who wished her identity concealed . . . or be doing it on his own.

It would be awfully easy for somebody who shared Lesa's bed to get a tracking device on her, and the assailants in the street had known where to find them. The chip in Vincent's pocket swung against his thigh as he followed Robert across the cool floors. The pieces might be falling together after all.

They passed through a heavy, old-fashioned door that swung on apparent brass hinges. Given House's ability to reinvent itself, Vincent assumed they were a cunning approximation. On the other side was a tiled, pleasant porch whose sides lay open on a balmy afternoon, a courtyard in which four or five children played with a pair of khir. The feathered quadrupeds were nimble and agile, coordinated in their movements as they raced after whooping and tumbling children.

Inside the balustrade, a group of adults sat at ease. Obviously dominating the group, Elena Pretoria wore cool cream and peach, her bare feet callused along the edges though the toenails were painted. Beside her, Lesa sat on a wicker stool, her feet hooked over the bottom rung, Katya sprawled on bolsters at her feet. Michelangelo had arranged himself cross-legged on a cushion on the other side of a low glass table suitable for resting mugs and feet upon. It was the lowest vantage in the room, but it had the advantage of putting his back to an angle of wall so the only one behind him was his security officer, a wiry berry-eyed young woman with a golden-brown fox's face.

Shafaqat leaned beside the door. She gave Vincent the right half of a smile as he came in, and didn't acknowledge Robert at all. Robert patted Vincent's elbow and kept walking down the stairs, out among the children and pets. "Please, Miss Katherinessen," Elena said without rising. "Join us."

Vincent took the gesture at face value and crossed the

tile to a cushion beside Michelangelo's, wincing as he lowered himself. Michelangelo raised an eyebrow. "A Colonial would forget that UV radiation is dangerous."

"It doesn't hurt until later," Vincent answered.

"That's why it's dangerous." Michelangelo might have said something more—he had that tension around his mouth—but apparently Vincent's discomfort was showing in his face. Instead, Angelo reached out lightly, without seeming to shift, and brushed the back of his knuckles against Vincent's knee. A slight curve lifted one corner of his mouth, and he spoke even more softly. "The big brute at least take good care of you?"

Vincent sighed. Forgiven. Or at least Angelo was willing to pretend he was. "Not his type," he mouthed, and was rewarded by a slightly broader smile. "How was your day?"

"Edifying." Michelangelo raised his voice, reincluding the rest. "The warden was telling us about your admirers."

"They must have been tailing us for some time," Vincent said. "Waiting a break in the crowds. And we gave them one." He shrugged, then regretted it. "I'm relieved to see Lesa and Shafaqat made it out all right."

There was an unspoken question in the words. Lesa fielded a glance from the security agent and took on the question. "They were carrying nonlethal weapons. And I don't think they expected Vincent to shrug off two tanglers quite so nonchalantly. If he hadn't, they would have concentrated harder on entangling Shafaqat and me, to slow us while they made their escape with Vincent."

Shafaqat's eyebrow asked a question. Vincent nodded, as a shadow entered the door and a cool drink appeared at his hand, already sweating beads of condensation onto

the rippled glass tabletop. The servant placed a pitcher of
amber fluid flecked with herby green on the table, removed an exhausted one, and withdrew. Vincent noticed
that the others already had glasses, picked his up, and
sipped.

"They weren't prepared to deal with my wardrobe's
defense systems," he said. "Next time, they'll be fore-
warned."

"First one's free," Michelangelo muttered.

Down in the courtyard, one of the children shrieked
laughter as Robert caught him under the arms and
hoisted him overhead, before settling the child on his
shoulder. Khir leapt and reared around him, chittering
and yipping.

"Walter, *down*," Robert said firmly, as the larger
khir put its paws on his chest and pushed. For its size,
the animal must be light. The big feet flexed, but
Robert didn't. The animal dropped to all fours and
leaned against the man, exhaling heavily enough that
Vincent heard it from where he sat.

"Is that safe?" Michelangelo asked quietly.

"Robert's good with children," Elena said.

Katya, who had not spoken, blinked at her. "Yes,"
she said. "You'd hardly know he was a stud male."

Vincent winced, and Lesa shot her daughter a look,
but for Elena the irony must have passed unnoticed.
"Exactly."

Michelangelo nudged Vincent lightly. Vincent wondered how long it would take them to process this particular cultural divide, in all its peculiarity. Michelangelo
had been asking about the animals. Not Robert, who bore
a striking resemblance to the boy on his shoulder, and
whom the child obviously adored, as he clung to his father, pulling Robert's ears.

And then Walter, spurned, trotted up on the steps

and sniffed Vincent curiously. Vincent forced himself
not to flinch from the brush of sensitive feathers, despite a close-up look at flaring nostrils and odd, pink
pits lining the scales along the animal's upper lip. Then
the creature walked around him, sniffed Michelangelo,
too, and flopped down on the cushions beside him
with the feathered back of its head pressed to Angelo's
thigh.

It sighed, braced its feet against the base of a nearby
chair, and shoved, moving him into a more comfortable position—for it—and appropriating part of the
cushion.

Michelangelo paused with both hands raised toward
his face. He lowered them slowly, and glanced down at
the khir. Walter turned slightly, stretching its neck out,
and wheezed a small snore as Katya and Lesa shared a
laugh.

"They like to sleep in confined spaces," Katya said.
"And back up against a pack mate, if they can."

"I'm a pack mate?" Michelangelo kept his hands up,
at chest level, as if afraid a sudden move would startle
the animal.

"You can touch it. It likes to be scratched at the base
of the skull," Lesa said. "And you're in its den, and the
rest of the pack is feeding you and treating you as welcome, so you must belong here. They don't differenti-
ate between khir and humans, if they're socialized.
They just know friends and strangers."

Gingerly, Angelo lowered his hand to the khir's
shoulder. It whuffled, but didn't wake. His fingertips
brushed scales and feathers, his face assuming a curious expression, slack and focused, and Vincent found
himself watching, breath held.

Vincent reached out and picked up his drink, folding his palm around cool, wet glass. It smelled minty

and astringent as he used the rim to hide his face. The beverage was cold, but helped the chills that crawled across his stinging shoulders.

Michelangelo looked up, his fingers moving in the sleeping animal's ruff, and gave Vincent a quizzical smile. The relaxed vulnerability around his eyes was more than Vincent could bear. He had to work for that, and nobody else got to see it, ever.

It was a hint of what Angelo would look like at peace.

"Right." Elder Pretoria leaned forward, sliding her own glass across the table with her fingertips. She lifted it and sat back. "Miss Katherinessen, have your adventures left you any appetite? Or should we see about getting you home?"

He glanced away from Angelo, who looked back down at the khir. "Oh," he said, "I think I could eat."

Dinner was served in an even more informal style than the supper and reception they'd endured on their first night on New Amazonia. Kusanagi-Jones found himself separated from his partner—not forcefully, but with the ease by which an accomplished hostess maneuvers her guests—and seated at a long low table in a spacious room. The carpetplant on either side and at the head and foot was protected by thick rugs, the floor underneath banked into comfortable seats. Another table ran crosswise at the foot of the first, and Kusanagi-Jones was surprised when he realized that it was populated by the household males, children, and servants. He'd expected that they would be required to eat separately, and perhaps after the adult women and "gentle" guests—but once the food was brought out, the cook and two male and two female servants settled themselves alongside the table and began passing plates and chattering along with everyone else.

The total assembly was about twenty-five. Five males other than the servants, counting Robert and an older man to whom he deferred, two boys, three girls, and the balance made up in teen and adult women, with the addition of Cathay, Shafaqat, Vincent, and Kusanagi-Jones himself. Michelangelo noticed that the female and what he presumed were gentle male servants sat between the stud males—recognizable by their scars and the street licenses worn on leather cuffs at their wrists like barbaric jewelry—and the children, and the males largely conversed among themselves.

He also noticed that the same dark-complected boy of about six or seven New Amazonian years—who had been riding Robert around the courtyard earlier— slithered out of his seat as soon as the cook's back was turned, scrambled into the big man's lap, and no one seemed to think much of it.

The table arrangements had left Kusanagi-Jones seated next to Katya Pretoria on one side, and another woman—Agnes Pretoria, who he gathered was something like the household chatelaine or seneschal—on the other. "Is that your brother?"

Katya followed the line of his gaze. He looked down and continued ladling food onto his plate. Someone had apparently asked the cook to take pity on them, because the food on offer included legume curry, rice, bread with a nut butter, and a variety of other animal-free choices. He'd have to find out to whom to send the thank-you note.

"Julian." Katya's quick glance at Lesa gave away more than she probably knew. "Yes. He's the last of Mother's obligation. I don't think she'll marry until he starts the Trials, though, and finds a position. Unless..."

Kusanagi-Jones caught her eye and then looked down, waiting her out while applying himself to the curry.

Her hesitation became a shrug. "Mother hopes he's gentle," she said. "He's very smart."

Kusanagi-Jones washed his food down with a mouthful of wine. The consideration of a good meal itself was enough to lower his defenses. "Like his father?"

"You noticed. Yes. Robert's special..." she paused, and picked up her fork. "Julian and I are full siblings. The third, Karyn——" The fork clicked on the plate. "She was older. Mother's first. She died in a duel."

"And do you duel?" he asked, because she didn't seem to wish her discomfort noted.

She twirled her fork. "No," she said, glancing up to locate her mother before she spoke. "It's a stupid tradition."

After dinner, the servants rose to clear the plates and bring more wine, coffee, and cakes before reseating themselves. Lesa surveyed the table and brushed Vincent's sleeve. "There's no butter, honey, or eggs in those."

He didn't flinch away from the contact—a small positive sign—and served himself from the indicated plate with tongs. "Thank you for this afternoon," he said.

She snorted. "Just doing my job."

"Any word on who might have been behind it? Or what the goal was?"

She shrugged and slid a pastry onto her own plate. "We'll know soon enough. I wounded one of them. As for what they wanted—a hostage? To open negotiations of their own? To demand a Coalition withdrawal in return for your life?" She lowered her voice and obscured her mouth behind her hand as she ate. "It all depends what faction we're talking about."

Which was a code phrase, one that should have identified her as his contact, based on the information in the chip he'd slipped Robert. But he just rolled his eyes and sipped his wine, far too relaxed for her to believe he had made the connection. "Then security will be tighter from now on."

"No more slipping through the streets incognito," Lesa agreed. She glanced at Elena; Elena frowned and tilted her head. *Back off.* Yes. Lesa thought she'd know if Vincent were dissembling. He might be just as good as she was, but he wasn't any better. Instead, Lesa leaned around Vincent and caught Robert's eye, beckoning with a buttery finger. "Would you like to meet my son, Vincent?"

He followed the line of her attention. "Very much," he said. "You have two children?"

"The obligation is three," she answered. "My eldest died, but I've met it, yes. I could start my own household, become an Elder in my own right."

"If you wanted?"

"There's a male whose contract I want to buy. Until it's available, there's no point."

"You wouldn't have to breed to get married if New Amazonia accepted the Coalition," he said, dryly.

She smiled. "And you wouldn't have three sisters and a brother if Ur had fallen into line a few years sooner."

The look Katherinessen gave her was ever so slightly impressed. It was public record, and Katherine Lexasdaughter's conceit in naming each of her five children—Valerie, Victoria, Vivian, Vincent, and Valentine—made the bit of data stand out in Lesa's recall. As Robert came around the table holding Julian's hand, she smiled at them and scooted back, opening a gap. Her son tugged loose of his sire's grip and came to her, plopping himself onto her thigh. It wouldn't last, of course. Any day now, Julian would decide he was too old for sitting on laps and listening to Mother, and not long after that, he'd enter the Trials. If he lived, he'd earn a contract in some other woman's house.

Unless he beat the odds, of course. And grew up gentle. "Julian," she said, when he had wiggled himself comfortable and Robert had settled down cross-legged, not far away. "I'd like you to meet Vincent Katherinessen. He's a diplomat like me."

"He's a male," Julian said, with childish solipsism. "He can't be a diplomat. That's for girls."

Whatever he thought of Vincent, he held out his hand anyway, and Vincent accepted it. "Pleased to meet you, Julian."

"Vincent's gentle," Lesa said. She met Katherinessen's golden-brown eyes, noticing the splinters of blue and yellow around the pupils. "He can be anything he wants."

Their hands interlaced, Julian's smaller and darker and more callused, and Julian winced. "You got burned."

"I did," Vincent said. "My sun protection failed."

"That was silly. You need a sunpatch." He pointed to the shoulder of his jerkin, craning his neck so he could see what he was pointing at—a small patch in colors that matched the one Robert wore on his wrist cuff. "It changes color when you get too much UV. So you know to go inside."

"I think I do need one of those. May I look?"

Julian nodded, but Vincent had been looking at Lesa when he asked. She slid her hand against her son's neck and lifted his hair aside, tacit permission. Julian wriggled; the touch tickled. But he sat mostly still as Vincent leaned forward to inspect the sunpatch, oblivious to Kusanagi-Jones watching from farther down the table with an expression that even Lesa found unreadable adorning his face.

"Where do you get one of those?" Vincent asked. He addressed Julian directly again, and Julian, charmed, smiled shyly and looked down.

"House," he said.

"Do you think House would make me one?"

Julian ducked further, still smiling, and nodded, his courage for strangers exhausted.

"If you asked," Lesa supplied.

Vincent leaned back, a half-second after Lesa would have, and let Julian tug away. He drew his knees up and buried his face against Lesa's shoulder, hands in front of his mouth. He was a warm compact bundle of muscle and bone, and she closed her eyes for a moment, leaning her chin on his hair. "He likes astronomy," she said. "And computers."

Vincent picked up his wineglass and leaned back, raising his eyes to the slow gorgeous burn of the Gorgon transmitted to the ceiling overhead. "Bad planet for getting to look at the stars from," he commented, without audible irony.

"I know," Lesa said. "Are *any* of them any good?"

12

THROUGHOUT DINNER, KUSANAGI-JONES WAS AWARE OF AN
increasing level of noise from the street. Vincent
gave him an arch look at one point—the invitation
had been for food and Carnival—but Kusanagi-
Jones answered it with a sidelong shake of his head.
*I'll chain you to a wall if you even suggest going out
there.*

Fortunately, in the constellation of VIPs that
Kusanagi-Jones had secured over the years, Vincent
ranked as one of the few who was capable of learning
from a mistake. He tipped his head, mouth twisting as
he acknowledged the undelivered ultimatum, and
turned to Elena Pretoria. "Elder," he said, when there
was a lull in the conversation, "may I inquire as to our
plans for the evening?"

"We have balconies," Elena said. "I think you'll be
sufficiently safe from abduction there. And you'll get
to see at least some of the proceedings."

Kusanagi-Jones bit his lip. Abductions were one thing. He was worried about snipers.

To say that Pretoria house had balconies was akin to saying that Babylon had gardens. Vincent would have liked to go to the edge of the one they occupied, three stories or so above the street, and lean out to get a better view of the merrymakers. But Angelo and Shafaqat had other ideas; they kept their bodies between him and the street, while Lesa and Katya flanked him. Elena, Agnes, and the older man that Vincent had met at dinner were off to the left and slightly above his vantage point, and the rest of the household scattered about, above and below.

Miss Pretoria had been right. It was indeed a pretty good party.

The street that the balconies overhung was narrow, the buildings opposite lower and more rolling than the twisted spire of Pretoria house. And even three stories up, Vincent could *smell* the mass of humanity below. Not just the liquor or the perfume or the crushed flowers draped around their necks and threaded through their hair, but the meaty animal reek of all that flesh pressed together. They moved like a many-legged, meandering insect, singing and laughing, banging drums, playing portable instruments that were remarkable to Vincent in their familiarity—gourds and flutes and saxophones and kalimbas.

There were a lot of weird worlds, a lot of political structures based on points of philosophy. Not all the ships of the Diaspora had been faster than light, even; humanity had scrambled off Earth in any rowboat or leaky bucket that might hold them, and dead ships

were still found floating between the stars, full of
frozen corpses.

Vincent found it alternately creepy and reassuring
when he considered that no matter how strange the
culture might be, every single world out there, every
instance of intelligent life that he had encountered,
claimed common descent from Earth.

As the Gorgon brightened overhead, the crowds
grew heavier. Someone on stilts paraded past, her head
nearly level with Vincent's feet. He returned her wave,
laughing, and she tossed him a strand of holographic
beads that cast pinpoint dots around them as they
whirled through the air. Vincent reached to catch
them, but Michelangelo intercepted and enfolded
them in his hands.

For analysis, of course. His wardrobe wasn't doing
anything that Vincent's couldn't, but it was Vincent's
job to let Angelo take the risks for him. He hated it.

Angelo finished his analysis and threat assessment
and handed Vincent the necklace. It was spectacular,
some light, cool substance with a high refractive index
and pinpoint LEDs buried deep within, so the facets
cast multicolored sparks in all directions. More brilliant than a necklace of diamonds, and not dependent
on available light.

Below, there was more music, more dragon dancers.
A roar echoed from the street's narrow walls as tumblers passed, given so little room by the crowd that it
seemed they must stumble into bystanders at any moment. Vincent ran a backup analysis on the beads—
nothing, not even a microprocessor—then pulled the
necklace over his head and let it fall across his chest. It
settled over his wardrobe, casting dancing pinpoints
down his torso and across his shoulders, up his cheeks
and into his hair. He turned to grin at Angelo, half

wishing they were down on the street amid the revelers, and caught Angelo looking at him with a particular, aching, focused expression that set him back.

Angelo blinked and looked down quickly, leaving Vincent adrift with one hand half extended. It might almost have been an honest reaction.

"What's that?" Michelangelo asked, pointing down the alley. The music was swelling again, a new group of performers pushing by. Katya Pretoria pressed a cold drink into Vincent's hand.

On the left, amid the coiling river of pedestrians, a group of men clad in red carried a platform on their shoulders. At first Vincent thought it was another Carnival float, and the person slumped cross-legged on the litter would begin throwing beads or lift up a trumpet at any moment.

But his head lolled against one powerful shoulder, and when Vincent leaned forward, peering down into the street—trying to see in the half-light provided by flickering torches and the glowing hemispheres that adorned the building walls—he could see that the man was propped up between slats, and his hands were bound together before his chest. The litter bearers were singing, Vincent saw, their voices rising over the tumult of the crowd, and even the dragon dancers made way for them.

Angelo nudged Vincent, and Vincent stepped back. "He's—"

"It's a funeral procession," Katya said. "It's an honor."

When Vincent turned to her, she stared straight ahead, her eyebrows drawn close above her nose. "Is it an honor afforded to women, as well?"

"If they die in combat," Katya said. She nodded down over the railing, then looked away from the litter

and the dead man's singing bearers. She pulled a
wreath of beads and flowers from the balcony railing
and shouted down to a teenage boy walking unat-
tended amid the tumblers. The boy looked up, and
Katya tossed the necklace into his hands.

Vincent didn't see his license, but he suspected the
young man wouldn't be allowed out alone if it were
not Carnival; he glanced about himself wide-eyed, and
waved the bruised flower over his head, calling out to
Katya.

"Combat?" Vincent asked.

She stepped back from the railing. "That's Philip
they're burying, who was of Canberra house. He was
killed in the Trials yesterday."

Vincent's voice came out of nebula-tinted darkness,
just loud enough to carry over the cries of merrymakers in the street. "Do you remember *Skidbladnir*?"

Kusanagi-Jones, who had been poised on the edge of
sleep, came sharply awake, his heart jumping in response to an adrenaline dump. "Vincent?"

A warm hand rested above his elbow. Too warm, and
Vincent was shivering. "The ship. Remember her?"

Kusanagi-Jones turned, eyesight adapting, collecting heat-signatures and available light. "Your temperature is up."

"Sunburn," Vincent said. "Robert warned me. I'm
cold."

Which was an interesting problem. "How much
does it hurt?"

"I've got chemistry," Vincent answered. Which was
Vincent for *a lot*. He didn't use it if he could avoid it.

"May I touch you?"

"Please."

But when he reached around Vincent's shoulders, Vincent yelped behind clenched teeth. Kusanagi-Jones jerked his hand back. "I'm more sore than I thought," he said.

"How's your chest?"

"Not bad. Not as bad. Just a little sore at the top."

"Well then." Kusanagi-Jones flopped on his back, shaking the bed, and tented the covers. "Get comfortable."

Vincent slid over him, a blessed blanket of warmth in the chill of the over-climate-controlled night. Kusanagi-Jones was used to sleeping warm everywhere but on starships, and he found himself sighing, relaxing, as Vincent spread out against his chest. Vincent made a little sad sound and stiffened when the blankets fell against his back, but settled in once his wardrobe established an air cushion. He propped himself on his elbows so he could look Kusanagi-Jones in the face. *"Skidbladnir."*

"What about it? Seventeen years ago." Kusanagi-Jones rearranged himself so Vincent could stretch comfortably between his legs. In the middle distance, someone was singing, and he shifted uncomfortably, remembering the dead man on his litter.

"It was the last time——"

When they were still half convinced they could keep their relationship a secret. When they thought they *had*, and the sex had, all too often, been furtive and hasty, and——

"Yes." The words scratching his throat. "I remember."

"Do you remember what you said to me?"

He knows, Kusanagi-Jones thought. He stroked Vincent's hip lightly, feeling heat and skin slick with moisturizer and analgesic. "Told you," he said, picking over each word, "no matter what happened, I wanted you to know I——" He shrugged. It wasn't something he had the courage to say twice in one lifetime. "I did. Want you to know."

"And something happened."

"Yeah." Kusanagi-Jones closed his eyes, filtering out the charcoal-sketch outline of Vincent's face. "Had to eventually."

"I didn't answer at the time," Vincent said. "I——"

Michelangelo reacted fast. Just fast enough to get his hands into Vincent's braids—careful of his burned neck—and pull Vincent's mouth down to his own before Vincent could say anything stupid. Before Vincent could give him back his own words of nearly two decades before.

Vincent's voice trailed off in a mumble that buzzed against Michelangelo's lips for a moment before Vincent's mouth opened, wet, yielding, returning fierceness for fierceness and strength for strength. The confession, however it might have begun, turned into a pleased, liquid moan. Teeth clicked and tongues slid, and Michelangelo arched his spine to press their groins together, not daring to hook his ankles over the backs of Vincent's calves. Vincent pulled back, panting, drawing the scratchy cords of his braids through Michelangelo's fingers.

"Nothing's going to happen," he ordained. *"Nothing."*

"Nothing?" Vincent asked, archly, lowering his head to claim another kiss.

"Nothing interesting."

Gray on gray in Michelangelo's augmented sight, Vincent's eyebrows rose. *Nothing,* Michelangelo thought, *because I'm going to sabotage this mission, too. Because I'm going to give you up again. I have it in my hands, sod it, and I don't…care…enough to sacrifice a whole culture for you.*

So I'm going to help New Amazonia get away, the

*same way I helped New Earth get away, and they're go-
ing to take me away from you again.*

What he said was, "Vincent. Your turn tonight."

*Kii understands. The bipeds do this themselves. They
choose. As the Consent chooses, in its own time. The way
of life is growth and consumption, blind fulfillment.*

*This is not the way of the Consent. As the Consent
chooses to enter a virtual space and achieve a burdenless
immortality, the bipeds, unpredatored, invent a predator.
Something that keeps them in balance. Something that
kills their culls, forces them to evolve when they outstrip
their native predators.*

A stroke of genius. An entire society bent to poetry.

They are esthelich, *after all.*

Vincent waited while Angelo pushed the pillows aside
and stretched on his stomach, breathing shallowly until Vincent covered Michelangelo with his body again,
licking the warm curve of Angelo's ear as Angelo
turned his head to breathe. Vincent caught Angelo's
hands in his own and pressed them to the bed. Playing
at restraint.

Angelo squirmed, panting, muscle rippling as he
pushed against Vincent, so powerful and so contained,
and so soft where it counted. He had always loved
this, loved and feared it, rarely permitted it, almost never
asked. He hated letting anybody, even Vincent—perhaps
especially Vincent—far enough inside his armor to see
the vulnerabilities underneath. To see him need *anything.*

And he would never forgive Vincent if he understood how transparent he was, in this one particular,

and how well Vincent understood this aspect of his
psyche. Because Michelangelo was a Liar—and while
Vincent couldn't tell when Angelo was lying, he knew
how it worked. Their talents were the same at the root.
But Angelo's was broken.

Vincent had been born with a cognitive giftedness.
He was a superperceiver. Michelangelo had the same
gift. And if he had grown up in the environment
Vincent had, chances were he would have been as
skilled at understanding and compromise and gentle
manipulation. But he'd been raised under harsher circumstances, and Michelangelo's gift had been shaped
by a history of verbal abuse and neglect into something else. Where a less talented child would have been
driven into a borderline personality, Michelangelo had
been warped into a perfect machine for survival. A
chameleon, a shape shifter.

A glossy exterior that showed only the reflection of
the person looking in.

Except for now, when Michelangelo lifted himself,
asking, and Vincent came to him. Exertion stung the tender skin on Vincent's back and buttocks and sweat dripped
into his eyes, scattering over Michelangelo's shoulders as
Angelo stretched under him. Vincent's wardrobe was
overloading again; he didn't care. Headfucks and Venus
flytraps and feedback loops were all right, but they didn't
satisfy the inner animal the way good, old-fashioned, biological *sex* did. Heart rate, brain chemistry, blood pressure—it all benefited from this: competition, cooperation,
intercourse. Conversation, as much game as release.

He rocked against Angelo, hands and mouth busy
on whatever he could reach. Michelangelo answered
him with sounds that might have indicated pain, if
they hadn't come in tandem with the eager motions of
his hips and the clench of his hands in the bedclothes.

Michelangelo flexed to meet his final, savage demands, and then they slumped together and pooled, relaxing.

Everything's better with a friend, Vincent thought, snorting with laughter.

"Glad to know I amuse you," replied the dryly muffled voice, Michelangelo slipping into their code.

Vincent resettled against his back, racing heartbeats synchronizing. "What did that Ouagadougou woman want with you?"

"You caught that?" Angelo sounded sleepy. "One of ours."

"Coalition?"

"Mmm. Our contact. Slipped me a map this afternoon. Might do some exploring in a bit."

"Alone?"

"Easier to countermeasure one than two, and I spent more time in the gallery than you did."

"What's the gallery got to do with anything?"

"Seems to be how you get there, if I'm reading this thing right—" Shoulders already whisked dry by utility fogs rose and fell against Vincent's chest. "What'd you find out?"

Vincent thought of the unexamined chip concealed under the table edge, and dropped his chin on Angelo's shoulder. "House— The city, I mean. Lesa called it House."

"Yeah?"

"I think it's an AI. Not sure if it's sentient—I mean, self-aware—or not, but it's sure as hell sapient. It problem-solves. And works from limited data to provide a best-response."

"Tells us how the marines died."

"Sure. The city just...lured them where the Elders

wanted them brought. And then walled them up. For as long as it took."

That brought a long silence, and then a sigh. "Hope the countermeasures work."

Vincent grunted. Michelangelo stretched again, the restless motion of hips and shoulders that meant *get off me, oaf*.

Vincent rolled clear. "How will you bypass security?"

"Don't be silly," said Angelo. "Going to turn invisible."

Lesa made sure Agnes knew she wouldn't be expecting Robert that night. She sat before her mirror, combing the brighteners into her hair, and contemplated the blankness with which Vincent had met her code phrase. A code phrase encoded on the chip *he'd* provided, at the meet prearranged by Katherine Lexasdaughter.

Which Robert had taken directly from his hand, palmed, and pressed immediately into hers. Vincent didn't know who he was to meet on New Amazonia. Couldn't know, before he made planetfall. It was too dangerous for everyone concerned.

Which was why the elaborate system of double blinds and duplicity. Isolation. Containment. Any good conspiracy needs fire doors. Lesa had required a chance to assess Katherinessen before she—and more important Elena—revealed herself. But when she'd tried to make the final connection . . .

Robert had palmed the chip and handed it directly to her.

Lesa's comb stopped in her hair. Robert had also been left alone with Vincent for at least half an hour before Lesa attempted to seal the contact.

She untangled the comb carefully, reversed its field with a touch on the controls, and redacted the brighteners. When her hair was clean, she folded the comb into its slot in the wall and stood. She stepped over Walter to reach the house com on the wall by the door. "House, please contact Agnes."

A moment later, Agnes answered, and Lesa told her that under no circumstances was Robert to leave the Blue Rooms. Agnes wanted details, and Lesa was forced to admit she had none to offer, "—but trust me on this."

She was already pulling on her boots as she said it. When House ended the connection, she called through the fabric of a thin black mock-neck for a car. She strapped on her honor, pulled her hair back into a plain tail, and hit the door at a trot.

The car was waiting at the end of the alley. There were some perks to being a government employee.

There were days when Kusanagi-Jones wished he were better at lying to himself, and then there were the days when he was pretty sure he had it down to a science. While Vincent made idle conversation, he split his wardrobe under the covers of the bed they had made love in, left the remainder to assemble a warm, breathing, nanometer-thick shell, and set what he retained to camouflage mode. When he stood up, as promised, he was invisible.

Well, not *truly* invisible. But his wardrobe handled minor issues like refracting light around him through the same process by which it could provide a 360-degree prospect in a combat situation, a lensing effect. It contained his body heat, presenting an ambient-temperature

surface to any thermal imaging devices, and it filtered
carbon and other emissions.

The drawback was that it would get hot and stuffy
in there rather quickly. He would have to move fast.

Kusanagi-Jones stood against the wall beside the
door as Vincent opened it and called Cathay inside on
the excuse of wanting a late snack. She came, yawning,
and Kusanagi-Jones slipped past her before the door
could iris shut.

The second security agent outside wasn't Shafaqat.
They must be trading off. In any case, she was standing
against the wall, admirably placed to see anyone coming in either direction down the short curved hall, but
with only a peripheral view of the door at her back.
Kusanagi-Jones slipped past in complete silence, the
only clue to his passage the dimpling of the carpetplant underfoot. She didn't notice.

The lift was a challenge, but it was out of sight
around the curve of the hall. He spoke softly and the
door glided open. He stepped inside. He wanted to
breathe deeply, to savor feeling alive in his skin and the
lingering tenderness of sex. But he kept his breaths
short and slow, giving his wardrobe as much help as he
could. He couldn't afford to dwell on pleasant memories when he was here to fail the man who created
them.

Vincent waited until Cathay returned with a tray, toast
and tea for two. He thanked her, then cleared Angelo's
solar collector from the edge of the open window. He
sat on the ledge to eat the toast and drink the tea. Then
he climbed back into bed beside the homunculus and
repeated Angelo's trick of mitosis. When he stood, he
collected the unviewed chip from its hiding place and

slotted it into his reader. The chip contained a map. He studied it while leaning out the window, examining the teeming city below.

Then he put one foot up and rose into the frame.

Anyone in the room would have registered nothing. No movement, no shifting of the light except a faint sparkle of mismatched edges if they had happened to look at the window just as he stepped up into it.

It was a long way down. Vincent let go of the window frame, lifted his arms, and stepped out.

Unlike a parachute, there was no shock as his wardrobe unfurled, growing filaments and tendrils festooned with catch pockets. The air resistance slowed him before he could build up falling velocity. He ballooned down like a spider, steering for a smooth dimple at the base of the tower, and landed squarely where he'd aimed. But faster than he should have; he rolled with it, but his knee twinged, and his wardrobe couldn't quite absorb the shock enough to protect his sun-seared shoulder. He whimpered when he hit, but the street noise was enough to cover that. In camouflage mode, his wardrobe would damp most of the noise anyway.

Once the wardrobe contracted, he slithered down the curved roofline to drop to street level, earning another twinge from his knee. He checked the map; the meeting place was one square over, in the open. No proof against listening devices, but if his suspicions were right, a member of security directorate would be making sure no records remained.

He slipped through the crowds into darkness, following the map through quieter streets. There were only a few reeling revelers here, and he avoided them easily. Somewhere in the distance, he heard fireworks or gunfire.

He fully expected that the shadow awaiting him in the darkness under an arched walkway would be Lesa Pretoria. He hadn't been sure until that evening, but the complex of her kinetics over dinner had convinced him, though she'd never dropped a recognition code. He paused in shadows to cancel the camouflage, dressed in local fashion and mocked up something that would pass from a distance for a street license with a quick accessory program—he didn't have a license for a hat, but he had one for a wrist cuff—and presented himself boldly alongside the arch, circumnavigating merrymakers as he went, restraining the urge to press his hand to his aching shoulder. The pain was nauseating.

He was drawing a breath to greet Miss Pretoria when an entirely different voice interrupted him, and a woman older and stouter than Lesa stepped into the light. "Miss Katherinessen," she said. "I'm pleased you could get away."

"Elder Kyoto," he choked. "This is a surprise."

Once Kusanagi-Jones reached street level and slipped into the night, he moved faster. The unrippled pavement was sun-warm under his feet, and he had little trouble winding through the scattered revelers by Gorgon-light. The gallery lay across the square. Penthesilea's government center was compact, and it wasn't the center of the party. Kusanagi-Jones only had to cope with the overflow.

He heard music from elsewhere in the city, cheers and laughter that suggested a parade or theatrical event. He triggered the full-circle display, the fisheye appearing in the lower corner of his sight where peripheral vision would pick it up. Years of training meant he'd react to it as fast as to a flicker in the corner of his eye, and as accurately.

He passed between drunks and singers, hesitated at the report of gunfire and an echoing siren. Four shots, but they were distant and spaced like a duel, and though heads turned, nobody reacted more strongly. He crept around to the back of the gallery, to the broad doors where more trucks of repatriated art were being unloaded and the protectively wrapped bundles carted in, to be hung in accordance with the afternoon's plan.

He skulked inside.

The lifts were running regularly. He simply stepped into an empty one, rode it down, ducked around a group of incoming laborers—mostly licensed men, and two armed women—and found himself at liberty in the gallery space.

The instructions Miss Ouagadougou had provided were quite precise. He crossed the first gallery and ascended the stair under the watchful eyes of the frieze. When he reached the far corner, he paused. This adventure would have been considerably less nervewracking if there were some mechanical means of opening the passage, something that could be hacked or bypassed.

If Vincent was right, there was a machine intelligence watching him. And Kusanagi-Jones could only hope its instructions didn't include the casual destruction of off-world human males poking about where they shouldn't be.

It wasn't as long a gamble as it seemed. He had, at best, speculation that the city might take action if it construed a major threat to its inhabitants—such as a ships' complement of Coalition marines. But Penthesilea remained an alien artifact, and if it could be efficiently reprogrammed or trained, he had no hope of carrying out his mission. And yet, here he was, against reason and sanity, doing what he did in the hope it didn't have protocols in place to deal with saboteurs and spies.

It was the old ambiguity that set his heart racing and dumped adrenaline into his bloodstream. Nobody sane would be here. But then, nobody sane would have taken this job in the first place. Especially when the most likely scenario, in the wake of the afternoon's attempt on Vincent, had Miss Ouagadougou luring him to a lonely place where he could be abducted or disappeared.

He lowered the audio damping, checked the fisheye display to make sure the gallery floor was clear, and asked House, please, to open the wall.

Before he finished speaking, the frieze before him parted like drawn curtains. He stepped forward into an arched tunnel, unsurprised when the opening sealed itself behind him. An indirect glow rendered his light amplification redundant; he dialed it down, but in deference to his mistrust of Miss Ouagadougou he left the camouflage protocol intact.

The tunnel was undecorated, smooth sided, the walls velvety and dark. It tended downward, the walls corded with shielded cables. Lesser ran into greater to form a vast, inverted mechanical root system, which thickened toward a trunk as he descended. The overall effect was Gigeresque, though the textures were more reminiscent of Leighton's velvets and silks.

He breathed easier. It was an access tunnel. Which meant, at least potentially, that Miss Ouagadougou had sent him to the right place. "Thank you," he said, feeling slightly foolish. The city didn't answer, but neither did the ongoing sense of observation (like a pressure between his shoulder blades) ease. He snorted softly when he realized he had expected it to, and kept walking.

Brightness spilled up the corridor as it leveled. He paused to let his eyes adapt. His wardrobe handled dazzle, but didn't ensure fine perception.

Fifteen seconds sufficed. He blinked once more, to be sure, and stepped forward into a chamber not much larger than the suite he shared with Vincent. It was bowl shaped, the walls arching to meet overhead in a smooth, steep-sided dome. He knew he was underground, but the depth of field in the images surrounding him was breathtaking. They were not just projected into the walls, but a full holographic display.

If it weren't for the tug of gravity on his boots, he might have been adrift in space. New Amazonia's primary, Kali, glowed enormous and bittersweet orange on his left hand, smeared behind watercolor veils. On his right, totally out of perspective, floated New Amazonia, a cloud-marbled berry with insignificant ice caps, incrementally closer to its primary than Earth was to Sol, partially shielded from Kali's greater energy output by the Gorgon's polychrome embrace.

The fisheye showed him stars on every side. He turned toward the sun. And a peculiar thing happened. The nebula dimmed, parted along his line of sight, and left him staring at the filtered image of Kali. He knew it was filtered, because his wardrobe wasn't blinking override warnings about staring into it, and everything around it didn't flicker dim as the utility fog struggled to compensate. The bruise-limned darkness of sunspots hung vivid against the glare, the ceaseless fidgeting of the corona marked abruptly by the dolphin leap of a solar arch. It seemed close enough to reach out his hand and touch, enormous, though his palm at full extension eclipsed the sphere.

Teeth rolling his lower lip, Kusanagi-Jones returned
to New Amazonia. The veils swept back from it as well,
focus tightening, and as the holographic point of view
swept in, he found himself retracing the rough course
of the lighter that had brought him to this planet. He
circled Penthesilea, and there the image hesitated.
Waiting, he realized. Hovering like a butterfly on
trembling wingbeats, accommodating the wind.

"House, show me the power generation system, please."

The image swooped again. A flying creature's preferred perspective, as internal decor mimicking wide
open spaces and empty skies would be comforting to a
creature with wings, where an ape's descendent might
feel cozy with limited perspectives and broken sight
lines, the indication of places to hide.

The sense of falling made his fingers flex, trying to
clutch a railing that wasn't there. He mastered himself, despite the sense that there was nothing to stand
on as images rushed past incomprehensibly fast. And
then they paused, arrested sharply, and he found himself staring at the back of his own head, the wooly
curls of a dark man in a star-spangled room.

His fisheye—and his own eyes—showed him that
the image *he* watched hadn't changed. But the room
around the virtual Kusanagi-Jones dissolved, vanished
into clear air, leaving him standing at the bottom of a
sphere whose every surface writhed with twisted cable.
It was a strangely organic growth, fractal in the way it
merged and combined, coming together in a massive,
downward-tending trunk beneath Kusanagi-Jones's
feet.

The hologram had stripped away the chamber's
walls, showing him what lay behind them. His neck
chilled. He rubbed his palms against his thighs.
"Follow the cables, please."

The perspective zoomed down—*through* him, and he blinked at the glimpse of meat and bone and wiring and a momentary cross-section of a pulsing heart— and chased the tunneling cables down, down, to bedrock and a cavern in the depth-warmed darkness.

He was no electrical engineer. But an encyclopedic education, RAM-assisted parsing, and the information he'd chipped when he came out of cryo identified most of the machinery. Capacitors, transformers, batteries, a bank of quantum processors big enough to run a starship: essentially, an electrical substation the size of some Earth cities.

And no sign whatsoever of a *generator*. Just the power endlessly flowing from the quantum array—

From the quantum array.

"Shit," Kusanagi-Jones said. He had an excellent memory. He could recall Elder Singapore's slightly amused tone precisely, as she had said, *But you can't get there from here*. "The power source isn't on this planet."

A flicker of motion in his fisheye alerted him a split second before an urbane, perfectly modulated voice answered him. He turned, binocular vision better than peripheral, the fisheye snapping down on the sudden motion and giving him a blurred preview that didn't remotely prepare him.

The head that hung over him was a meter long from occiput to muzzle, paved about the mouth and up to the eyes on either side with beady scales that ranged in color from azure to indigo. Flatter scales plated under the jaw and down the throat, creamy ivory and sunrise-yellow. A fluff of threadlike feathers began as a peach-and-cream crest between the eyes, broadened to a mane on the neck and down the spine, spread across the flanks, and downed the outside of the thighs. The forelimbs, folded tight against the animal's ribs, raised towering spikes on either side of its shoulders—the outermost fingers of hands that were curled under to support the front half.

Support it couldn't have needed, because the entire four-meter-long animal was lucently transparent. It was a projection.

"You are wrong, *esthelich* Michelangelo Osiris Leary Kusanagi-Jones. Planetary margins are irrelevant. The cosmocline is not in this *brane*," the ghost of a Dragon said, and paused before it continued.

"Good morning, *esthelich*. Kii greets you. Kii is explorer-caste. Kii speaks for the Consent."

BOOK TWO

The Mortification of
the Flesh

13

"YOU OPPOSE CONSENT," KII SAID, THE SPIKED TIPS OF folded wings canting back as it settled onto its haunches, knuckles extended before it like a crouching dog's paws. Its long neck stretched, dipping slightly at the center as it brought its head to Kusanagi-Jones's level. Its phantom tongue flicked out, hovered in the air, tested, considered. "You are disloyal."

Kusanagi-Jones had no answer. He was poised, defensively, ready to move, to attack or evade. But there was nothing here he could touch, and the creature's capabilities were unmeasured.

It paused, though, cocking its head side to side as if to judge distance, and nictitating membranes wiped across wide golden eyes. It seemed to consider. "Perfidious," it tried, and Kusanagi-Jones could see that the thing wasn't actually speaking. The voice was generated stereophonically, so it seemed to originate near Kii's mouth—if Kii was the animal's name, and

not its species identifier or a personal pronoun or something Kusanagi-Jones wasn't even thinking of—but
the mouth didn't work around the words, and its
breathing flared and flexed nostrils, uninterrupted.
"Treasonous," it considered, lingering over the flavor
of the word, and then shook its head like a bird shaking off water. "Disloyal," it decided gravely. "You are
disloyal."

Michelangelo found himself quite unintentionally
disarmed by this haphazard pedantry, though he
fought it. He straightened, breathing slowly, and let
his hands fall to his sides. He kept his balance light,
weight centered on the balls of his feet. He would
move if he had to and try to look calm in the meantime. The preliminary indicators were that Kii was
nonaggressive. It might be a sort of . . . user-friendly interface bot designed for a Dragon. The alien's equivalent of an application assistant.

"Request clarification," Kusanagi-Jones said.

Kii's tongue flickered. It settled another notch, lowering itself to its transparent belly, drawing its head
back, neck a sinuous curve. The tension in Kusanagi-
Jones's gut untwisted another notch, the lizard in the
back of his skull reacting to a lowering of threat
level—as if the Dragon's appearance of ease mattered
at all. Any attack, if it came, need have nothing to do
with a hologram; a laser concealed in a wall port would
suffice.

"You are a member of a population in competition
with the local population," Kii said. "But your trans-
missions indicate that your allegiance to your own population is . . ." It paused again, head rocking and eyes
upcast. Kusanagi-Jones imagined the Dragon was
searching for an unfamiliar word again. "—spurious."

Kusanagi-Jones licked his lips. It wasn't *technically* a

question. More an observation. Maybe he could return a question of his own. "Are you House? Wait, belay that. Are you the intelligence known as House?"

"Kii is..."

Kusanagi-Jones thought that the approximations occurred when it was searching for a word in New Amazonia's patois that matched a concept in its own language. He waited it out.

"Kii is not-House," it said. "House is House. House is a construct. Kii is of the Consent."

Not I. Kii. Maybe not a personal pronoun. But it understood them—it used *you* fluently enough. So there was some reason it didn't think of itself as I. Or even *we*, the logical choice if it were a hive-mind. "Kii is a virtual intelligence?"

"Kii is translated." It stopped again, nictitating. "Transformed. *Molted*," it said, and then, triumphantly, the spiked fingertips flipping up to reveal cream-and-ultramarine wing leather in blurred, torn-paper patterns: "Fledged!"

Kusanagi-Jones put his hand against his mouth. He pressed it there, and thought. "You're a transcendent intelligence," he said. Kii blinked great translucent eyes. "What do you want?"

What he meant was, *why haven't you killed me the way you killed the last Coalition forces to land here?* But that seemed an impolitic question. *I'm not trained for first contact—*

But this wasn't first contact either. First contact was *handled*. First contact was more than a hundred Terran years ago. It didn't matter if the New Amazonians knew that the Dragons still inhabited their cities, after a fashion—which was something that Kusanagi-Jones wasn't prepared to assume—because the Dragons definitely knew rather a lot about humans.

"Your population is expansionist," Kii said, after it had given Kusanagi-Jones adequate time to consider the stupidity of his blurted question. "But intelligent. Kii wishes to encourage détente." It showed him teeth, back-curved spikes suitable for holding and shredding meat. "Kii is not eager to repeat, no, reiterate a massacre."

"I am not eager to be massacred," Kusanagi-Jones replied. "You've ethics."

"You have aesthetics," Kii said. "But no Consent. No true Consent." It hissed, frustrated. "You act in ways that are not species-ordained."

"And you do not?" It was surprisingly easy to relax with the thing. For all its alienness, it made no threatening gestures, did nothing but occasionally tilt its head and twitch the spikes of its wingtips into a more comfortable pose.

"Kii follows Consent," it said. That ripple of the downy feathers on its neck almost looked like a skin-shiver. "Consent is ... ordained."

It was watching him. Trying the words in turn and seeing how he reacted. Testing them on him, until something—his body language, his scent—told it he was understanding as it wished.

"I follow my leaders, too."

Could that be the thing's answer to a smile? After 150 years of observation, it must comprehend human body language. Especially if it was reading his responses.

But he was a *Liar*.

"Biochemical," it explained after another pause.

Oh. *Ah.* Not a group mind, then, but something closer to a political structure ... albeit one enforced by biology. Or programming, in the case of a life form that wasn't biological anymore. "Consent?"

"Yes."

"Can't argue my people out of coming here. They'll—" Kusanagi-Jones shrugged and spread his hands out, pale palms up, dark backs inverted. *They won't leave something like you at their flank.* A raw frontier world with a powerful bargaining chip, they *might* negotiate with, if the cost of occupation was deemed higher than the benefit gained. But a Transcendent alien species, with no apparent defenses, and the promise of all that energy, all that technology—

The Coalition had proven its acquisitiveness. On Ur, on New Earth—spectacular failure though *that* had been—and on half a dozen other worlds. *This* would be one bastard of an interesting brawl in Cabinet, in any case. It might be worthwhile to send combat fogs into the population centers just on the chance there might be pieces to pick up later.

"If you cannot convince your population to leave Kii's...pets, Kii's associates, in possession of these resources," Kii said, "Kii will kill them. As necessary."

Lesa had made Cathay and Asha wait in the hall as she passcoded the door to the Coalition agents' suite and went inside. The simulacra in the bed were effective, but they wouldn't bear up to a touch. Still, she stood over them, listening to the sound of their breathing— "Vincent's" a regular hiss, "Michelangelo's" touched by a faint hint of snore—and closed her eyes.

Robert had end-run her. And the essential link to Ur and rebellion could be walking into a trap right now— or, worse or better, arranging a deal with a rival faction.

Lesa knew her mother. If Elena wasn't in charge, Elena was unlikely to play. And if Elena didn't play——

——Lesa's own chances of getting Julian off-planet to Ur, if he didn't prove gentle, went from reasonable to infinitesimal.

Ignoring the monitors (she'd be the one who examined the recordings), she tugged the covers up slightly, as if tucking in a couple of sleeping spies, and padded back toward the door. It opened and she passed between Asha and Cathay without a word.

"Everything all right?" Asha asked, hooking lustrous dark hair behind her ear with a thumb.

"Fine," Lesa said over her shoulder. "Sleeping the sleep of the just. Make sure they're up at five hundred for the repatriation ceremony?" She paused and turned long enough to throw Cathay a wink. "I think they wore themselves out."

The lift brought her down quickly. Her watch buzzed against her wrist; she touched it and tilted her head to her shoulder to block external noise. Her earpiece needed replacing. "Agnes?"

"Lesa, Robert's not in the rooms," Agnes said, her high-pitched voice shivering. The words came crisp and clipped, as if she'd had them all lined up, ready to rush forward as soon as her mouth was opened. "Do you want a constable on it?"

Lesa's mouth filled with bitter acid. "Does Mother know?"

Agnes paused. "I called you before I woke her." Which was a violation of protocol. But Lesa would have done the same.

There were any number of possibilities, but only two seemed likely. Robert was a double. Which meant he was working for either a free male faction, like Parity or—she prayed not—Right Hand Path. Or he was working for security directorate, and she'd just bought herself a sunrise execution.

"You did the right thing," Lesa said. As she walked out into Government Center she passed the community car she'd taken here, which was parked silently at the curb waiting for its next call. She paused, frowned at her watch, and then continued, "And send me Walter, would you?"

She leaned a hip and shoulder against the wall as she waited, closing her eyes to cadge a few moments of dozing. Less than ten minutes later the whuff of hot breath on her hand and the tickle of feathers alerted her. She stroked a palm across Walter's skull, laying his ear fronds flat and caressing warm down and scales. He panted slightly with the run, but he'd had no trouble finding her. Penthesilea wasn't a big city in terms of area; he was trained as a package-runner, and he regularly went on errands with Robert or Katya. Agnes would have just told him *find Lesa at work,* and once he was at Government Center, he would have traced her scent.

"Good khir," she said, and gave him her other hand, the one she'd stroked through the Coalition agents' bedding. He whuffed again and went down on his haunches, not sitting but crouching. He lifted his head, ear-fronds and crest fluffing, and waited, his eyes glowing dimly with gathered light.

"Find it, please," Lesa said. Walter nosed her hand again. "No cookie," she said, shaking her head. She had nothing to bribe him with. "Find."

He whuffed one last time, disappointed, and bounced up into an ambling trot, nose to the ground. She waited while he cast back and forth, darting one way and then the other, feathery whiskers sweeping the square. They framed the end of his mouth like a

Van Dyke, above and below the labial pits, and served a dual purpose—as sensitive instruments of touch and for stirring up, gathering, and concentrating aromas.

Then, not far from the doorway she'd exited, he made two short, sharp dashes at right angles to each other and glanced over his shoulder with quivering ear-fronds for a decision.

They hadn't gone the same way.

Lesa raised her hand and pointed at random. Walter took off like a spring-loaded chase dummy, and Lesa bounded after, running until her knees ached and her lungs burned.

The scent was fresh.

Elder Kyoto closed her fingers around Vincent's biceps and drew him under the archway. "Any problem getting away?"

She kept her voice low, down in her throat like a lover's, and Vincent answered the same way. "None. Given who passed your note, I expected Miss Pretoria—"

"What a pity to confound your expectations," she replied. "You have a message from your mother, I understand?"

"I am empowered by the government-in-anticipation of Ur to seek alliances, if that's what you mean." He checked his fisheye: slightly more subtle than glancing over his shoulder. "We're unmonitored here?"

"Jammed," she said, and held up her wrist. The device strapped to it looked like an ordinary watch. She smiled. "I apologize for my boorish behavior at the reception, by the way."

"Quite all right." He draped himself around her shoulder, leaning down as if to murmur in her ear. "Elder Singapore isn't sympathetic, I take it?"

"Elder Singapore is convinced that the Coalition can be bargained with." She snuggled under the curve of his arm, her shoulders stiff behind a mask of insincere affection.

"Yes," Vincent said. "So was my grandmother. Is it worth trying to convince her?"

It was so easy now, now that it was happening. The tension of waiting and secrets and subtleties released, and he was here, working, calculating. "On a male's word?" Kyoto shrugged. "There isn't. Singapore was Separatist before her conversion to mainstream politics, and her closest associates—Montevideo, Saide Austin—are still deeply involved in antimale politics." Kyoto grimaced. "Pretoria house might be sympathetic—actually, we used sleight of hand to talk to you first—"

"We?"

"Parity."

"Excuse me?"

She tossed her hair back roughly. "That's our name. Parity. What you might call a radical underground movement. We're pro men's right's, anti-Trials, in favor of population control. Opposed to Coalition appeasement—"

"And illegal."

"How ever did you guess?" She might have become someone else since the night before, the cold mask replaced by passionate urgency.

"You're a *Liar*," he answered. "I would have known—"

"I'm not. And you don't know everything. I'm on your side."

"My mother's side."

"The rebel prince," she mocked. She folded her arms across her chest. "Do you actually *care* what your mother stands for, or did you just grow up twisted in her shadow? Katherine Lexasdaughter is a famously charismatic leader, of course. But what do *you* believe in, Vincent Katherinessen?"

His lips drew tight across his teeth while he considered it. "You think it's wise to overthrow the entire planetary social system as a prelude to an armed revolt, Elder Kyoto?"

"Armed revolt first," she answered. "*Then* revolution. We have a hundred thousand combat-trained stud males on this planet. We have half a million armed, educated, fiercely independent women. I don't want to see them come to blows with each other. I want to give them an enemy in common."

He watched her, still, and she shifted uncomfortably under his gaze. Maybe not a Liar, then. Not a trained one, anyway. Just very controlled, very good. "I was *supposed* to contact Lesa Pretoria, wasn't I?" he asked. "You intercepted the codes."

"We needed you first. It's not just about the Coalition—"

"It's about the Coalition first."

She raised an eyebrow. "What about personal dignity? Personal freedom?"

"Never mind the *Coalition*." His hands wanted to curl into fists. Tendons pressed the inside of his bracer. "Never mind New Amazonia. Do you think there's any of that under the Governors?"

"I think," she said, "the Governors come first. And then the internal reforms."

He bit his lip, leaning forward, voice low and focused, taut with wrath. "Elena *Pretoria* can bring me the New Amazonian government, once Singapore is out of the way. Can you? My mother *will* supply the Captains' council. We can guarantee New Earth. That's three. It's not enough, but it's what we've got, and once things are started, a few more may take their chances. You were right when you said my mother is famously charismatic. But this is a civil *war* we're discussing, Antonia, and one Old Earth will fight like hell to win, because every planet it loses means one less place for the population to expand to. Will your half a million armed women fight for you, fight against Coalition technology, if they think you're going to take away *their* spot at the top of the pecking order?"

"They'll fight to keep New Amazonia free. We can explain the rest afterward," Kyoto said. Determination squared her. She unfolded her hands and let them drop against her thighs, the right one hovering close to her holster. "And, if you wouldn't mind putting the rest of the lecture on hold for a minute, Miss Katherinessen, we have company."

Vincent had caught the motion in his fisheye, and was already putting his back to the wall. Someone walked toward them, a tripled shadow cast by multiple light sources splayed on the pavement before her. The unfastened safety snap bounced against her holster and her hair caught blond and crimson and fuchsia highlights off the domed street lights lining the walls of the half-empty square. A big animal—a khir—stood beside her, the angular silhouette also casting three long shadows that interlocked with the woman's.

"You shouldn't raise your voice so, Miss Katherinessen," Lesa said, pausing, her thumb resting on the butt of her weapon. "It's unseemly to shout."

He slid his arm off Elder Kyoto's shoulder and stepped back with a sigh. Kyoto glanced at him and he shrugged. He didn't say it, but he didn't think you'd have to be a superperceiver to read the *I told you so* in the twist of his mouth. "Miss Pretoria," he said. "Welcome to the party. Is Robert coming?"

Lesa let her hand drift away from her holster as she came forward, but didn't fix the snap. Kyoto hadn't unbonded her honor; it wouldn't slow her down much, if she opened fire—but probably enough. Considering how people treated Lesa when she had a weapon in her hand.

"I don't know," Lesa said. She stepped under the arch, into the shadows, and Walter trotted beside her, fluffed up and cheerful. "You'd have to ask his true mistress." She tilted her head, frowning at Kyoto under the fall of her hair, and lowered her voice. "In between plotting treason in the streets. Where's Kusanagi-Jones, Vincent?"

"Keeping busy with a little industrial espionage. You leave Angelo to me. That's not negotiable."

Kyoto glared for a moment before she nodded. "All right," she said. "Vincent. You are authorized to deal for your mother."

"Full authority," he said. "New Earth, too."

Kyoto nodded and turned to Lesa. "Then we'll join forces. One good Coalition deserves another."

"Mother won't like it."

"I'll handle your mother." And now Kyoto's hand dropped to her gun butt. Vincent stiffened, ready to grab her wrist and trust to his wardrobe to save him, but all she did was stroke a thumb across the snap, assuring herself that it was closed.

Lesa snorted, but she echoed the gesture, causing a *click*. "I'd like to see that. Who else do you have in Pretoria house?"

"Nobody," Kyoto said. Vincent believed her; he glanced at Lesa to see what *she* thought. He was still half convinced that Kyoto was a Liar. Or the next best thing.

Lesa was nibbling her lower lip, leaning forward aggressively as if completely oblivious that she was facing down her superior officer. "Then where's Robert tonight?"

"I beg your pardon?"

"Robert left the Blue Rooms somehow. He's gone."

Vincent had rarely seen somebody's mouth actually drop open. Kyoto's did, and stayed down for seconds while she thought it over. "I'm sorry," she said at last. "I have no idea."

"Shit," Lesa said. She thumbed her watch and turned slightly away, as people did for politeness when taking remote calls. Her eyes unfocused slightly. "Agnes? Yes. Sweetie, I'm sorry . . . we have a fairly serious problem."

"When you're done with that," Vincent said, "I'll need a distraction while I sneak back into my room."

Kusanagi-Jones returned to the guest suite half an hour before dawn, walking camouflaged through the door when the security guards knocked to awaken Vincent. He slipped into the bed as Vincent was shaking the covers in an ostensible attempt to awaken him, reabsorbed the mannequin, and sat up, rubbing his eyes. "Morning already?"

"You don't look very rested," Vincent said. He walked toward the shower as Kusanagi-Jones rolled out of bed.

"Somebody's snoring kept me up," he said between push-ups.

"Your own?" Vincent replied.

Kusanagi-Jones's eyes were gritty with exhaustion. He wasn't young enough to shrug off a sleepless night anymore, if he ever had been; he couldn't remember. He quit at twenty-five push-ups and knelt, ducking his head over his wrist as he adjusted his chemistry. A rush of energy swept the cobwebs away, leaving him taut and jittering but awake.

He climbed to his feet and went to join Vincent in the shower. Vincent stepped aside, letting Kusanagi-Jones have the spray. He lifted his face into the patter of water, fighting the uneasy urge to flinch. He didn't like it drumming on cheeks and eyelids. "Did you find it?" Vincent asked.

Kusanagi-Jones stepped out of the water and looked at him before answering the same way. "Found something. I know where the generator is, anyway, though it's going to be a bigger problem than I want to contemplate getting to it. *Disrupting* the power supply, I might manage. At some risk. The point of transmission is guarded. The rest... it's going to take awhile to explain." He paused for a breath, and to shake the water off his lashes. "Why are you limping?"

Vincent was lathering himself. His hands were over his face, but Kusanagi-Jones saw him hesitate. "Am I?"

"Favoring your knee."

"I must have hit it wrong last night," Vincent answered, turning into the water to rinse. "It's sore."

"Sure picked the right day," Kusanagi-Jones answered, as Vincent stepped past him, reaching for a towel. "We're going to be on our feet every minute."

14

IT WASN'T QUITE AS BAD AS THAT. THERE WERE CHAIRS AT the breakfast table. Which was fortunate, for by then occasional sharper stabs punctuated the ache in Vincent's knee. It was manageable, however, with the assistance of the same chemistry that mitigated his sunburn.

Elder Kyoto caught him wincing as they took their seats. "Third day is the worst," she said.

"Oh, good," he answered. "Something to look forward to." Across the table, Michelangelo reached out to press a fingertip to Vincent's wrist. The heat made him jerk his hand back.

"Remember this," Angelo said, finishing it with a glower. The sting of the touch wasn't what made Vincent's eyes burn.

He looked down hastily, examining what was on offer this morning. Apparently, somebody had alerted the chef to the dietary restrictions of the Coalition agents, because the breakfast options included a kashalike

grain, cooked into porridge and served with some sort
of legume milk and a sweetener reminiscent of mo-
lasses in its sulfury richness.

There were new people at this meal, husbands and
wives of dignitaries who hadn't attended the supper
two days previous. Vincent filed all the introductions
under mnemonics. The one on his immediate left,
however, he suspected he'd have no difficulty recalling:
Saide Austin, the artist.

She was an imposing woman. Almost two meters tall
and not slight of build, with short, tight-coiled hair shot
through with gray threads like smoke and wide cheeks
framing a broad, fleshy nose. Her skin was textured
brown, darker around her eyes and paler in the creases
between her brows, and her half-smile reinforced the
lines. Heavy silver rings circled several of her fingers,
flashing like the mirrors embroidered on her robe.

Her hand was warm where she shook Vincent's, and
she gave him a little pat on the forearm before she let
him go. Over her shoulder, he saw Michelangelo frown.
Their eye contact was brief, but definite, and the flickering glance that followed ended on Claude Singapore.

So Austin was the one pushing Singapore's but-
tons.

"I very much admired your sculpture," Vincent
said.

"*Jinga Mbande?*" The smile broadened, showing
stout white teeth. "Thank you. How do you think your
government will feel about touring artists, when negotiations are concluded?"

"I'm sure they'd welcome them," Vincent said. He
slid his spoon into the porridge and cut a bite-sized
portion against the edge of the bowl. "I'm surprised
you'd be willing to send New Amazonian art to Old
Earth, though, after—"

"The Six Weeks War?" She spooned honey into her tea. He looked away. "Isn't the Coalition bent on showing goodwill?"

"Your countrywomen aren't all so sanguine," he answered.

She shrugged and drank. "What did you expect? I'm not sanguine either. But I'm prepared."

Vincent nodded, reaching for his own tea. Yes. This was the person the Coalition meant him to deal with, the one who could bargain without running home to check with her mother. And according to Kyoto—if he could trust her —one he had no real chance of bargaining with. A separatist, somebody who'd as soon see New Amazonia live up to its name to the extent of eradicating men entirely.

So why was she wasting his time?

Across the table, Michelangelo was drinking coffee, apparently engrossed in conversation with Miss Ouagadougou, but he was listening. Vincent suppressed that twinge again, half guilt and half anticipation. "I've heard a rumor," he said, "that your voice is one of the respected ones urging détente. We're grateful."

She sipped her tea, set it down—aligning the cup and saucer carefully with the cream pitcher—and lifted a forkful of scrambled eggs into her mouth. Vincent waited while she chewed and swallowed. "How would the Coalition react if New Amazonia opened itself to limited immigration?" she asked, as if idly. "There must be women on Old Earth who would come—"

It was possible she was trying to see if he would startle, or how he would react. It was possible the offer—with all its attendant benefits and problems—was genuine. He could see half a dozen ways it could be politically or idealistically motivated. In any case, he'd been expecting some sort of dramatic maneuver, and he managed to neither bite his tongue nor drop his spoon. "I think they'd be very interested," he said. "It might help relieve population pressures a great deal."

"Of course, it would be unlikely that the government would allow them to import Old Earth technology." She touched his sleeve, rubbing the fog between finger and thumb. "They'd be homesteading. Any men would live under New Amazonian law."

"Of course." He put the spoon down and leaned back, turning to face her. Suddenly, he wasn't all that hungry. "This wouldn't substitute for negotiations regarding the exchange of technology for the remaining unrepatriated art, though."

"Why not?" She finished her tea, the resinous scent of her perfume wafting from her clothes as she moved. "We'd be giving the Colonial Coalition something it desperately needs—"

"Because," Vincent said, "you benefit as much as we do. You're having genetic issues, of course."

Her fingers rippled on the table. She watched them beat three times, then let go a held breath and nodded. "Not yet."

"But soon."

"We do not permit genetic manipulation."

"Indeed," Vincent said. "In a closed population, that's likely to cause problems. Especially if the radiation exposure your colonists suffered in transit was anything like what we contended with on Ur."

"You're a clever bastard, Vincent Katherinessen," she said, and lifted her fork again.

He matched the gesture. "It's what I do."

As the breakfast reception ended, Lesa made her way around the table to collect Katherinessen, leaving

Kusanagi-Jones looking slightly trapped under Elder Montevideo's care.

She waited while Katherinessen courteously ended his conversation with Elder Austin and turned before she offered her hand. He shook it lightly and followed as she led toward the door. "Robert?" he asked quietly.

"No sign. We reported him as a runaway. Anything else was too much risk." She'd been proud of how level her voice was, but it didn't spare her Vincent's glance of sympathy.

"Are we ready for the ceremony, then?"

"Claude and Elder Austin will be on their way down shortly. But I thought you and Miss Kusanagi-Jones would appreciate a trip to the washroom beforehand," she said. "House has the stage set up, and there's quite a crowd."

"You'd expect everybody would be too hung over."

As easily as he read her suppressed grief, she picked up the tension under his flip reply. "Penthesileans pride themselves on never being too hung over for a party," she answered. She lowered her voice and leaned in, as if making an off-color comment in his ear. "Any problem with your partner?"

"Not at all," he answered, turning to wink. "I'm afraid he didn't get any rest, though."

"Miss Katherinessen, you're a very bad man."

"I know," he answered. "Isn't it grand?"

Lesa caught Kusanagi-Jones's attention and he fell into step as they slipped through the crowd milling by the door. Two security agents—Shafaqat and someone new—joined them as they entered the hall, and waited with Lesa during a brief pause outside a lavatory. When the males rejoined her, they both looked ineffably fresher. Lesa resisted a brief pang of jealousy.

The wardrobes were indeed nice technology, but who would want to pay the price?

The sun barely crested the rooftops as they reached the square. Three more security agents joined them as they stepped outside, and Lesa noticed that not only did Vincent know how to move with them—close as a shadow, his body always partially obscured by theirs—but that Kusanagi-Jones fell into the pattern as flawlessly as a stone into a ring, covering both Katherinessen and Lesa herself. The crowd parted to let them pass, and to Lesa's trained eye, Vincent's unease at the situation lay open. He concealed it from everyone else, smiling and waving graciously, shaking whatever hand was offered, while Kusanagi-Jones exhibited a grim stoicism that probably masked painful worry.

Lesa guessed that on Old Earth, an emissary would never be suffered to come in such close contact with crowds. If the mind of the mob were to decide it wanted Vincent Katherinessen dead, he would be, though the cost in New Amazonian life might be stunning. But the New Amazonian system was based on personal contact, kinship and friendship systems, alliances and bargains hammered out during drawn-out suppers.

The populace wouldn't tolerate any deal they felt was made in secrecy. And if Pretoria house was going to succeed, especially with the added complication of something as unpopular as Parity in the soup, Lesa needed the people comfortable with, even fond of, Katherinessen. He'd have to take the risk, even in the wake of the attempted abduction.

They climbed the stairs to the stage and took their seats. House had provided several rows of chairs for the occasion, along with a canopy to offer shade and some protection from the inevitable afternoon squall, if proceedings lasted that long.

Except for Shafaqat, security fell away as they climbed. The rest of the detail lingered near the foot of the stage or mingled with the crowd. And Lesa, drawing a deep breath, looked down at her hands and composed herself as Claude Singapore and Maiju Montevideo, Saide Austin, Antonia Kyoto, Nkechi Ouagadougou, and four pairs of artists and dignitaries chosen to represent other settlements passed through the crowd in their own ring of security, pausing to exchange small talk and shake hands with those who came forward. "When they come up," Lesa said, in case her charges didn't know, "you'll rise and shake hands with them."

"Of course," Kusanagi-Jones said, the left-hand corner of his mouth twisting up. "What else'd we do?"

"You could always break somebody's neck," Lesa answered. "Do you take recommendations?"

Kusanagi-Jones turned to check before he was certain she was smiling at him. It was a small, tight smile, such that he wondered at the subtext, but a secondary peek at Vincent yielded no further information.

He sighed and ran his fingertips across his wrist, activating the sensors in his watch. "Not more chemistry," Vincent said.

"Just dialing my wardrobe down," he said. "Hate to zap the minister of produce."

"Do they have a minister of produce?" Vincent asked, between unmoving lips. Their eyes caught, and Vincent smiled, just with the corner of his eyes.

Michelangelo looked down quickly, disguising the sudden, tight pain in his chest. There had to be a way.

There *had* to be a way. There was a way out of every-thing.

It was just a matter of finding it, and then having the guts to grab it and the strength to hang on. And stand-ing ready to pay the cost. Kusanagi-Jones's choice was a little too clear cut. He could be loyal, desert Free Earth, and keep Vincent—maybe. If they could pull this off. If he could bring home the brane technology—far more critical to their reception on Earth than any alliance with New Amazonia—it might be enough to buy him Vincent. All it meant was abandoning the ideal of free-dom from the Governors that he'd been working toward for thirty years.

He even saw an angle that might work. All he had to do was convince Kii to give it to him as the price of keeping the Coalition out of New Amazonia. Destroying the Consent wouldn't work. He didn't think the virtual space they inhabited was housed in the Kali system. Or even in the local universe.

If it were him, and he had the technology to ma-nipulate branes, to build himself a pocket universe of his desire, he'd build one where the cosmological rules encouraged a stable existence, or maybe lock it to an event horizon. What was the point of Tran-scending to virtual immortality if it just meant you still had to die when entropy collected its in-evitable toll?

After long consideration of the night's odd conver-sation, Kusanagi-Jones even thought he understood the theory. The technology was another issue, of course—but based on what Kii had said, that suggestive word *cosmocline,* and a technology apparently based on ma-nipulation of quantum probability and superstrings, Kusanagi-Jones could make an educated layman's guess at what was going on.

The mysterious energy might be generated *between* universes, in a manner analogous to a thermocline. Some quality—the cosmological constant, gravity, something even more basic—varied along the cosmocline, to use Kii's word. And that variation produced a gradient, which produced potential energy, which could be converted into *useful* energy. They could stick the far end of a wormhole into the general vicinity of a star, even, he supposed, though he wouldn't vouch for the integrity of the star afterward.

This was a species that could grab hold of a superstring and open up a wormhole to another universe as if tugging aside a drape. Kii's promise to obliterate the Coalition stem and branch if it threatened Kii's pets was not idle posturing.

It was just Kusanagi-Jones's fortune that the Dragon was ethical and preferred to avoid atrocity. When convenient. And that he was constrained by the programmed equivalent of a neurochemical tether; he was physically (if that was the right word for a Transcended intelligence) incapable of acting against his species' interests.

Leaving Kusangi-Jones the choice of siding with Vincent, and leaving most of his species under the threat of Assessment and the Cabinet's less-than-generous governance—or of lying to Vincent, and protecting New Amazonia from the Coalition and the Coalition from the Dragons, and losing Vincent for good.

He could always *tell* Vincent. But the questions would inevitably lead to New Earth, and the death of the *Skidbladnir*.

Not that it mattered. The choice wasn't a choice. It was just torture, and part of the pain was knowing how it would end.

"I need an Advocate," Kusanagi-Jones muttered, as Saide Austin paused at the bottom of the steps to shake three more hands and then, adjusting her heavy rings, her robes swaying around her sandal-corded ankles, ascended majestically.

"After lunch," Vincent answered, with a curious glance.

Kusanagi-Jones nodded. The stage had the same curious resilience as the pavement; it felt almost buoyant under his boots as he retraced his steps and reached out to assist Elder Austin up the last stair.

Her hands matched her girth and her shoulders, wide fingered and strong. Her rings pinched him as he hauled her up, and when he pulled back his hand there was a line of blood in the crease of his finger.

She stepped closer, concerned, when he raised the hand to examine. "Did I hurt you?"

"Nothing serious," he said. His docs were already sealing the wound and a reflexive check for contaminants showed nothing; his watch lights blinked green and serene under the skin. One thing about intelligence work in the diplomatic corps: they paid for the best. "It won't bother me long." And as she smiled, chagrined, and turned aside to take Vincent's hand, he reached out to greet Elder Kyoto.

This time he waited until she reached the top of the stair.

Like the hoary joke about the flat-Earther arguing with the geologist, it was speeches, speeches, speeches all the way down. Vincent had spent three months on *Kaiwo Maru*, which Michelangelo slept away in cryo, studying the sparse information they had on New

Amazonia—fragments sourced from long-term agents on the ground, like Michelangelo's contact, Miss Ougadougou—and reinforcing chipped and hypnagogic language lessons with live study, for which there was no effective replacement. New Amazonia's patois was as unique as Ur's. And Vincent didn't have the easy, playful facility with languages that Angelo went to such lengths to conceal.

But it had given him an opportunity to work on his own speech. On a Coalition world, he'd have been confident that most people would hear nothing but a few carefully selected sound bites, if the adaptive algorithms in their watches let that much get through the filters. An infotainment system that could determine when the user was bored or not paying attention—and later, efficiently filter out similarly boring content—was handy. But sometimes limiting.

New Amazonia was different. As on Ur, politics was the subject of a good deal of social and personal focus, and the repatriation ceremony would hold the planet's eyes.

Vincent waited and listened while Claude Singapore welcomed him and Michelangelo and their precious cargo to Penthesilea. Her own speech had been surprisingly short and to the point, and when she turned to introduce him, he paused a moment to admire her grasp of rhetoric before rising and stepping out of the shade of the canopy.

He barely resisted the urge to adjust his chemistry as he stepped up to the lectern, Michelangelo at his side as faithful and silent as any politician's wife. Sunlight pushed his shoulders down. Like the rest of the speakers, he wasn't wearing a hat, and the heat seeping through his wardrobe scorched and prickled burned shoulders. He touched the pad on the lectern and said "active" to key the public address system to his voice. He lifted his eyebrows at Michelangelo; all he needed to do. Angelo knew. Vincent's focus would be on reading and working the crowd from here on in, shaping their energy and giving it back to them, flavored with what he wanted them to think. Judgment, safety, discretion—those had just become Michelangelo's job.

Vincent took a breath, squared his shoulders, and drew the crowd's energy around him like a veil.

Audiences were like perfume. Every one a little bit different, but with practice, you could identify the notes. He read this group as expectant, curious, unfriendly. Neither Vincent Katherinessen nor the Coalition was welcome here.

Giving Vincent a mere cable bridge to balance. Because he didn't care to rehabilitate the Coalition in their eyes. But *Vincent* needed to retain their respect.

And he wasn't about to address the *citizens*.

"People of New Amazonia," he began, raising his voice and pitching it so the audio motes would recognize it and amplify it across the crowd. "I stand before you today in hope—"

It was as far as he got. Michelangelo shouted *"Shooter!"* and Vincent, as he was conditioned to do, went limp.

The next sensation should have been a blow, the impact of Angelo's body taking him down, covering him.

But it didn't happen quite that way.

Certain things happened when Michelangelo saw the gun come up, and all of them happened fast enough that if later asked, he would have been unable to provide their sequence. He registered the weapon before it was sighted in, shouted a warning, pointed, and dove for Claude Singapore. A split-second judgment, based on the realization that the weapon was tending toward her, that Vincent's wardrobe would afford him protection, and that Vincent had partial cover behind the lectern.

Shafaqat Delhi was half a step behind him, and she landed atop Vincent, who had recovered from his surprise enough to dive with her to the floor of the stage and land facedown, arms around his head. Michelangelo lost sight of him then; he felt the shock and smelled the *snap* of ozone as something struck his wardrobe and he struck Elder Singapore.

A second gunshot cracked, louder and longer—two fired at once?—and Michelangelo's skin jumped away from transmitted pressure as his wardrobe caught that one, too. Shouting echoed around the square: more gunfire, now. Not surprising, when most of the crowd was armed, but it seemed fairly restrained, and no more bullets were arching over the stage.

And the prime minister was shoving at his chest and cursing him as his wardrobe snapped painful sparks at her. "Stay down," he hissed. He slapped the cutoff on his watch so it wouldn't electrocute her, and caught her hand as she was reaching for her weapon. "Let security handle it."

By the time he dared to lift his head and let her lift hers, they had. Elder Singapore shoved him away violently and sat. "You'll hear about that," she snapped.

He permitted it only because they were behind a screen of security agents, and—to be honest—he wanted to get to Vincent, who was making much less fuss about an equally rough takedown.

Two bullets hung beside Kusanagi-Jones, trapped in the aura of his wardrobe like hovering bees. He dialed a glove and plucked them out of the fog.

Shafaqat already had a transparent baggie ready, and she took the bullets—pristine, despite having been stopped by the antishock features of the wardrobe fog—and made them vanish without so much as catching Kusanagi-Jones's eye. He could get to like that woman.

"Vincent." He crouched as Vincent pushed to his knees.

"Unharmed," Vincent answered, despite the evidence of a scratch across his cheek and a bloody nose. "Good work."

Kusanagi-Jones smiled in spite of himself, standing. People in the square were shouting, shoving. Something shattered against the stage, and Vincent ducked reflexively. "All I did was yell. Local security swarmed the shooters. Let's get you off the stage, Vincent. They're not pleased about the security—"

"Hell, no," Vincent answered, wincing again—this time, Kusanagi-Jones thought, from the pain of moving in his own stiff, burned skin. His hand, fever-warm, slid into Kusanagi-Jones's, and he levered himself up. "I have a speech to give."

Kusanagi-Jones, watching Vincent shove ineffectually at his braids and mop blood onto his hand as something else was hurled and broke, bit his own lip hard to stop his eyes from stinging.

Because now he knew what he was going to do.

15

IT WAS FORTUNATE THAT VINCENT HAD PRACTICED HIS speech until it was as automatic to his recall as his system number, because later, he couldn't remember having recited a word of it. He knew he extemporized the introduction, and if it hadn't been recorded he never would have known what he said. He must have made quite an impression with the blood caking his face and the split lip, clinging to the edges of the lectern like a drunk in an effort to keep the weight off his knee. His wardrobe provided a brace, but that hadn't helped absorb the impact when he went down.

At first, the crowd had been restive, muttering, rustling like a colony of insects with passed whispers. More security agents arrived while Vincent was speaking, filtering through the audience, but they didn't reassure him as much as Michelangelo's silent warmth at his elbow. Or the way the crowd calmed as he spoke, subsiding like whitecaps after a passing storm.

When he stepped back from the lectern, he had silence. A long moment of it, respectful, considering. And then first snapping, scattered as the first kernels of corn popping, and then stamping feet and shouts—some approval, some approbation, he thought, but nothing else shattered on the stage.

He waved and nodded. Lesa was on his right side, also waving, and her left hand threaded through his arm as she tugged him back. Michelangelo was right there, too, covering Vincent with his body, as Saide Austin stepped forward.

"Like to see her match that," Angelo murmured.

"I did okay?"

Angelo touched him carelessly. "Real good."

"Good," Vincent said, aware that he sounded petulant, and not caring. He was seeing stars now—literally, sparkles in front of his eyes—as the adrenaline wore off. "My nose hurts."

"And your back?" Lesa asked.

"My back," he said, with tight dignity, "hurts more."

Vincent looked gray, the blood draining from his face as he sat stiffly upright on the chair, his leg stretched out before him to ease the knee. Kusanagi-Jones slipped his hand across the gap between chairs and took Vincent's, squeezing, hiding the action with their bodies. Vincent sighed and softened a little, his shoulders falling away from his neck, though he had the sense not to lean back. Shafaqat handed Vincent a wet towel while Elder Austin was still talking. He took it right-handed, and didn't release Kusanagi-Jones's hand with his left while he dabbed at the crusted blood on his lip. "At least my nose isn't broken."

Kusanagi-Jones widened his eyes and spoke in an undertone. "It's supposed to look like that?"

"The Christ, don't make me laugh." He winced, and then flinched, as if the act of wincing hurt.

Vincent handed the bloody cloth back to Shafaqat and glanced at his watch, and Kusanagi-Jones knew he was thinking about upping his chemistry and dismissing the idea. He was still idly checking readouts when Austin's speech came to an end, a study in deceptive inattention, but when he glanced up, his eyes were sparkling. They stood when everybody else did, herded by security agents, and filed down the steps and through the crowd again. Kusanagi-Jones covered Vincent as much as possible, varying distance and pace within the crowd, and for the first time was actively angry that all of the New Amazonian security was female and that Vincent was taller than any of them and all the New Amazonian dignitaries. And, of course, taller than Kusanagi-Jones. There was nothing to block a head shot, if there was another shooter somewhere in the crowd.

Which meant relying on the agents assigned to crowd coverage and Vincent's wardrobe to get them through safely. And Kusanagi-Jones thought that just possibly, he would rather have severed his own fingers with a pair of tin snips than made that endless, light-drenched walk. Though the crowd was calm, respectful, their attention oppressed Kusanagi-Jones like the weight of meters of water, cramping his breathing.

He managed a free breath when they stepped out of the square and into the cool shade of the gallery lobby. A brief bottleneck ensued as politicians pulled off shoes and hung them on the racks, but it wasn't as bad as it could have been. Only the dignitaries, security, chosen observers, and a small herd of media would travel past this point.

When he looked up, Kusanagi-Jones found himself on the periphery of a glance exchanged between Elder Kyoto and Vincent that Kusanagi-Jones would have needed all of Vincent's skill to interpret. Lesa caught it, too, and by her frown she understood it far better than Kusanagi-Jones—but she said nothing.

Now that he had a plan, the wait was nauseating. He knew how Vincent, having formulated his strategy, would be behaving in Kusanagi-Jones's shoes. He would already have assessed the possible ways in which the subject might react, and he'd have a contingency for each. He'd have alternates mapped and a decision tree in place to deal with them, with counterplans in the event of failure or unexpected consequences.

Kusanagi-Jones had only one idea, and it involved doing something he hadn't willingly done in his adult life. And he was basing it not on facts, probabilities, and meticulously calculated options, but on three entirely illogical factors.

The first of these was Kii. Kusanagi-Jones didn't know what to do about the Dragon's ultimatum. He was as torn as Hamlet; Kusanagi-Jones did not, in all impartiality, consider himself capable of making the demanded choice. He wasn't a decision maker. He would do anything possible to avoid being placed in that position of responsibility.

It was a strength in some ways. One of the things that made him an accomplished Advocate was his ability to argue both sides of a predicament to exhaustion. But he'd been able to rely first on Vincent to make the tough calls, and then, after Vincent, on the fact that he was limited by scandal to unimportant missions to pre-

vent it from becoming a weakness. It was Vincent's job
to decide, and Kusanagi-Jones's job to back Vincent up.

Except when he was betraying him over politics, but
that, while ironic, was orthogonal to the argument.

The second factor was Vincent himself. Kusanagi-
Jones couldn't face stepping away from him again.
He'd done it once, ignorant of the cost, as the price of
something he had thought more important than either
of them. He *still* thought it was more important. But
he wasn't sure he would live through it twice.

And yes, it would mean his life if Vincent reported
him. He had no illusions. Except, perhaps, for the
illusion that Vincent wouldn't do it. Vincent's loyalty
to the job had always been unimpeachable... but
Kusanagi-Jones was about to gamble that his loyalty to
the partnership would outweigh it.

In the final analysis—to dignify his gut belief
with an entirely unjustified word—he didn't believe
Vincent would kill him. Which led to the third factor.
Which was what Vincent had said to him in bed, regarding *Skidbladnir*, that had flexed Kusanagi-Jones's
shoulders and neck in a shivering paroxysm. But it was
possible—just—that Vincent had done it on purpose,
had chosen his moment and found a way of letting
Kusanagi-Jones know he suspected, without allowing
it to become an accusation or an admission of retroac-
tive complicity. More, it was possible that Vincent was
letting him know that Vincent was about something
equally dodgy himself, and wanted his help. It was a
daydream. Denial. Fantasy that didn't want to deal
with the reality of how compromised he truly was. But
like pearls seeded in oysters, great treasons from small
irritations grow.

He couldn't mount a better option. Michelangelo
Osiris Leary Kusanagi-Jones, Liar, was going to have to

tell someone the truth. And now that he'd decided, the wait was killing him.

As they broke into groups for the lifts, Kusanagi-Jones caught Vincent's eye and gave him the subtlest of smiles, nothing more than a crinkle of the corners of his eyes. Vincent returned it, careful of his bruises, and Kusanagi-Jones swallowed a forlorn sigh.

It was going to be a long, long day.

He repeated those words like a silent mantra all through Elder Singapore's and Elder Austin's second round of speeches, these taking place against the un-polished back of the black granite panel that blocked the view of the rest of the display from casual eyes, and continued it as Vincent stepped up to the focal point. He didn't need his mind engaged to run security. After fifty years, his reflexes and trained awareness did a better job of it if he kept his consciousness out of the way.

His thoughts still chased an endless, anxiety-producing spiral when Vincent joined Elder Austin and Miss Ouagadougou to lead the group around to the polished, graven side of the wall. Kusanagi-Jones in-sinuated himself at Vincent's side, and so he was one of the first around the corner to observe—

—an empty space in the middle of the gallery floor.

Phoenix Abased, all four and a half metric tons of her, was gone.

What followed was more or less predictable. Elder Kyoto took charge of the scene, and Vincent found Lesa hustling himself and Michelangelo to a car, pass-ing through a crowd of insistent media with very little pause for politeness. For a moment, Vincent thought one of them might reach for her weapon, but Lesa fixed the woman with a calm, humorless stare that seemed to persuade her of the better part of valor, and then slid into the backseat opposite Vincent and Angelo.

The door sealed and Lesa slumped. "Miss Katherinessen. You certainly know how to keep a party interesting."

"Surely you don't think I——" Vincent fell silent at the wave of her hand. A few minutes passed, silence interrupted only by the blaring of the groundcar's horn as it edged through streets jammed with Carnival revelers.

"You haven't the means," she said. "It had to be somebody with override priority on House."

"Override? . . ."

Her eyebrow rose. He fell silent. Sticky leather trapped the heat of his burned skin against his body, and he shifted uncomfortably. Angelo's regard pressed the side of his face like a hand. Angelo, of course, had been in that gallery until nearly dawn. But he hadn't said he'd seen anybody, in particular near *Phoenix Abased,* and Vincent hoped he wasn't thinking that Vincent was likely to hold him accountable for the theft.

"Override priority?" he asked again.

Lesa looked up from the cuticle she was worrying with her opposite nail. "House has three modes. It automatically adapts to any regular use to which it's put. This is how most of the architecture develops. It will also do small things—forming a fresher in an unused space or rearranging the furniture—for anybody who spends a fair amount of time in a particular spot, and provide other favors such as directions or a drinking fountain"—she tilted her head at Vincent—"for anyone, anywhere."

"And stealing a three-meter statue from a public venue?"

"There's the problem," she said. "We didn't build House. We just adapted it, learned how to program it."

"And adapted to it. You're saying there's no security feed from the gallery?"

"I'm saying that anybody who could take that statue out could tell House not to remember. We'll check the records—"

"Of course." He managed it without a glance at Angelo. He'd been cloaked when he entered. The chances he could be detected were slim. "Please do. That means it's somebody with clout."

"Somebody in Parliament, if it wasn't a ranking gallery administrator," Lesa corrected after a reluctant pause. "We don't let just anybody engage in urban re-newal."

"This isn't the way back to the residence unless we're going the long way," Kusanagi-Jones said a little while later.

"No," Lesa said. "I'm bringing you to Pretoria house. I know who has access to the priorities there."

"And security?"

They'd left the agents behind. Lesa seemed to understand the nuances of his question. "Shafaqat and Cathay are running a decoy operation," she said. "Asha will follow us. Pretoria house has its own security, of course—"

"Of course," Vincent interrupted, ever so dry. "And there's no evidence that *it* could be compromised."

"Not by a male," Lesa said.

Kusanagi-Jones raised an eyebrow at Vincent, who

rolled his eyes. "Angelo is probably finding your re-mark somewhat cryptic."

"One of our household males has taken advantage of the recent confusion to run away," Lesa said. "We are trying to recover him before it becomes public knowledge and we have to make an example of him when we catch him. Thank you very much for airing our dirty laundry, Miss Katherinessen."

"Anything you can tell me, Angelo can hear," Vincent said, which earned him another arch look from the Penthesilean. There was a subtext there that Kusanagi-Jones wasn't catching, and for a moment, he understood what it must be like for others, on the out-side of his rapport with Vincent.

"The male," Kusanagi-Jones hazarded, his hands folded between his knees. "Robert, was it?"

Lesa, looking out the window, nodded.

Kusanagi-Jones frowned. "Your secret is safe with me."

He half expected to be installed in the harem, or whatever they called it, but he and Vincent were given a small, comfortable room with a balcony that opened onto Pretoria house's inner court and left alone to com-pose or, Kusanagi-Jones thought, incriminate them-selves.

A young male servant who was familiar from the previous night's dinner brought them warm sand-wiches of scrambled, spiced vegetable protein and mixed greens, the bread made from some unfamiliar grain, and bottles—not bubbles—of a carbonated drink with a pleasing bitter aftertaste reminiscent of chocolate. They sat cross-legged on the bed, the tray balanced on the covers between them, and picked at the food.

Neither one of them was hungry, but they were

both determined to eat, which made the meal an extended comedy of dragging silences and lengthy chewing, interrupted by occasional distant cracks of thunder and the sound of music and shouting drifting from nearby streets. Nothing as minor as the attempted assassination of a head of state would put a cramp in Carnival.

Kusanagi-Jones finished first and waited while Vincent picked bits out of his sandwich and poured drink into his glass one mouthful at a time. He waited poorly, bending his fingernails against the edge of the tray and wishing Vincent would break the silence with a conversational offer.

But Vincent seemed preoccupied, withdrawn. "All right?" Kusanagi-Jones said finally, and then bit the inside of his cheek in frustration.

"Yes," Vincent said, prodding his nose delicately with the tip of his finger. "Sore, exhausted, and full of released toxins, but I've been worse. Something's preying on you."

And if he was presenting strongly enough that Vincent could tell, Kusanagi-Jones was doing even worse than he'd thought.

"Need to talk," he said. And then, unable to bear the close intimacy of the two of them leaning together over their food, he swung his legs off the low New Amazonian bed and levered himself to his feet. The carpetplant dimpled under his soles. He strolled to the archway leading to the balcony and paused inside the air curtain, currents stirring the fine hairs on his arms.

The first fat drops of a tropical downpour splashed the green-blue translucence of the balcony as the ceiling inside paled to simulate the storming sky. As the light outside dimmed, that within seemed to brighten in comparison, so when Kusanagi-Jones glanced over his shoulder he was caught by the luster of rust-colored highlights on Vincent's hair.

He looked down, folded his arms to hide the way his hands were shaking—again—and stepped through the air curtain and out into the rain as if stepping through a spun glass drapery.

His wardrobe shunted it away, creating a shimmering outline centimeters from his skin. He pulled his folded arms apart and ran fingertips over his watch, opening the utility fog.

The water was warm. Blood-warm, warmer than his skin, corpulent drops hitting hard enough to sting. He closed his eyes and tilted his face back, letting the rain wash him. It passed through his wardrobe without dampening the simulated cloth or affecting the hang of the outfit, soaking him, sluicing down his chest and thighs, saturating his hair.

He heard Vincent's footsteps and saw his shadow cross the fisheye before Vincent spoke. "Do you suppose it's safe?"

"Safer than the sunlight."

"There could be pollution. Parasites."

"Could be," Kusanagi-Jones said. Even when he dropped his chin to speak, water splashed into his mouth. It tasted strange, not neutral but crackling with ozone, faintly salty, sweet. From below, Kusanagi-Jones heard voices, a woman's and those of children, and the slap of bare footsteps running on wet pavement. He turned his right hand up to let the rain wash across the sealed nick on his palm. "Don't seem too worried."

Water pattered on Vincent's hair and shoulders as he came outside. He paused at Kusanagi-Jones's shoulder, and Kusanagi-Jones leaned back slightly, so their wardrobes meshed. The coded channel was carried on a single-photon beam—an unimpeachable transmission. But it didn't hurt to shorten the hop. "Vincent—"

Vincent's hand on his shoulder almost made him jump out of his wardrobe. "If you're about to tell me that you're seizing command of the mission, Angelo, I don't blame you. But I will put up a fight. Can't we come to an accommodation?"

Kusanagi-Jones stopped hard, with his jaw hanging open. He put one hand out, found the balustrade, and used it to pivot himself where he stood. "Beg pardon?"

To see Vincent staring at him, similarly gape-mouthed and blinking rapidly against the rain that dripped from his lashes. "I thought—" He stepped away, let his hand fall, and tilted his head back. "The Christ. I thought you'd made me."

"As a double," Kusanagi-Jones said, understanding, but needing the confirmation.

Vincent snorted, shaking his head, water scattering from short, randomly pointed braids. He rocked back and slumped against the wall beside the doorway. "Well, now you know. It's a good thing *I* don't claim to be a Liar."

"Who?"

"You know I can't tell you that—"

"Vincent. I won't hand you over. Or your connections."

"I still can't tell you."

"What organization?"

The smile was tight, Vincent's hands curled into fists beside his thighs. He didn't look down. Kusanagi-Jones hadn't thought he would. "One that doesn't have a name."

Kusanagi-Jones shouldn't have been riding a rush of relief and joy; emotion made you stupid. But it welled up anyway. He reached out and took Vincent's arm, the dry wardrobe sliding over wet skin beneath. "Know what I'm thinking?"

"Do I ever? It's part of your charm—"

Michelangelo took a breath and let the words go with it when he let it out. "I threw the mission on New Earth."

"The *Skidbladnir* suffered a core excursion," Vincent said. "You couldn't have had . . ." And then his voice trailed off. He tugged away from Kusanagi-Jones's hand, but not hard, and Kusanagi-Jones held on to him. "Angelo."

"I'm Free Earth," he said. "Have been for decades. I killed *Skidbladnir*, Vincent, and everybody on her."

"To keep New Earth out of the Coalition."

"To give them a fighting chance."

Vincent licked his lips and looked down, jaw working. Kusanagi-Jones imagined he was toting up the dead—the ship's crew, marines, civilians. He started to pull his hand back and Vincent caught it, squeezed, held. "Do you mean to do it again?"

"Here?"

"Yes."

"If I have to."

"Good," Vincent said. "Me, too. We need a plan."

If there was any tap on the door to the hall, neither one of them heard it over the sound of the rain, but Kusanagi-Jones could hardly have missed it irising open. He pressed Vincent's arm before stepping around him, turning him. Then he walked under the dripping door frame before pausing to shake the water off his hair. A shower of droplets bent the leaves of the carpetplant until his wardrobe took care of the rest, wicking moisture away so his clothes seemed to steam. "Come in," he said to the young woman who waited outside in simple off-white clothing with a Pretoria household badge embroidered on the breast.

She carried a slip of some sort in her hand, and was on the hesitant cusp of offering it to Vincent, who came through the door a moment after Kusanagi-Jones and held out his hand, when she glanced at Kusanagi-Jones for permission. *Odd*, he thought, and nodded, but not before he said "Wardrobe," to Vincent.

He didn't want him actually *touching* that thing.

The faint sparkle around Vincent's fingertips when they touched the slip said Vincent had anticipated him. "Thank you," Vincent said to the young woman. She nodded and stepped back, the door spiraling shut before her. Vincent glanced down, the slip dimpling lightly between fingers that didn't quite contact its surface. "It's for you."

"Who from?"

"It doesn't say." Vincent generated a thin blade and slid it into the slip, along a seam Kusanagi-Jones couldn't see. A slight tearing sound followed, and then he tapped and inverted it, sliding out a second, matching slip. Vincent turned it in his hand and frowned at the black, ornate lettering.

"Another party invitation?" Kusanagi-Jones asked, letting his mouth twist around the words.

"No," Vincent said, raising a thin sheet of old-fashioned card stock, wood pulp unless Kusanagi-Jones missed his guess. "You seem to have been challenged to a duel."

16

KATHERINESSEN APPEARED AT LESA'S DOOR IN THE COM-
pany of Agnes, who had been working in a study near
the on-loan bedroom, and wordlessly presented her
with a challenge card inscribed in Claude Singapore's
writing. Once she read it, he told her, minimally, that
Kusanagi-Jones wasn't any more loyal to the Coalition
than he was, and that it was his considered opinion
that they should bring him in.

She sent Agnes back upstairs to fetch Kusanagi-
Jones while Katherinessen appropriated the cushions
by her work surface. Kusanagi-Jones appeared and stationed himself against the wall on the opposite side
of the room, arms and ankles folded, still enough to
go forgotten. Except for the slip of paper that
Katherinessen had laid on her desk for examination,
but would not permit her to touch.

Legally speaking, Kusanagi-Jones *couldn't* fight.
Gentle or not, foreign or not, he was a male, and men

didn't duel. As she had expected, Katherinessen waited until she finished explaining and asked, "Then what's the point in issuing a challenge?"

"He cost her face," Lesa said. "Bad enough she's in a delicate political situation for pandering to the Coalition—"

"Cost her *face*?" Katherinessen leaned forward, disbelieving. "He saved her life."

"That *is* costing her face." Lesa pressed palms flat on either side of the indicted card, and wrinkled her nose at it. "You laid hands on her, which is illegal and a personal affront. If you were a stud male, it would go to Tribunal. Because you're a gentle male, if an arraignment found no intent to harm, she could still challenge, and the women in your household would have the option of meeting it."

"She can't take him to trial," Katherinessen said. "He has diplomatic immunity."

Kusanagi-Jones broke his silence without looking up. "Which is why she went straight to the challenge."

"Precisely." Lesa stood, turning her back on that cream-colored card, and traced a hand along House's interior curves as she walked away from the desk. "Do you want a drink?"

"Please," Kusanagi-Jones said with fervor.

Lesa turned, surprised, and pointed at Katherinessen. He nodded and held up two fingers.

Ice rattled into glasses. She dropped it from higher than necessary, for the satisfying thump. "It isn't personal."

Katherinessen frowned at his thumbnails while Lesa filled the glasses and waited, curling her toes into the carpetplant, waiting to see what he would logic out. He looked up and stood to take two glasses from her and pass one to Kusanagi-Jones. "We...I...walked out of that assassination attempt with a PR advantage. She needs to nullify that."

"Theft had to be a blow," Kusanagi-Jones added.

"Yes." Lesa tested her drink. Too much ice. "And she can't be seen to be beholden to the Coalition. And now it seems that you are willing to go to some risk to protect her."

"She needs to shift the apparent relationship back to a more adversarial footing, or lose support. But why a challenge, when Angelo hasn't got—"

"A woman to fight for him?" Kusanagi-Jones said, rattling the ice in his glass. "You can say it."

Lesa snorted. She came around the desk, easing the formality of the situation, and perched one hip on it, though the position made her holster pinch. "If he were Penthesilean, and no one in his house would stand up for him, Claude could take him in service."

"Good way to get rid of unwanted houseguests."

Katherinessen frowned over his shoulder. "But he's not."

"No. So if he can't field a champion, he loses face as a...debtor who doesn't meet his obligations. Claude looks tough on the Coalition and the two of you are sent home in disgrace, your viability as negotiators devastated. If I were a conspiracy theorist, I'd half-bet she set up the assassination herself; it couldn't better suit her needs. How long would it take the Coalition to scrape up another team?"

"Of 'gentle' males? How long do you think? So it's a stalling tactic."

"Precisely." Lesa slammed the rest of her drink back and dropped the glass on the edge of the desk.

"But if she wants the rest of the art repatriated—"

"Look." Lesa wiped her mouth with the back of her

hand. "She'll leap on the opportunity to keep Coalition agents off New Amazonian soil; she never wanted you here in the first place, whatever face she gave the Coalition. So she splits the difference, if I know Claude. She stalls and bribes and cajoles and commits diplomacy by packet bot rather than facing an immediate threat. And moreover, making you look uncivilized reflects on public opinion regarding the Coalition."

"Charming. We're deadbeats. We're going to be very popular with the Coalition Cabinet when we get home."

"If you can't, as I said, field a champion."

"Well, I can't fight for him——" Katherinessen blinked. He sipped his drink thoughtfully and stared at the glass after he lowered it from his mouth. "You can't be serious."

"You could ask."

The stretch of that silence gratified. "You'd shoot Claude Singapore for me," Kusanagi-Jones said after several ticks.

She grinned. "I'd shoot Claude Singapore on general principles. Actually, it's perfect. We use her attempt to discredit you to discredit or kill her. Much more efficient than a vote of no confidence."

Katherinessen rubbed his fingers together, unconvinced. "And if she kills you?"

She wondered if he knew just how unlikely that was. From the worried press of his lips, she didn't think so. "Deal with my mother and Elder Kyoto, then. And get Julian off-planet."

"Your son."

"He deserves better than I can get him here. He's a very smart boy." She paused, looked down, and swept her hand across the surface of her desk. "Take him to Ur. That's my price."

She hadn't expected Katherinessen to pause and turn, and give that slow, considering look to Kusanagi-Jones. Whatever Kusanagi-Jones's expression disclosed in return, Lesa couldn't read it, but it seemed to satisfy Katherinessen.

"All right," he said, when he looked back. "I'll try."

Which was the best he could honestly offer. She waited a beat, to see if anything else was forthcoming, and nodded twice. "At least if I win, it saves us staging a coup."

"Sure," Katherinessen replied. "All we have to do is fix an election. And provoke a revolution."

Lesa smiled, nudging the still-cold glass farther from the edge of the desk with the backs of her fingers. "Or two."

Kusanagi-Jones buried his face in his glass and breathed deeply, letting eye-stinging fumes chase his muddle-headedness away. "How did you two make contact?" he said to Vincent.

"New Amazonia turns out to be a hotbed of political unrest." Vincent scratched the back of his neck, wincing. Kusanagi-Jones had to lace both hands around the glass in front of his groin to keep from reaching to stop Vincent's hand as he said, "Who'd guess? But Lesa hasn't told you the best part."

Kusanagi-Jones lifted his chin. "Suspense is killing me."

"As I mentioned in the car, Robert's vanished. The bad news is, he was the primary contact between Vincent and myself. Unfortunately, he was also working for Elder Kyoto, who, we learned last night, is secretly involved in a radical male-rights movement called Parity."

"Who wants in on the conspiracy."

"She's in," Vincent replied. Kusanagi-Jones gave him the dirtiest look he could manage, and Vincent met it bold-faced.

"Nice private little junta you've whipped up."

"It's what you call an arrangement of convenience," Vincent said. "The bad news is, Robert is missing—"

"And Robert knows about all three of you."

"And my mother," Lesa said. "Who is not, however, aware that we're hoping to rearrange New Amazonia's social order quite as much as we are."

"And it's safe to talk about this in her house?"

Lesa smiled. "My security priorities are higher than hers."

Vincent straightened, moving stiffly. "Ur's prepared to go to war, if necessary. This doesn't have to stay secret long."

Kusanagi-Jones shook his head. He suspected that if he were even remotely psychologically normal, he *should* have been feeling worry, even panic. But it was excitement that gripped him, finally, the narrow color-brightening focus of a *purpose*. "I've hopped a cresting wave."

Vincent smiled. "Something like that. We're committing treason against two governments; everybody with a grudge can ride. Do you think your Free Earth contacts can help?"

"Depends what the plan is."

"What was yours?"

"Sabotage. Prevent Earth from getting its hands on the technology by any means necessary. Very straightforward. Easy enough for a lone operative to accomplish."

Lesa looked up. "What made you go to Vincent, then?"

"Vincent knows. He's satisfied." Well, he knew the hasty outline at least, Kusanagi-Jones having filled him in quickly about Kii's ultimatum before they decided to bring the challenge to Miss Pretoria's attention. Hadn't been time for details.

"Anyway," Kusanagi-Jones continued, when Lesa had been staring at him for a little longer than was comfortable. "How many factions *are* there in the New Amazonian government?"

"That I'm aware of?" She shrugged, too. "For current players, we have to count all of us, Parity, whoever Robert is working for, the isolationists, the appeasement faction, and the separatists, who want the males—*all* the males—off New Amazonia. And whoever it was who tried to kidnap Vincent, whoever attempted to assassinate Claude—"

"Though there may be overlap." Vincent made a face. "Do we at least have a DNA type on that woman you wounded yesterday?"

"Take at least a week," she said, and Kusanagi-Jones wasn't sure if he or Vincent looked more startled. "Backwater colony, remember? As you were so eager to point out to us just the other night. Besides, genetic research is a very touchy subject here."

A pained silence followed. Vincent cleared his throat. "Anyway, our plan was a little more complex."

"It always is." But Kusanagi-Jones lifted his glass to his lips and drank, politely attentive. "You had said something about fomenting revolution."

"Revolution here. Eventually," Lesa said.

"If you're busy fighting a civil war—"

"*After* we bring our support to a rebellion on Coalition-controlled worlds. That means replacing the government, but we do that every three years anyway, and if we make Claude look bad enough, when we call for a vote of no confidence we'll get it. The Coalition's advances come in handy, actually. There's nothing like an external enemy to unify political opponents." She smiled. "You can even send home reports that you're working to weaken Claude's administration, and be telling the truth."

Kusanagi-Jones rubbed the side of his nose. "The other issue. Robert."

Lesa nodded, biting her lip.

"He knows all this?"

"We'll bring him in. Don't worry. If he'd gone to Claude, I'd be in custody, and she wouldn't be trying to discredit you."

Kusanagi-Jones snorted. "Unless she's waiting to see who else we implicate. You suppose diplomatic immunity will keep Singapore's people from shooting us as spies?"

"Depends," Vincent said, "on how badly they want a war."

Later, after a more in-depth discussion of the details of alliance with Lesa, Vincent paced the bedroom while Angelo curled, catnapping, on the bed. Angelo was breathing in that low, gulping fashion that meant nightmares, but Vincent set his jaw and didn't wake him. He needed the sleep too much, no matter how poor its quality.

And Vincent needed the time to think.

Axiomatically, there came a point in any secret action where the plan failed and the operative was left to improvise. And when that happened, the best option was a *lot* of options. He wasn't about to close off any doors until he had to—with Lesa, or with Kyoto.

Or with Michelangelo.

Angelo's second report on Kii had been more detailed, including not just the ultimatum, but some of Angelo's conjectures as to what "Consent" might be. Enough to set Vincent's fingers twitching. Angelo's revelations about the city's resident—Transcendent—Dragon were the most interesting development, especially when combined with the unforeseen complication of having taken refuge in Pretoria house.

While their temporary accommodation was restful, with the storm passed and the walls revealing a panoramic view of expanses of jungle canopy, seen from above, it was also inconveniently far from the gallery. And the interface room Michelangelo had discovered there.

And Angelo thought Vincent should talk to Kii.

Vincent was disinclined to argue. What an intoxicating idea: an alien—a *real* alien. A creature of mythic resonance.

Intoxicating, and terrifying. Vincent wasn't remotely qualified to handle this. And there was the practical problem of how to get there without telling Lesa about the Dragon in her basement, since Angelo seemed to think she didn't already know. He paced slowly, trying to make the space he had to walk in seem longer, and became aware that Angelo had awakened only when he spoke.

"Should ask to examine the crime scene in the morning." He sat up as Vincent turned to him, leveling his breathing. He didn't look any more rested.

"Dreams?" Vincent asked. Angelo dismissed the question with one of his sideways gestures, as if deflecting a blow, but Vincent leaned forward and gave him the eye-brow.

"*Skidbladnir*, if you must know." Angelo turned away, not bothering to hide the lie. "Can we be transferred back to our original rooms tonight? For convenience' sake?"

"Once you've accepted Elder Singapore's challenge."

"Once Miss Pretoria has accepted it for me," he replied, leaning back on his elbows. "How's your back?"

"It hurts," Vincent said. "But improving. I think the docs are getting some purchase on it." He used their private channel to continue. "You don't suppose your new friend is limited to appearing *there*, do you?"

"Pretty silly if he were."

"So he probably knows what happened to the statue."

Angelo was out of bed before Vincent realized he was standing. "He probably knows all sorts of things. The question is, if he's ethical, will he *share* them?"

Volley and return. Sometimes surprising things came up that way. Vincent batted it back. "How do you suppose his ethics stack up to ours? Do you think they have anything in common?"

Angelo paused, scuffing one foot across the carpet-plant. "He'll avoid the unnecessary destruction of sentient organisms. Or, *esthelich*, his word. Get the feeling it's not exactly what we'd call sentient."

"Right. And he likes pets."

The look Angelo gave Vincent could have fused his wardrobe. "Ironic, isn't it?"

"Quite."

"So what do we do?"

Vincent rocked on his heels, folding his arms. "We ask?"

"Here?"

"Why not? It's not as if anyplace in this city is free of surveillance, and we have to assume Kii has some control of House, if he's observing the citizens—"

"—denizens. Think he's as concerned for the khir as he is for the Penthesileans."

"Granted." Vincent bit his lower lip and frowned at Angelo until Angelo licked his lips and looked down.

And then he dropped channel and said aloud, "House, Vincent and I would like to speak to Kii, please. Privately."

For a moment nothing happened. Then the rippling leaves of the rain forest canopy fluttered faster, sliding together like chips of mica swirled in a flask, layering, interweaving, a teal-colored stain creeping through the gathered mass until it smoothed, scaled, feathered, and blinked great yellow eyes at them. "This chamber is private," the hologram said. "Greetings, Vincent Katherinessen. You speak to Kii."

Angelo's description hadn't prepared Vincent for the reality of Kii. That serpentine shape emerging from camouflaging jungle triggered atavistic responses, an adrenaline spike for which his watch barely compensated. He took one unwilling step back anyway, shivering, and forced himself to pretend calm. "Kii," he said, as soon as he could trust his voice. "I'm very pleased to meet you."

And then he bowed, formally, as he would have on Old Earth, rather than taking a stranger's hand. Kii seemed to bow as well, its head dropping on its long neck as it took advantage of apparent depth of field to slither a meter or two "closer."

"You oppose your government's agenda for this population?"

Vincent swallowed. Angelo stood at his shoulder, silently encouraging, and it was all Vincent could do not to glance at him for support. But he didn't care to take his eyes off Kii. The Dragon's direct, forward gaze was intent as any predator's, and meeting it made Vincent very aware that he was small and—mostly—quite soft-fleshed.

"We wish to assist you in protecting New Amazonia from Coalition control. We wish to preserve that population as well."

"But not its Consent."

"No," Vincent answered. "Not its Consent. Its... Consent is not the will of the governed."

Kii hissed, just the breathy rush of air from its jaw, without any vocal vibration. It wasn't actually *talking*, Vincent realized. He was hearing sounds, but they didn't match any vocalizations the Dragon made. "You are very strange bipeds," it said. "The Consent is that Kii shall not aid you."

It was not, Vincent told himself, unexpected. He closed his eyes for a moment, though it was an effort breaking Kii's regard. "So you deliver your ultimatum, and leave us to it?"

"It is the Consent," Kii said, unperturbed. "It is Consented that Kii may observe and speak with you, and continue Kii's attempts to help your local population adapt. And protect them and the khir, as necessary."

Vincent sank down on his haunches, tilting his head back, up at the looming Dragon. It was comforting to make himself smaller. "Kii, can you use your...wormhole technology to connect points in the local universe?"

"Spatial travel? No. Only parallel branes," Kii said. "The wormholes must lie along a geodesic, and they must transect, or be perpendicular, *orthogonal* to the originating, no, the initiating brane. It is not the Consent to provide technology."

"So you didn't just plunk one down beside your sun for power," Angelo said, resting one hand on Vincent's shoulder, his knees a few inches from Vincent's tender back. Kii's nictitating membranes slid closed and open once more.

"We couldn't give it to them anyway, even if Kii would provide it," Vincent said, craning his neck to get a look at Michelangelo's face. "Maybe a power feed. Not the generator technology. It's not an option under any circumstances."

Angelo scratched the side of his nose, staring down at Vincent as if it were an everyday occurrence for Kii's holographic head to hover over both of them while they argued. "If they can't use it for travel, or as a weapon within this universe, tell me why."

"Gravity," Vincent answered. He licked his lips and tilted his head back again, addressing Kii directly. "Just because you can't make a wormhole open under your enemy's feet doesn't mean you can't use this as a weapon. Kii, correct me if I'm wrong, but do your manipulations of branes cause tidal effects?"

"We amend for them," it said. "But you are correct. There is gravitational pollution. Some we harvest as an additional energy source, or to create effects in the physical universe."

"Such as tucking a nebula around your star to hide it from random passers-by?"

The Dragon's smile was an obvious mimicry of human expressions, on a face never meant to host them. Its ear fronds lifted and focused, the feathery whiskers that made its muzzle seem bearded sweeping forward, as if focusing its senses on Vincent. "Such as," it said.

Vincent held his face expressionless as much by reflex as by intent. Michelangelo shifted, broke contact, and sat down on the carpetplant with a plop. "Can't give the Coalition that. If they didn't break something on purpose, they'd break it by accident."

"Can they be educated?"

"Have you *met* my species?" Michelangelo snapped.

Vincent burst out laughing and caught his arm. "Kii, can the Consent limit what it provides?"

"The Consent is not to provide."

"If it did—does the Consent ever, uh, change its mind?"

"The Consent is sometimes altered by a change in circumstances," Kii said. "But the current probabilities do not indicate it likely. The Consent is to defend."

Vincent rolled to his knees and pressed himself to his feet, careful of his twinging knee. He thought better if he walked, despite the unsettling oscillation of Kii's head as it followed him. Michelangelo scooted back against the bed, out of the way. "If we could present a convincing argument, do you think the Consent would authorize us to build receivers? Only? Or even provide them, as a solid-state technology, for trade? That export would provide the Consent with leverage over the Coalition. They would have something to risk, in opposing you."

Kii sunk lower, resting its chin on the interlaced knuckles of its wing-joint digits, the extended pinkie fingers folded against its sides. "You wish a crippled technology?"

"Why not?"

"It could be arranged. The Consent will contemplate it." Kii considered, and tilted its long head toward Michelangelo. "This, Kii is not forbidden to impart, Michelangelo Osiris Leary Kusanagi-Jones. There is a weapon in your blood."

Kusanagi-Jones heard the words plainly, but they didn't process at first. He was tired, overstimulated, still unsettled with the dream he'd lied to Vincent about. It hadn't been *Skidbladnir* at all, but the old dream, the one of Assessment. But it hadn't been his death he'd dreamed this time, or his mother's.

It had been Vincent's.

He looked down at his hands, as if expecting to see what Kii meant, and then his eyes flicked up again and he bounced to his feet. "Bioweapon."

"Yes."

Of course, Old Earth didn't need to invade New Amazonia. They could do it the easy way. And the months in cryo to help time the latency right. "The Coalition didn't—"

Kii reached forward, as if to sniff, or sweep its whiskers and labial pits across Kusanagi-Jones. But its head was nothing more than a projection in the holographic wall, and Kusanagi-Jones was treated to the bizarre perspective of the Dragon seemingly lunging for him, and never arriving. Kusanagi-Jones locked his hands on the edge of the bed and held his ground, when he wanted to flinch and shield his eyes. *It isn't real.*

"Since yesterday," Kii said. "The infection is new."

Kusanagi-Jones turned toward Vincent, who stood framed against the evening light filtering through the doorway to the balcony. "Saide Austin," he said. "Bitch."

Vincent stepped forward, and Kusanagi-Jones stepped away. Since last night. Which meant that Vincent had no more than casual exposure, and—"How long?"

"It is a tailored retrovirus," Kii said. "It will affect only certain genetic strains of the human animal."

"Mine," Kusanagi-Jones said.

"Yours. In females, it will not express to disease. Kii estimates the latency period to be on the order of part-years."

"The Penthesileans turned you into a *bioweapon*?" Vincent took another step forward, and this time Kusanagi-Jones let him.

"Time bomb." Kusanagi-Jones bent over his watch, running diagnostics, search routines, low-level scans, calm despite the twisting tightness in his chest. "Not even a blip. My body thinks it's me. Supposed to carry it back to Earth and—*pfft!*" He waved his right hand in the air, still hunched over the green and blue lights glowing under the skin of his wrist.

"The New Amazonians think genetic tailoring is anathema."

"Not anathema enough—"

Kii shifted, fanning and refolding its wings, a process that involved leaning back on its haunches to get them clear of the ground. "Kii has subroutines to contain the infection," it said. "The Consent is indifferent with regard to Kii's dealings with individuals. Kii may intervene in this thing."

Vincent grabbed Kusanagi-Jones's arm and pulled him forward, front and center before the hologram. "You can cure him."

"Kii can," Kii said. The ragged-edged patterns on its wing leather showed bold against blue sky as it beat them twice. Kusanagi-Jones flinched from expected wind, but felt nothing.

"Wait."

"No wait." But Kusanagi-Jones shook Vincent's hand from his arm and dropped to their subchannel.

"You trust him? You can't *process* that thing, you know."

"You don't think there's a virus? It makes Claude Singapore's plan make a hell of a lot more sense, doesn't it? Get you sent home, in disgrace, maybe brought before the Coalition Cabinet to testify, make all their separatist friends happy." Vincent glanced sideways at Kii.

"First thing we do, let's kill all the men."

Kii, filling an apparent silence, said, "Your genotype proves resistant, Vincent Katherinessen."

"Don't *know*," Kusanagi-Jones said, over Kii. "If there is, it's hiding in plain sight— You trust him."

"It's not human body language."

"You trust him anyway."

Slowly, Vincent nodded. He reached out gently and took Kusanagi-Jones's arm again, folding his fingers around the biceps and holding on like a child clinging to an adult's finger.

"Bugger it," Kusanagi-Jones said out loud. "So do I." He waved at Kii. "Do we know it's fatal?"

"Kii estimates a 93 percent mortality rate."

"Cure him," Vincent said.

And again, Kusanagi-Jones stepped away from his partner and said, "Wait."

17

LESA DID NOT WANT TO TALK TO HER MOTHER. SHE MOST particularly had no desire at all to tell Elena the truth about Robert, and she was still working out her spin when the door to her office irised open again, admitting Katya. Her hair was bound back in a smooth, straight tail, and—an out-of-character note—her honor was strapped over garish festival trousers.

"I'm going out," Katya announced, a conclusion Lesa had already drawn. "Do you want anything?"

"No. Thank you. Home for supper or out all night?"

Katya looked down. "It depends if I find a good party."

The relationship between Lesa and her middle child had always resembled an arms race. Katya had been determined to become unreadable since she was a small child and she was often successful. But Lesa could almost always tell when she was hiding something, if not what she was hiding.

Lesa laid her stylus across the finished response to

Claude she had been staring at, and folded her hands over it. *Please let it be something innocent.* A secret lover, a questionable hobby. Anything Katya thought Lesa should disapprove of.

Anything, but knowing where Robert was and concealing it from the rest of the household.

"All right," Lesa said. "Try to stay out of fights."

"Mom." Katya paused before making good her escape. "Oh, and Grandma wants to see you. She's up in the solar."

"Wonderful." Lesa levered herself from her chair, leaving the stylus laid across the desk but slipping the card into an envelope. "That's what I was waiting for. Thank you, Katya."

"No problem." Katya grinned before slipping out the door.

Lesa followed, but turned right instead of left. She worried at her thumbnail with her teeth as she strode down the short, fluted corridor and climbed the stairwell past the second floor, where Vincent and Michelangelo were temporarily housed. Sweat trickled down her neck by the time she reached the third story and stopped in her own room.

It was full of evening light. Walter dozed in his basket, warmed by a filtered ray of sun, and for three or four ticks she contemplated activating the beacon in his collar and sending him after Katya. But that would hardly be subtle; it wasn't as if he could be told to *hide* from her.

Lesa would have to track Katya herself, after she spoke to Elena. That would give Katya enough of a head start. In the meantime, Lesa combed her hair, changed her shirt, and went to talk to her mother.

Elena's solar was at the top of Pretoria house, and Lesa took the lift. That climb was above and beyond the call of casual exercise in the service of keeping fit.

The room was pleasantly open, airy and fresh, with the windows on the sunset side dimmed by shades currently and the other directions presenting views of the city, sea, and jungle. Elena stood at the easternmost side, staring over the bay and its scatter of pleasure craft and one or two shipping vessels cutting white lines across glass blue.

"How much trouble are we in?" Elena asked before Lesa could announce her presence.

Lesa crossed the threshold, stepping from the smooth warmth of House's imitation of terra-cotta tile to cool, resilient carpetplant. "It's less bad than it could be. Antonia Kyoto has injected herself into the situation."

"What?" Elena's voice shivered; through the careful modulation, Lesa read the blackness of her mood.

"She's Parity. Robert was doubling for her."

Elena laid her hands on the window ledge and tightened her fingers until the tendons on her wrists stood out. "Of course he was. I'll have him flogged for that."

"It gets worse."

Elena turned away from the window. "By all means, draw out the suspense."

"He didn't run away to Antonia."

"Then where, pray tell?"

Lesa held her hands up, open and empty.

She heard Elena take two slow breaths before she spoke again. "Oh," she said. "I see."

"There's good news," Lesa added hastily. "I've talked with Katherinessen, and it seems I was wrong about Kusanagi-Jones. He's sympathetic, and brings Free Earth assets to the table."

The latest indrawn breath hissed out again in a sigh. Elena closed her eyes briefly and nodded. "That is good news. And the deal with Katherine Lexasdaughter?"

"Proceeds. She stands ready to present a united front

with us. Vincent—Miss Katherinessen—came very well prepared. Kusanagi-Jones less so, in that he'll have to carry word of our plans to his contacts on Old Earth personally."

"Of course, out of twenty named worlds, the defiance of three won't make much difference in terms of military might."

"No," Lesa said. "But House will protect us. And it will mean something in terms of leadership. We just need to show that the Coalition *can* be opposed. I've provided a full report on the Coalition agents, anyway." She stretched her back until it cracked, and pitched her voice higher. "House, would you send the report to Elena's desk, please?"

The walls dimmed slightly in answer, and Elena nodded thanks. "There's something else."

"News travels fast."

Elena's smile only touched one corner of her mouth. "Agnes said Kusanagi-Jones received a challenge card."

"From Claude, yes."

"What's he going to do about it?"

It was Lesa's turn for a collected smile. "I'm going to fight for him."

"Wait?" Vincent snapped, but Angelo met his gaze with that infuriating impassive frown. Vincent's fingers tightened against his palm, as if there were any way in the world he could make Angelo do anything he hadn't already meant to do.

"Can you think of a better plan?" And oh, his voice was so damned reasonable when he said it. "Cheaper than a war."

"It's not what I would call ethical," Vincent said. He glanced up at Kii for support, but the Dragon only watched them, feathered brows beetled over incurious eyes. "You've no way to control it, and it will cost a lot of innocent lives."

"It will," Michelangelo said, folding his arms, his face relaxing into furrows of worry and grief. "And at least one not so innocent one."

He meant himself. And he was letting Vincent *see* him, the whole story, nothing concealed. The intimacy rocked Vincent in sympathetic waves of Michelangelo's fear and desperation. He was scared sick. It was in the creases beside his eyes, the crossed arms, the slight lean back on his heels. Scared, and he thought it was worth doing anyway.

Killing off nearly half the population of Old Earth would sure as hell limit the threat of the OECC as a conquering power, Vincent would give Michelangelo that. He still didn't think it was the world's greatest solution to the problem.

"You're not doing this," Vincent said. "That's an order."

"The alternative is letting Old Earth drag the Coalition worlds into a fight that Kii and the Consent would end when it got to New Amazonia. Probably get twice as many killed on both sides. Nuclear option, Vincent. It will save lives."

Kii's feathered tufts ruffled and smoothed. "We would not be pleased to do so."

"No," Vincent said. "I don't imagine you would. Kii, I have another option. Would the Consent, uh, consent to teach my people to create Transcendent matrices such as yours?"

"Your species may not be suited."

"What do you mean?"

"My species chooses to copy our psyches into an information state, and to permit our physical selves to grow old and fail."

"Of course," Vincent said. It wasn't as if one could actually *upload* one's personality, stripping the man out of the brain and loading it into a computer like a Raptured soul ascending bodily to heaven. One made a copy. And that left the problem of what to do with the originals.

"We accepted that to do so, our physicalities must die without progeny. The Consent was given, and so it was... wrought. No, so it abided." Kii angled its nose down at them. "Kii thinks biped psychology is unamenable to such constraints."

"Bugger," Angelo said into the silence. "Shove it down their throats if we have to—"

"No," Vincent said, rubbing his hands through his braids so the nap of his hair scratched his palms. "We'd have to sterilize the lot. An entire planetary population for whom procreation is the most cherished ideal? It wouldn't change anything, except we'd have Transcendent copies of them in a quantum computer leading productive virtual lives. The plague's a better idea. Which is not to say it's not a lousy idea."

He glared at Michelangelo, and Michelangelo unfolded his arms, a gesture of acceptance but not surrender. "We'll wait," he said. "For now. Try to come up with something better."

"You're content to walk around breeding retrovirus for the next two weeks?"

Angelo echoed Vincent's gesture, palms across his scalp, but his version added a yawn. "Sounds a regular vacation, doesn't it?"

On the way out, Lesa stopped in her room, discovered that Walter had apparently gone to the courtyard to stretch his legs, and got a leash before heading down to collect him. Far from gamboling with the children, the khir was sprawled in a sunbeam, sides rising and falling with steady regularity.

Awakened from his nap, he stretched lazily front and back and trotted around her twice on her way to the door, as if to prove that lesser khir might need to be leashed, but he certainly didn't. All his blandishments were in vain. She clicked the leash to his collar as they stepped out the front door, and then crouched to tap the veranda with her forefinger and say, "Find Katya."

Walter whisked his muzzle across the deck and picked his way down the stairs, pausing at the bottom to sniff again before angling left, toward the bigger thoroughfare, threading between merrymakers at a rate that had Lesa hustling to keep up. She trotted, too, keeping the leash slack, though Walter occasionally turned to glare. "I'm running as fast as I can!"

He didn't seem to believe her, but he was too well trained to lunge at the lead, even when irritated by streets clotted by buskers and food vendors. It had been Lesa's idea to train the household khir as messengers, when she was Katya's age, an idea that had turned out well. So well that other households had copied the trick once they found out how adept the khir were at memorizing routes.

The pace he set was better than a jog. Her honor jarred on her thigh with every footstep; her hair disarrayed and stuck to her forehead with sweat. She clucked to Walter, slowing him as they threaded between people so they wouldn't accidentally trample other pedestrians and spark a duel, or overrun Katya and have rather a lot of explaining to do.

That Katya had gone on foot heightened Lesa's suspicions. If she'd called a car—either public transport or Pretoria house's communal one—her destination would have become a matter of record. Walking for exercise was one thing, but it was early for parties, even in Carnival, and if Katya *were* going to parties, she wouldn't want to arrive sweat-saturated and stinking.

Lesa had always encouraged Robert to know her children, to develop relationships with them, far beyond the customary. He had, and both Robert and the children had seemed to enjoy it.

And now Katya was making Lesa pay for it.

It had seemed like a good idea at the time.

After their dead-end conversation with Kii, Vincent had happened to be watching when Lesa appeared in the courtyard, whistled for her pet, and snapped a leash onto his collar. "Angelo," he'd said, without turning, "follow her."

Which was how Kusanagi-Jones came to be slipping through the steadily increasing press of cheering, staggering, singing men and women behind Lesa and her animal like the sting on an adder's tail, following the rest of what he took to be a long and somewhat complicated snake. Vincent remained at Pretoria house, nursing his sunburn and wrenched knee and covering Kusanagi-Jones's tracks, but the drop from their balcony was only four meters and Kusanagi-Jones could have done it without tools, stark naked and on a sprained ankle.

Fully equipped, he could almost take it as an insult how easy escape had been.

Robert's decampment was more interesting, and Kusanagi-Jones was still trying to comprehend it. Based on his imperfect understanding of the layout of Pretoria house, the men's quarters were isolated well up the tower and guarded. It was a descent that could not be made inobviously on ropes, especially in the middle of a festival, and if the guard had not been overpowered, the obvious solution was that somebody inside the house had assisted Robert in getting out.

Kusanagi-Jones wasn't surprised to discover that Vincent wasn't sanguine as to Lesa's involvement. Robert certainly wasn't the only double in Pretoria house, and neither Vincent nor Kusanagi-Jones wanted to trust Lesa more than necessary.

Which was somewhat ridiculous, given how much Kusanagi-Jones was trusting Vincent. But at this point, if he wasn't going to choose to trust Vincent he might as well go home, hand in his commission, and wait to be surplused. For the first time in his life, political and personal ideals were aligning, and if that wasn't worth dying for, he was in the wrong line of work.

And so as they left the side street graced by Pretoria house, he dropped the camouflage function on his wardrobe as he stepped into a shadow, and stepped out again dressed to blend with the Carnival crowd. His wardrobe had no license of a mask, but it could provide something that would pass for a street license, barring inspection—and, it being Carnival, there were a lot of men on the thoroughfares. Though Kusanagi-Jones didn't think he'd have cared to try it any other time of year.

The moderately illegal modifications to the cosmetics subroutine he carried—under Cabinet seal, as patching a wardrobe was beyond even Vincent's skills—made it easy to change his skin tone and alter his facial features. Programs for haircut, color, style, length, and texture came standard.

He couldn't do much about his height—beyond heeled shoes—or his build, and those were distinctive

enough to cause him worry. Fortunately, Lesa Pretoria
was either stringing along any potential tail, or she
just wasn't very good at spotting one. She knew what
she was supposed to do—the techniques were there—
but the application was crude. And even had she been
more accomplished, she was hampered by the animal
that accompanied her. An animal that was going somewhere.

The streets filled as sunset approached, the air
growing heavy with perfume, food smells, and the
slightly rancid aroma of flowers fermenting in their
garlands. Kusanagi-Jones saw khir other than Walter,
some of them accompanied and some of them alone,
all moving with a sense of purpose that reminded
him of footage he'd seen of Earth predators. Moreover,
all of them seemed to be treated with a casual respect
that surprised him. People and vehicles granted the
khir the right of way, to such a degree that Lesa made
better time jogging through the crowd beside the animal than she would have on her own. Kusanagi-Jones
was hard-pressed to keep up.

The game of follow-the-leader ended when Lesa
and the khir turned off the main road down a curved,
narrow, unpopulated street that Kusanagi-Jones
couldn't enter without becoming obvious. He hung
back, waiting for Lesa to round the corner, and didn't
step into the mouth of the street until her silhouette
slipped out of sight.

If he were her, he'd have paused then, on the chance
that he might get a glimpse of anyone following. So he
didn't race after. Instead, he chose a sedate path along
the inside curve of the street, maintaining the wall's
cover for as long as possible. He paused to listen at the
most extreme point of the arc—one of the drawbacks
of New Amazonian architecture was the lack of useful

reflective surfaces at street level—and mused briefly that eyes on the back of his head were all very nice, but he really wished that one of the tricks his wardrobe could perform was generating a periscope. For the space of three heartbeats, he listened, but heard nothing, not even the patter of a woman's boots and a khir's paws.

And then voices, softly, but too low for him to make anything useful of, given the echoes off tight walls. With careful steps, he rounded the corner. Lesa was not in sight, but the street ended in a T-intersection, and a pedestrian was moving toward him on hurried steps, her eyes fixed on the street as if she needed to pay close attention to where she was putting her feet. She walked steadily, though—no trace of staggering.

It was reassuring to encounter other traffic. He nodded deferentially as she passed, even stepping aside to provide her a comfortable margin, but she paid him no notice. He continued on, allowing himself to hurry now, and paused before entering the intersection.

Another patch of ground where a couple of nice, big, street-level windows would come in very handy. Kusanagi-Jones frowned and stared at his feet. "House," he murmured, "which way did Miss Pretoria go?"

He was not answered, not even by a flicker of color absorbed from the deepening sky overhead.

He licensed a hand mirror and used it to check both ends of the cross street, crouching so when he extended it, his arm lay parallel to and near the ground. There was movement to the east, but the mirror was too small to reveal more.

His fisheye, however, showed him that the pedestrian was safely out of sight. He released the mirror and touched his wrist, keying the wardrobe back into camouflage mode. Then he stepped forward.

Lesa Pretoria was there. Back against a wall, her hands spread wide but not raised, exactly, so much as hovering, and Walter beside her, balanced on his hind legs like a miniature kangaroo, with his forelegs drawn under his chest and the feathers on his long, heavy tail fanned wide. They were surrounded by five armed women, and a man Michelangelo knew from the reception the first night: Stefan, a light-complected fellow with unusually fair hair, more so even than Vincent's.

The man had his back to the alley and his bulk hid part of the scene. Beyond him, what Kusanagi-Jones had taken to be two attackers was revealed as an attacker and a hostage with her arm twisted behind her back, her own confiscated weapon by her ear.

The hostage was Katya Pretoria. Which explained Lesa's careful, motionless poise.

Vincent would have known the instant he saw the bystander hurrying away. He would have read it in her gait, the guilty downcast of her eyes, the haste.

Kusanagi-Jones *would* have to walk in on a mugging blind.

Or maybe not a mugging. Having Katya as a hostage—miserable, trying with pride not to flinch away from the muzzle of her own weapon—would tend to indicate that something more complex was occurring. Lesa had made casual comment about people kidnapped by pirates, after all, and not in a sense that indicated she was, entirely, joking. And there was the incident with Vincent—

As Kusanagi-Jones moved, he obtained a more complete perspective. The stranger was holding the weapon cocked beside Katya's head. Not actually in contact, but close enough to make the point in a professional manner.

Lesa's weapon was still holstered, but the other women were all armed, and only one of them hadn't drawn. Kusanagi-Jones didn't take her for the ringleader, though. More likely a scout.

A poorly trained scout. She repeatedly glanced over her shoulder at the confrontation, rather than facing the approach, weapon ready.

Actually, her right hand was bandaged and splinted, and though her weapon was rigged for left-hand use, he thought that hand flexed awkwardly over the holster.

Sometimes you got a lucky break.

Well, Michelangelo thought, *at least I'm invisible.*

For now. He thought he could rely on the New Amazonians to figure things out once he acted. And while his wardrobe *could* stop bullets, it couldn't do it forever. It cost in power and in foglets, and the technology needed time to recharge and repair.

He wasn't without assets, though. She might be female, but Lesa was deadly enough with a sidearm to win Vincent's respect, as Vincent had impressed on him after the discussion in Lesa's office. Katya was another factor. Duelist or not, Kusanagi-Jones didn't think she was the sort to just stand there and weep. And, of course, the khir. Kusanagi-Jones could only guess from old media how useful it might be in a fight, but he knew police and military had used dogs as attack animals before Assessment, and the khir was bigger than any image of a dog he'd seen.

He hoped they hadn't overstated the case.

If Lesa was the…gunslinger…Vincent had intimated, she'd initiate something when she saw an opening. Which meant Kusanagi-Jones needed to *give* her that opening, while being alert for any moves she might make on her own, and standing ready to abort and follow her lead. He just hoped she didn't do anything hysterical, or freeze up because of the gun to her daughter's head.

He was getting blasted tired of trying to second-guess people smarter than he was. And it wasn't made any easier when they were *women*.

If this was the same crew that had attempted to abduct Vincent—as the lousy perimeter guard's bandaged hand tended to indicate—they might be armed chiefly with nonlethal weapons. They would want everyone alive.

Which would be why the woman controlling Katya was using Katya's weapon. Because *it* would be loaded with lethal rounds, and Lesa would know that. If one meant to threaten, it never hurt to reinforce your intention with a little evidence.

If one meant to act, however, sometimes the element of total surprise came in handy.

Kusanagi-Jones moved forward. The wardrobe's camouflage function was designed to bypass automated security. Mere human senses never stood a chance as he picked his route between the attackers. The target was of average height, for a New Amazonian. Her dark brown hair was cropped short and brushed forward into a coxcomb, dyed cherry-red at the tips. She held Katya's weapon with confidence, and her voice carried.

"Please place your hands on your head, Miss Pretoria, and turn to face the wall."

Lesa seemed to be obeying, slowly and with deliberation. Her hands rose, her eyes unswerving on the gunwoman's face. Walter's leash still slid looped around her left wrist, and the khir hissed as she turned, its nostrils flaring. Michelangelo wondered how long it could balance on its hind legs—it showed no signs of strain yet—and he wondered also why the cherry-haired woman didn't just drop it. Whatever need kept them from harming Lesa, he couldn't imagine it applied to her pet.

That was, he hoped, secondary. He found a position behind the gunwoman before Lesa finished her hesitation-march pirouette. His moment would come when Lesa's back was fully turned. The target's attention should shift, momentarily, from controlling Lesa and Katya to ordering her troops.

That would be the moment when Katya would be at the least risk from his intervention. And he saw it coming in the shifting of the target's weight, the instant when she drew a deeper breath, preparatory to speaking.

New Amazonia had specified that the negotiators come unarmed, all security to be provided by Penthesilean forces. And so Vincent and Kusanagi-Jones had carried no obvious weapons. But a utility fog was, by its very nature, adaptable technology, and they carried data under diplomatic seal. And among those data were licenses for weapons banned on every Coalition world.

The cutting wire that formed between Kusanagi-Jones's hands as he raised them wasn't actually a monofilament. It was composed of a single chain of hand-linked foglets, and it was neither as strong nor as sharp as a monomolecular wire.

It didn't need to be.

He formed his arms into an interrupted loop, as if to capture her in a surprise embrace, and brought the wire down.

It caught the target below the elbows. Slight resistance shivered up the invisibly thin wire as it made contact, and Michelangelo jerked down.

The target made no sound. For a hopelessly long time—a third of a second, longer—she stared in shock at the abrupt termination of her arms. Both her hands fell, and Michelangelo had just enough time to hope the pistol didn't discharge from the shock when they hit.

And then the target's heart beat and blood sprayed from her stumps, soaking Katya and spattering Lesa, Walter, and the wall. A thin moan filtered through her teeth, cut off abruptly as Michelangelo slit her throat, passing the wire through flesh with a quick, sliding tug that didn't sever her spine because he snapped the filament off before it pulled completely through.

He stepped clear as she fell. Shock would buy him split seconds, but there were five more enemies to account for. With any luck, Katya would reclaim her weapon and help even the odds.

Michelangelo surrendered to the mercy of trained reflexes. He spun, moved to the next target, slipping in blood. Its pewter stink and the reek of urine rose as he took a second woman down, striking nerve clusters in the neck and solar plexus. A bullet sank into his wardrobe, the sting unbalancing, but he recovered as she fell. Lesa's gun spoke; the fair-haired man grunted as Walter plowed into his chest.

It would be good to have at least two for questioning. Michelangelo used feet and fists and elbows, gouged and kicked. A tangler splashed against a wall, shunted aside by his wardrobe. He heard a second one discharge, but it wasn't close. He didn't see where; it was a blur of motion in his fisheye, and he was distracted by the passage of blows with a gap-toothed woman whose hair lay in flat braids behind each ear.

She couldn't see him, but she could fight. Air compression or instinct, she parried six blows, each one flowering blue sparks as his wardrobe shocked her. She gave ground as he advanced. She would have caught the seventh on the cross of her arms if she hadn't slipped in blood.

The grin was a rictus as she raised her hands, seared patches showing on her forearms, one foot coming up, bracing to roll her over and aside. Too slow. Michelangelo stepped forward between her knees and kicked her hard, in the crotch.

Her expression as she coiled around the pain was almost worth three very long New Amazonian days of being treated like a child-eating monster, and a not very bright one at that.

Lesa's gun was silent, and as Michelangelo kicked his latest target in the temple to keep her quiet, he saw her snared in webbing, writhing against the strands in an effort to free her weapon hand. Walter was down, too, sprawled on his side with a gash through feathers and scales across his ribs. Katya pushed herself to her feet, so drenched in blood as to be barely recognizable, but with her sidearm clutched in one sticky hand. The last two assailants left standing were casting left and right for any sign of their invisible attacker.

Katya lifted clotted hair from her eyes left-handed as she brought her weapon up. "Stand down," she said.

The women stepped forward. Michelangelo kicked the one on the left under the chin; they ducked sideways as the other woman discharged a chemical firearm. The three-shot burst stuttered against his wardrobe, transferred shock emptying his lungs.

"Stand *down*!" Katya yelled, before he regained his balance, but the other woman didn't lower her weapon. He turned, moved toward her——

——and Katya shot her through the heart. Michelangelo didn't even see an impact. Flechette rounds, maybe. She went down anyway, looking shocked, and hit with a liquid thud.

"Shit," Katya said, wiping her bloody mouth on a hand that wasn't any better. "Shit."

Kusanagi-Jones spared a glance around the battlefield. "Nice shooting for a girl who doesn't duel."

Katya put a hand down and pushed herself to her feet, then planted both hands on her knees and stood doubled over, panting, for a moment. "Mom made sure I knew what I was doing with weapons. It isn't her fault I think shooting people for points of honor is stupid. Michelangelo?"

"It's me," he said, snapping off his wardrobe's filters as she came upright.

She blinked, looked down at the weapon in her hands, and back up at him. "Wow."

"Good trick, huh?"

She swallowed and didn't nod. Instead she came toward him, pistol hanging from half-curled fingers, shaking so hard her shoulders trembled. He looked down, frowned, checked one more time for enemies in a position to do damage, and uncomfortably dialed his wardrobe down to offer the girl a hug.

Not even shaking, *shuddering*, from the nape of her neck to the soles of her feet, and the only reason her teeth weren't clacking was because her jaw was clenched so tightly the muscles stood out under her ears. "Never killed anybody before?"

She shook her head.

He squeezed her roughly and backed away, pushing her in the direction of the downed khir. "Gets easier. I'll untangle Miss Pretoria."

She went, silently. He checked the casualties one more time while picking his way between them to get to Miss Pretoria. It never hurt to be sure.

And Katya was a good kid, for a girl. He was even more impressed if this was her first fight.

He left the wardrobe dialed down. He'd need to touch Lesa to get the tangler off. "This won't take long," he said, picking through licenses as he crouched beside her, looking for the right antiadhesive formula.

He was loading it when Katya shot him in the back.

18

AT DINNERTIME, THE HOUSEHOLD DISCOVERED MICHELAN-
gelo was missing, and Vincent was subjected to a brief,
cursorily polite interview with Elena on a wicker-
furnished sun porch overlooking the central courtyard.

"He left with Lesa," Vincent said, shading the
truth.

Elena, seated with her back to the courtyard, the
evening's balmy air blowing the scents of fireworks and
wilted flowers around her, frowned over her datapad.

"Lesa's not answering her com," she said with the
air of one bestowing state secrets. "And Walter, one of
the household khir, is missing."

"Let me guess," Vincent said, unable to keep the
dryness out of his voice. "Lesa's especial pet."

"It would be a mistake to think of khir as pets, exactly."

She had kept him standing, and he consciously

arranged himself at parade rest, weight on his heels, body relaxed, spine hanging from his skull like a string of beads straightened by gravity. "Though you collar them?"

"We identify who the responsible humans are. But the khir are perfectly capable of resettling if conditions don't suit them. They have their own packs and family arrangements. It's considered unwise to intervene." She pushed idly at the iced drink resting on the low table before her, tracing fingertips down the glass-beaded side. "This was their city first. In any case, in the light of yesterday, we must consider foul play."

Vincent folded his arms, firming his mouth. Nothing as daunting as Michelangelo's frictionless mask, but he wouldn't be much of a diplomat if he couldn't lie with a straight face. "I find it surprising they would have left without security."

"They didn't make you aware of their destination, then?" The furrow between Elena's eyebrows creased deeper. She sat back abruptly, flicking moisture off her fingers like a cat. "I assumed the lack of security meant it had something to do with"—a dancing gesture, back and forth—"private matters."

"Between you and me?"

She nodded.

"It might have," he said. "I presume Lesa passed along the substance of our conversation last night."

"She said you were unforthcoming enough about your partner's politics to make her curious."

"I was," he said.

Elena sat forward. "I'll have contact codes for your mother, documents, a timetable. Coordination is going to require discretion and effort."

"Elder Pretoria," he said, leveling his voice with far

more effort than he allowed to show in it, "what about Angelo and your daughter?"

"Katya and Agnes have taken out search parties," she said. "I've informed Miss Delhi and the rest of her security team, and no doubt they are scouring the city as well. In the meantime, it's not as if our other business will wait."

"In the *meantime*," he replied, "I don't suppose you've made any progress in locating the missing statue."

"*Phoenix Abased?*" She studied her fingernails. "I believe security directorate is looking into it."

"If it's not located," he said, "I may have some difficulty convincing the Coalition Cabinet that it's wise to repatriate the rest of the liberated art. To a city that can't manage to keep track of the jewel of the collection for twelve hours, once it's released to their authority."

"That would be unfortunate," she said. "Because New Amazonia would no doubt interpret that as further evidence of the Coalition's perfidy. And I think even Claude would find it challenging maintaining generalized acceptance of neutrality or appeasement under those circumstances."

"The Christ," he said, biting his lip to keep the grin under control. "That's worthy of my mother."

Elena tipped her head. "It's hard to imagine a higher compliment."

Lesa had said it. Only a member of Parliament could have pulled off the theft. One such as Elena Pretoria, the Opposition leader. "So you have a plan to foment revolution. Convenient. What do you plan to do about Robert?"

She spread her fingers wide. "He's just a stud male. An unusual male, but a male. His chances of

successfully accusing three well-placed women are
slim. Unless he had hard evidence—which I don't
believe—his testimony is easily discredited. It's a minor scandal how much Lesa spoils him, anyway."

The chill that crawled across his shoulders might
have been the sunburn. "So you're unconcerned."

"Honestly," she said, "given Claude's blunder in
challenging Miss Kusanagi-Jones, I find it hard to see
how our situation could be better. Assuming, of course,
that they are located quickly."

"Assuming." He took it as leave to go when she
lifted her drink and turned to the window. She could
mask her worry from her family, but not from him,
and it made them both uncomfortable.

Still, he managed to avoid panic until after night-
fall, when a commotion in the courtyard roused him
from unprofitable ceiling staring, watching the repro-
duced image of the Gorgon slowly color the darkening
periwinkle of a crepuscular sky. He rolled off the bed
quickly and hurried to the arch, his injured leg lag-
ging. The pain medication helped, but couldn't obscure
ongoing twinges.

He came out under the real sky, washed by city
lights until it shone less bright than the reproduction
inside, and paused with his hands on the balcony railing. A stem of carpetplant stuck between his toes, and
he momentarily forgot the ache of his knee and the
seared shivers crossing his tender back. Below, several
dark heads gathered, women rushing barefoot from
the house, and a doorway in the courtyard wall—a sort
of garden gate without a garden—stood open on the
street beyond, two girls observing through the crack
with gamine eyes.

He spotted Elena easily as she strode into the courtyard, the others giving way before her, except for one.

Katya Pretoria stayed crouched beside an exhausted, bedraggled khir. The animal's head curled up on a long neck, trembling, but otherwise it lay spread on its side, and Vincent could see the white glare of bandages against scaled, feathered hide.

"Dammit," he said, stepping back. "Dammit, dammit, dammit."

A few limping steps brought him inside, into the gentler light projected from the ceiling. He stopped, stared up at the pale colors of the nebula, and forced himself to breathe slowly.

The door irised open at his approach. An alert and concerned-looking guard met him, setting aside the datapad she was reading to rise from her bench. "Miss Katherinessen?"

"Why wasn't I informed?" he snarled. She stepped back, arms crossed, and he sighed and modulated his tone. "I'm sorry," he said, through the taste of gall. "I need to speak to Elder Pretoria immediately."

"I'll see what I can do. If you'll return to your room..."

"No. I'm going with you."

She stared, but he refused to glance down. She wasn't wearing a weapon, unlike most women, and he was glad. Otherwise, he thought she might shoot him if he stepped any closer. At least he had height and age on her. He lifted his chin and folded his arms, feeling like the heroine in a Victorian drama.

Her arms dropped to her sides. "This way."

He followed meekly, rubbing grit from the corners of his eyes. He was *not* losing Michelangelo. Not with long-elusive dreams about to settle on his hand like butterflies. War, revolution, treason——these seemed minor considerations now.

He almost didn't recognize the emotion. It was

hope. And it was also hope settling into his gut with a painful chill. He'd forgotten what it was like having something to lose. But apparently he hadn't forgotten how much it hurt to lose it.

Along the walk, he learned that the guard's name was Alys, and that she wasn't a member of Elena's family, but was raised in a less wealthy household and working in service until she could afford her own citizenship stake. She led him down stairs and along another curved corridor tiled in faux terra-cotta, which combined with the thicketed landscape of the walls to suggest a jungle path. At least the movement eased the ache in a knee further strained in descending the stairs.

"Your culture believes in the beneficial power of walking," he said as they paused for Alys to consult her datacart and locate Elder Pretoria.

"Saves on chemical antidepressants," she quipped, and frowned slightly when he didn't laugh.

"And I would have guessed the jungle was rich in useful pharmaceuticals." He knew he should have bitten his tongue, and couldn't be bothered. Michelangelo was still missing, he was being kept deliberately in the dark, and she had the nerve to look disappointed at his lack of attention to her jokes.

"I believe you should discuss that with Elder Singapore," she said coolly. "Elder Pretoria is on the porch, Miss Katherinessen. She'll see you."

Her pique amused him, and it might have been impolitic to let her see it, but he was beyond caring. So he nodded and smiled as he walked past her down the short corridor to the veranda, through an open archway and into the still-warm night.

Elena waited as promised. She placed a rough pottery cup in his hand before he spoke a word. The shape clung to his fingers, and the contents perfumed the air above with the fermented tang of alcohol. He set it down without tasting it, brushing garlands off the ledge to make room, and drummed his fingers beside it.

"Katya must have checked in, mustn't she? Before she brought the khir in for medical treatment."

"We didn't want to distress you with imperfect data."

"Of course not." The ledge was very smooth, and lattice laced with flowers and sticks of incense stretched above it to the veranda's overhanging roof, so he had to peer through the chinks as if through a veil to see the courtyard beyond. The khir had been brought inside. Neither Katya nor any of the household staff and family members who had descended to assist her were present. "I understand that you wouldn't want to disturb my fragile emotional equilibrium."

The finger drumming was unlikely to convince her that he was calm. With an effort, he smoothed his hands and curled them around the base of the cup. The pottery wasn't cool, but compared to the sun-retained warmth of the ledge, it seemed so.

"My apologies, Miss Katherinessen. It was thoughtless."

He licked his lips, lifted the cup, and turned back. She stood as he had left her, hands folded around a similar cup—he couldn't be sure of the color in the dark—and her face half shadowed, half picked out in pinpricks from nebula and courtyard light filtering through the lattice. "Tell me now," he said.

"Katya found Walter in a street about six kilometers from here. In Cascade, which is not the best neighborhood. He was wounded, unconscious, and there were signs of a fight."

Vincent realized the cup was at his lips only when it clicked against his teeth. "What signs?"

Elena rocked back on her heels. "Blood. A great deal of it. Marks of bullet ricochets and tangler fire."

"Bodies?"

"None."

He closed his eyes, breathed out, and breathed in across the liquor. The sting brought tears to his eyes. "What now?"

"There may be a ransom note," she said. "Or an extortion demand. Security directorate is investigating. A house-to-house search has been authorized——"

"Unacceptable."

"Miss Katherinessen," she said, her dignity unmoderated by the interruption, "my daughter is missing as well."

"Yes," he said. "You haven't even been able to find one 'stud male' in a city where he can't legally walk the streets without a woman's permission. And I'm supposed to take your efforts to ensure Angelo's safety seriously?"

"It's *Carnival*, Miss Katherinessen. You've seen what the streets are like this time of year."

"And yet nobody witnessed anything? I want to see the scene."

"And expose yourself further?"

"You had no qualms about exposing me when I was shot at——"

"Now we do," she said. She looked down at the surface of her beverage. He wondered what she saw reflected. "Relax," she said. "Not only is Elder Kyoto very interested in getting Miss Kusanagi-Jones back, but Saide Austin has become involved. And she is *very* well connected. If anybody in Penthesilea can find Lesa and your partner, it's the pair of them."

Of course Saide Austin wants him back, he thought. *It'd be a crying shame if her time bomb died on New Amazonian soil, far from the people he was meant to infect.* What he said was, "I wish to return to the government center. I will feel safer there, under proper security."

"I'll see to it tonight," she said. "Go make your farewells to the house, if you have any."

He went quietly. The guard Alys was not waiting in the hall. He glanced left and right, but saw no trace. She must have expected Elder Pretoria to send for her when she was required.

Or Elena had sent him out intentionally unescorted for some purpose of her own. He paused in the hall, recalling the route back to his borrowed rooms unerringly. He could retrace it...or he could do a little unofficial wandering under the guise of being lost.

Don't be silly, he told himself, following the corridor back the way he'd come. *You're inventing busywork to keep your brain off Michelangelo. It's as likely an oversight; she's a crafty old creature, but not everything is conspiracy, not even on this planet, and not even everything in Pretoria household happens to Elena's plan.*

Lesa Pretoria was proof enough of that.

He paused at the foot of the stair, one hand raised to rub at his nose, and froze that way. Of course. Elena couldn't arrange for him to visit the scene of the kidnapping, if it were a kidnapping and not a murder—and the Christ damn this outpost of hell for its archaic technology anyway. If they could manage an engineered retrovirus, they ought to be able to swing a twelve-hour DNA type. But she could buy Vincent a sliver of time in which to speak to Katya in private about what she'd seen. And Katya would doubtless be with the injured khir.

"House," he asked, "which way to the infirmary?"

The ripple of brightness was expected this time, a pattern of motion designed to catch a predator's eye just the way light snagged on the V-shaped track of a big fish underwater.

If he had to take a guess, he'd wager that was what Dragons ate. It made sense of the jaw full of slender, needle-sharp back-curved teeth, the sharply hooked talons. Following the light, he thought about that, distracted himself with images of arrowing, broad-winged green-and-blue beings hauling great silver fish squirming from the protected waters of the bay.

They were far superior images to the one that persisted when he did not force himself to think of something frivolous.

The rill led him through cool rooms and several corridors, his feet passing over carpetplant and what passed for tile the way the strand of light passed over moving images of jungle understory. He memorized this route, too. It was always good to know how to get out of whatever you were getting into.

He smelled cut greenery, and then cooking, and finally the hospital reek of antiseptic, adhesive, and synthetic skin. The pale glow lingered around a closed iris. Vincent paused and rested his fingertips against the wall beside the door.

"House, open the door, please."

It spiraled obediently wide. This was a public space, and there was no reason for House to forbid him entrance.

The murmur of voices washed out as he stepped inside. Or a voice, anyway. Katya bent over a flat-topped table covered with layers of folded cloth, one hand on the neck of the animal she whispered to and the other on his muzzle. It looked as if the bandages had been changed.

Girl and khir were alone in the room. Katya glanced up, tensing, at the sound of the door. Walter might have lifted his head, but she stroked his neck and restrained him, and he relaxed under her hand. She also seemed to calm when she saw Vincent, but he knew it for a pretense. Her shoulders eased and her face smoothed, but no matter how softly she petted the khir's feathers the lingering tension in her fingers propagated minute shivers across his skin.

Vincent cleared his throat. "Just how smart is a khir?"

She smiled. "Smart."

"As smart as a human?"

"Well," she said, stroking Walter's feathers back along the bony ridge at the back of his skull, "not the same kind of smart. No. They don't use tools or talk, but they understand fairly complicated instructions and they coordinate with humans and with their pack mates."

"So they must communicate."

"Oh, yes."

"Pity he can't talk," Vincent said, sadly.

Katya colored, olive-tan skin pinking at the cheeks. "Miss Katherinessen," she said, "I'm sorry about Miss Kusanagi-Jones. I want to offer my personal assurances that I and everyone in Pretoria house will do everything we can to find him and bring him home safe. Agnes is coordinating the search now, and I'll relieve her in the morning."

As if her words were permission, he stepped over the threshold and came fully into the room. The white tile floor was cool, even cold, shocking to feet that had already grown accustomed to carpetplant and the blood-warmth of House's hallways. "I shall be praying for your mother," he said, "and her safe and timely return."

"Thank you," she said after a hesitation, and licked her lips before she looked up again. "Do you pray often?"

"Sometimes."

"Ur is a Christian colony."

"Founded by Christians. Radicals, like New Amazonia."

She kept her eyes on the khir, as if watching him breathe. He lay quietly, the nictitating membrane closed under outer lids at half-mast. She smoothed his feathers again. "We're taught that Christians were among the worst oppressors of women. On Old Earth. That they held women responsible for all the sin and wickedness in the world."

He chuckled. "Not my branch of the Church. We're heretics."

"Really?" She brightened as if it were a magic word. "Like Protestants?"

He shook his head and reached out slowly to lay his hand on Walter's flank behind the bandages. The khir's hide was soft and supple under scales like beads on an evening gown, pebbled against his fingertips. The khir sighed as another breath of tension left his muscles. Vincent's own heart slowed, the ache across his shoulders easing in response.

"Descended, philosophically speaking, from the very first heresy of all. One that was eradicated by the Paulines about two and a half thousand years ago, for being prone to sentiments that were thought to undermine the authority of the Church."

He had her interest. She brushed the back of his hand and he could feel her trembling, though she restrained the appearance of it well. "But was it really a...church yet?"

"There was a bishop." She laughed, so he continued. "Who didn't approve of their ideas, such as that the Christ might speak to anyone and not solely through the Apostles, and that God was both masculine and feminine and thus women might serve equally as well as men, and that the passion of the Christ was a physical ordeal only, and did not affect his divine essence, and so martyrdom was kind of silly. You know, the usual heresies."

"And you believe all that?"

He smiled and turned his hand over, pressing it to hers palm to palm. "I was raised to. My mother's philosophy is a utilitarian one. She believes the purpose of religion, or government, is to maintain the maximum number of people in the maximum possible comfort. And so it suits her to believe that what the serpent offered Eve in the garden wasn't sin, but self-knowledge. Enlightenment. *Gnosis.*"

Katya shook her head. "That's supposed to be the story that was used to justify oppressing women."

"But what if the snake did her a favor?"

"Then Eve's not the villain. Your mother's supposed to be some kind of a prophet, isn't she? On your home world?"

"Gnostics believe that anyone can prophesy, if the spirit moves them. She is"——he shrugged——"very good at getting people to listen to her. On Ur, and elsewhere. Enough so that even Earth has to deal with her."

She squeezed lightly before she pulled her hand away. "Okay, you said you were raised to believe that. But you didn't answer my question."

He grinned and let her let go. "Do you believe everything you're taught, Miss Pretoria?"

When she paused and swallowed, it was all there in
her expression, for far longer and much more plainly
than she would have liked. How Lesa had missed it,
Vincent couldn't imagine.

Of course, he'd missed Michelangelo's duplicity.
And even for a Liar, that was an impressive trick. The
hardest people to read were the ones one was most
emotionally attached to, because one's own projections
and desires would interfere with the analysis. One
would see what one wanted to see.

There was no surprise in not noticing the knife in
Brutus's hand.

Katya Pretoria stepped back, shaking filthy locks of
hair out of her eyes. Flecks of blood stuck the strands
together. "Of course I don't," she said. "Now, if you
will excuse me, Miss Katherinessen, I'm going to get
Walter upstairs and try for some sleep myself. I have to
relieve Agnes in the morning."

*Kii watches the rust-colored biped climb. Its heartbeat is
fast, blood pressure elevated, serotonin levels depleted,
blood sugar dropping, lactic acid levels high, breathing
shallow. It is, in short, exhausted, hungry, and danger-
ously emotional.*

*Kii waits until it regains its temporary refuge and is
alone, in what the bipeds call privacy. Then he clears the
wall and appears. "Greetings, Vincent Katherinessen."*

*"Kii," it says. "I was just about to call you. I know the
Consent is that you will not assist me—"*

*"You wish to know if Kii can locate Michelangelo
Osiris Leary Kusanagi-Jones."*

*"I wish it, yes." The biped pauses its speech, but not its
motion. If anything, the short quick steps appear to Kii*

like a futile struggle against the inevitable edict. "And Lesa. Katya Pretoria knows what happened."

"It shoots Kusanagi-Jones in the back," Kii says.

The russet biped rounds on Kii's projected image, manipulators clenching. "What?"

"Your mate is unharmed," Kii adds speedily. "It is struck by a sedative capsule. No permanent damage inflicted. Lesa Pretoria is also uninjured, and is restrained in a tangler."

This linear, discursive mode of communication is vastly limited and inefficient, prone to misparsing. It requires finesse to communicate accurately in this fashion. How much more elegant to present information in poem matrices, with observed, stipulated, speculated, and potential elements clearly identified and quantified by the grammar of the construct.

The Katherinessen biped sinks on the edge of the bed, elbows on its legs, manipulators that seem powerful for its size dangling between its knees, knuckles facing. "Where are they?"

Kii accesses records, flicks through House's files. At last, reluctantly, Kii says, "They are not in range of House's nodes."

"They're out of the city. In the jungle?"

"That follows as a strong potential."

"Hell," the biped says. "Now I have to tell Elena that her granddaughter is a traitor. I do not get paid enough for this."

19

LESA WOKE COLD, A NOVEL EXPERIENCE IN PENTHESILEA
in summer. Her hands in particular were numb (the
left one beyond pins-and-needles and into deadness),
her ankles sore, her neck cramped from lying slumped
on her side. The hair that dragged through her mouth
was foul with blood and dirt and the acrid bitterness of
tangler solvent, and she spat and spat trying to clear it
away.

She lay on an earthen floor, and she could smell the
jungle. Smell it—and hear it. Night sounds, which explained why her eyes strained at darkness. The canopy
filtered daylight, but blocked the Gorgon's light almost
entirely. She heard birds and insects—and a fexa's
warble, closer than she liked, even if she was lucky and
there was a stout stockade between them.

She flexed and kicked but didn't learn anything that
surprised her. Her wrists were bound at the small of
her back and her ankles strapped. When she lifted her

head, her neck amended its status from painful to ex-
cruciating, and she fell back, trying to ease the spasm,
crying between her teeth.

Incapacitating pain was the first priority. That, and
getting her weight off her left arm.

A wriggle of her hips flopped her onto her back,
yanking her wrists against the cords. This position was
no kinder to her hands, but she bore the pressure and
the cutting tautness for the sheer, blessed relief of letting the earth support the weight of her head.

Something feather-quick and many-legged scurried
across her ankle, but she managed not to react.
Pointless caution. She'd made enough noise already
that one little thrash and scream would cause no harm.
But most New Amazonian "insects" were completely
disinterested in any Old Earth fauna that wasn't actively forcing them to defend themselves. Lesa guessed
that when it came down to it, human type people just
smelled wrong.

Something stretched on her left side, close enough
that she could feel the heat radiating from it and hear
the slow hiss of breathing, in and out. Now that Lesa
could concentrate on something other than the pain in
her neck, she smelled unwashed male over her own
sweat and tangler solvent. The solvent explained why
she was cold. The stuff was something like 95 percent
isopropyl alcohol.

Michelangelo. She got her knees drawn up, straps
cutting the tendons of her ankles, and with one hard
shove flopped onto her right side. Pain seared up her
neck and her left arm sizzled violently to life. She had
preferred it, she decided, when it was flopping from
her shoulder like the corpse of a dead animal.

Kusanagi-Jones wasn't cold. She pressed against his
back, but he breathed regularly, his body swaying in

response to her nudges with the fluidity of deep un-consciousness. Her right shoulder and upper arm scraped earth painfully as she squirmed closer, writhing over broad shoulders to press her face against the close-clipped base of his skull. As she cuddled up, she realized she heard two sets of snores—Kusanagi-Jones's, faintly, and muffled as if through walls, a louder rasp.

I hope Vincent's not the jealous type. Gallows humor. The pain of one bitten-off chuckle brought tears to her eyes.

"Miss Kusanagi-Jones." She heaved herself against him. Every movement jostling her neck felt as if some-body had run electrified wires under her skin. "Miss Kusanagi-Jones!"

His breath caught and a light moan fluttered at the back of his throat, but he didn't wake. She lowered her head and shoved, smacking her head into his neck. "Dammit, Michelangelo."

He vanished.

A second later, air cooling against her chest, she re-alized she *had* felt him move. One moment, Kusanagi-Jones was a yielding obstacle rocking in time to her efforts. The next, she was alone in the dark, and some-thing thumped—a meat-on-bare-earth sound—followed by silence.

And then a voice, barely a breath. "Miss Pretoria?"

She sighed, trying not to dwell on the strength it would have taken to flip himself to his feet while bound wrist and ankle. "Very impressive. So how are you at square knots?"

Michelangelo's wardrobe wasn't functioning, informa-tion delivered quite unceremoniously by the weight of imitation cloth on his shoulders. He couldn't tell if it had failed due to power drain or because of exposure to an electromagnetic pulse weapon of some sort.

The wardrobe was shielded, but shielded was not *invulnerable*. His low-light add-ons, his watch, and his other sense enhancements weren't functioning either, which told him it was a power problem and not just the wardrobe. But in the case of failure, the fog assumed a default configuration. In Kusanagi-Jones's case, his gi—and that was what hung around him now with a strangely *material* weight.

A quick triage would not rank a malfunctioning wardrobe as the greatest of his problems. The foglets would have made short work of his restraints, but he was trained to operate without them. No, the immediate problem was one of where he was being held, and how to get out of there.

"Keep talking," he said. "I don't want to step on you."

"What would you like to talk about?"

The voice located her. He sat in a different direction, with as slight a thump as he could manage. The rammed earth didn't give. He rolled onto his back, lifting his legs, forcing his arms down against cords that cut at his wrists.

"Talk about anything," he said, keeping his voice as level and soft as he could. She didn't need to know about his pain.

"I heard someone snoring before you woke. I think our guard is napping against the wall."

"Who do you think is holding us?"

"Right Hand," she answered immediately.

Discomfort escaped him on a hiss as he stretched to work his arms around his hips, dragging his shoulders down. "Why?"

"Well," she said, "we know it's not Parity. And whoever it is has dragged us off to a hut in the jungle, where you might expect bandits and runaways."

His hands were free suddenly, with a scraping pop. Or, not exactly free, but bound behind his knees rather than behind his back. Awkward, but easily remedied, and once he got them around his feet, he had teeth. A bloody good thing they hadn't had shackles. "You weren't kidding about pirates."

"No," she said. "Damn Robert to a man's hell anyway."

Kusanagi-Jones brought his legs up, hooked his hands under his heels, and stretched and wriggled until blood broke through his scabbed wrists and trickled across the skin. If he had Vincent's loose-limbed build, this would be easy, but long flexible arms were another of the advantages that hadn't made it into Kusanagi-Jones's heritage.

He made it happen anyway, and then sprawled on his back, panting as quietly as he could manage while blood dripped off his thumbs and spattered his chest. It wouldn't soak into the gi the way it would real cloth, but it could seep between the minuscule handclasped robots that made up the utility fog, and there was no way he was getting it out of there—short of wading into the ocean—until he found a power source.

"Ow," he said. "Ever noticed this doesn't get easier?"

"Indeed," she said. "I have."

A good smearing of blood and sweat hadn't made the thin cords binding his wrists any simpler to manage. They were tight enough that they'd be more accessible if he gnawed his thumbs off first. Also tight enough that he wouldn't even feel it much.

Which would defeat the purpose of getting his

hands free. Instead, he dug at the cords with his teeth, scraping at the fibers and working as much mayhem on his own flesh as on the bindings. But eventually he heard a pop and felt a cord part, and the constriction loosened.

The next thing he felt, unfortunately, was his fingers. Which made him wish for one long, brutal instant that he'd just been a good well-behaved secret agent and lain there peaceably waiting for the firing squad.

The pain filled his sinuses, flooded his nostrils, floated his eyes in their orbits. It was physically blinding—he couldn't see the darkness for the flashes in his vision. Beyond pain, and into a white static he couldn't see or move or breathe through. Michelangelo gritted his teeth, pressed his forehead to thumbs while tears and snot streaked his face, and held on.

It would crest. It would peak and roll back.

All he had to do was live through it.

All he had to do——

He wheezed, hard, when his diaphragm finally relaxed enough that he could get a breath, and then threw his head back, panting. "Bugger," he said indistinctly, and let his hands fall against his chest.

His fingers felt thick and hot, and they bent only reluctantly, but he could feel them, and they hurt less now than did his wrists.

"You ever needed to disprove the existence of a Creator God," he said, "the miracle of efficiency that the human body isn't would be a fucking good place to start."

"Miss Kusanagi-Jones?"

Deities or not, there was obviously still room in the world for miracles. Miss Pretoria honestly sounded scared.

"Under the circumstances, call me Michelangelo. Will you roll onto your stomach, please?"

Her wrists were more important than his ankles. He knelt over her, hands on either side of her waist, and used his teeth on these cords, too. His fingers weren't strong enough.

She whimpered once or twice, but overall, he thought she made less noise than he had.

When he was done, and she was taking her turn coiled shaking around the agony of returning circulation, he sat up and began fumbling at the strapping on his ankles. It was adhesive, wound tight, but he managed to feel the torn edge. It came off noisily, along with a generous quantity of hair.

A ripping sound in the darkness, followed by a series of half-breathed "ow"s, informed him that Miss Pretoria didn't need any instruction in order to follow his example. "Now I understand why males complain so much about waxing their backs for the Trials," she murmured, barely audible under the sawing and bowing of whatever animals infested the jungle night.

Kusanagi-Jones stifled a laugh. "Hold onto that strapping," he said. "Might come in useful."

"It's sticky."

"And strong," he answered, attempting to disentangle his own length so as to wind it around his waist. "See anything yet?"

"Now that you mention it, it might be graying. Slightly."

He thought so, too. If the walls were boards, as he suspected, and the roof was thatch, the slivers of faint brightness he saw might very well disclose the first grayness of morning. The exotic noises outside were increasing in volume, frequency, and complexity.

Dawn was coming.

"You don't have a theory why pirates would want to kidnap a couple of diplomats, do you?"

"Not yet," she answered, and now he could make out enough of her silhouette to see her, head bent, tucking the strapping around herself like a sash. "I'm also curious about how they've come to recruit so many young women."

"Including your daughter."

She lifted her head to stare at the dimly outlined wall. Her lips were pursed. Her eyes caught the growing light, glistening. She didn't blink. "Maybe they're all the daughters or sisters or lovers of males associated with the Right Hand. Maybe..." She sighed and shrugged. "I don't know. If they can infiltrate Pretoria house, they could be anywhere."

"Could be facing a revolution."

She licked her lips, turned, and blinked at him. "Did you think for a moment there was a possibility we aren't? Come on. Let's make a break for it."

She shook herself and moved toward the door they could now see outlined against the far wall, her hand twitching toward a nonexistent weapon. The door was chained around the post, but Kusanagi-Jones thought he could handle it. He touched the chain, stroked it, rust rubbing off on his fingertips. That chain would hold against anything he could manage barehanded.

The planks of the door, on the other hand...

"Sneak, or rush?" he asked Miss Pretoria.

She crouched beside him, examining the door. "There will be a stockade," she said. "If they have any sense. A kind of barrier of cut thorn trees."

"A zareba."

She blinked at him. "I don't know that word."

There was enough light now to show a smile, so he made it a good one. "If you had ever lived in Africa, you would. Before the Diaspora, people walled themselves in with stockades made of thornbushes, to keep out predators like hyenas. Village was called a kraal or enkang. Stockade was a zareba."

For a moment, he thought she was about to ask him what a hyena was, but instead she returned his smile and dusted her hands on her knees. "Miss Kusanagi-Jones, I think that's the longest speech I've heard you make."

He grunted his answer and stepped back, gesturing her to one side as he squared himself before the door. She went, standing with her back against the wall, but the curve of her lip told him she wasn't about to leave it alone.

"Why do you let people assume you're the lump of dumb meat on Vincent's elbow?"

"Suits me," he said, after a long enough pause to let her know she'd overstepped. His own fault for giving her the opening. "You never said: got a better route out of here than kicking the door down?"

"No," she answered, rubbing her wrists. "I don't."

She'd missed the opportunity to really see him move when he'd saved Claude Singapore's life, and during the previous evening's skirmish she'd been only peripherally aware of what he did, the phenomenal efficiency and speed with which he'd managed three armed women.

"Farther left," he said, waving her aside. "Splinters."

Another time, she might have taken him to task for his lack of deference, but she didn't want to break his focus, so she edged two more steps away from the door frame and flattened herself against the wall, breathing steadily, ready to spring out and intercept the swinging panel on the rebound. She shielded her face with her hand, but couldn't resist watching between her fingers as Kusanagi-Jones took one deep breath.

"If I go down," she said, "run and keep running."

He didn't spare her a glance. "Try not to be the one that goes down."

Without breaking the steady rhythm of his breathing, he took two fluid steps, spun, and kicked out, hard. The door shattered against the chain, and Lesa kicked off the wall and slung herself through it, catching the rebound on her flat hand. Flesh tore on splintered wood, but she didn't hesitate.

As she cleared the doorway and broke into a bare, scuffed-dirt yard, the unwary guard lunged for her and missed. The unshod footsteps behind her were Kusanagi-Jones's. She heard the grunt and thud as he slammed into the sentry and hoped Michelangelo had body-checked him hard enough to break bones.

Not hard enough to shut him up, unfortunately, because he was shouting before he'd picked himself up on his elbows. But Michelangelo was still with her, pulling up beside her, running hard as the camp boiled like a kicked nant's nest.

Gunfire spattered around her, ended by a curse. Chemical accelerant had a distinctive sound. These were lethal loads, and they came close enough to sting her with kicked-up earth and splinters. Kusanagi-Jones grunted as he dropped back a step, falling in behind her, shielding her body with his own.

She wasn't going to get him shot by running slow. Lesa dodged around the side of a low hut constructed of thatch and daub over a wooden frame and dove past two unarmed males, elbowing the nearer in the jaw as she went by. Judging by the collision, Kusanagi-Jones took the other one down without breaking stride.

"Go," Kusanagi-Jones yelled as she slid around the

second corner, between the shelter and the thorn wall. She could see green jungle through the gaps in the canes, and the wall was no more than a meter beyond the hut. His footsteps stopped, his breathing no longer close on her heels.

He was buying her time to get out, turning to make a stand.

Below the edge of the overhang, Lesa bent her knees and jumped. Not for the thorn wall—the long curved spines of wire plant rendered it as impossible to climb as a heap of razors—but for the roof. Her fingers slipped in rain-slimed thatch, and insects and shreds of vegetation showered her face and shoulders. The top layers were wet, but underneath the fronds were dry— old enough to need replacing—and her hands sank through to latch onto the beam underneath. Wood cracked under her weight, and for a moment she dangled, cursing. Then she got her motion under control, pumped her legs, and half swung, half scrambled up, arms trembling and chest aching with the strain.

This was not a roof built for walking on. She lay flat and turned to pull Kusanagi-Jones after her.

"Go," he said, with a glance over his shoulder. He had a weapon in his hands that he must have liberated from the first, unwary guard, and he was bleeding, red dripping from the right sleeve of his gi and spreading over his fingers, more than his torn wrists could explain.

There was no time for thanks, for apologies.

She went.

She slithered across the hunchbacked roof on her belly, turning so she faced the thorn wall, and paused where rafters gave way to the unsupported fringe of thatch. The flat sharp cracks of three more gunshots echoed through the trees, the birds of morning shrieking and then silent. The bullets came nowhere near their position. Encouraging, because the hut wouldn't offer Kusanagi-Jones anything except visual cover, but she hoped the partisans might think they were working their way toward the gate.

Kusanagi-Jones conserved his ammunition, making them find him and *then* deal with his ability to shoot back. Smart boy. She'd seriously underestimated the Coalition males.

Lesa clenched her hands around that last flaking roof beam and drew her feet forward into a crouch. It was hard to judge distances in the gray morning light, but she could hear calls through the camp now. Another two or three random shots might serve to raise the alarm for any distant sentries. She stared at the thornbreak one last time, closed her eyes, and jumped for her life.

She might have made it if she could have gotten a running start. As it was, she kicked off hard, stretched, tucked, rolled, and almost cleared the wall. She made it over the top, but the sloped sides were too wide. Thorns tore her shins and forearms, lacerated her shoulders, pierced the hands she raised to shield her eyes and throat. Brittle canes shattered under her weight, and momentum sprawled her clear, lungs emptied, diaphragm aching from the impact.

She gasped and shoved herself up, shaking off bits of twig and barb, driving thorns into her palms and knees as she scrambled to her feet, piercing her unshod soles as she staggered forward through the rubbish. She was leaving a trail of blood and bits a girl could follow, but there was nothing to be done for it now.

Tears and sweat stinging her lacerated face, she ran.

20

ELENA HANDLED KATYA'S ARREST HERSELF. SHE SUM-
moned Agnes—a Pretoria cousin who had the same
stocky build and epicanthic folds as Lesa—and requested Vincent wait for their return. He was left
alone on the sun porch that served as Pretoria house's
center of operations, but deemed it unwise to wander
about the house with Elena in the mood he'd put her
in. So instead he paced the length of the veranda, re-
viewing documents on his watch that he already knew
by heart.

He'd accomplished everything he'd come here to
do—the real reasons, not the surface justifications.
He'd met his mother's opposite number, deemed her
honest, established a secure line of communication, exchanged the necessary codes.

Now all he had to do was wrap up two kidnappings,
a sabotage operation, a first-contact situation, a duel to
the death, convince Michelangelo he didn't want to

play kamikaze, and figure out exactly how he was going to get rid of the Governors *and* protect Ur and New Amazonia from the imperial ambitions of the Coalition. Oh, yes, and at least give his ostensible task—that of reaching some sort of détente with whoever was in charge of the New Amazonian government by the end of the week—enough of a lick and a promise that he could justify declaring the mission accomplished and heading home. Or, potentially, blow it so badly that he and Angelo were both discharged in disgrace, which would save him the additional delicate operation of prying Michelangelo loose from the OECC.

Because Michelangelo *was* coming home with him. Just as soon as Vincent reclaimed him.

Piece of cake.

He closed the documents and stood in the darkness, running fingertips along the slick leaves and soft petals garlanding the lattice. A flicker of movement in his fisheye alerted him to company, and he turned his head, but it wasn't Elena or any of her servants. Instead, a child stood framed in the doorway, pressed close to one of the posts as if he thought he could meld into them. A boy child, nine or ten Old Earth years, six or seven New Amazonian.

Lesa's son, the one she so desperately wanted to be gentle.

"Hello," Vincent said.

"Hello," the boy answered. He came forward a few more steps, from the lighted hallway to the darkness of the porch. "Are you really a diplomat?"

Vincent smiled. The boy—Julian—was hesitant and calm, but the lilt in his voice said he was curious. And Lesa thought he was a genius, and wasted on New Amazonia.

She might even be right.

In any case, if Vincent was likely to wind up smuggling the kid home in his suitcase, he might as well get to know him. "I am, among other things. Your mother's very proud of you."

The child sidled along the wall sideways, back to the house but meeting Vincent's eyes defiantly. "She says if I want to be a mathematician I have to be like you."

"Like me?"

Julian nodded, his hands linking behind him, shoulders squeezing back as he crowded against the wall. "Gentle. Otherwise I'll be sent to foster and train soon, and then I'll go to the Trials and be chosen by another house."

"And you won't have time for mathematics then?" As Vincent understood it, not everybody was as...permissive...with their stud males as Pretoria house. His heart skipped painfully while he waited for the answer. *Poor kid.*

"Mother says," Julian said, tilting his head back as he recalled her words, "that women don't like males who seem too smart. They find them threatening."

What an elegant little parrot she's created, Vincent thought, and wanted to bury his face in his hands.

"So she says I can only play with computers and numbers when I grow up if I'm gentle," Julian continued, still childlike enough to take his silence for rapt attention. "Like you. So I must be gentle..."

"Because you love numbers so much."

Julian nodded. "But it's not bad, being like you, right?"

Vincent found the edge of Elena's wicker chair, sat down on it, and leaned forward with his elbows on his knees. The cosmic irony of the moment didn't elude

him. This child was no more a budding homosexual
than Michelangelo was thick-headed, and Vincent had
to fold his hands together to keep them from shaking
as he thought about Julian embarking on a life of sexual deception so he'd have an option of careers. "No,"
he said. "People can be cruel. But being like me isn't
bad. I had to lie about it for a very long time, though,
and pretend to be something I wasn't to keep my job."

The boy's eyes were wide. "I thought you were a
diplomat because you're, you know, because you don't
fight."

It cost Vincent a painful effort to keep the smile off
his face. The last thing this fumbling child needed was
to think somebody he was looking to as a role model
found him amusing. "Things are different on Old
Earth," he said. "Gentle males are...stigmatized. Do
you know that word?"

"The stud males run everything and don't like gentle ones."

"Yes."

"Like the other boys make fun of me for playing
with numbers."

"Yes."

"How come?" An earnest question, not plaintive, as
Julian's hands fell to his sides as he forgot himself
enough to step away from the wall.

It deserved an honest answer. "I don't know."
Which was as honest as he could be. "Your mother says
you're very talented."

The boy's skin was dark, darker than Lesa's if not as
dark as Robert's. In a better light, Vincent wouldn't
have been able to see him blush. "She said that?"

"She did. She asked me if I would sort of be a men-
tor for you." Not too much of a stretch, and Vincent
didn't feel bad about it. The child's mother and father

were missing, his sister was under arrest, and if he felt alone and frightened, he didn't have to feel *that* alone and frightened.

Julian glanced over his shoulder toward the door, the sidelong look of somebody operating under a guilty conscience. "Do you know anything about programming quantum arrays?"

"Not a thing," Vincent admitted. "But I listen well. You can teach me."

He set his watch to record, and let the boy chatter on about transforms and quantifiable logic and fractal decision trees and a few thousand other things that might as well have been Swahili. No, not even. *Urdu,* because thanks to Michelangelo's remarkable—and habitually concealed—gift for languages, Vincent actually spoke a fair amount of Swahili.

In any case, Julian talked, and Vincent made encouraging noises. And before too long, he started to wonder exactly what Julian was doing wandering around the house alone in the middle of the night, when from what Vincent had seen even young males didn't go about unescorted. Except, of course, during Carnival.

The boy had to pause for breath eventually. "Julian," Vincent said, "how did you get out of the Blue Rooms to come talk to me? Did somebody give you a pass?"

Julian's mobile mouth thinned and he shook his head jerkily. "No pass."

"So how?"

Because as far as Vincent knew there was supposed to be only one route out of the harem, and it was supposed to be guarded. By Agnes, usually, who had been out of the house trying to locate any trace of Lesa and Michelangelo, and whom Elena had just summoned home to help deal with Katya.

"Did you just walk out?"

"My sire showed me," Julian said, quietly. "There's a secret stair. I'm not supposed to tell anybody."

Which explained how Robert had escaped. "Julian," Vincent said, "I think you'd better go back before your grandmother catches you out of bed."

"But—"

"It's okay. I promise we'll talk some more tomorrow." He stood up, slouching enough to minimize his height advantage on a kid who hadn't hit his growth spurt yet, and came over to Julian, hunkering down a little to speak to him eye to eye. He put his hand on Julian's shoulder and felt the boy shudder, as if the companionable contact was a threat.

In his society, a sane reaction. "It's okay," Vincent said again. "I'll help. Right now, we have to get your mom back, and my partner. After that—"

Julian nodded jerkily and stepped back into the doorway. They stared at one another for a moment, and then a moment later Julian sidestepped and was gone.

Kii is restless.

This is not a sensation Kii is any longer accustomed to, and Kii is some time in identifying it. Restlessness is not one of the emotional routines that Kii finds useful in Kii's work.

Kii is somewhat disconcerted at first. Inspection, however, reveals the source of the emotion; it is an outflow of the Consent. The Consent wishes more information regarding Kaiwo Maru *and regarding the life forms that inhabit her.*

They are made things, like the khir, and like the khir,

they are guardians. They are intelligent, and they are designed, but they are not people.

There are differences. The khir serve. They guard the Consent's endless dreamings, but these Governors, while designed to serve a purpose, serve it by ruling over the esthelich *creatures who created them.*

It is an inversion.

Perhaps the bipeds are truly alien enough to place their destiny in the hands of monsters. Or perhaps there is a miscalculation, and this is the result. Kii cannot yet be sure, and the Consent is chary of deciding on so thin a pattern.

Kii continues to research. The Governors are an advantage to Kii's bipeds—the local colony, that is. The bipeds Kii identifies as Kii's pets, and which the Consent is to abet.

The Governors advantage Kii's bipeds because they severely curtail the growth of the nonlocal population.

But they are a disadvantage as well. They create a population that is extremely creative and active, without the drain of substandard individuals. In other words, by ensuring that only extraordinary and accomplished individuals survive, and by skewing that population toward those most practically creative, the Governors nourish innovation. They force the Coalition outward, groping, grasping, subsuming other colony worlds.

They are the engine that drives the expansion that Kii has informed Michelangelo Osiris Leary Kusanagi-Jones that Kii will not permit in local space-time.

The Consent is temporary. The potentialities are complex, the patterns not yet emergent. The current solution is to prepare for three eventualities deemed likely. The first requires no action, as there are possibilities in motion that carry the Coalition away from local space-time for the foreseeable potentialities. The second is the need to eradicate the Governors as a species, which will alleviate immediate population pressure on the Coalition worlds and thus the immediate threat to the local colony. This solution carries an attendant ecological cost and an eventual pattern that may mean dealing with stronger and larger Coalition feelers. The third is to prepare to exterminate as much of the nonlocal population of bipeds as is deemed necessary to prevent their encroachment, if the emerging pattern proves them belligerent.

When the waves collapse, Kii will he glad to no longer worry. But they are not yet resolved, and so Kii is worried, and the Consent is not open to Kii's advice.

Kii believes that a preemptive strike would be more effective. Kaiwo Maru *is the nexus of probabilities, the center of the indeterminacies. If* Kaiwo Maru *is destroyed, so many waves collapse—*

Kii is overruled. The Consent is that there are too many esthelich *intelligences aboard* Kaiwo Maru *in addition to the Governors, and the* esthelich *do not act yet in belligerence. The Consent is to observe and prepare.*

The Consent takes hold, and Kii ceases to recall why Kii, in an alternately collapsed wave, would have felt differently.

When Elena returned in the growing light of morning, Vincent's fisheye showed that she'd been crying. He hadn't resumed her chair after Julian left, and instead stood in the shadows near the lattice, watching things like moths and probably named for them come and go among the dead, plucked flowers, ignoring what threads of music and laughter drifted in from the streets. They were jangling, frantic sounds. *Have fun quick, before someone comes and stops you.*

"You don't like the garland," Elena said, when he realized she was waiting for him to notice her, and turned. Her voice rasped. She coughed and rubbed her mouth with her hand.

"They're dead. It strikes me as macabre to hang murdered plants all over your buildings. How much longer is Carnival?"

"Seven days," she said. "Ten all together. And the flowers are dead because nothing grows in a Dragon city. Except carpetplant. They do their own weeding."

"I didn't think of that."

"That's how the cities survived intact." She came closer and joined him at the lattice, peering through the blooms to the empty courtyard. "Katya's not talking," she said. "We're going to have to go to Claude."

"Not an option," he said, and bit his lip. "I didn't mean to say that. Some sneaky, underhanded diplomat I am."

She didn't step closer, but he felt her warmth against his arm. It reminded him that his shoulders itched, and he tightened his fingers on the ledge of the porch railing.

"You're more worried about him than you pretend."

He looked at her standing there, open-eyed, empty-palmed, and for a moment almost managed to think of her as human.

"We need to involve security and the militia," she continued when it became apparent he had nothing to say. "I can't do that without Claude."

"Elder Kyoto is on our side."

"Elder Kyoto wouldn't keep her job long enough to be of any use to us if she tried to sneak this past the administration. Why are you so opposed to involving them?"

"Other than her challenging Angelo to a duel?"

"Political maneuvering," Elena said with a wave of her hand. "There's more."

"All right," Vincent said, and let his hands fall open, too. "I believe she and Saide Austin are aware of—no, in collusion with—the operators of an illegal genetics lab somewhere on New Amazonia. And that they used that lab to create a retrovirus with which they then infected my partner, with the intent of spreading a deadly epidemic across Old Earth."

"You have proof?" Elena asked, as of course she would.

"It's in Angelo's bloodstream," Vincent answered. "We hadn't had time to get it taken care of yet."

"Oh." She took a half-step forward, belly against the railing, her hands curled hard on the edge.

"Yeah," Vincent said. "I'm not sure talking to Claude is the best possible solution."

"No," Elena said. "The genetic engineering, though. If we could prove that, we wouldn't even have to have her killed."

"So all we have to do is find a genetic lab so well hidden nobody in Penthesilea knows where it is."

"You've never had to find an illegal drug lab?" Elena said. "Somebody always knows. I just wish Lesa were here."

"Out of danger?"

"To help find it. Security directorate is what she does."

21

LESA KNEW HER WAY THROUGH THE BUSH. UNARMED, barefoot, injured, and clad in the rags of city clothes, she managed to stay ahead of the pursuit for almost twelve hours, through the afternoon rain and well into the evening of the long New Amazonian day, until the sounds of voices faded and the only man-made sound she heard was the occasional distant, echoing signal by gunfire, followed by a crescendo of animal complaint.

She regretted not having a bush knife most of all. A gun would have been nice, and it chafed not to have her honor at her hip, but a knife would have made travel infinitely easier. It also would have left a defined trail, of course, but crawling under still more thorny wire-plant, her scratched hands and forearms swelling with infection, she didn't think she'd care. At least the tender redness was likely just her own skin flora; most New Amazonian bacteria didn't like the taste of Earth meat any better than did the New Amazonian bugs.

Once the sun was up, she had managed a good bearing, though that wasn't much use without a reference point. Then, for lack of options, she had headed east. If the Right Hand hadn't brought her too far from Penthesilea, she'd find a coast in that direction. And if they'd transported her any distance—well, this looked like home jungle, and if it wasn't, something was very likely to eat her before she starved.

Unlike the "insects" and the "bacteria," some of the larger New Amazonian life had absolutely no objection to the taste of mammal. And fexa were quite territorial.

In any case, it was bound to be a long walk.

At least she could entertain herself as she picked her way over borer-addled trunks and through drapes of waterlogged vines by trying to decide how she was going to explain to Vincent that she'd left Kusanagi-Jones behind.

The conscious edge of her brain wasn't helping her anyway. What she needed was the inner animal, the instincts tuned to shifts of light and the cries of big-eyed, ringtailed treekats awakening for the night and the black-and-violet, four-winged Francisco's macaws settling down in their roosts. She thought about fashioning weapons, but that would take time, and her advantage right now was in staying ahead of her pursuers—well-armed men who knew the lay of the land.

She did pick up a stout branch, green and springy. It had a gnawed, pointed gnarl at the base where it had been disarticulated by a treekat after the infestation of bugs in the heartwood. The smaller twigs had withered since it fell, but only a few rootlets protruded; she stripped them away, broke the slender end off, and found herself possessed of a serviceable three-foot-long club.

The rich scent of loam rose from under her denting footsteps, and insectoids scurried from overturned litter. She made an effort to walk more lightly, picking past clumps of moss that would show her footsteps, hopping between patches of wild carpetplant that flourished where sunlight managed to pierce the canopy in long, flickering rays. It wouldn't bruise, even when she jumped on it, and it beat sticking to game trails. Those would lead pursuit right to her.

She needed to find a place to bed down for the night.

Lesa had slept rough before, but she had no illusions about her odds of surviving a night in the jungle un-armed, without shelter, and without daring to build a fire even if she had the wherewithal to do so. It might keep off animals, but it would be as good as a beacon to the Right Hand.

At least being dive-bombed and picked clean by sirens or strangled by a fexa would be quick.

She found a crevice under a fallen log big enough to cram herself into, heaped leaf litter under it to con-serve warmth, and hauled a drape of living wire-plant over the top to serve as a barricade to any wandering animals, savaging her hands further in the process. She picked the thorns out of her palms with her teeth, and dropped them in the cup of a rain-collecting plant among wriggling tadpoles so the water could help hide the scent of her blood.

The pungent stinging scent of wire-plant sap would serve to conceal her own body odor.

She crammed herself into her impromptu shelter as dusk was growing thick under the trees, controlled her breathing, and resolutely closed her eyes.

Kusanagi-Jones sighed and tugged idly at his shackles, galling his wrists and pulling at the shallow knife cut on his forearm. He didn't shift either the three-

centimeter-thick staple they were locked to or the
beam behind it. Apparently better bondage equipment
had arrived during the night. And when he'd been lying on the ground in the center of camp, flat on his
back from the paralytic agent the insurgents had used
to bring him down, he'd seen several more good-sized
shelters all overhung with holographic and utility fog
camouflage. At least two aircars had gone out after
Lesa. The entire camp was under a false rain-forest
canopy, all but invisible from the air, probably protected by IR and other countermeasures.

Coalition technology. Which also explained how
they'd managed to shut down his wardrobe. Miss
Ouagadougou wasn't the only Coalition agent on the
ground here.

Somebody was running guns.

And the nasty, suspicious part of Kusanagi-Jones's
mind—the one that tended to keep him alive in situations like this—chipped in with the observation that
he and Vincent hadn't been trusted with the information. Which told him that they weren't the primary operation in this theater.

They were the stalking horse. And the real operation was an armed insurrection.

Who'd miss a couple of disgraced old faggots anyway? And if Vincent happened to get himself killed in
theater by enemy action, it wasn't as if Katherine
Lexasdaughter could complain, no matter how much
pull she had with the Coalition Cabinet. Which made
sense of yesterday's unutterably stupid grab for
Vincent in Penthesilea, too. It gave the Coalition one
more big black check mark in the *invade New
Amazonia* column to present the Governors.

At least he was more comfortable now. They'd permitted him access to a privy, and the shackles gave him

enough slack to stand, sit, or even stretch out on his back if he crossed his arms over his chest—and enough slack to kick the "food" they'd brought him almost far enough away that he didn't have to smell charred flesh every time he turned his head.

The water, he'd drunk; it was clean, and there had been plenty of it, and if they wanted to drug him they didn't need to hide it in his rations when another dart would work just fine. He had tried a few bites of the bread, but there was something cloying about the taste and texture that made him suspect it contained some ingredient he didn't care to consume.

He'd wait. He wasn't hungry enough for it to affect his performance, yet.

It was best that Lesa had escaped. She had a better chance of getting back than he did, and a better chance of being heard when she did so. And Kusanagi-Jones was safer in captivity anyway. Less likely to be raped or tortured—and they hadn't tried anything yet, though he wouldn't bet his ration number on it—and more likely to survive the experience if they wanted to use him to extract something from Vincent.

He wouldn't be held as a bargaining chip, though. Not if they were already receiving Coalition aid. Presuming they knew who they were receiving it from. Which was presuming a lot.

He shifted again, wishing he could rub the torn skin under his manacles or his cut shoulder. His docs weren't dependent on the power supply of his watch or his wardrobe; they used the kinetic energy of his own bloodstream to power themselves, a failsafe that kept them operational as long as his heart was beating. And they were doing an acceptable job of preventing infection, and even speeding healing, but the wounds could hardly have itched more.

Another damned irritation, like the hunger and the dehydration making him light-headed in the heat.

He closed his eyes, leaned his head back against the post, and tried to think as Vincent would. What purpose would holding him serve? What was he doing alive?

There was the obvious answer. Bait.

"You know," Kusanagi-Jones said to the air, "he really only brings me along so they'll have someone to take hostage."

He was bait. A hook in Vincent. Because the Right Hand had missed Vincent, and the Right Hand was taking aid from the OECC. And if anything happened to Vincent, while Katherine Lexasdaughter couldn't very well take the OECC to task for it, she could certainly demand some kind of retaliation against New Amazonia for so carelessly disposing of her son. And if she didn't, the Coalition could.

Vincent's abduction and death was probably a good enough excuse that the Governors would allow the OECC to go to war against New Amazonia. And if anybody in the Cabinet suspected that the recalcitrant leader of the Captain's Council on Ur was plotting with a bunch of hysterical and heavily armed Amazons, the death of Katherine's son at the hands of such might be seen as a good enough way of putting an end to any revolutionary alliances.

And wasn't it just a damned shame that Lesa had already left, and Kusanagi-Jones didn't have any way of transferring that particular startling deduction to Vincent.

He could reconstruct the scenario easily enough. Lesa had followed Katya, caught her about to join Stefan and the rest of the revolutionaries, and Katya's controller had taken Katya "hostage" with a weapon

they both knew was loaded with stun capsules, but
which Lesa would think lethal. After Kusanagi-Jones
rode to the rescue, Katya had had the presence of mind
to establish herself on the winning team by incapacitating her colleagues...until Kusanagi-Jones let his
guard down long enough to get shot in the back like a
rookie. And the Right Hand had seen a chance to reset
its trap for Vincent.

Kusanagi-Jones closed his eyes again, settled his
shoulders against the unfinished wood of the beam,
and tried to ignore the pain in his shoulder enough to
nap. It looked like he'd be wanting to escape after all.

He dozed intermittently through the heat of the afternoon. His disabled wardrobe dragged at his body and
trapped the heat against his skin, raising irritated
bumps, but the docs were working well enough to seal
his wound. Occasional shadows across the gap under
the door told him when he was observed, and the sweat
rolled across his forehead and down his neck to sting
his eyes and his cuts.

He didn't think they'd unsecure him after dark, and
was surprised when, as the light was failing, the chain
around the doorpost finally rattled and slid. A moment
later, the door cracked open and a big silhouette filled
the frame.

The door shut behind it and Kusanagi-Jones heard
the chain refastened by someone outside.

"Michelangelo," the man said, as Kusanagi-Jones
was still blinking his eyes to refocus them after the
light. "I am truly sorry about this."

It was Robert. As he approached, Kusanagi-Jones
pushed himself up the post, determined to meet him
standing.

He found the apology somewhat specious, but this didn't seem the time to explain. So he grunted, and considered for a moment how best to absorb the injury if it came to blows.

But instead, Robert crouched just out of range of Kusanagi-Jones's feet and began pulling things from the capacious pockets of his vest. He laid them on the floor, bulbs of some cloudy yellowish fluid and three pieces of unfamiliar fruit. One was knobby and purple-black in the dim light, the other two larger and creamy yellow, covered in bumps that reminded Kusanagi-Jones unpleasantly of his current case of prickly heat.

"I brought something you can eat," Robert said, without rising. His shiny black boots creased across the toes as he balanced lightly, the insteps and toes daubed with clotted mud. Bloused trousers were tucked into the tops just below the knees. His head jerked dismissively at the flat leaf Kusanagi-Jones had shoved as far away as he could. "I didn't expect they would have taken any care about it."

Robert edged the offering forward, while Kusanagi-Jones watched, feet planted and chained hands hanging at his sides. He kept his eyes on those creases across the toes of Robert's boots, and not on the hands, or on the food. Or, most important after the endless heat, the liquid.

"What's in the bulbs?" he asked when Robert had pushed them as close as he meant to and settled back on his heels.

"Dilute bitterfruit. Electrolytes, sugars, and water. Factory sealed, don't worry."

"Can't exactly pick it up," Kusanagi-Jones said, moving his hands enough to make the shackles clank.

Robert folded his arms over his knees and looked up,

mouth quirking, the faint light catching on the scars that marked his shaven scalp. "Don't you know how to juggle? Use your feet."

Kusanagi-Jones sighed. But he knew how to juggle.

He leaned against the pole, angled one leg out and braced it beside the offerings, and used the ball of the other one to roll the first bulb onto the top of his toes. Then he planted the second foot, shifted his weight, and used the first to flip the bulb into his hands.

Robert applauded lightly, so Kusanagi-Jones lifted an eyebrow at him and angled his body from the waist, a bow amid clanking. Then he raised his hands to his mouth, the cool, sweating bulb turning the filth on his palms into mud. He tore through the stem with his teeth.

The beverage was an acquired taste. It stung his mouth like tonic water.

It might be nasty, but it cleared his head. He drank slowly, so as not to shock his system, and then retrieved the second globe the same way as the first before he said anything else to the patient, motionless Robert. "So," he said, weighing the soft-sided container in his palms, "what price charity?"

"No price." He hesitated. "If you gave me your promise of good behavior, I could see you moved to better quarters."

"Don't pretend concern for my welfare."

"I am concerned," Robert said. "We're freedom fighters, not barbarians. And I'm sorry your arrival here was so rough. It was improvised. They were under instructions not to harm you or Vincent, or Lesa."

"You make it sound almost as if we're not bargaining chips."

Robert smiled, teeth flashing white in the darkness. "You're almost not. You won't give me your word?"

And Kusanagi-Jones opened his mouth to lie—

And could not do it.

He could justify his failure in a dozen ways. The simplest was to tell himself that if he gave Robert his word and broke it, here, now, under these circumstances, he would become useless as an operative in any capacity relating to New Amazonian culture, forever. Their system of honor wouldn't tolerate it. But it wasn't that.

"Thanks for the drinks," he answered, and shook his head.

And Robert grunted and stood, and made a formal sort of bow with folded hands. "Don't forget your fruit," he said, and turned to rap on the door, which opened to let him leave.

By the time Kusanagi-Jones finished the fruit, the hut was as dark as the one he'd woken up in. He dried slick hands on his filthy gi, and then clutched his chains below the shackles, holding tight. Leaning back on his heels, pulling the heavy chain taut, he began to rock back and forth against the staple, trying to limit the pressure on his wounded arm.

Something sniffed Lesa's lair in the dark of night, the blackness under the shadow of the trees. Whatever it was, it found the wire-plant discouraging and continued on its way. Lesa slept in fits, too exhausted to stay awake and too overwrought to sleep. She'd never spent a longer night.

In the morning, the cheeping and whirring of alarm calls brought her from a doze as the skies grayed under an encroaching sun. Lesa froze in her paltry shelter, jammed back against the leaf litter that cupped her meager warmth, and held her breath.

There were three of them, two males and a woman.

All carried long arms—the woman in addition to the honor at her hip, while the men had bush knives—and one of the males and the woman held them at the ready. The third had his slung and was nodding over a small device in the palm of his hand. They conferred too quietly for Lesa to make out the words, and then the woman leveled her weapon and pointed it at Lesa's tree. "You might as well come out, Miss Pretoria. Otherwise I'll just shoot you through the vines, and that would be ignominious."

Lesa's cramped limbs trembled as she pried herself from her cave, collecting more long superficial scratches from the wire-plant as she pushed it aside. She stood hunched, her resting place having done nothing to help the spasm in her neck, and stared at the taller of the two males. His hair was unmistakable, a startling light color that Lesa was almost tempted to call blond, though nobody classically blond had survived Assessment. He was out of context, though, and it took her a moment to place him. The shock of recognition, when it came, was disorienting. Stefan. Stefan, the gentle male who worked as a secretary in the Cultural Directorate. Under Miss Ouagadougou.

Not a direction in which Lesa had been looking for conspiracy.

"Your hands," the woman said, continuing to cover her while the second male slid his detecting equipment into a cargo pocket and came forth to immobilize her wrists. No cords this time, but ceramic shackles joined by a hinge that allowed only a limited range of motion.

At least he cuffed her hands in front of her and the smooth ceramic didn't irritate her lacerated wrists. He stepped back three quick steps and grabbed Stefan by the shoulder, turning him away.

The woman didn't let her rifle waver, and Lesa watched her for several moments, and then sighed and sat down on the mossy log, her bound hands in her lap.

Backs turned or not, she could hear more than they intended her to. And it wasn't reassuring. Robert's name was mentioned, followed by a mumble that made the woman snap over her shoulder, "I don't give a damn what *she* thinks."

"If we take her back to camp, it's just one more decision to make in the end," Stefan said. He turned, and caught her gaping before she could glance down. His mouth firmed over his teeth, an expression she understood. A duelist's expression, and one she'd seen on the faces of stud males before a Trial.

"It's too much risk to keep her alive," he said, and Lesa let the breath she seemed to be holding hiss out over her teeth, and, for a moment, closed her eyes.

"And too much risk to shoot her," the woman said. Lesa opened her eyes in time to see Stefan answer her with a flip of his hand, but she continued. "She has family in the group, Stefan. I don't think anybody's going to be comfortable with the idea that their relatives aren't safe—"

"Do you suppose they thought we'd be able to overthrow the government without bloodshed?"

The woman bit her lip. "I don't think they expected their lovers to be shot out of hand."

Stefan nodded, still staring at Lesa, who managed another shallow breath around the tightness in her throat. "It'll have to look natural, then," he said. "That's not hard. There are plenty of ways to die in the jungle. Exposure, fexa, sneakbite."

He glanced around, and Lesa wobbled to her feet. The woman leveled her rifle again, her squint creasing the corners of her eyes. *Thank you*, Lesa mouthed at her, but she only shrugged and shifted her grip on the rifle.

"Here," Stefan said. "Mikhail, give me your gloves."

The second man pulled a pair of hide gloves from another cargo pocket and passed them to Stefan. He tugged them on, his eyes on his fingers rather than Lesa as he made sure they were seated perfectly. And then he walked toward her, past her, and began tugging at the mess of wire-plant until the bulk of it was on the ground, the long stems dragging down from their parasitic anchor points in the canopy. Nests fell in showers of twigs and twists of desiccated parasitic moss, two yellow-gray eggs shattering on the ground and one bouncing unharmed on a patch of carpetplant.

When he'd freed most of the vines, Stefan placed his hands carefully between thorns and gave the plant a hard, definite yank, enough to sway the strangler oak it rooted in and bring another shower of twigs and dead leaves down. A glistening black Francisco's macaw swooped down, shrieking, and made a close pass at his head, fore-wings beating wildly and the hind-wings folded so close to its body that the gold primary feathers merged with the tail plumage.

Stefan ignored it completely, even when it made a second pass, close enough for the claws of its hind-wings to brush his hair. "Bring her up here."

Mikhail and the woman started forward, though she waited until Mikhail had a good grip on Lesa before lowering the rifle.

Lesa made them drag her. A few scuffs in the earth might be revealing, if the right person found her body.

If anyone ever found her body.

She shook her head. Negative thinking. She *would* find a way out of this.

Mikhail unlocked her cuffs, but by then Stefan had

her arms too tightly restrained for her struggling and feet-dragging to make any difference. But she kept squirming and kicking anyway, until fighting made the thorns of the wire-plant Stefan wound around her bite that much deeper. Then she sagged, dead weight, but he hung her on the plant like so much laundry anyway, vines winding her wrists and crossing her chest, thorns sunk like hooks into her skin.

When Mikhail released her and the thorns took her weight, she couldn't even scream. She choked out a whimper, bit her lip, managed to pull it back to the barest whine. Her flesh stretched against imbedded thorns.

Mikhail backed up, scrubbing his palms against his capaciously pocketed trousers, and the woman looked down as Stefan draped a few more vines artistically across her chest. Then he also moved away, frowning at his handiwork. Lesa could barely see him, though the morning had grown bright. Her vision was empty at the edges, and every breath, no matter how shallow, sank the vine's three-centimeter thorns more deeply into her skin. Some of them shattered, stripping off the vines, but there were many more, and they were fresh and green.

They took her weight.

Stefan dropped out of sight. Lesa heard scuffling, but couldn't turn her head. A moment later, he reappeared, sliding from under her log with her improvised club in his hand. He weighed it across his palm, and then took good hold of it and smashed at the ground with a croquet-mallet swing.

Whatever he was doing, a few blows satisfied him. He whirled the club overhead, and slung it tumbling deep among the trees. Mikhail stared down at his feet, and flinched when Lesa couldn't hold back another whimper.

"Right," Stefan said, grabbing the woman's wrist in a liberty that would have shocked Lesa under other circumstances. "Come on," he said, and paused long enough to smile up at Lesa. "Pleasant dreams, Miss Pretoria."

Then he herded his companions away.

They were out of sight, and Lesa considering her options for the least painful method of breathing, when she felt the first savage, stinging bite on the edge of her foot and jerked stupidly against the thorns, and cried.

Stefan had broken open a nant's nest. And while they might not think humans were good eating, they were more enthusiastic about driving off something that might be the predator that had attacked their home.

Except this predator didn't have anyplace to run.

22

KUSANAGI-JONES WAS STILL AT IT LONG AFTER SUNRISE, but he thought the staple might be loosening. He heard a faint clicking now when he rocked it against the wood. When it went, it would go all at once, and he'd find himself sprawled flat on his back in the dirt. At least the chains and the staple were steel, unlike the manacles. They'd make a reasonably effective weapon, once the other end was no longer bolted down.

The clatter of the door lock left him plenty of warning that somebody was about to enter, if the murmur of voices hadn't been enough. He released his grip on the chains and began pacing, wearing out the brief arc permitted. Two steps and pivot, two steps and pivot the other way. Exactly what Vincent would have been doing in his position.

He had less than a meter of slack.

Light spilled in when the door opened with the brilliance of midmorning. Kusanagi-Jones averted his eyes, staring toward the darkest corner of his domain, and waited until the door banged the frame again and the brightness dimmed.

"Michelangelo." Robert again, standing by the door, his left hand cupped beside his thigh as if he held something concealed in the palm.

"Breakfast already?" Kusanagi-Jones asked. "Seems like you just left."

Robert's smile was tight. "Do you remember what I said about the Right Hand not being the barbarians we're painted?"

Kusanagi-Jones folded his hands in front of him and nodded slowly, the chains pulling against his wrists.

"I was wrong," Robert said, and flipped something through the air.

Kusanagi-Jones caught it reflexively. A code stick, the sort that worked as a key. He held it up inquiringly, the shackles stopping his hand before it came level with his face.

"Go ahead," Robert said. He crouched, and began digging in the capacious pockets of his vest. Objects piled on the packed dirt before him. Kusanagi-Jones recognized emergency gear, a primitive datacart of the sort that seemed ubiquitous on New Amazonia, a two-foot knife that Robert pulled from under his vest, a pocket lighter, and the crinkly packaging of a sterile med-kit.

He didn't stand and gawk. He skipped the code stick over the manacles and pried them open with a sigh, careful not to let the chains clang against the pole when he lowered them. He dropped the code stick on the floor and kicked dirt over it, and stepped toward Robert.

"You're helping me escape."

"We're going together," Robert said. "The team that went after Lesa came back."

"Without her?" Kusanagi-Jones sank onto his haunches and began picking items out of the pile and slipping them inside his gi, where the belt would hold them in place. Robert had also provided socks and a pair of low boots, which Kusanagi-Jones jammed his feet into.

"Stefan and Mikhail said they found no sign of her."

Kusanagi-Jones was not Vincent, but even he could read the irony in that tone. He hefted the knife—he would call it a machete—and shoved it through his belt like a pirate's scimitar. The hilt poked him under the ribs.

"There was a third with them. Medeline Angkor-Wat. The tracker. Who told me the truth, after Stefan and Mikhail went to get coffee."

Kusanagi-Jones waited.

Robert lifted his head, fixed Kusanagi-Jones with a look that froze his throat, and filled the silence, the way people did. "We might have a chance to get to her while she's still alive," he said, and shoved a water bottle into Kusanagi-Jones's hand. "There's a GPS locator and a map in the datacart. If we get separated. Medeline's best-guess location for where they left Lesa is plotted. It won't be off by more than a few hundred meters. She's good."

Unless she's lying to you. Kusanagi-Jones pressed his elbow against the pad inside his gi, without voicing the comment. "What about the guard?"

"I brought Chun breakfast," Robert said. "He should be unconscious by now. And the guards at the gate won't know you. Here." He produced a wadded-up dark green shirt from somewhere, and tossed it at Kusanagi-Jones's chest.

Kusanagi-Jones shrugged it on over his gi. It looked less out of place, and the bottoms were dirty enough to pass for the same sort of baggy tan trousers that Robert was wearing.

Robert stood and rattled the door. "Chun?"

There was no answer. Kusanagi-Jones breathed out a sigh he knew better than to have been holding, and waited while Robert pulled the chain through the hole in the door and used another code stick to unfasten the lock.

They had to heave Chun's unconscious body aside to slip through. The sentry had passed out leaning against the door with his plate in his lap. Kusanagi-Jones carefully reclosed the door, pulled the chain free and slipped it into his pocket, and propped Chun back up as he had been. There was no need to leave the place looking like an escape in progress.

And then, side by side, Robert chatting aimlessly about some sporting event, they headed for the gate.

"Easier to steal an aircar," Kusanagi-Jones suggested in low tones. "I can hotwire those."

"They all have beacons. Besides, it's only about fifteen kilometers. We'll be fine."

The boots were too tight and pinched across the ball of Kusanagi-Jones's feet. He could already feel every step of that fifteen kilometers. "I hope you can run," he quipped, which earned him an arched eyebrow.

He wondered what Vincent would have made of that look, of the jaunty set of Robert's shoulders.

And if it would have meant anything. Because if Robert had been fooling Lesa for as long as he must have been, the only explanation was that either he was a Liar, too, or he'd been very lucky never to find himself in a context that Lesa could pick up what he was concealing from her.

Of course, it was possible that the New Amazonian women just didn't talk to their men very much.

The guard at the gap in the zareba barely gave them a glance. They emerged into a camouflaged clearing that extended a few meters beyond the stockade, and crossed it quickly, Kusanagi-Jones blinking gratefully when they entered the shade of the trees. He slid a hand under the borrowed shirt and retrieved the data-cart, wincing at the beep when it activated.

Amateurs.

Something took flight overhead, invisible among the branches.

"What are you doing?" Robert asked.

"She's east?"

"So Medeline said." Robert stepped into the lead, using his own long knife to lift vegetation out of the way rather than slashing at it. Of that, at least, Kusanagi-Jones approved.

The map was easy to use. Lesa's estimated position was marked by a yellow dot, that of Kusanagi-Jones and Robert by a pulsing green glow. All he had to do was make the second match the first.

He'd done harder things in Academy.

Robert never knew what hit him. Michelangelo stepped left, the chain from the door doubled in his right hand, the lock swinging freely. It struck Robert at the base of the skull, on a rising arc that snapped his head forward and sent him crashing forward into the brush. His knife went flying.

Michelangelo had to search to find it, after he straddled Robert and broke his neck.

It was a pity, because Michelangelo had sort of liked him. But he'd already proved he would switch sides over a woman he'd betrayed at least once, and

unlike Vincent, Michelangelo didn't believe in re-
demption.

And you couldn't trust a Liar.

Lesa would have taken the night before over the day
that followed. At least nants weren't much for climbing,
and few of them bothered to scale the inside of her
trousers past where they bunched at the knee. After a
while, the scathing agony of each individual bite, like a
heated needle slipped into her skin, dulled into consis-
tent pain as her flesh puffed up, honeycombed with
lymph.

And when she could manage not to flinch reflexively at every bite, she didn't wind up imbedding the
thorns farther into her skin. Thrashing wouldn't help
her anyway. The wire-plant's barbs were backcurved
like fishhooks, and every twist impaled her more. But
if she could get her hands around the vines...

They were strong enough to take Stefan's weight. If
Lesa could manage a grip on them while she still had
the strength, she could lift herself off the barbs. They
hurt, but they weren't long enough to threaten her unless they tore her throat or eyes, or punctured her inner
thighs where the femoral arteries ran shallow.

It meant freeing one arm, however, while her entire
weight rested on the wire-plant wrapping her other
arm and her torso, and every movement earned her an-
guish.

The thorns didn't come out any sweeter than they'd
gone in. She closed her eyes in concentration and
lifted, edged, bending her wrist in an arc that encouraged the burred vine to drag down the back of her
hand. She couldn't just yank herself off the thorns
without impaling herself on others; she had to coax it.

It was like giving birth, one centimeter, two centimeters. A slide and a moan and a fraction closer to freedom.

Flecks of sun dotted her face through the fluttering leaves of the strangler oak, and her tongue swelled in her mouth by the time she got the last serrated coil to scrape down her arm and drop away. She swayed with reaction and gasped painfully, the vines crossing her torso tightening.

Lifting her head, blinking sweat from her lashes, she studied the vines on her right side, looking for a place with fewer thorns. The motion made her light-headed, the jungle a green whirl around her as she tilted her head back. But it would go faster now. She had a hand free, through careful work and resolute refusal to panic, and there was a spot about a half-meter to the right and slightly over her head where the thorns might be thin enough that she'd only shred her hand grabbing onto the vine, rather than crippling it.

It beat dying here.

She reached out and took hold, gritting her teeth against the pain as she forced herself to close her hand.

Some of the thorns broke, while others cut deep, but she held on. Held on, and tensed the shoulder, and flexed the biceps, and *pulled*. She felt the tendons in her forearm take the strain, the searing heat flash up her neck, blinding white static, and a concomitant lessening of pain as her weight came off the thorns.

This might just work.

When Vincent had asked to talk to Katya, he hadn't expected Elena to consent. They both knew *talk* was a euphemism. But she showed him into the room and left him there, and almost two days later, there he still sat, across a low table from Katya, his bare heels resting on the strictly decorative rungs of a stool that was an outgrowth of House rather than a piece of individual furniture. He was already growing accustomed to single-purpose objects, wasteful as they were. The little cultural differences could seem absolutely homey, compared to the big ones.

Katya stared sullenly, her hands folded in her lap as if to hide the manacles linking her wrists. She wouldn't shift her gaze from his chin, which was meant to be disconcerting.

Vincent wouldn't permit it to succeed.

She was good. Very practiced, very serene, offering open, neutral body language nearly as controlled as Michelangelo's despite exhaustion that had her swaying in her chair. Many years of practice in lying to her mother had given her that edge.

But Vincent wasn't Lesa, and he didn't have a mother's blindness, her self-deception.

Katya Pretoria had no power over him.

They had been sitting here, with brief intermissions, for sixty-one hours, most of two New Amazonian days. Katya had been sitting longer than Vincent, because Agnes took over when Vincent left the room, and Katya . . . didn't leave the room.

Agnes, Katya would plead with. Vincent didn't envy the older woman that.

Vincent could have taken longer breaks, but he contented himself with catnaps barely longer than microsleeps, because they were in this together. She needed never to realize he had been gone long enough to rest . . . and when she broke, he needed to be there. He needed to be making a difference, doing something, anything. Even if it was wrong.

And besides, he had something neither Katya nor

Agnes had. He had chemistry, and his superperceiver's skills.

He hadn't seen Elena Pretoria since the interrogation started, and he didn't blame her. He didn't have a granddaughter, but if he did, he didn't think he'd care to watch her browbeaten, cajoled, misled, manipulated, and entrapped by the likes of Vincent Katherinessen.

Especially if his child's life hung in the balance.

He could only hope that wherever she was, Elena was putting as much effort into locating Saide Austin's illegal genetic engineering lab as Vincent was into prying any potentially useful information out of Katya. And having better success.

He thought she might be weakening, though. The pauses were growing longer, the disconnects between her sentences had become disconnects between phrases, and she could no longer maintain the thread of a lie—or even a narrative. Her wobble on the stool had become a sway.

She would break. All he needed was time. And to put away the sinking, invalid knowledge that Michelangelo could already be dead. *That* was unbearable, the idea that something could have happened, and Vincent would not know. He wanted to believe there was some connection, that somehow he'd understand if anything happened. It was self-delusion. Magical thinking.

Even breaking her wasn't without risks. After a certain point, she'd tell him anything just to get him to leave her alone. If she lied, he was counting on his ability to catch it. Almost as much as he was counting on her actually possessing the information he needed, which might be a little more problematic. But he'd deal with that crisis when he got there.

"Katya," he said as he hopped off his stool and came

around the table to stand beside her, "if you tell me where they took your mother, I can let you sleep. I can get you something to drink and put you in your own bed. Wouldn't that be nice?"

She blinked, wrapping her fingers around each other, her legs splayed wide as she tried to balance herself. Her toes curled into the carpetplant, flexing tendons playing across the tops of her feet. "Can't tell," she said, in a tired little-girl voice that could have broken his heart. "S'important."

She sounded drunk. But she still wasn't to the point of giving him any old answer he asked for just to placate him.

"Your mother's life is in danger," he said, and managed not to frown when Katya shook her head.

No impatience. It wasn't his style. And however long it was for him, it seemed twice as long to her. Katya couldn't know it, because House had been asked to conceal time cues in the ceiling and walls (which Vincent also hoped was disconcerting to someone who had spent her life under, more or less, natural light), but the sun was setting outside, and Lesa and Michelangelo had been in captivity since the afternoon of the day before yesterday.

And the evening and the morning were the second day, Vincent thought, and stroked her hair, pushing dark strands off her clammy forehead. Admittedly, the insurgents had taken great care to capture them alive, and if it was the same group that had tried to snatch Vincent, they had been almost solicitous.

But his training and his experience told him hostages that weren't rescued within seventy-two hours usually weren't rescued. The logistics of keeping somebody alive in detention started to wear on the captors, arguments started, and mistakes...were made.

"Your mother needs you. You can save her, Katya."

"My mother's *fine*," she insisted, words slurring out after such a delay that he startled at the sound.

"What if she's hurt? What if she needs medical attention? You made some bad choices, Katya. But nothing we can't fix, if we get to her in time."

"They wouldn't hurt her." A chink, the first admission she'd made that she knew who had Lesa. She didn't seem to realize her error. Instead, she waved her hands for emphasis, but the manacles brought her up short and the weight of her own arms overbalanced her. Like Vincent's, her stool was an extension of House. It didn't tip.

But Katya did, flailing, and fell hard. Vincent caught her, cushioned the impact, but he was tired, too, and she slipped through his hands and landed on her shoulder on the carpetplant with a sharp sound. She pulled her knees up as if to hide her face against them.

Vincent crouched beside her, none too steady himself. He had to pause and adjust his chemistry, or he would have joined her on the floor. Energy rose through him like sap. It didn't fool him; he could feel the ache of weariness in his bones, the sensation of every joint in his hands swollen and fouled with grit. The itch and ache of peeling skin on his back, thighs, and shoulders wasn't helping. At least the sun toxicity had faded, and his fever, muscle pain, and nausea had broken. If he wasn't so damned tired, he might even be thinking clearly.

It was a small enough consolation.

Katya giggled as he got his hands under her armpits and hauled her upright. It morphed into a sob when he deposited her back onto the stool, balancing her carefully before he stepped away. Agnes, wherever she was watching from, was probably scandalized. Vincent really didn't care.

With Katya swaying behind him, he crossed to the door and tapped it open. As he'd predicted, Agnes waited there, arms crossed, chin tilted belligerently when he stepped into the corridor.

"Would you get us a drink?" he asked. "Something sugary. Fruit juice. With a stimulant in it."

She nodded and turned away. He waited just outside the door until she came back, two cups in her hand. He took only one of them, smiled, and stepped back into the small chamber that had become an interrogation room.

Katya, miraculously, was still on her stool. He set the cup down on the table, out of her reach, and stood between her and it. "Come on, Katya," he said, quietly. "Help me out here."

She lifted her eyes, focused on his face. Another crack in the armor. His heart rate picked up. Sometimes, when they broke, it happened all at once. Like pebbles rolling down a hill. "I want to sleep," she said, more distinctly than he would have thought she could manage.

"Me, too." He reached around behind him, picked up the mug, took a sip of the juice. It was cold and sweet, with bits of pulp that burst on his tongue when he swallowed. By an act of will, he managed not to drain it.

Katya watched what he was doing, and couldn't stop herself from licking her lips. She wouldn't beg, though.

He came to her, put his hip against her shoulder, and with one hand encouraged her to lean back against him. He brushed her hair, stroked it gently, smoothed the tangled strands. "Talk to me, sweetie," he said. "We both want to sleep. You can end this, you know, anytime."

"Can't," she said. Her hair was dirty; the greasy strands coiled between his fingers when she shook her head. She probably would have fallen over again if he hadn't braced her.

His fingers wanted to tighten in frustration, but hurting her wouldn't net him anything. "Not can't," he said. "Won't. I can save her, Katya, but you have to let me."

She leaned her head against his belly, and he stroked her hair and held the cup to her mouth so she could drink. Her manacled hands cupped around his, and she drank in long, lingering swallows, licking the edge of the empty cup before she'd let him take it away.

The sugar and stimulants worked fast. He felt her stabilizing before he finished reaching over her to set the empty cup down. She shifted on the stool, but didn't fall or pull away. Instead, she leaned her head against his stomach, closed her eyes, and sighed.

He didn't say anything, just kept stroking her hair. Gently, impersonally, as he would stroke a child's hair. She was relaxing, slowly.

People were surprisingly easy to tame, when you knew how to go about it. A little kindness at an unexpected moment could create a bond. An interrogation was a relationship, and relationships were based on developing trust. All seductions worked the same way; the seducer must create empathy with his target. He must project himself into the target's emotional space and create a connection. Such connections were only effective when they ran both ways.

Vincent couldn't remember if this had ever bothered him.

"Would you like another drink?"

"Please." She hesitated. "Could I use the toilet, please?"

She hadn't been so polite thirty hours ago. "In a moment," he said, and steadied her with one hand before he stepped away. He made sure to collect the empty cup before going to the door. It was light and rounded, shatterproof, not much of a weapon—but any weapon was better than none.

He'd once seen a man killed with an antique paper fan. It was the sort of experience that stayed with a person.

He exchanged the empty cup for the full, ignoring Agnes's glower, and returned. Katya's eyes were closed. This moment of clarity would be brief, and before long she'd crash harder than ever. Borrowed energy would be repaid with interest.

He held the cup for her again, and again her hands came up to cover and control his, the ceramic of her manacles warm against his wrist. She drank half, paused, and drank again, licking her lips when he took the empty cup away. "Do you really think she's in danger?"

Vincent turned and put his backside on the edge of the table. He folded his arms over his chest and waited, letting his silence be his answer.

"You're really worried." Her voice still had that vague, frail note, more strained now though the hoarseness had faded.

"I'm scared stiff." He made it into a confidence, leaning forward over his folded arms. "And I do want to help. Your mother, and Robert. And my partner."

She bit her lip. He crossed his ankles and waited, insouciant though it was everything he could do not to jitter against the table edge.

"Whatever they told you, there will be bloodshed," he said.

"Claude's going to sell us out to you. To the Coalition."

"Claude's your best hope of keeping the Coalition out," he said. All Kii's confidence aside, Vincent wasn't certain that the Dragons could handle the combined might of the Governors and the OECC. "Claude, or your grandmother. If the people you're working for succeed in overthrowing the government, who do you think will be here to pick up the pieces? A civil war is exactly what they would want."

"What you would want, you mean. I don't think so." She still wasn't thinking well. It was evident in her squint, in the pauses between her words. "If the Coalition wanted a, a change of government, you wouldn't be arguing against it."

He sighed and straightened, came to her, and smoothed her filthy hair again. "Sweetheart, I don't work for the Coalition."

Her eyes were closed. She was listening.

"I work with your mother," he continued. "And I agree with you, things have got to change on New Amazonia. But wiping each other out for the convenience of the Governors is not the way. Trust me on this, as one born on a repatriated world."

She pressed her face into his wardrobe.

"Get me a map," she said. "And a pot of coffee."

Vincent craved a shower, long and hot and decadent and New Amazonian. Anything to wash the deceit off his skin. Instead, he bent down and kissed her on top of the head. Agnes was already on the way in with a datapad in her hand when, silently, her shoulders shaking, Katya started to cry.

When Kusanagi-Jones found Lesa, he judged by the drag marks that she had hauled herself at least fifty meters after disentangling herself from the thorns. The sun was high, the air breathless and heavy under the great arched trees, but the afternoon had not yet dimmed with the clouds that might bring rain, and Kusanagi-Jones had not heard thunder. Lesa lay curled among the arched roots of some smooth-boled, gray-skinned tree, her hands locked over her face, her back wedged into a crevice more of a size for a child.

Kusanagi-Jones could smell the blood from two meters off. He couldn't see her breathing. And he was panting hard enough that he couldn't have heard her.

His knees ached, his calves were shaking, his heart pounding hard enough that he saw its rhythm in his trembling hands. His feet were chafed raw and blistered in the boots, the borrowed socks soaked to uselessness with sweat and serosanguinous fluid. He'd run the fifteen kilometers.

He wasn't as young as he had been.

Time to get out of the field, he thought, and considered for a moment the serious possibility that he might be suffering a myocardial infarction. But the hammering pulse, the stabbing pain across his chest, and the dark edges around his vision faded rather than worsening, and he managed to stumble close enough to go down on one knee beside Lesa, even as he didn't quite manage to avoid thinking of her as *the body.*

And now, finally, he heard thunder and a distant pattering like dry rice shaken in a container that might be the sound of leaves brushed aside by rain. The jungle was big and disorienting, full of things to trip over and ground too soft to run on without twisting your ankle, the trees teeming with flickering animals, black birds with feathered hind-limbs that they used like a second pair of wings and screaming green-feathered lemurs with bright, blinking eyes.

Too late, he told himself as he gathered himself to touch her, bracing for disappointment, taking in the seeping, swollen lumps of her feet, the glossiness of the infected scratches on her hands. He could kill without hesitation, but it took him seconds to gather the courage to reach out and push her matted hair away from her face.

Warm.

Of course, she would be. The air was hotter than his skin. She didn't stir, and he reached to brush her hair back, to afford her whatever privacy in death he could.

But something caught his attention and held it, and he heard himself bringing in a slow, thoughtful breath, full of the scents of blood and infection and the warm sweet yeasty smell of the moss and the fermenting earth.

Her eyes were closed. Closed all the way, closed softly and completely, the way a dead woman's eyes would not be.

He grabbed her wrists and dragged her huddled body out from under the curve of the root, laying her flat on her back as rain began to patter on the leaves overhead, not penetrating the canopy at first but then pounding down, splashing his face, soaking a dead man's shirt, washing the grime and sap and blood off the deep angry scratches on Lesa's face.

Kusanagi-Jones leaned back on his heels, gathered Lesa up in his arms so the water wouldn't pound up her nose, and tilted his own face to the warm rain, mouth open, feeling her heart beat slowly against his chest.

She awoke fifteen minutes later, while he was dragging her into a hastily constructed shelter, rain still smacking their heads. The first thing she did when she blinked fevered eyes and saw him bent over, half carrying and half-shoving her under a badly thatched lean-to, was start to laugh.

"One thing I never understood," Lesa said, rainwater dripping down the back of her neck. "Why the Coalition is so set against gentle males—"

"What's not to understand?" Michelangelo might seem brusque and hardhanded, sarcastic and cold, but he touched her damaged skin with exquisite care. He'd gotten a medical kit somewhere, and a shirt he was tearing into bandages. Whatever he was doing made her feet hurt less. Which wasn't surprising; her ankles looked like the trunks of unhealthy trees, and could hardly have hurt more.

He had started at the soles of her feet, mummifying her from toes to ankles, and was now dabbing the red, swollen bites on her calves.

"It's not like you contribute to population growth," she said, frowning. He pressed the sides of a bite, clear fluid seeping between his fingertips. "Ow!"

"Sorry." He smeared that wound, too, glossy leaves dimpling and catching under his knees as his weight shifted. The motion tumbled another scatter of rain down Lesa's neck, and a few jeweled drops made minute lenses on his close-cropped cap of hair. "No, it's not. Not by accident, anyway."

"But?"

"You're operating on spurious assumptions, so your conclusions are flawed."

"How— Ow! How so?"

"One, that sexual preferences have anything to do with reproduction. Doesn't matter who you *fuck*. Only way to have an unauthorized baby on Earth is to plan it." His hands shook as he tucked in a stray end of bandage, and she thought, startled, that he wasn't lying to her now.

"Two?" she pressed, when he'd been silent a little longer.

"Human societies aren't logical. Yours isn't. Mine isn't. Vincent—" He coughed, or laughed, and shook dripping water out of his hair. "—well, his is at least humane in its illogicality."

"So why?"

"You want my theory? Worth what you pay for it."

She nodded. He looked away.

"Cultural hegemony is based on conformity," he said, after a pause long enough that she had expected to go unanswered. "Siege mentality. Look at oppressed philosophies, religions—or religions that cast themselves as oppressed to encourage that kind of defensiveness. Logic has no pull. What the lizard brain wants, the monkey brain justifies, and when things are scary, anything different is the enemy. Can come up with a hundred pseudological reasons why, but they all boil down to one thing: if you aren't one of us, you're one of them." He shrugged roughly into her silence. "I'm one of them."

"But you worked for . . . 'us.' "

"In appearance." He reached for another strip of cloth.

It was damp, but so was everything. She shivered

when he laid it over seeping flesh. "How long have you been a double?"

The slow smile he turned on her when he looked up from the work of bandaging her legs might, she thought, be the first honest expression she'd ever seen cross his face. He let it linger on her for a moment, then glanced down again.

"I can tell you one way your society does make sense," Lesa said. "The reason Old Earth women don't work."

"And New Amazonian men? But some do. Not everyone can afford the luxury of staying home."

"Luxury? Don't you think it's a trap for some people?"

"Like Julian?" Harshly, though his hands stayed considerate.

She winced. "Yes."

The silence stretched while he tore cloth. She leaned against rough bark. At least her back was mostly unbitten. "During the Diaspora," Lesa said, "there wasn't *work* on Old Earth. Industry failed, demand fell, money was worth nothing. The only focus was on getting off-planet. Then, after the Vigil, after the Second Assessment, when the population stabilized, there was an artificial surplus of stuff left over from before. The Old Earth economy relies on maintaining that labor shortage. So women's value to society is not as professionals, but as homemakers or low-paid labor. And then you fetishize motherhood, and tell them that they aren't all good enough for *that*..."

She trailed off, looking down to see what he was doing to her legs. More salve, more bandages. Meticulous care, up to her knees now. That was the worst of it.

"The Governors' engineers were mostly female," Michelangelo said, as if to fill up her silence. "Seemed like a good idea at the time."

"And Vincent didn't know about your sympathies?"

"To Free Earth? He didn't. Not the sort of thing you share. If I wind these, it'll make it hard to walk."

"Just salve," she decided, regretfully. The pressure of the wraps made the bites feel better. "He knows now, though."

"We both know. Delicious, isn't it?"

She'd never understand how he said that without the slightest trace of bitterness. "So you grew up gentle on Old Earth, and you became a revolutionary."

"Never said they were linked."

"I can speculate." She touched his shoulder. His nonfunctional wardrobe couldn't spark her hand away.

He tucked the last tail of the bandages in, and handed her the lotion so she could dab it on the scattered bites higher on her legs, her thighs and belly and hands. He sat back, and shrugged. "It's not common. Maybe 4 percent, baseline, and they do genetic surgery. Mostly not an issue to manage homosexual tendencies before birth. In boys. Girls are trickier."

His tone made her flinch.

"Did I hurt you?"

"No," she said. "Just . . . genetic surgery. You're so casual."

"As casual as you are about eating animals?"

It wasn't a comment she could answer. "And your mom didn't opt for the surgery?"

"My mother," he said, sitting back on his heels as the imperturbable wall slid closed again, "planned an unauthorized pregnancy. And concealed it. I wasn't diagnosed prenatally. And I don't think anybody expected me to make it to majority without being Assessed."

"And you weren't."

"No," he said, quietly. "She was."

This time, when he touched her ankle, she shivered. But not because of him. She covered his hand with her own, leaning forward to do it, breaking open the crusted cuts on her palm and not caring. "I'm glad you weren't," she said. And then she leaned back against the smooth gray aerial root of the big rubbermaid tree that formed the beam and one wall of the lean-to, and slowly, definitely, closed her eyes.

23

VINCENT COULD SEE NOTHING FROM THE AIR, BUT THAT failed to surprise him. He perched on the observer's seat of the aircar, beside the pilot, and made sure his wardrobe was active and primed. The Penthesileans wouldn't give him a weapon, but as long as he had his wits, he wasn't helpless.

A weaponized utility fog didn't hurt either.

"They must have a camouflage screen up," he said over his shoulder.

Elena, in the backseat, grunted as the aircar circled. "Or Katya lied to us."

"Also possible," Vincent admitted, as the pilot reported finding nothing on infrared. "I don't suppose any of these vehicles have pulse capability."

"This one does," the pilot answered, after a glance to Elena for permission.

There were seven aircars in the caravan, armored vehicles provided by Elder Kyoto through the Security

Directorate. According to Katya, that should be more
than enough to handle the complement of this particular Right Hand outpost.

And again, Katya might be wrong. Or she might be
decoying them into a trap, though Vincent's own skills
and instincts told him *she* believed she was telling the
truth.

Of course, he'd also trusted his own skills and instincts about Michelangelo. But Angelo was the best
Liar in the business—and close enough in Vincent's af-
fections that any reading would be suspect anyway.

"Take us higher, please," Vincent said. The pilot
gave him a dubious look, but when Elena didn't intervene she shrugged and brought them up. Somewhere
down there, indistinguishable from the rest of the
canopy by Gorgon-light, had to be the camouflage
field. Invisible—but not unlocatable.

Vincent's wardrobe included licenses for dozens of
useful implements, among them an echolocator. It was
designed for use in situations where there was no available light and generating more would be unwise. In
this case, he was obligated to patch through the aircar's
ventilation systems to externalize the tympanic membranes, but that was the work of a few moments.

The readout projected to his implants was many-
edged, shifting, translucent, but perfectly detailed, each
individual leaf and branch discernable over the spongy
reflection of the litter-covered ground. And just off to
the south was a gap in the fragile, shadowy echoes of
the canopy, a mysterious, rough-edged hole floored
with sharp regular echoes and softer elevated patches.

"There," Vincent said, and pointed. "South by
southeast, 40 degrees descent."

"It's all trees," the pilot said, and Vincent frowned at
her—the frown he reserved for people who obviously

couldn't have meant to disappoint him, and so must
have done it through some oversight. "It's a utility fog,"
he said. "A limited-license one. It pattern-matches the
surrounding territory. Look, see that tree?"

There was one, in particular, a bit taller than the
rest and a bit paler in color, as if it hadn't entirely
leafed out yet or were growing in iron-poor soil.

The pilot nodded. Elena leaned over the chair back
to see better, laying a possessive hand on Vincent's
shoulder.

"There's another one," she said, and pointed left.
The angle was different, and so the silhouettes didn't
quite match, but there they were, as alike as if cloned.
"Which is real?"

Vincent indicated the second one with a jerk of his
thumb, making an effort not to shrug her hand away,
no matter how it irritated. *And* reminded him of the
tenderness of peeling skin.

At least the damned sunburn hurt less than it had
and his wardrobe was doing an adequate job of coping
with the sloughing epidermis. Which was unpleasant.
But, by comparison, didn't hurt enough to be worthy of
the term.

"Is it safe to descend through the canopy?"

He hesitated. "Theoretically."

"Meaning?"

"Meaning it's a utility fog, and they can be
weaponized. Elder Pretoria—"

Her hand flexed on his shoulder. He hid a flinch.
"Yes, Vincent?"

Not *Miss Katherinessen* anymore. "Does anybody on
New Amazonia use fog technology? Because something Lesa said led me to believe it wasn't warmly considered—"

"No," Elena said. "They don't."

He nodded. "Then I can't guarantee what we'll run into."

"Right," she said, and released him. "Jayne?"

"Elder Pretoria?"

"Bring us down onto the canopy, would you? And let the others know what we're doing, and why."

The aircar didn't have the flexibility of programmable vehicles that Vincent was used to, but he had to admit that the landing nets were impressive. Jointed insectile limbs unfolded, stretching glistening mesh between them, and the aircar settled onto a forest canopy made mysterious by nebula-light. The trees dimpled and groaned under the distributed weight, and Vincent heard wood creak and twigs snap wetly, but they bore up under the weight. On each side, the other aircars settled into the canopy, surrounding the camouflaged clearing, pastel swirls of night sky reflected in their glossy carapaces so they looked like enormous, jeweled beetles resting on spinners' webs.

"How do we get out?" he asked, because he knew it was expected of him.

And Elena smiled, ducked down, folded the center rear seat up, and tugged open a hatch in the floor.

The camp was deserted, which surprised Vincent even less than its invisibility. The security personnel had body armor, weapons, metal detectors, and khir trained to sniff for explosives and hidden people, and he was content to let them conduct the search. He stuck close to Elena and to Antonia Kyoto, who had arrived in a separate car, and eavesdropped on incoming reports with their complicity.

It took them less than half an hour to secure the camp, which showed signs of having been abandoned with great haste and insufficient discipline. Supplies had not been taken, and one of Kyoto's people uncovered a cache of weapons under a bed in one of the ten or eleven huts clustered within the zareba.

It was Shafaqat Delhi who found Robert Pretoria's body, though, and hurried back into the camp to inform Vincent and Elena—and then had to jog to keep up with him on the way back out, while Elena followed more sedately.

Somebody had rolled Robert over, but that wasn't how it had fallen. Vincent crouched beside crushed greenery and traced the outline of the body in the loam, running fingers along the deeper, smoother imprint where someone had shoved Robert's chest into the ground while he broke his neck.

Vincent turned and ran his fingertips across the base of Robert's skull, below the occiput. The distended softness of a swelling met his fingertips, exactly where he expected.

"Vincent?"

"Blow to the head," he said, wiping his hands on Robert's shirt before he stood. The dead man's pockets had been rifled, and any gear he had with him taken, and the leaf litter in the area of the body was roughed up as if from a scuffle.

There hadn't been any scuffle. He'd been as good as dead the minute he turned his back.

Vincent stood, his feet where Angelo's feet would have been when he struck, and turned a slow pirouette. And there it was, exactly at a height to catch his eye. A single hair, black and tightly coiled, snagged in the rough bark of a tree about four meters from the murder scene.

It could have been Robert's hair, if his head wasn't shaved. But it wasn't.

Vincent covered the distance in three long steps and stopped. The forest floor was undisturbed, leaves and sticks and bits of moss exactly as they should be. He crouched again, feeling alongside the roots of the trees, combing through the litter with his fingertips. Worm-eaten nuts, curled crisp leaves, sticks and bits of things he couldn't identify—

—something smooth and warm.

His fingers recognized the datacart before he un-earthed it, although Michelangelo had wrapped it in a scrap torn from a dirty shirt. Vincent brushed it care-fully clean, aware that Shafaqat and Elena were watching him in breathless anticipation. A sense of the dramatic made him hold his silence until he could turn, drop one knee to the ground to brace himself, and raise the datacart into their line of sight before he powered it on. There was a password, but Vincent could have entered it in his sleep.

He had been meant to guess it.

It didn't beep. Somebody had disabled that function. But it did load something: a glowing electronic image of green and golden contour lines and insistently blinking dots.

"What's that?" Shafaqat asked.

Elena put one hand out, pressing her palm to the bole of a tree to steady herself, and sighed as if she could put all her pain and worry onto the wind and let it be carried away. "A scavenger map," she said. And then she stood up straight and rolled her shoulders back. "Come along, Miss Delhi, Miss Katherinessen. No rest for the wicked yet."

Even by Kusanagi-Jones's standards, it was a pretty cinematic rescue. He awoke from a fitful doze at dawn, when a frenzy of animal cries greeted half a dozen digital-camouflage-clad New Amazonian commandos rappelling through the canopy. They landed in the glade where Lesa had been half-crucified on the thorn vines and unclipped, fanning out with polished professionalism. Half a dozen commandos—and Vincent, dapper and pressed and shiny-booted as always, handling the abseiling gear as if he spent every Saturday swinging from the belly of an ornithopter.

Kusanagi-Jones rolled onto his back and reached out to nudge Lesa awake, but she was already propped up on one elbow, peering over his shoulder. Her face, if anything, looked more lined with tiredness than it had the night before, and more of her scratches were inflamed, but the smile curving her lips was one of relief. "Come on," Kusanagi-Jones said, holding out his hand. "I'll carry you down there."

"Fuck that," she answered. "I'll walk."

And she did, or hobbled, anyway, leaning on his elbow harder than either of them let on.

Kusanagi-Jones didn't even really mind when the first thing Vincent did was hug him hard enough that it knocked him back a step. Especially when the second thing he did was piggyback their watches together, and give Kusanagi-Jones's wardrobe a kick start and a recharge to baseline functional levels.

Later, after the medics had seen to his injuries, and while he was still tucked into bed hydrating on an IV while they worked on Lesa's more serious wounds, Vincent brought him a tray, and spread jam on crackers for him to eat. They sat silently, shoulder to shoulder. Kusanagi-Jones had edged over to make room, and

Vincent leaned against the headboard with one foot on the floor and one propped up on the bed.

"Can't go home yet," Kusanagi-Jones said at last, over their private channel, when it became evident that Vincent wasn't going to bring it up.

"No," Vincent answered, after letting the statement hang for a bit. And then he said out loud, "Eat the soup. It's good."

"I hate lentils." But he ate it, thick and pasty and full of garlic, and it was better than he expected. He needed the protein, anyway. And the salt. "There's Claude to deal with."

"There is," Vincent admitted, "still a negotiation to complete. And a duel to fight if we can't find that lab, and link Singapore and Austin to it."

Kusanagi-Jones glanced down at his watch. Every light shone clean and green, except the blinking yellow letting him know fatigue toxins were building to the point where chemistry wasn't cutting it anymore. He held it up so Vincent could see. "There's also this."

"You know what I think," Vincent answered, his voice chilly and flat. Kusanagi-Jones reached out and curved his fingers around Vincent's wrist, and Vincent didn't shake him off.

Kusanagi-Jones couldn't remember how he'd ever decided anything on his own. Maybe he hadn't. Maybe he'd just done what other people told him. "What are we going to do?"

Vincent shrugged to hide his shudder, and pushed another cracker in front of Kusanagi-Jones.

"There are no limits to brane technology," Kusanagi-Jones said, ignoring the cracker.

Vincent slid off the bed, but gently, and moved away. There was a window in the room, shaded by louvers that broke the tropical sunlight into bars. He stood before it and laced his hands behind his back. "Once there were no limits to what you could discover with a sailing ship."

"False analogy——"

"Fine. It's false. What's the moral implication of the damage we do to the planets we colonize? What about *gravity pollution*, for the Christ's sake? Can you even begin to come up with a list of potential ill effects? Black holes? Supernovae? Planetary orbits? It's not a clean technology. It just pollutes in ways we can't begin to cope with."

"Are no clean technologies," Kusanagi-Jones reminded.

Vincent continued as if he hadn't said a word. "What if we expand into species less companionable than the Dragons? There's a lot of what-ifs."

"Do what we've always done," Michelangelo said. "Trust the next generation to solve their problems the way we've solved ours. Risk is risk. We live with it."

"By hitting the cosmic reset button one more time. That's a technical solution to an ethical problem. Hell, it's not even a solution——it's a delaying action. That's what got us into this situation in the first place."

"Entropy," Kusanagi-Jones said, "is a bitch. There's still the retrovirus——"

"Angelo, I will shoot you myself."

Their eyes met. Vincent wasn't a Liar. He meant every word. "All right," Kusanagi-Jones said. "There isn't the retrovirus."

"There's another solution," Vincent said coolly, although the pit of Kusanagi-Jones's own stomach lurched when he realized what his partner meant. "We leave the Governors in place."

"No!"

"Yes," Vincent said. "Listen to me. There's magic in it. Because once we learn to control ourselves—"

"Oh, no. Vincent, you are not *saying* this."

"—the Governors become obsolete. On their own. If we clean up after ourselves, Angelo, they have no reason to intervene." Vincent let his hands fall and squeezed them into fists, as Kusanagi-Jones squeezed back against the headboard, as if he could crowd himself into the wall and somehow get away.

"Then we all die in a fucking Colonial revolt. You, me, your mother, Lesa, Elená. For a bunch of geniuses, you're all idiots for thinking you can stand up to the Coalition."

"New Earth stood up."

"New Earth had help. And even if the Governors wouldn't permit an open Coalition intervention, how many New Earthers do you suppose died in the covert retaliations for what I did to *Skidbladnir*? Wasn't me that paid that price."

Vincent's answering silence was long. "The Dragons?"

"Might defend the New Amazonians. Not Ur. And this is the human society you want to protect? I don't think so."

He could hear Vincent breathing. He wondered if he knew what Kusanagi-Jones was about to say. Kusanagi-Jones, his eyes shut, rubbed his knuckles across his face.

His voice dropped. "Consent."

Vincent's flat expression, when Michelangelo opened his eyes again, seemed an attempt to convince himself that he hadn't actually understood. Kusanagi-Jones's face felt numb.

He kept talking.

"Kii won't give us the brane tech. What if we offer

him another way out of a war? He's ethical. We offer Kii the opportunity to engineer a virus that modifies the human genome, that *induces* Consent, and we get the fucker to downgrade self-interest as a motivating force."

"The Christ," Vincent whispered. They stared at each other.

"Vincent. This is ... this has to be exactly—"

Vincent's larynx bobbed as he swallowed, a shadow dipping in the hollow of his throat. "They were the first ones to die, you know. You can't accuse them of hypocrisy. The Governors Assessed their creators first."

"Cowards," Michelangelo said. He shoved the tray aside and swung his feet out of bed, wincing as blistered flesh contacted the tiled floor. "Cowards who didn't want to watch their program carried out. Could cause a genocide, but couldn't stand to live through it."

"This is just how they felt."

"Heady, isn't it?"

"Angelo—"

"No. Don't argue. *Think.* What do you have that's better?"

"Who are we to choose for an entire species?"

Michelangelo gave Vincent his sweetest smile. "Who better?"

Vincent backed up to lean against the wall and folded his arms. "Every solution is going to present us with new problems down the line. And this would put an end to Lesa's problem, too. The way to stop men from preying on women without treating the entire sex as criminals is simply to remove the predatory urge. If we can't be trained, we can be broken."

"You're Advocating."

Vincent winked, but Kusanagi-Jones saw his hand shake when he checked his chemistry, taking a moment to revise the adrenaline load down to something manageable. "All right. I'll Advocate. I'm Lesa. She would say it was immoral to tamper with human biology, and more defensible to institute social controls to the same effect."

"So slavery is more moral than engineering out aggression."

"It's not chattel slavery."

"No," Kusanagi-Jones said. "An extreme sort of second-class citizenship."

"Not much worse than women in the Coalition."

"Women in the Coalition can vote, can work—"

"Can be elected to the government."

"Theoretically."

"Practically?"

"Doesn't happen." Kusanagi-Jones swallowed. "Who'd want a woman in charge?" Except on some of the repatriated worlds. But Ur was the only one with the nerve to send a woman to the Cabinet. The conviction had dropped from his voice. "I can't even Advocate this anymore, Vincent. It's just *wrong*."

"No fanatic like a new fanatic," Vincent said. He came to Kusanagi-Jones and crouched beside him, and patted him on the knee. "We'll figure something out."

"Scared," Michelangelo said, a raw admission meant as much for himself as for Vincent.

And Vincent knew it. Michelangelo could tell by his expression, the arched eyebrows, the line between them. "Having your preconceptions rattled is unsettling."

"No," Michelangelo said. He dropped his face to his hands, pushed fingertips against his eyelids until the pressure hurt. The pain didn't help his focus, so he dropped his hands and looked up instead. "Scared we've already figured it out."

Vincent stood, all lithe grace, and let his hand rest

warmly on Michelangelo's shoulder. "Whatever," he said. "Let's at least talk to Kii about getting that weapon cleaned out of your bloodstream, shall we?"

Michelangelo nodded. "And then tell Lesa about Kii, and see what *she* bloody thinks."

Vincent and Michelangelo found Lesa on Elena's beloved veranda, her bandaged feet propped on the softest available cushion, a plate on her lap and a sweating glass beside her as she watched Julian and some other children romp in the courtyard with a couple of khir. Vincent didn't think Elena would have left her alone willingly. It must have taken a spectacular temper tantrum.

She didn't acknowledge them at first, as he and Angelo came up beside her—unescorted—and took places on a wooden bench. It was polished smooth, the wood warm in the muggy afternoon, and Vincent leaned forward with his elbows on his knees, watching in fascinated horror as Lesa worked her way around a piece of shellfish sushi rather like a snake ingesting a too-large mouse: lingeringly and with many pauses.

"I'm sorry about Robert," Angelo said finally when the silence had gone on longer than Vincent expected.

Lesa didn't look. "I'm not," she said. "But don't let Katya find out about it, okay?"

Vincent felt Michelangelo shrug. "I won't."

She did turn, then, and give them a painfully dilute smile. "I've just heard from Antonia Kyoto. She wanted me to pass along her thanks for your information as well, Michelangelo. And let you know that Miss Ouagadougou and Stefan have been arrested. And are under . . . considerable pressure to name the rest of the Right Hand apparatus."

He grunted. "Miss Ouagadougou wasn't working for the Right Hand," he said. "She's Coalition."

"Yes," Lesa said. "Antonia just led a raid on another encampment and found more Coalition tech. It might save us an insurrection if we can find enough of them."

Vincent said, "And Katya?"

"She'll go to prison." Lesa said it so calmly that Vincent looked at her twice. The tension lines around her eyes told another story. "But she's young. And it won't be forever."

Vincent had no answer. He leaned on Michelangelo and didn't try to come up with one.

Lesa cleared her throat. "And I also heard from Claude."

"And?"

"She wants to set the duel for the sixth of Carnival."

Vincent glanced doubtfully at Angelo, but Angelo's gaze was on the children in the yard. "Three days. Will you be able to walk by then?"

That homeopathic smile didn't flicker. She picked up another piece of sushi and contemplated it before she said, "I don't need to walk to shoot somebody, Vincent."

"And are you as fast today as you were the other afternoon?"

She didn't answer, and he thought about her silence while she chewed. Angelo shifted on the bench, leaning closer while Vincent pretended not to notice. Funny how he could always tell exactly where Michelangelo's attention was, even when Angelo was pretending it was somewhere else.

"We need to find that lab. Then there won't be a duel."

Too late, he remembered she didn't have the context, and was opening his mouth to explain when she silenced him with a wave. "Mother told me."

"I thought she would."

"And I told Antonia," she continued. Vincent opened his mouth, and she silenced him with one raised finger and a chipped stone glare. "If I don't live through the duel, she needs to know what Claude is capable of."

Vincent didn't answer, but he swallowed and nodded. All right.

Lesa turned to Angelo. "Are you going to get the infection taken care of? *Can* you get it taken care of?" She spoke to Michelangelo rather than Vincent, but Michelangelo didn't look at her.

"We can," Vincent said. "And will. Which reminds me. There's somebody we want you to meet."

"Where?"

"Inside."

"Hand me my crutches."

Michelangelo was still at his shoulder when they came into the house, following the stubborn staccato of Lesa's crutches. She managed them well, stumping forward grimly—though she winced when her weight hit her hands. Thick batting padded the handles; it obviously wasn't enough.

She paused before the lift rather than heading for the stairs. Just as well, because Vincent didn't fancy carrying her up them, and Michelangelo's feet were in no shape for chivalry.

Stubborn or not, Lesa was swaying by the time she stopped, and Vincent steadied her with a hand on her shoulder as he commanded the lift. The venom had left her weak, febrile, and probably aching. Inside the lift, she propped herself on him without seeming to, and he smiled as he tilted toward her. He hadn't slept in days, and though he still had chemistry it was wearing thin. If Michelangelo was too proud to lean, Vincent wasn't.

The lift brought them to the third floor, and Lesa paused before the doors to her bedroom. "Excuse the mess," she said, and gestured them inside.

Michelangelo went first, covering Vincent, and for once Vincent reveled in it rather than chafing. But there was no one inside except a sleepy khir in a basket, who lifted his ear-feathers at them but seemed otherwise disinclined to stir. Vincent recognized Walter by his bandages and almost thought the khir grinned at him—if khir grinned.

He turned to assist Lesa in managing her crutches through the door, but she didn't need him. She clumped to her bed and flopped down, letting the crutches slide to the carpetplant alongside. She closed her eyes, face sallow with pain, and didn't seem to notice when Angelo bent down, picked up the crutches, and silently braced them upright against the wall between her bed and her nightstand.

"All right," she said. "This is as private as I can manage on short notice."

Vincent nodded and raised his eyes to the wall. "Kii, would you introduce yourself to Miss Pretoria?"

The swirling effect in the wall panels was just as before, though Vincent noticed that Lesa had turned off the jungle scenes in this room, leaving blank taupe walls. First eyes and then a tall lithe body coalesced from swirling pixels, and Kii lay at ease, its wings folded comfortably along its sides so it could recline on its elbows. It settled its plumed head between its shoulders like a somnolent bird and blinked at them.

"Greetings, Lesa Pretoria," it said. "Greetings,

Vincent Katherinessen and Michelangelo Osiris Leary Kusanagi-Jones. Kii anticipates your questions."

At the sound of the mellow, neutral voice, Lesa lurched upright on the bed, hands braced to either side. "Dragon," she said, and shook her head, many-colored hair flying around her.

She looked to Michelangelo, not Vincent. "Simulation?"

"Transcended," Vincent answered, when Michelangelo didn't. "Kii, Michelangelo would like to accept your offer of medical treatment."

Kii's head settled more solidly between ridged shoulder blades. "Michelangelo, is that so?"

Michelangelo kept his eyes straight ahead, though Vincent was waiting for the glance. "Yes, Kii."

"It is done," Kii said. "You will find a document for your life support device available in the datastream. It should enable your implants to locate and eradicate the infection."

"Kii," Vincent said, "can you tell me where to find the lab where that virus was tailored?"

"It is not within Kii's range of access," Kii said. It angled its head and stretched its neck, as if regarding Lesa more closely than before. "The khir like you, when you come. The Consent is that you may stay, to please the khir. We are fond of the khir. And Kii is grown fond of you."

Lesa sat very still, the bedclothes knotted in her hands. She licked her lips, pulse visible at her throat, and Vincent found himself in sympathy with her nervousness. The Dragon's regard had a tendency to make him feel like a snack, as well.

"That's you-humans, not you-Lesa?" Michelangelo, surprising Vincent.

"The khir approve of Lesa Pretoria," Kii said, the

long neck swaying slightly, plumage ruffled by an un-
seen breeze.

In his basket, Walter flopped on his side and hissed,
showing his belly to the air. Lesa turned her head and
looked at him, leaning forward on the bed without
lowering her feet to the floor. Not trying to stare the
Dragon in the eye seemed to ease her. Vincent remembered some Old Earth legend about snakes and hypno-
sis, or maybe turning people into stone.

"The khir really aren't smart enough to...talk...
are they?" she said. Walter lifted his head, neck craning around like a hand puppet, and blinked back at her
with triangular-pupiled eyes.

It was that look that did it. He'd been telling himself,
over and over, that his gift shouldn't apply to Dragons or
to khir. That their kinesthetics, their *everything* was
different from that of humans, and deceptive.

But that intellectual knowledge hadn't stopped him
from reading them, and reading them correctly—
Dragon and khir.

Because the khir had been living with New Amazonians for 150 years, and the khir—nonverbal, with a
predator's extended jaw structure and limited facial
expressions—were quite perfectly capable of commu-
nicating through kinesthetics, the rise and fall of their
peculiarly expressive plumage that ruffled independent of any wind.

Just as the Dragons must have, when they were
meat.

"Actually," Vincent said, "I think the khir tell the
Dragons rather a lot, don't they?"

"The khir are invaluable," Kii said. "They are the
protectors of the old world. We make them safe den-
ning, and they give the city purpose. As now you do as
well."

"Because the city is *esthelich*, isn't it?"

"That can be no revelation, Vincent Katherinessen."

"No," Vincent said, aware of Michelangelo shifting a half-step closer to him, a warm pressure at his elbow. "I've known that for a while. Since it helped me hide from the kidnappers. If it's *esthelich* by your standards, it must have an aesthetic. And its aesthetic is... comfort? The care of its inhabitants?"

"Would you create a domicile that thought otherwise?"

"No."

Lesa had looked away from Walter and was now sitting curled forward, the bedclothes dragged over her lap as she stared at Vincent. "And of course," she said, "even if you were Transcendent, there's always the chance that something could go wrong with the system, isn't there?"

Smart woman. Which was no more a revelation than House's taste in art had been. "The possibility exists," Kii said, hunching between its wings.

Vincent said, "And if you needed physical bodies again? Could you read your... personality onto an organic system?"

"The possibility exists."

"The khir are a failsafe."

"The khir are not disposable," it answered, contracting again, pulling itself back on its haunches.

"Kii," Michelangelo said. "If you had to translate *esthelich*. What would you say it meant?"

The Dragon hesitated. Its head swung side to side, the tongue flickering through a gap in its lower lip. "It does not translate into merely one of your words."

"Try."

"Fledged," it said, with no weight of emotion on the word.

If Kii were human, Vincent would have scrupled to press. He would have known he was millimeters from a moral pit trap, a bit of doublethink that would expose a violent defensive reaction when triggered. But the Dragons had Consent. They were as physically incapable of experiencing moral qualms about following orders as Vincent's own hand was of rebelling when his consciousness instructed it to pull a trigger.

He said, "They're not a separate species, are they?"

And Kii shifted, its wings furled tight against its sides, and blinked slowly. "The khir? They are not."

"They're young Dragons. Neotenous. With their growth and intellectual development intentionally retarded."

"They are not *esthelich*. They have no Consent. We provided for them, and they protect us."

"That's horrible," Lesa said. She dropped the bedcovers and climbed to her feet, wincing as her bandages touched the carpetplant. "You ... engineered your own children into *slaves?*"

"Pets ... no, domestic animals are not slaves," Kii insisted. "They are without aesthetic. They are not people. Your infant creatures are immoral—no. *Sociopathic*. They are not *people*."

Vincent reached behind Angelo to put a hand on Lesa's arm, steadying. She shook it off. "But they could have been."

"Not these, no. They were conceived to this purpose, and they breed true. They are animals, and would never have been born, otherwise."

"Unless you remove the, what, the chemical inhibition? And then they transform into adults. Only with the minds of Transcended Dragons downloaded into their skulls, rather than whatever they might have become?"

"It is," Kii said, "the Consent."

Lesa might have wanted nothing to do with Vincent, but Michelangelo stepped closer, shoulder to shoulder, and Vincent leaned on his warmth, their wardrobes melding. "What if we lobotomized girl babies," Angelo said. "Kept them as cattle. Destroyed their higher functions—"

"They would not be *esthelich*," Kii said. "They would be as domestic animals, as the khir. But it would be immoral to destroy the potential to be people in one born with it."

"But the Consent finds no ethical failing in creating the khir?"

"The Consent finds no ethical failing in the selective breeding of domestic animals."

"Lesa," Angelo said, "please sit down. It hurts to watch you."

She stared at him, head drawing back as her neck stiffened, and then she nodded and sank down on the unmade bed. "I have another question for the Consent," Vincent said.

Kii lifted its chin, ear-feathers forward to cup sound. Alert and listening.

"If you can reprogram Michelangelo's docs, can you rewrite other code?"

"We can."

"The Governors," Vincent said.

And with a careful, human gesture, Kii shook its head. "It is discussed. The Consent is that it is unwise. And also that the Governors are not *esthelich*, but that they are art. And not to be destroyed."

"Fuck," Michelangelo said, and Vincent didn't blame him. "Then it's a war."

24

THE MALES LEFT SHORTLY AFTER THE DRAGON DID, LEAV-
ing Lesa alone in her bedroom with the sleeping khir.
Michelangelo wouldn't let her rise to see them to the
door, his stern glower as effective as a seat belt, but hiding a striking chivalry that Lesa wouldn't pretend not
to chafe at and couldn't understand how she'd earned.
It still carried a taint of chauvinism, but Michelangelo
seemed to think it indicated respect.

It didn't matter. He was trying to learn, to accom-
modate. And she'd have fought for him even if he
wasn't. Her own honor was at stake now.

When the door spiraled closed behind Vincent and
Michelangelo—and stayed closed; Lesa was wise to that
trick—she pried herself off the bed again and settled
wearily on the carpetplant beside it. The pain was bad
enough, though analgesics and anti-inflammatories
were some use—but the vertigo was truly incapacitating.

She could live with pain.

Her citizenship piece was still missing. Lost to her forever, probably, along with her daughter and her mate. But she had more than one weapon and it wasn't as if she could go about unarmed. There was a pistol and an old holster in the bottom of the nightstand.

Lesa pulled the box out, inspected the weapon—clean and smelling muskily of gun oil—and strapped the soft, worn leather of the gunbelt around her waist. Then she loaded the honor, safetied it, and laid it on the bed. It took the same caseless ammunition as her citizenship piece.

Standing was unpleasant. But she couldn't settle the holster properly while hunched on the floor, and whatever bravado she'd issued to the males about not needing to be able to walk to shoot, she had to be able to stand to duel.

She slipped her new honor into the holster, checked twice to make sure it was locked and no round was chambered, and pulled one of the crutches away from the wall to brace herself on.

"House," she said, "I need a mirror."

The long interior wall with no doorways was her usual mirror. It misted gray and glazed reflective as Lesa limped toward it, transferring as much weight to the crutch as possible to keep it off her feet. She paused two meters from the wall and stared at her reflection in true color.

She looked like ragged death. Her face was puffy around the scratches and shiny with antibiotic ointment. Her hands were red-fleshed and torn, her forearms more scab than skin. She wobbled, and leaned against the crutch hard enough that her whole body canted left. The fingers of her right hand, hovering over the butt of her honor, looked like undercooked sausages, and the gouges on her palm had cracked open again and were leaking pinkish fluid.

"I am," she whispered, "so fucked."

The draw was reflex, wired into nerve and muscle by decades of practice. She shouldn't have to think about it. She should barely be conscious of feeling it happen.

The air dragged at her wrist, thickened around stiff fingers. The hand was slow, the fingers inflexible; they didn't hook the butt of the honor and glide inside the trigger guard as they should. The weight was wrong, the balance off—

Her honor skipped from her hand, spinning, and hit with a thud butt-first on the carpetplant, tottering a moment before toppling onto its side. The crutch skipped, and Lesa hit a split second later, down on one knee, her right hand slamming the floor with all her weight behind it.

The pain was asphyxiating. She fought for breath— diaphragm spasming, the gasp more like a whine if she was being honest—and blinked until her vision cleared. And then she picked up her honor, holstered it, found the crutch left-handed, and forced herself up, to face the mirror again.

The twenty-fifth attempt was no more successful than the third.

Pain couldn't force her to stop, but eventually the bleeding and nausea did. She holstered her honor one last time, resettled the crutch under her armpit, and hobbled to the balcony. Julian was still down there with the other boys, running and laughing. The echoes of his voice carried to her room before she stepped outside, and she found a smile for that. The only thing he loved better than handball was his numbers.

Lesa hitched to a stop a few steps shy of the railing.

She stared down, at the running children, at the watching tutors. Her gouged hand tightened on the crutch; she barely noticed.

She took two steps back, into the frame of the doorway. "House," she said. "I need to speak to Julian. Please have Alys send him down."

When Lesa summoned them again, even Kusanagi-Jones could tell she had not been resting. Her color was worse, her hair tangled and the knees of her trousers stained with chlorophyll. And then there was the matter of the slender dark boy curled on the seat before her terminal, pecking at the keys with concentrated precision.

"Miss Pretoria?"

She gave him that eyebrow, but stepped aside to allow him into the room, Vincent at his heels. The door clicked as it contracted shut behind them, and Kusanagi-Jones paused and glanced over his shoulder. Vincent caught him looking, of course, eyebrows quirked and the faintest hint of a smile—an expression that slid through Kusanagi-Jones's heart like a skewer. He would have sworn he could feel the muscle contracting around penetrating metal, trying to beat and only managing to shred itself a little further.

Three months, on the *Kaiwo Maru*. Three months they could have had. And he had been too much of a sodding coward to even *reach* for it.

Then Vincent's half-smile turned into a real one, as if he knew exactly what Kusanagi-Jones was thinking, and loved him for it, or in spite of it. And Kusanagi-Jones smiled back.

So it went.

Kill or be killed.

Vincent took him by the elbow and steered him into
the room. "You have the look of a woman with a plan,"
Vincent said, and the corners of Lesa's eyes crinkled,
an expression that made Kusanagi-Jones homesick.

"Can you shield this room?" she asked.

"Shield it from what?"

"Electromagnetic monitoring."

Vincent glanced at Kusanagi-Jones, who looked
right back, silently. "Yes," Vincent said. He touched his
watch. "The whole room?"

"It'd be more convenient. I've already isolated it
from House."

"Angelo?"

Kusanagi-Jones nodded, and slaved his wardrobe to
Vincent's. Between them, they had enough foglets to
manage a Faraday cage, since their wardrobes—given
time—could manufacture more as needed.

The process took a few minutes, and Lesa said nothing further throughout, which seemed an indication
for communal silence. "There," Vincent said when it
was done. "I've added eavesdropping countermeasures."

Lesa didn't answer. Instead, she stared at Kusanagi-
Jones and asked, "Did you download Kii's medical program?"

"He did," Vincent answered.

"Do you still have it?"

Julian, who hadn't spoken, came up beside Lesa,
close enough to feel her body heat without the childish
admission of actually touching her or stepping behind
her. Kusanagi-Jones looked at him, not at Lesa, and
held up his left arm, stripping the sleeve off the forearm to show the status lights on his watch. Only one
blinked green now, the slow flicker of the nanodoc

condition readout. The rest glowed red or dark amber, for critical infection.

There was more amber than there had been an hour before, and not just because Kusanagi-Jones had grabbed a nap.

"I need that," Julian said.

Kusanagi-Jones let his arm fall, and his sleeve drop over it. "The program?"

"A copy of it." He shuffled forward, forgetting that he had been half hiding behind his mother, and grabbed Kusanagi-Jones's wrist to pull him toward the terminal.

Bemused, Kusanagi-Jones was about to step forward and follow, until Julian froze and turned back, gazing up at Vincent with stricken eyes.

Vincent, sod him, was waiting for it. He smiled at Julian and waved him away, Kusanagi-Jones included.

Nice to know I've still got his mark stamped between my eyes. But he went, as Vincent must have known he would.

"What frequency does it use?" Julian asked, and Kusanagi-Jones told him. And then queued and transferred the archive copy of Kii's program as soon as the protocol connected.

"What exactly are you planning?" Vincent hadn't done more than step sideways and lean back against the wall before the door. Kusanagi-Jones knew without turning that his chin would be dropped insouciantly toward his chest, his ankles crossed.

"Julian's been working on quantum decision trees," Lesa said.

"Fractal," Julian corrected, without looking up from his displays and the holographic array floating in the air before him. "Fractal decision trees."

"Which means what, in layman's terms?" It almost

sounded as if Vincent knew what was going on. Which was fine with Kusanagi-Jones, because he certainly didn't. He could code a little, hack a wardrobe license as well as anybody—which was to say, not very well at all—but whatever Julian was doing with confident, sweeping gestures of his hands over the holopad was beyond him.

"House has its own programming language," Lesa said. "Julian's been learning to code for it."

"It uses four-dimensional matrices," Julian said. "You would not believe how tricky." He looked up, and seemed to realize that Kusanagi-Jones was still standing behind him, peering over his shoulder with a befuddled expression. "This is going to take *awhile*," he said, with a child's sublime confidence in his field of expertise. "You might as well get something to eat. I won't have anything done before tomorrow."

"But what," Kusanagi-Jones said, folding his hands together to keep his fingers from tightening, "are you *doing*?"

"Kii's a computer program, right?" Lesa said. "I mean, he's Transcendent. He's a machine intelligence. So theoretically you could rewrite him—"

"A virus," Vincent said.

"A *worm*," Julian corrected. "Or more like...like... repurposing the worm he wrote for Miss Kusanagi-Jones."

"Call me Angelo," Kusanagi-Jones said, unable to contemplate the specter of this infant calling him Miss anything. A week was overtime on this planet. Ten days was beyond the call of duty.

Julian glanced sideways enough to grin. "Anyway, we've got a worm. I just have to, you know, tweak it."

"It's not Kii," Kusanagi-Jones said reluctantly. It

was such an arrogant, audacious plan. Exactly the sort of thing Vincent would come up with, really.

He hated to punch holes in it.

"What do you mean?" Lesa asked. She had sat back down on the bed, and Kusanagi-Jones was glad. He'd *seen* her feet, even if she was determined not to show the pain.

And Vincent was looking at him, too. When he'd rather hoped that Vincent would pick up the thread and do the explaining. "It's the Consent," Kusanagi-Jones said. "Not a hive mind, really. But the community makes up its mind and Kii does what the Consent decides. Democracy by decree. Everybody votes, and whatever gets voted up retroactively becomes everybody's idea. Biochemical. So when Kii says it's not his decision, he's not saying anything more than the truth."

And anyway, he didn't care how good the New Amazonians were at programming for their adopted domicile, he didn't believe for a second that the child could actually hack a Transcendent brain. And he didn't think any of them wanted to live with the consequences of failure.

Lesa stared at him, eyebrows crawling under streaked hair, and then folded her hands over her lap. "Biochemical."

"Yes."

"Except it can't very well be biochemical if he doesn't have any damned biology, can it?"

"A programmed approximation of biology," Vincent said. "The important part is he's not an individual once the decisions have been made. He's a happy cog, a bit of the machine."

Lesa nodded slowly. And then she looked at Julian. "So what do you think he'd do if we cut him off from the Consent? Isolated him? Let him...make up his own mind?"

This time, it was Vincent's gaze on the back of his head that turned Kusanagi-Jones around. They traded a look, and Vincent slowly shook his head. "I get the impression he's been edging up to the limits of his authority to help us. Julian, do you think you can do that?"

Julian shrugged. Lesa drew one foot up onto the bed, wincing. She cleared her throat. "I *told* you he was a genius."

Julian, head bent over the terminal, snorted. "Mom. *Please.*"

Kii listens.

The bipeds plot. Clever, delicious bipeds, random and amusing. They are eager for change, ravenous for it, the antithesis of the Consent. The Consent are firm in their judgment, unambiguous, and Kii is in agreement. It is too dangerous to become involved with such a chaotic species, one prone to generating and collapsing wave-states with mad abandon. The wave-states that originate in the possibility of the Consent intervening on behalf of the bipeds are unpredictable, and some of them endanger the Consent itself.

The possibilities that stem from noninvolvement are safer. Predictable. There is a war, and the defense of the local population of bipeds, those that the khir are fond of.

Most of the others do not survive.

Kaiwo Maru *remains a nexus. Where she enters the local system, the potentialities propagate. Where she leaves, they collapse. One choice is safety. The other—*

—unpredictable.

There is no intervention. That is the Consent. The ac-

*tions of the Governors and the Coalition Cabinet follow
predictions to a nicety. Kü is one with the Consent in this.*

*But Julian's involvement is an emerging pattern, one
not forecast. It is a new wave. And Kü is not reporting
yet, for Kü has neither instruction nor Consent.*

*Kü is fond of the bipeds. Kü is explorer-caste. Kü is
alien to the Consent in many ways, a valuable, diverse
voice in the chorus of similar voices, an evolved risk
taker, an outside perspective that exists to be heard and
then ignored.*

*Kü does not resent this. Kü is in agreement with the
Consent. Kü will always be one with the Consent.*

*But the bipeds are so interesting when they're plot-
ting. And Kü knows that the Consent will be to prevent
their plots from coming to fruition. And once the
Consent is reached, Kü will be in agreement of it. Will
always have been in agreement with it.*

*Kü will report it when the plotting ceases to be inter-
esting. But Kü is explorer-caste.*

Kü wants to listen first.

They slept while Julian was working. It didn't matter
that it was bright afternoon, hours before siesta and
the rains not even a hint of darkness on the horizon;
Lesa dropped off midsentence, slumped on her bed
with her feet propped on pillows, and when Vincent
turned to share a grin with Michelangelo, he found his
partner leaned against the wall with his head tipped
back and his eyelids fluttering, hands palm-up on his
thighs.

Just as well, Vincent thought. He was in the best
shape of any of them, and he was running on ninety-
odd hours of chemistry and snatches of sleep. He told
Julian to wake him if anything interesting happened,

sat down next to Michelangelo and made a pillow of his shoulder, and was asleep too fast to realize exactly how uncomfortable the position actually was.

He noticed it waking, however.

It was dark in Lesa's bedroom, the image of the nebula overhead banished as surely as the jungles of the walls. But there was light from the door to the balcony, and Vincent could make out Julian's silhouette crouched beside him. Any lingering grogginess fled before the lancing pain when he lifted his head. "How long have I been asleep?"

"It's almost morning," Julian said. "Agnes came at supper time, but she said not to wake you. The household's in bed."

Michelangelo stirred against Vincent's shoulder, lifting his head and wincing, too. "Done?"

Trust Angelo to cut to the heart. "I'm not sure," Julian said. "I might be. I'm as done as I know how—"

"Right," Vincent said. He checked his watch: two hours before sunrise. He'd slept across twenty-one hours and felt like he could use another eight. Lying flat, preferably; his neck was not forgiving of an evening spent slumped against his partner and the wall.

He scrubbed crusts from his eyes and reached over to push Michelangelo's sleeve up, checking the status lights on his watch. They burned amber and green, and in their reflected light Angelo's lips twitched. "Aw."

Vincent kicked Angelo's ankle. "Let's wake your mom up, Julian, and see if we can make your plan happen."

Even if they had been inclined to skip eating, someone must have requested that House alert the kitchen when Lesa rose, for by the time she'd emerged from the fresher with a towel wrapped around her head,

Alys had arrived at the door toting a tray of coffee, toast, fruit, and preserves, along with an assortment of less appetizing things. House produced a small table and four chairs for their use and then Alys had left them alone with their breakfast.

It wouldn't have occurred to Vincent to feel guilty for the hour if Michelangelo hadn't mentioned it, but despite that momentary pang of conscience his stomach thanked him for the care and the coffee—which they must grow locally, the way they went through the stuff. On Ur, it was an expensive, imported treat, but Ur was notably lacking the sort of tropical climates in which the plants thrived. In Penthesilea, you could probably grow them on rooftops, if the city had permitted it.

Of course, on Ur, a potentially invasive alien plant would never be legally cultivated, though Vincent knew there were black-market greenhouses. It marked another way in which New Amazonia's government was environmentally permissive.

Vincent, watching Lesa nurse her third cup of coffee while Angelo took his turn in the shower, noticed that she wasn't wearing her honor, and tried not to think that today was the day of the duel.

Lesa'd dressed in a skirt and a tunic and freshened her bandages, and though she still hobbled on crutches, Vincent thought her feet and ankles looked less swollen. He could make out the outline of bones and muscle under the tightly wrapped gauze, anyway, which he couldn't have done yesterday.

She seemed calm as she watched Julian pack food away, and not at all like a woman contemplating a Dragon. Or a duel.

The human animal's ability to acclimate to nearly anything hadn't ceased to amaze Vincent. And confound him a little, he thought, as he poured another cup of coffee for himself. The flavor was bitter, satisfyingly rich and full-bodied, and he cupped both hands around the cup and hooked one heel over the seat of his chair so he could rest his elbow on his knee.

Michelangelo, clean and steaming faintly, his wardrobe arranged in a plain royal blue shirt and black trousers, came padding out of the fresher and kissed Vincent on the top of the head in a shocking display of affection. He still walked gingerly, his feet dotted with blood blisters and raw places, but even those looked better since yesterday.

There was a kind of pleasing domesticity to this little scene—woman, child, khir catching tossed scraps of toast, uncharacteristically pleasant Michelangelo— and it amused Vincent when he caught himself thinking so. This was *nice,* the dim room lit by the glow of Julian's coding display and the gray-gold sky outside, stained along the rooftops with a peach hue that echoed the color of the tatter-patterns on Kii's wing leather. It was a taste of something he'd left behind on Ur, lazy rest-day mornings with his sisters and brother and mother and both of her husbands sprawled about the atrium, quoting news stories and satire to each other. And it pained him to think of this, and that, arrayed in frail defiance against the machines of the Coalition.

He and Angelo ranked as *subtle* weapons.

When he looked up from the broken rainbows scattered across the oily surface of his coffee, Lesa was frowning at him. "You're thinking about what happens if this doesn't work."

He shrugged. She probably knew what he was thinking as well as he did. "If it doesn't work, we fight."

"Assuming I beat Claude today." She glanced guiltily at Julian—who was hunched over the terminal, getting toast crumbs in the interface—and then looked down at her hands, both curled clumsily around her coffee mug, and frowned. When she set the mug down and turned her hands up to examine the palms, the fingers stayed curled, and Vincent could see how the heat had puffed and softened her wounds, which were glossy and slick looking where she'd showered the scabs away.

Michelangelo was full of surprises this morning. He crossed behind Vincent, trailing his fingers across his shoulder, and took the four steps to crouch down next to Lesa's chair with something like his old grace. And then he reached out gingerly and slid thick fingers around her wrist, drawing her hand out and turning it over so he could brush a kiss across the back. Old Earth chivalry.

"Capable hands," he said, while Lesa stared down at him with twisted lips and a wrinkled brow. "You'll manage."

His fingers flexed on her wrist, and then he replaced her hand in her lap and stood, patting her lightly on the shoulder.

She turned to follow him with her eyes. "And if I lose?"

"If we have to fight, we fight," Michelangelo said, but Vincent wouldn't let him get away with that particular lie.

"We go home in disgrace," he interjected. "Claude takes New Amazonia isolationist, and Dragons defend it. And Ur and New Earth do what they have to."

"And everybody gets their asses kicked except us," Lesa said, staring at Julian's oblivious back. Vincent tried to remember what that kind of focus felt like and couldn't. Forty years since he might have been like that, but that was forty years of enhanced sensory input and eyes on the back of his head ago, forty years of living or dying by his wits while trying to fill five or ten mutually exclusive assignment objectives simultaneously.

"You could just let her send us home, mission incomplete," Michelangelo said.

"Dishonoring myself and discrediting my mother, and leaving Claude in an even stronger position than if she shoots me."

"Besides," Vincent said, "that's an acceptable risk for me. Not for you, Angelo. Not after New Earth."

It hurt, the way Michelangelo's shoulders rose and fell, the way he dismissed his own life as acceptable losses. He wasn't expecting to live through this, Vincent realized. He didn't think their trick with Kii would work. And he wasn't even bothering to hide it.

He was just telling the truth.

It was the most plaintive admission of defeat Vincent could imagine.

"Claude will want that art," Lesa said, as if driven to shatter any silence so strained. "And even if Claude doesn't, Elder Austin will. They'll have to work something out with the Coalition eventually."

After the Coalition crushed whatever fragmentary revolution Katherine Lexasdaughter managed to cobble together without New Amazonia and its unrepatriated trade partners. After the...flawed New Amazonian social structure got a kick in the pants that could keep it going strong for another hundred years. There was nothing like a little outside pressure to get people to stick to a stupid philosophical position.

The Coalition was proof enough of that.

"Right," Lesa said, looking down. "Let's hope this works, then. Julian?"

He didn't twitch.

"Julian?" she repeated. "Are you ready?"

The second use of his name penetrated. His head snapped around. "I've been ready for hours."

When she insisted that she wasn't meeting any more Dragons sitting down, it was Michelangelo who went to help Lesa stand, an arm around her waist to ease the pressure on her feet. Vincent closed down his countermeasures, and resolutely chose not to think about the possible vengeance an angry Dragon could wreak on four humans who meddled with its programming.

"Kii," Angelo said, "we'd like to speak with you, please."

The Dragon appeared in its trademark twist of colored light, seated on its haunches with its wings half unfurled. "Greetings..." it began, and then blinked. And blinked again, the entire eyelid, rather than just the nictitating membrane.

"I feel strange," it said.

It took Vincent half a second to figure out why exactly that simple sentence made Michelangelo curse with such heartfelt relief. By the time he'd worked it out, Angelo was talking. "Forgive us, Kii. We needed to talk to you without the Consent."

Kii beat wings hard, and Vincent ducked reflexively, but of course they weren't really there. Not even so much as a draft flipped his braids around, and after a moment he controlled himself and stood upright. "I am..." the Dragon began, and then flipped wings closed and settled down, the delicate fingers on the leading edges of its wings scrabbling lightly at nonexistent stone. Vincent almost imagined he could hear the *scritch scritch* of immaterial claws. "There is no Consent," it said, its head subsiding between hunched shoulders. "What have you done?"

Michelangelo looked as if he wanted to step forward. He couldn't, though, not with Lesa leaning on him. "Kii," he said, "we needed to talk to you *alone*."

The argument lasted the better part of three hours, but Lesa only participated in the first fifteen minutes. Her feet hurt, and moreover, Julian was sitting turned around in the chair in front of her terminal, his knees drawn up under his chin and his back braced against the desk, blinking at Kii wide-eyed as a boy watching his first Trials.

Michelangelo barely noticed when Lesa disentangled herself from him, other than to give her a grim little smile as she limped away to sit down beside her son.

This was Vincent's job, this negotiation. She didn't have the faintest idea of where to begin. And Julian deserved praise and a hug. One he wasn't too grown up, today, to return.

She watched the discussion closely, however, and she quickly got the impression that Kii actually wasn't opposed to helping them. That it might in fact be inclined to do so, but a sense of duty was stopping it. And so, when she interjected, she only had one point to make; Vincent had covered the rest.

"Kii," she said, when Vincent had taken two deep breaths of frustration and curled his fingers into his palms, "sometimes the status quo *needs* rearranging. No matter how safe it is."

"The Consent would not agree," Kii said, its eyes

filming white for a moment and then clearing, sun-brilliant again.

"The Consent aren't here to ask, are they?"

Its feathers smoothed, and it stared at her.

"Kii," she said, "what do *you* think?"

"I think the Consent is too conservative," it said. "I think the diversity of your species should be protected. I think preserving a small local population when there is a . . . menagerie . . . no, a panoply of you to experience is foolish." It settled, and furled its wings. "You're all so *different*," it said plaintively. "And I've only gotten to meet a few of you."

"Take you to Earth," Michelangelo said. "If you make me a promise about the Governors, Kii. If you'll take them apart."

Kii recoiled, wings fanning. And Lesa dropped her hand to the butt of her weapon and took a single slow, deep breath. If she died today, it didn't matter. Either the plan to subvert the Governors would work, and there would be no war—or she would have to have faith in her mother's ability to discredit Austin and Singapore.

And there was Vincent's promise. One way or another, Julian would be okay.

"Decide quickly," she said. And when they turned to her, she shrugged, her lips pulled tight across her teeth to keep them from trembling. "We have to leave within the hour if we're going to meet Claude and her seconds before noon."

Ninety minutes later, Vincent, Lesa, and Michelangelo met Claude, Maiju, and another woman at the challenge square. It was otherwise empty, and Claude and her people had beaten them there and stood, waiting, not far from the center of the open court. Saide Austin was nowhere in sight, and Michelangelo couldn't decide if he found that expected or surprising. New Amazonian dueling apparently didn't bow to such niceties as seconds; other than the men she dueled for, Lesa went alone.

She limped in stiff boots that were the next best thing to braces, and she had refused Michelangelo's offer of an analgesic. "I'd rather suffer than be slow."

She'd gotten Agnes to cut the trigger guard off an old weapon for her, and wrapped the grip in cloth so that if her palm seeped through the sealant it wouldn't slick the gun.

Michelangelo wished he thought it would be enough.

Even across the intervening distance, he saw Claude's chin go up when Lesa rose, wobbling, out of the groundcar. Michelangelo offered his arm, but she brushed past with stubborn pride. Claude didn't say a word, although the glance she exchanged with her wife said everything.

Michelangelo squeezed Lesa's shoulder before he let her stagger forward alone. She flashed him an ashen grin and went, trying to stride but hobbling, and Claude's retinue withdrew.

The duelists would meet at the center of the square. Alone. They would pace off ten steps, turn, and fire.

One shot only.

Which explained why more New Amazonian women didn't die over a point of honor. Of course, most of them probably wouldn't bother prosecuting a case as thickheaded as this one unless they had an ulterior motive—like Claude's.

Michelangelo didn't react or step back when Vincent laid a hand on his uninjured shoulder and squeezed. The least he could do was refuse to look down.

Lesa was halfway across the square when Antonia Kyoto stepped from an open doorway, flanked by Shafaqat Delhi and two other uniformed security agents, and called out her name. Lesa dragged to a halt, turning slowly, as if it took a moment for the cry to penetrate her awareness. And then Kyoto came toward her, the women fanning out on either side, and Lesa spread her hands wide. Michelangelo started forward, but Vincent's hand was still on his shoulder, unrelenting now, holding him in place. He could have broken the grip, but he would have had to hurt Vincent to do it, so he shuffled his feet and stayed where he was.

Lesa never even reached for her weapon. She let Kyoto take her elbow and lean close to speak into her ear. And whatever Kyoto said, Lesa responded first by shaking her head and then drawing back, startled, and glancing at Claude.

Claude, faced by two security agents herself, did drop her hand to her weapon. If she ever actually intended to shoot, the gesture came too late, because Shafaqat grabbed her arm and dragged it behind her, and the next time Michelangelo paused to think, he was moving, and Vincent had him by the elbow and wasn't trying to slow him down.

Lesa and Kyoto reached Claude before they did, about the same time as Maiju and the other woman were intercepted by more uniformed women. Hands were waved and voices raised, though Michelangelo didn't hear all the conversation. That muttering grew louder when Claude's gestures and Kyoto's determined head shaking grew more vehement, and cracked into silence when Lesa turned and gestured Michelangelo over.

He came to her, hiding his limp, Vincent still at his side. "Yes?"

"Claude," Lesa said without looking at him, "would like to know if you're willing to accept a vaccine for the virus in return for keeping the existence of the laboratory secret."

He hid his shock with the old reflexive skill, but couldn't resist a glance at Kyoto. She winked, but not so Claude would see it, and from Vincent's sudden tension the answer must be in her face, but Michelangelo couldn't read it.

He could act, though. He dropped his gaze from Kyoto's to the pavement in front of his toes and made a show of thinking about it, and then he smiled, looked Claude in the eye, and lightly shook his head. "Don't think so."

He almost felt bad for enjoying it so much until Lesa's hand snuck out and squeezed his own.

"It was good work," Elena said, and Lesa smiled under the praise despite herself. She wouldn't go so far as to call it a victory party, but she, Vincent and Michelangelo—whom she could no longer think of as the Coalition agents—Antonia and Elena were seated comfortably around the demolished remains of a very good supper, and even Michelangelo looked halfway relaxed. Very relaxed, for a man going to his execution.

But Lesa wasn't going to think about that tonight. "So," she said, when Antonia finally pushed her dessert plate away, "how did you find the lab?"

Elena enjoyed playing hostess. She was already filling a coffee cup, which Antonia accepted gratefully. "Old-fashioned investigative work," she said. "We pulled House's records of everywhere Saide Austin had been for the past six weeks, and found out that she'd checked out a rifle and taken a three-day hike right before Carnival. We sent out tracking teams, located where the aircar met her, and used satellite imagery to track it to the base. We actually knew last night, but it was more fun to arrest Claude in her moment of triumph."

Lesa caught herself shaking her head in annoyed admiration and had to force herself to stop. Vincent snorted, and sat forward enough to pick up a dessert plate before reclining back on the floor. He leaned against Michelangelo and sighed. "Are you sure you're not a Liar, Antonia?"

"Just an old warrior," she answered, and blew across her coffee cup, but her eyes twinkled over it. "There's no guarantee we'll be able to hold Claude for any length of time, of course—or Saide either. They have enough political resources to weasel out of it, I'm afraid—though the scandal should at least clear them out of Parliament."

Elena coughed lightly. "You might want to search Austin's studio," she said with a casual smile. "While you have probable cause and might stand a chance of getting a warrant."

Antonia blinked at Elena while Lesa bit her lip, watching her mother the way a khir kit watches a fexa. "Oh?" Antonia said.

"You never know," Elena said. "You might find contraband."

Saide Austin's public shock when the stolen statue was discovered concealed under a tarpaulin, among her waste marble, might have been convincing under other circumstances. But given the furor already surrounding her links to the genetic engineering scandal, even her reputation was not enough to weather the storm unscathed.

Her eventual jail sentence, however, was somewhat lighter than Claude Singapore's.

When it came down to it, it wasn't the New Amazonian's virus that was the problem. It was Kii. Getting it to Earth and with it, its promise to eradicate the Governors.

Those on *Kaiwo Maru* were easy. The ones on Earth, and the Coalition worlds, and infesting the starships that traveled between them were another issue entirely. As was ensuring that Kii got to Earth intact and protected.

Michelangelo had never had a fight with Vincent that *began* to match that one. Vincent began adamant: Michelangelo was to go AWOL, go native on New Amazonia. With Antonia Kyoto as the heir apparent to the prime minister's chair—once, of course, the unpleasant business of Claude Singapore's impeachment and prosecution had gone forward—he would be safe there, even a valued member of Kyoto's team. And with the remnants of the Right Hand still eluding sweeps in the jungle, he would have no trouble keeping busy. Meanwhile, Vincent would hand-carry Kii's data bomb back to Earth.

It was a beautiful plan, and completely unworkable. So Michelangelo had kissed him, and called him a fool. "My patron can see to it that I get a show trial to end all show trials," Michelangelo said. "A hearing before the Cabinet. They'll download my watch, Vincent, and the details of this mission will be presented as part of the evidence."

Purged of such details as the fact that Michelangelo

had not been acting alone, of course. His patron would see to that, too.

And the evidence would be shared among the Governors, forwarded via shipping and mail packets to the farthest outposts of the Coalition, so that the Governors could return a consensus regarding whether they would carry out the Assessment. It would take about four months out and four months back for the verdict to be returned.

An inevitable verdict. But the forms would be observed. And the Governors would swallow the poison pill of Kii's virus with the evidence upon which they would return Michelangelo's sentence. Which would be Assessment. That, he already knew.

And that, moreover, was the poetry that had convinced Kii, finally, to do as Michelangelo said.

"It's a death sentence," Vincent said.

"Yes," Kii said. "But it is elegant."

Michelangelo nodded, at peace and whole in his heart. That was, after all, the plan. The only pain came in hurting Vincent. But Vincent would recover. He had always been the stronger one.

"It's nothing I can't do as well, with a better chance of surviving."

"Vincent," Michelangelo said patiently, "you're *Katherinessen*. Won't put you before the Governors. They'll ship you home with a discharge and pretend you never left Ur."

"Angelo—"

Vincent's voice cracked. Michelangelo couldn't stand it. He shook his head. "Let me be the fucking hero just once, you son of a bitch," he said, and kissed him on the mouth.

And Vincent, eyes closed, kissed him back, and murmured, "Kill or be killed," against his lips.

Michelangelo repeated the same words, and if they meant martyrdom rather than bravado now, they were still a benediction, of sorts.

That first leg of the journey was a little less than two months, and Vincent was both grateful and grieved that Michelangelo did not spend *this* trip in cryo. They had that, at least, and it had a kind of end-of-the-world sweetness that alternately tore and honeyed him.

The results of the New Amazonian election caught up with them at Cristalia, via a fast packet bot, and they weren't surprised to hear that the new head of the security directorate was Lesa Pretoria.

Between her and Prime Minister Kyoto, Vincent doubted if he'd ever have to make good on his promise to take Julian back to Ur.

At Cristalia, Vincent and Angelo parted ways.

Vincent tendered his resignation through the mail packet that would reach Old Earth on the same ship that Angelo would and boarded the *Pequod* toward Ur. Michelangelo's ship was named the *Argo*. They didn't laugh about it.

Vincent's family was surprised to see him, except for his mother, who was pleased. Captain Katherine Lexasdaughter was finally showing her age, her hair thinning now, and bright silver in its careful coif, but the steely resolve hadn't left her. She was even more pleased to hear that the revolution could go forward.

But not as scheduled.

Vincent suggested she wait, eight months or ten, to see if it would even be necessary to start a war. And she listened.

Katherine always listened. And she made other people listen, too. So it happened that once the Governors ceased issuing their dictums, there was no need to bring revolution to Old Earth.

Old Earth managed very well on its own.

Vincent had never tracked incoming ships before, but now he did, waiting for any scrap of news, though the trial received only moderate coverage—and none at all once the fighting started and the Cabinet was dissolved. The Governors would never return Angelo's sentence. They'd be gone before the mail could get back to Old Earth.

That didn't matter: it would be obvious to anyone with a calendar and a brain where the virus had originated. Vincent knew the Coalition.

Someone would do the work himself.

Vincent was consumed—possessed—by the need to know the date, the exact time of Michelangelo's execution. As if in knowing, he could fix the sun in the sky, control the death, contain it, crystallize it. As if he could *own* it.

Ridiculous, when he didn't even stand under the same sun.

He knew how it would be. He would observe the anniversary. He would grieve. Every year at first, and then perhaps after the fifth iteration or the tenth, he would forget, skip a year—and then it would be once a decade, a period of ten years frivolously chosen because his species had ten fingers for counting on, with no more cosmic significance than an astrological unit. A convenient meter, a king's foot. An arbitrary standard, where Kii would count by eights.

And then Vincent, eventually, would be dead as well, and there would be nothing left of Michelangelo Osiris Leary Kusanagi-Jones, except a string of dead men's names.

And Kii. Kii would remember him. And Kii, or

some propagation of Kii, might someday make its way home to New Amazonia, and the Consent would reclaim its prodigal.

They might not change. They might never accept change. It was not in the ethos of the Dragons, other than the explorer-caste, essential and ignored.

But they could appreciate poetry. And the story would have an ending, after all.

Epilogue

IT CAME, UNBELIEVABLY, ON THERMOPAPER. A DNA-CODED diplomatic packet, read-to-destroy, for Vincent Katherinessen, Old Earth Colonial Coalition Diplomatic Corps, Lt. Col., Ret.

Hard copy.

He'd never held one before.

He licked his thumb and pressed it against the catch.

The message within was brief:

With one thing and another, Rome fell before they decided to waste the bullet. Coming the long way round, but I'm coming. Hope you weren't kidding about introducing me to your mom.

Would you believe it?

All those years, all those worlds, and we were wrong.

About the Author

Elizabeth Bear shares a birthday with Frodo and Bilbo Baggins. This, coupled with a tendency to read the dictionary as a child, doomed her early to penury, intransigence, friendlessness, and the writing of speculative fiction. She was born in Hartford, Connecticut, and grew up in central Connecticut with the exception of two years (which she was too young to remember very well) spent in Vermont's Northeast Kingdom, in the last house with electricity before the Canadian border. She currently lives in the Mojave Desert near Las Vegas, Nevada, but she's trying to escape. Her recent and forthcoming appearances include: *SCIFICTION, The Magazine of Fantasy & Science Fiction, On Spec, H.P. Lovecraft's Magazine of Horror, Chiaroscuro, Ideomancer, The Fortean Bureau,* Polish fantasy magazine *Nowa Fantastyka,* and the anthologies *Shadows Over Baker Street* (Del Rey, 2003) and *All-Star Zeppelin Adventure Stories* (Wheatland Press, 2004). She's a second-generation Swede, a third-generation Ukrainian, and a third-generation Hutzul, with some Irish, English, Scots, Cherokee, and German thrown in for leavening. Elizabeth Bear is her real name, but not all of it. Her dogs outweigh her, and she is much beset by her cats.

Be sure not to miss

UNDERTOW

The next exciting novel from

Elizabeth Bear

André Deschênes is a killer, but he wants to be more. If he can find a teacher who will forgive his past, he can learn to manipulate the odds, control probability, become a conjure man. But the world he lives on is run by the ruthless Charter Trade company, and the floating city called Novo Haven is little more than a company town, where humans and aliens alike either work for the Greene family or are destroyed by it. In the bayous and back alleys, revolution is stirring. And one more death may be all it takes to shift the balance...

Here's a special preview:

UNDERTOW
Elizabeth Bear

Coming Soon!

Over the years, André had come to accept that his luck was often ridiculous, but he hadn't expected a shot at filling the contract his first night out. He folded his forearms over the handlebars of his wet-dry scoot and let it bob, lights dark, on the moonlit water of the bay. The floor pushed at his feet as it yawed; he ducked behind the faring so his head wouldn't silhouette on the horizon. The craft was low-profile; without the brightness of the sky or of Novo Haven's lights behind him, André was nothing more than a blacker patch on the water.

About that luck, he thought, watching Lucienne Spivak and her guest come chattering down the floating dock. Ridiculous wasn't the half of it. Epic, maybe. Operatic. *Farcical.* Because even by moonlight, with his lowlight adapt kicked up, he recognized the woman walking alongside Spivak, leaning into her so that their shoulders brushed, ducking down as they shook their heads over some joke funny enough that André could hear their laughter across the water.

"You know," he murmured under his breath, "you couldn't make this shit up."

He wasn't going to kill anybody in front of his girlfriend. Some things were beyond the call of duty, and it would be difficult to make it look like an accident if Spivak suddenly went down, clutching her throat. *And* he wasn't in a hurry. Impatient men often didn't do well in André's line of work. *Luck will only get you so far.* Even ridiculous luck—

With his lowlight, he could make out the hunched shape of a minifab at the top of the dock, a white shell path leading up to it. The residence itself was in a sheltered inlet, not quite up the bayou—as Nouel had suggested—but on a channel and away from the open bay. A paramangrove swamp cut sight lines to the city, and the approach path of descending lighters lay directly over the house, which explained why this wasn't more popular property. That, and the inconvenience of being an hour and a half by scoot or boat from the city.

He'd wait for Cricket to leave, and then he'd slip close enough to get an overview of the location. It would be better if he could catch Spivak away from home, but it didn't hurt to know the turf. He'd have to be careful, though; Jean Kroc's house was a homestead, no plans on record, and he had no idea what sort of security devices the conjure man might use. Anything from tiger pits to tracking lasers were possible, and it would be embarrassing to take a load of buckshot in the fundament.

André folded his arms and waited, listening to

the women laugh. The breeze across the water was cool, carrying a taint of the heady sweetness from the parasitic flowers that swathed the paramangrove limbs. The scent carried over miles, and right now it told André that the wind was offshore. Which was also helpful to him; even if Kroc had a sniffer or a smart guard dog, it wouldn't pick up André's scent.

Yep. Luck was wonderful.

Pity he couldn't talk any conjure on Greene's World into helping him train it. Ah, well. He shifted on the hard seat of the scooter, pretending resignation to himself. No matter how much of a hurry Closs was in, it wasn't as if André had to kill anybody *tonight*.

Except it didn't look like Cricket was leaving alone. She climbed into the passenger chair of the waiting flashboat, and Spivak followed, settling in the pilot's seat. If she was just running Cricket down to the ferry, about fifteen minutes, then—

—André might not need the research after all. More luck, that he hadn't mentioned it to Cricket.

It could have put a strain on the relationship.

The engine of the flashboat was faster and louder than the caterpillar drive on the scoot. André waited until his prey was in motion before powering up. His scoot was dark gray, and the topcoat had a gloss-or-matte option that got a lot of work on night jobs. With the lowlight, he didn't need the running lights.

He concentrated very hard, thinking of Spivak dropping Cricket off at the ferry landing, just the other side of the paramangrove swamp, and turning back for home, maybe a little careless and tired. He couldn't take a blacked-out scoot into the city; if he didn't get run down by a barge, he'd get pulled over by traffic enforcement—and Cricket might recognize him or the vehicle under conditions of more light. The ideal, of course, would be for her to drop off Cricket, turn around, head home, and run into engine trouble. Unfortunately, André didn't think his untrained mojo was enough to pull off that set of coincidences, but he held the thought anyway, sharp and fine, visualizing it in detail.

But Spivak guided the flashboat toward the lights of Novo Haven. The universe wasn't listening. Or somebody else's free will was getting in the way again. Just plain inconvenient.

She opened quite a gap as she headed inward—his craft wasn't as speedy—but André wasn't worried. It shouldn't matter, as long as he could spot her running lights and the silhouette of her boat across open water.

Traffic was light at first, and there were no street- or channel-lights on the outskirts, other than the occasional door or dock lamp. But the traffic regs assured that Spivak couldn't just flash off and leave his slower vehicle behind. André made up some of the distance and then slotted his scoot in behind a water taxi two vehicles behind Spivak and Cricket.

He didn't even need to follow that closely. It was obvious pretty quickly that they were going to Cricket's new flat. André hadn't been there yet, but he had the address, and it was a neighborhood he knew.

He stuck close anyway, though, the tactile rubber of the scoot's handlebars molding his palms, the engine softly vibrating his calves. He pulled a hooded sweater on one arm at a time—keeping his eye on traffic—and slipped on eye protection. Too dark for dark glass in the goggles, but they changed the line of his face a little. He skinned the beard off, which wouldn't help if either woman was running connex, but he knew Cricket at least usually kept her skins live. She hypertexted like a mad thing in conversation, her agile brain tending to shoot off in six unrelated directions at once.

The scoot was a quiet little craft, and André was glad of that as he ducked it out of the traffic stream one bridge shy of Cricket's flat and diagonally across the channel. They unloaded quickly—a small favor from fate—and Cricket gave Spivak a one-armed hug as she climbed past her before turning away.

André crushed a pang of conscience. He'd be there to console her. It might even bring them closer together. Cricket had this unnerving tendency to flit just out of reach, as if she were covered in something slick and transparent. You could brush against her surface, but there was never any way to get a grip.

A minute later, Spivak finished fussing with her safety belts and pulled away from the landing, headed in the opposite direction, not back across the side channel where André lay in wait. He twisted the throttle and sent the scoot forward, pulling into traffic smoothly to avoid attracting attention.

Now his heart thumped his breastbone. The

crackle of tension spidered up his back to grab and prickle across his shoulder blades, and his stomach seemed to sway in his gut like a ballast bag of wet sand. His skin crawled taut across his thighs and groin; nausea chased bitterness up the back of his throat.

This was it.

The luck was running now.

It was ninety minutes before he got his shot. Spivak stayed in the city, visited a tavern André didn't follow her into—it was on a decommissioned ferry, moored along the east side of Broadbrook, and there was no way off it that wasn't immediately obvious—and returned to her flashboat after less than forty-five minutes. It might have been the meet, but his job wasn't to stop the meet, or to identify the other party. He didn't do that sort of thing.

Afterward she headed west, out of the city on bayside. Not back the way they had come, but this was a shorter route out of the city and she could always cut across the shipping lanes for a nearly direct route back to Kroc's house—a shortcut that would be ideal for André's purposes. Not only did lighters kick up a hell of a splash when they touched down—a splash that could turn over a small craft—but big ships sometimes didn't notice little boats, and accidents could happen.

André didn't like to smile over his work; it seemed disrespectful. But it was hard to keep this one down: maybe prayer was good for something.

He should have stuck to his demand to be paid a bonus for a twenty-four-hour closure.

The only potential problem was the top speed of his scoot. If Spivak raced home, there was no way he could keep up. But if she was cutting the lanes, she'd want to proceed cautiously, with one eye on the sky. That would be better.

And it seemed to be her plan. André hung back almost a half-kilometer, trailing Spivak until they were well clear of Novo Haven. The submerged lights of the shipping lanes glowed beneath the surface of the bay, but there was no real danger of being caught against them; they were meant to be seen from above. Only one lighter splashed down during the transect, and that one well off to the south and gently enough that by the time the wake reached André, he cut across it diagonally and noticed only what the skip and lurch did in his already nervous belly. The night was calm, still warmer than he'd expected, and the breeze from landward had faded off, leaving a few late-traveling sailboats motoring along the placid surface with their white sails hanging slack. Spivak, charting a stately progress, seemed inclined to enjoy the night. André had no problem with letting her do it. It was a point of honor with him that his targets never even knew they were in danger. Necessity did not have to be cruel.

Around the middle of the landing field, he goosed it. The caterpillar drive wasn't fast, but it was fast enough if Spivak didn't hear him coming, and quiet enough that she shouldn't. He set the autocruise, looped his hard memory, and—keeping one eye on the sky and the other on his quarry—began to assemble his weapon.

In most cases, André killed with a long-barreled sniping weapon, a combination rifle brand-named Locutor A.G. 351, for the year the design had been introduced. It adapted to either caseless standard ammunition—jacketed projectiles fired by a chemical accelerant—or crystalline slivers of hemorragine fired by compressed air, which dissolved in the victim's blood, causing symptoms of a cerebral aneurysm, then broke down into innocuous organic compounds within the day.

That was what he would be using tonight. He preferred a bullet; it killed instantly if you did it right, whereas the hemorragine left the victim sometimes as long as a hundred and twenty seconds to feel fear. And that was ugly and cruel.

The other issue with the damned things was they didn't fly far, and a fairly light cross breeze could deflect them. He'd have to be within a hundred meters, and he wouldn't get more than a couple of shots. Even in the wee hours of morning, people tended to notice when someone pointed a rifle at them and fired poisoned needles at the back of their heads.

He'd put one needle into her back, wait for her to go down, approach with caution, and download her hard memory for Closs—as instructed, just to be sure. Then he'd capsize her boat, lose the body someplace where it shouldn't be recovered for at least a day (long enough for the hemorragine to break down and for her hard memory to wipe), and pretend, in the morning, to be shocked when he heard the news.

The scoot purred forward. André extended the

telescope rest and slid the weapon-mount onto the peg. He squinted through the sight, focusing down through the scope because only an idiot would use connex for this, and took a sighting.

Lucienne Spivak was sitting upright in the pilot's chair, her braid whipping behind her, her shoulders square and facing him. Easy. The only way he could miss was by divine intervention.

He measured his breathing, matched it to the regular rise and fall of the swells, tugged his glove off with his teeth, slid his finger under the trigger guard. He waited for the moment when his breath would pause naturally just as the scoot topped one of the gentle waves.

The moment came. He squeezed the trigger. A jet of cool, grease-scented air stroked his cheek.

There was no sound.

The sun wasn't up yet when someone hammered on Cricket's doorframe. No doorbell, no chime of connex and the name of the importunate visitor, just the thumping of fist on paramangrove paneling.

"Oh, fuck," Cricket murmured, twisting her legs into the cool air. She slept nude; she dragged the robe she kept on the bedpost over chilled skin and stumbled barefoot across a morphing rug that this morning was off-white and shaggily looped. Her toes curled as she stepped onto the decking, as if she could somehow protect the tender instep of her foot from the crawling chill. "Fuck, who is it?"

"Kroc," came the voice from the other side of the

door, which answered the question of why he was knocking. No connex to ring her chimes. His voice shivered, high and sharp, almost shrill. "Is Lucienne with you?"

"Shit," Cricket said, and palmed the lock plate faster than she should have. "She left me around one hundred and one. She was going to get a drink and go home."

"She didn't make it," Kroc said, unnecessarily, because sometimes it was better making a noise. He ducked under her arm into the flat, and she locked up behind him. "Check your messages. If she sent anything—"

It would have been to Cricket, because Jean was not connected. She tightened her robe and scrubbed her eyes on the sleeve. "One second."

She dropped her connex at night, except for the flat security and a couple of emergency codes. If it had been really important, Lucienne would have spared the couple of extra keystrokes and sent to one of those.

But there were messages waiting. The one from André, which she hadn't answered. One or two from connex acquaintances, people she knew from online groups. And one from Lucienne.

She looked at Jean, so he would know. His face paled under his stubble, but he didn't speak.

Cricket opened the message.

And would have fallen if Jean had not caught her.

It was a sense-dump, night water and darkness, the smell of lubricant and the texture of the flash-boat's controls in her hands, all subsumed by a hypodermic stab to the left of her spine, the building pressure of a migraine like the handle of a knife pressed to her eye. She gasped but couldn't make her diaphragm work. Jean's hands on her shoulders guided her back, cushioning her until she slumped against a chair. The robe was everywhere, he must have been getting an eyeful, but he caught her under the chin and made her look into his eyes. "You need EMS."

"No," Cricket said, a shrill, spasming whine. She couldn't lift her hand to push at him, so she thumped the heel on the deck for emphasis. She felt him jump. "No doctor. Just . . . a minute."

Dying. Cricket—no, Lucienne was dying. Lucienne knew she was dying, and she knew why. And there was no time to explain.

So she showed.

The file was encoded, and Cricket's breath came back into her with a rush as the flood of numbers washed away the swelling pain in her head. Lucienne had swamped her connex, a massive core-dump—

Corrupt. Corrupt. Corrupt.

"Shit!" The word of the day, apparently. Cricket scrambled to save, to back up, to dump what Lucienne had sent her into a protected hold. Cricket was an archinformist. She had better security protocols than most governments. And she knew how to sling data, and how to repair it—

She went after it, the bones in Jean's wrists creaking as she clenched her hands. But the file was incomplete. And a non-holographic transmission, so what she had was a chunk of data, but not the sort of chunk that could give her a fuzzy picture of the whole. This was a linear string. And Cricket was pretty sure she could find the key, because Lucienne would have wanted her—or Jean—to crack the code. But she only had part of it...